To Kevin,

May your life be as adventurous as the books you read!

Sincerely,

FERN MAJESTIC

AND THE FALL OF A DRAGON

MASCOT BOOKS

www.mascotbooks.com

Fern Majestic and The Fall of a Dragon

Cover and map designs by Jasmine R. White

For more information, please contact:
Mascot Books
620 Herndon Parkway #320
Herndon, VA 20170
info@mascotbooks.com

Library of Congress Control Number: 2018902917

CPSIA Code: PBANG0718A
ISBN: 978-1-68401-600-6

Printed in the United States

To my youngest son, Richy,
who inspired me to begin.

To my eldest son, Jim,
who always sat to listen.

To my one-and-only daughter, Vicky,
who kept me going with encouragement and support.

To my wife (my worst critic),
without whom, I would have never succeeded.

And finally, to my faithful dog, Rascal,
who never left my side. Rest in peace old friend.

FERN MAJESTIC

AND THE FALL OF A DRAGON

JAMES STEVENS

WHITE SEA

DUNDIRE

LAND OF
THE DRAKES

Lake Burlin

EARTHINGLAND

Land of the Stone Trolls

Eshland Lake

LOUSTOF

Crags of Malice

VALOM

The River Dardown

ALKYLE

BLUE
MARSH

Burdensville

N
W E
S

ALBIANAC SEA

ULMECK MOUNTAINS

HARTH

CONTENTS

PROLOGUE

Before ice and snow ruled, before fire and rock ravaged the earth, before the world, there was, and is, the planet Harth. Mountain peaks touched the stars, grassy fields stretched like the mind, and barren wastelands decorated the north. Oceans drowned the coasts, rivers cut through valleys, and rain poured down like torrents. Dragons roamed the skies, turgoyles pillaged towns, and quaggoths lurked beneath the ground. Elves prospered, dwarves constructed, and fairies lived. Centaurs grazed, chamroshs flew, and sun bears served. Kings, lords, and peasants. Giant...Humans...Magic...Blood...ancient.

An elm tree grabbed the clouds in a nameless wood. Dry ground surrounded its base as a dying sun burned bright, crippled, casting radiant light down upon the soil. The earth began to crumble underneath the elm and five small fingers slowly emerged, thrusting dirt and stone aside. A hand rose from the ground as another joined it. Arms followed until a head covered in auburn hair pushed through the soil. A young boy nearly three years old stood beneath the elm covered in dust and dirt. Balled fists rubbed blue eyes as he cleared them from debris.

The child wandered through the woods as hunger suddenly took over. The sounds of a waking village caught his attention and he made his way towards it. Fresh bread cooling on window sills enticed him to come closer. A sudden scream from inside a small house startled the young boy.

"SAVAGE CHILD!! WHERE ARE YOUR CLOTHES? BE GONE WITH YOU!!"

The boy twisted around like a rope and darted through the streets. Yells and screams were shadows following him past homes and small businesses. Suddenly, an outstretched hand grasped him by the arm.

"Who are you? Where do you come from, child?" said an elderly woman.

But the boy could not speak. The words were the first to ever grace his ears.

"Here, put these clothes on before someone horse whips you," she said.

The boy stood, bare feet rooted to the ground like a tree, not understanding the old woman.

"Are you daft?"

She dressed the child, jerking him about like a rag doll. Noticing an inscription upon his arm, she gasped.

"TRAITOR SCUM! LEAVE MY SIGHT BEFORE I FEED YOU TO MY DOGS! PIT...GRUFF!"

Two large dogs bounded from a doorway towards the young boy. Quickly he spun around and raced towards the woods closely followed by the hairy beasts. The elm tree came into view and the young boy reached its trunk. With a jack-rabbit leap, he clung to the lowest branch, pulling himself away from the chomping jaws of the pursuing dogs. Their master's call was suddenly heard in the distance and the beasts quickly returned to the village, leaving the young boy clinging to the branch.

Hours passed, and the child eventually climbed down. Tears fell from the young boy's eyes as night fell from the sky. He sat curled in a ball swaying like a bird on a twig, trying to fight the agony in his stomach. His hunger had grown to an unbearable emptiness, aching as he stood to his feet. Determination painted the young boy's face as he set off towards the village once more.

Slowly, he crept as large silhouettes of homes appeared like monsters in the darkness, dark and looming. Large wooden barrels covered with lids sat outside the buildings. The young boy watchfully made his way closer and removed the top to one of the containers. A putrid aroma emerged, wafting into the boy's nostrils and burning his senses like fire. His hunger, insatiable, masked the smells, and he began to eat his fill. With the pain finally diminished, the young boy slumped against the barrel and fell into a deep sleep. Morning came.

"VAGABOND!! TRAITOR!! LEAVE MY PROPERTY BEFORE I CALL THE GUARDS!!"

The boy was a spring, jumping from his slumber as he was beaten with a hard object. A tall, burly man with a dark beard ran after the child waving a large broom handle in the air, but this time the boy did not retreat to the woods. Easily outrunning the grown man, he raced down the streets. The villagers soon came to see that he was no ordinary child.

Time creeped like an old man as the young boy grew older. Day after day he would return to the village searching and begging for scraps of food. He would often watch as other children played in the streets, and on numerous occasions tried to join them in their merriment, only to be cast away. The longing for friends stabbed the poor boy's heart, and the lack of companionship embittered his soul. His life was one of loneliness and solitude, and survival became his only thought.

With age, the boy learned words as he endured the villagers and their relentless yells and threats. For the longest time, the boy thought his name was "traitor," until the day he learned to read. That was the day he read the inscription upon his arm, and that was the day he learned his true name.

1

IN HONOR OF...

This story starts like most stories...with a hero. His name, Fern. Yes, yes, it is realized that Fern is not a very heroic name, but one does not choose her or his own name, or we would all have the names of heroes.

Of course, the fact that Fern was also a Majestic didn't make life easy, to say the least. No, he was not a person of royalty or nobility, which would have made life grand. Majestic was his surname. He was the descendant of a long line of traitors to the kingdom of Loustof. So, no matter how many heroic deeds he accomplished, there was no living down his inherited shame, or so he was meant to think.

Fern lived in the small farming village of Burdensville in the southern part of Loustof. He himself was not a farmer, but a blacksmith. As a matter of fact, he was the only blacksmith for miles around.

Fern had never been outside Burdensville, other than visiting the Ulmeck Mountains to the south, and although he had been in many battles and fought many creatures that wandered into his village, there was still much he had not seen. Reading tales from books or hearing the stories from travelers about the lands and creatures that dwelled beyond the kingdom of Loustof was Fern's only link to the outside world.

So every day, Fern would be hard at work repairing and producing farming tools to keep the village in running order. It was a normal, sunny spring day when his adventure began. Fern was up early repairing a plow a farmer brought to him the evening before, demanding in a not-so-polite way that it be done the following day. Although it bothered him greatly, Fern was used to such treatment. Living in the small town of Burdensville with the embarrassment of his name weighed heavily on his broad shoulders day in and day out. So, as usual, Fern agreed without argument and assured the farmer that it would be ready no later than noon.

It was barely six o'clock and the sun was just peeking up over the horizon. Fern was busy at work, beams of light streaming through a window on his right as he prepared the fires. Prodding the coals with an iron poker, he was suddenly rattled by a thunderous boom that rocked his workshop, nearly bringing him tumbling into the flames. *What now?* He quickly found his footing, regained his composure, and stammered out his front door onto the splintering planks of wood he used as a stoop. A large shadowy figure swooped overhead. There was smoke billowing all around him, and Fern knew at once what he was dealing with. *Not another dragon!*

More often than he would've liked, Fern had to risk his own life to defend against dragons, among other beasts, that attacked him and his village. Just last week, in fact, Fern was tending to a wagon wheel that had shattered on a large stone on his way to deliver some tools to the local butcher when a band of hobgoblins tried to sneak up behind him. Fern stood from a squatting position just as the leader tried stabbing him in his back, but instead, punctured his calf with the dull blade of a dagger. Quickly crushing a few of the tiny pea-green creatures with the same wagon wheel he had just finished repairing, Fern sent the rest of the horde running in fear. Suffice it to say, the wagon wheel needed repairing again. Unfortunately, this sort of thing was becoming a common occurrence.

So once again, Fern raced towards danger to face what could be the final moments of his life, chasing another dragon. His auburn hair moistened with sweat as he ran to the weatherworn opening of his workshop. He quickly entered, slamming the wooden door behind him. Grabbing a finely crafted iron door handle, Fern opened a supply closet on his right. He frantically searched the clutter and discovered what he was looking for. Emerging from his collection of hand-forged weapons, Fern stood upright grasping a longbow in one hand and a quiver of arrows in the other. Quickly he ran, nearly ripping the front door from its hinges with his inhuman strength.

Down the main street of Burdensville he raced, dodging screaming townsfolk and rising flames. The gravel from underneath his feet kicked in the air, ricocheting off homes and businesses he passed until he abruptly stopped and stared into the sky. His sapphire eyes caught the glimpse of the dragon as it soared through the crisp morning air. Ash from his smith's apron crumbled to the ground, and he took aim at the blood-red drake. His heart thumped rapidly as he drew back his bow with arrow poised. Through the diminishing smoke he released. Flying true and swift, the arrow found its target. The flying giant noticed his opponent too late as the arrow entered its heart. Slumping downward, the dragon's massive horned head became limp, and its outstretched wings collapsed as it plummeted to the earth. The village shook violently, bringing a multitude of wooden shingles from the rooftops crashing to the ground like playing cards. Fern swiftly ran towards his fallen foe, noticing the plain structures that he had become so familiar with as they burned to ashes. Scrambling like scattered chickens, the villagers tried their best to find water to douse the rising flames. Fern attempted to assist his neighbors in their plight, only to be shunned and pushed away, something that he had become accustomed to.

Can't they forget who I am, if only for these moments? How much do I need to show them? Shaking his head and wiping the sweat from his unshaven face, he continued his search for the fallen beast. By the time Fern reached the downed dragon, it was surrounded by townsfolk and barely visible. Children bounced on its corpse, treating it like a trampoline in a playground and cheering as if they were the ones who had defeated the beast. No applause welcomed Fern as he approached the dead dragon, nor the slaps on the back or praise one might expect for a man who just saved a village from sure destruction. Instead, he received blank stares and silence as the people of Burdensville butchered the dragon like a slaughtered cow. *Maybe someday they will appreciate this,* thought Fern as he walked away.

Hours had passed, and the excitement of battle was dying down. The flames were extinguished, and the townsfolk were busy repairing and cleaning the charred remnants of homes and buildings left from the dragon's fury.

Fern was in his workshop, hammer in hand with three lead nails clinched in his teeth, putting the finishing touches on the repaired plow when suddenly the front door swung open and a hooded man walked in.

"Are you the one who killed the dragon?" bellowed the man in a nasally tone.

"Yes, and you are?"

"That's not important. What is important is the fact that you just killed the king's personal dragon. The king has sent me to retrieve you. I have soldiers standing outside your door, so come quickly and quietly if you wish to retain your head." The intruder raised his black-gloved hand and pointed out the door.

6

Without a word, Fern set his tools down on a wooden workbench and walked hesitantly outside. He showed no sign of resistance and did not want to provoke his company, if in fact, this threat was real. After all, he had just fought a dragon and did not feel up to another battle. Not only this, Fern was quite curious about how the king of Loustof could possibly have a dragon as a pet.

As Fern closed the door to his workshop, five soldiers clad from head to toe in shining armor with long swords drawn quickly surrounded him. *This is more serious than I thought.* Fern furled his brows as the soldiers stepped forward.

"Shackle his arms and feet," the hooded man commanded, slapping his hands together.

Fern submitted, surveying his position and realizing that although his strength was mighty, his chances of defeating five trained soldiers of Loustof was not something he wanted to attempt, especially considering he was unarmed. The Loustofian soldiers grasped his wrists, clamping down like vices with their cold, metallic, chainmail gloves, and cranked his arms behind his back violently before securing them with rusty shackles.

Just beyond the soldiers was a simple horse-drawn wooden jail cart with its door open. Fern stepped within its dark depths, turning as the soldiers closed the door with a slam. His muscular arms, uncomfortably behind him, tested the strength of his bonds. *What have I done to deserve this? I can't seem to win.* Fern lowered to a sitting position and laid his head upon his knees.

He sat lost in thought bouncing on the hard, wooden floor as the cart rolled over the rocky, uneven road. His thoughts accumulated like falling snow as minutes turned into hours. Torturous visions gnawed at his mind and hovered around him in the darkness. The specters of townspeople surrounded Fern, eyes burning and nostrils flaring as they shouted *traitor* in his face. *Why are the Majestics deemed as such?* Fern's head snapped up. *The king! They are taking me to the king! Maybe... no, why would he... but, but maybe he will.* Answers that might finally be within arm's reach gave Fern light, and he smiled in the pitch black.

What seemed like an eternity later, they reached a great wall surrounding a magnificent castle. It was a pity that Fern could not see the sights of this fortress from his windowless confines, for it was an experience that most will never witness. No one was permitted inside without invitation, or in Fern's case, arrest.

As they approached the stone walls of Loustof, pines flanked the sides of the path, and what was once uneven and rocky, now became a smooth cobblestone road. Beautiful vines twisted and climbed, clinging to stone as they scaled the massive walls. Vibrant pink flowers burst open, and lush landscaping made for an awe-inspiring presentation. A set of solid wooden doors, twenty feet tall and adorned with golden hinges, slowly swung open as the jail cart rolled closer. A giant man, clad in soldier's armor, bounded to the middle of the entrance and commanded the cart to halt. The horse pulling Fern's mobile cell reared as the giant lifted his enormous hand, spreading plump fingers.

"State your business," bellowed the giant like a fog horn, towering over the horse.

"Move aside, Garrick, dumb beast. It is I, counselor to the king."

"U—Uh, I sorry, sir, I not recognize you," replied the giant in a submissive tone.

"I cannot understand how the king allows such an idiot giant to defend the only entrance we have to Loustof."

The giant could only lower his head with embarrassment, shuffling aside as the cart rode passed.

Inside the jail cart, Fern clung to every muffled word as he pictured the pitiful giant's downtrodden face. His heart clawed at his sternum, and the pain that he felt for the man welled inside him. Fern could easily deal with being mistreated, considering it was his way of life, but to hear another suffering such indignities was something he could not stand. *Why do some people feel they have the right to berate others? Why? If ever I get free from this, maybe I can teach this goon some manners.* Fern knew all too well the effect caused by such degradation. He desperately wanted to wring his captor's neck. *And a giant,* thought Fern! A being he had always wanted to meet. The stories he had heard of the massive creatures always intrigued him as a child. He even used to imagine himself as one, just to be able to scare the antagonizing townsfolk with his mere appearance. But to his dismay, he was stuck in a windowless cage unable to see his own hand in front of his face.

Fern laid his head on his knees and began to drift off as the cart came to a sudden halt. He heard the metallic scratching of the keys unlock the cart door. Flooding sunlight blinded Fern as the door creaked open. All five soldiers met him. Without warning, two of the men grabbed Fern just beneath his armpits, forcing him out, the toes of his brown leather boots dragging the cart floor. The remaining three soldiers jerked him to his feet. As Fern's eyes adjusted, he could see that he was standing outside what he could only assume to be the main entrance to the palace. The wonderment he witnessed was something that could not be forgotten. *This is unbelievable. How could anyone live like this?* Standing in a large courtyard,

Fern was finally able to view the magnificence of the wealthiest kingdom known to their world of Harth.

Multiple blue tanzanite fountains came to life as they sprouted water, and circular topiaries danced around them as a breeze suddenly came swooping in. Stone buildings were planted sturdily on the ground, no space between them. The palace itself sat like a king upon his throne, regal and proud. Large towers stood as guards, flanking the entrance. Fern held his breath in awe. *This is amazing!* He was a sponge, absorbing everything around him.

With a soldier on both sides, Fern staggered between them. The hooded man, stooped as he walked, making him appear rather short as he took the first step up the beautiful stone stairs to the doors of the palace. His wiry appendages moved like spider's legs, spindly and creeping.

Intricately sculpted statues pleaded as the company walked up the steps to the enormous entrance doors. Fern studied them as he passed. Each one yielding down upon their knees. First, a centaur with its stone head lowered. Second, a dutiful bugbear with a cringing expression. And, finally, a minotaur, compliant, on both knees with its head held high.

Once at the top of the steps, Fern cranked his neck around the hooded man's slumped posture and marveled at the doors. In the center of each door was a design crafted completely of polished silver. On the right was a glistening soldier with his sword raised above his head ready to strike, and on the left was another minotaur on his knees. Fern later learned that this scene was known as the "Loustofian Crest."

"Mallock of Loustof!" shouted the hooded man.

The doors opened inward to reveal an expansive hallway leading to another set of solid gold doors adorned with the Loustofian Crest. Along the walls on either side were fully armored guards standing still as statues. As they approached, two of the guards opened the second set of doors. They entered a room the size of Burdensville, or at least to Fern's eyes; it was the throne room to the king. He sat rigid and proud atop a large dais overlooking the expansiveness of his royal chamber. He was surrounded by more than a dozen armed guards making it impossible for Fern to catch a glimpse. So instead, Fern stood peering at the walls of the throne room. Comprised of beautifully stained-glass windows that depicted scenes of battling soldiers, Fern examined each. *I don't think my stay here is going to be forgiving. Best be humble,* he told himself.

"Come forth!" commanded the king.

Mallock bowed and motioned to the guards.

Fern was finally able to see Mallock with his hood off. He was quite young, younger than Fern. His greasy long black hair that hung in a ponytail bound by a leather strap flopped like wet noodles over his shoulder. He sported a sparse, well-trimmed, black goatee that gave him a rat-like appearance, and his eyes seemed dark and distant, reminiscent of a cavernous hole...deep, hopeless, and never ending.

The guards grabbed Fern by the arms, dragged him in front of the king and wrenched him down to his knees. Fern held his head up to get a better look at the king of Loustof.

The king approached, walking tall, back arched, and belly forward with his bearded face held high. Fern noticed a royal-blue, beautifully tailored robe that brushed the ground as the king brought his polished, brown leather boots to a halt mere inches from where Fern knelt. The burly king bent down for a closer look. His crown of gold and rare jewels caught the light, piercing Fern's eyes, but the crown did not falter from his head as he leaned forward, nearly nose to nose. His snow-white hair tickled Fern's face as it dangled in front at an angle, and the king's ash colored beard protruded from his chin down to his chest. Fern could feel the king's hot breath as it escaped from his mouth and had full view of his untrimmed nostrils. The waft of something familiar closed Fern's eyes. *Smells like fish. Oh, please...please, back away. Say nothing, Fern, say nothing. Humble... be humble.* Trying not to make eye contact, Fern noticed the age upon the king's face, rough and dry was its texture, as he realized that the king was more than thrice his own age.

"So, who do we have here?" asked the king in a deep aged voice.

"This is the one who murdered your dragon, your Majesty," Mallock exclaimed as he rose from his normal stoop, euphoria on his face, and smiled like a child on their birthday.

"What?" shouted the king.

"Yes, your Majesty, I captured him myself!"

"Idiot!"

"Your Majesty?"

"I told you to *retrieve* him, not *arrest* him. I swear you're as incompetent as that ignorant giant."

Fern swallowed his tongue trying not to giggle as Mallock dropped his head in shame.

"Release him at once!"

The guards immediately unlocked the shackles binding Fern's hands and feet.

"Stand," spoke the king as he arched his back, cracking his spine.

"State your name," commanded Mallock, though speaking in a softer tone than before.

"My name's Fern Majestic, your Majesty."

"Majestic? Hmm, interesting. No wonder," the king whispered beneath his breath. "I did not think there were any of you left. Who, and where, is your father?"

"I believe both of my parents died when I was a baby, and I don't know where they came from, to be honest," answered Fern, remembering his childhood: homeless and confused.

"Yes, yes, of course they're dead," mumbled the king.

Of course they're dead? What's that supposed to mean? Confusion framed Fern's face. The king began to pace the marble floor in front of his throne. Abruptly he stopped and turned to Fern.

"Follow me."

The king stepped off the dais, marching with conviction in long firm strides. Still puzzled, Fern turned and followed behind him.

The king walked leisurely, but still proud with his head held high and his nose pointed toward the ceiling. Fern kept one step behind him. As they passed through the throne room, Fern was astonished by the riches blatantly placed at every corner. Masterly crafted longswords crossed over intricately detailed escutcheons hung between the stained-glass windows. Large golden vases, ornately designed, with polished crimson rubies that accented the bases and rims, and filled with fresh cut pink orchids, sat neatly on marble jardinières. Crystal chandeliers hung low, with candles lit, as the flickering flames dazzled Fern. High above, decorating the ceiling, were spectacular paintings of beautiful women in formal gowns dancing on clouds of white and azure. Fern thought it strange to see such joviality when all he had witnessed thus far was pride of battle, and ignominious statues. *Hmm, this kingdom contradicts itself with its artwork. Though I must say, I like the dancing women much more than the submissive creatures.* Fern nearly cracked a smile at his thoughts.

After strolling by numerous arched doorways, they came to a halt. The king grunted the word *now*, and a set of large wooden double doors opened inward. Fern immediately noticed two young servant women dressed in tattered brown dresses clinging to the door handles with their heads held low. *Wonderful, now the humans are the submissive ones.* Fern was interrupted from his thoughts by the sound of his own name.

"Fern."

"Yes?"

"Walk beside me," said the king politely.

"Of course, your Majesty." Fern shuffled his feet quickly to the king's side.

As they exited the expansiveness of the throne room, a warm and cozy corridor comforted Fern. He could not see where it led, but every twenty feet or so were lit torches hanging from stone walls, and in between them were ornate wooden doors. Fern wondered if they were sleeping quarters and could only imagine the luxuries that decorated the inside of each one. Beneath his feet was a plush, artistically woven runner that cushioned his feet as he continued to walk beside the king.

Fern suddenly noticed the king staring at him. With a smile on his aged face, he spoke:

"So, tell me, what do you think of my fortress."

"Well, your Majesty, from what little I was able to see, I can say I've never seen anything quite so...quite like it in my life." Fern replied, trying to be polite.

"Ah, yes, it is breathtaking," The king said as the corners of his mouth pushed his cheeks towards his chestnut colored eyes. "I want to apologize for the treatment you received. It was not my intention to have you arrested."

"No apologies are necessary, your Majesty," Fern said bowing his head in respect. *Though, I'd think a king should know what his subjects are up to,* he thought, biting his tongue.

"My name is Edinword; please stop calling me 'your Majesty.'"

Fern cocked his head squinting his eyes.

"As you wish...Edinword." Fern's reply was uncomfortable, to say the least, as he bowed his head once more.

"And you can cease the head-bowing as well. Treat me as...as a friend, not a king, please."

"Yes, of course," Fern said, confusion mounting with every step as they strolled past more doorways.

Silence took over as darkness greeted them. Fern scratched his disheveled hair as they stood at the end of the corridor. Edinword reached forward and began scraping a stone wall directly in front of him. His hand abruptly stopped midway down. He plunged into a side pocket of his robe and grasped an unadorned brass key. Drawing it out, Edinword inserted it into a keyhole. A hidden door suddenly slid into the wall revealing three exceedingly wide, winding staircases that spiraled downward. More torches attached to the walls illuminated the stairway, and Fern took his first step noticing that the cushion under his feet had vanished. In place of a beautiful runner were dirt covered slate steps. Fern descended deeper into the belly of Loustof. The temperature changed rapidly, and Fern began to shiver.

The air became damp, and a putrid smell rose to his nostrils. Unexpectedly, they reached a door. Its structure was solid and made completely of iron, except for a small sliding hatch about eye level made of tin. Edinword knocked, and the hatch slid open, revealing a set of peering eyes. Without a word, the door unlocked, and a guard opened it from the other side.

"Welcome, your Majesty."

A guard with flowing red hair bowed as Fern and the king passed through the doorway.

"Have the arrangements been made?" The king asked.

"Yes, of course, your Majesty."

The king turned to Fern as he led them down a shrinking corridor. The stench intensified, burning Fern's nasal passages. He lifted his left hand and covered his nostrils. The burning aroma seemed to have no effect on Edinword.

"Tell me, Fern, how did you defeat the dragon?" he asked, suddenly turning.

"Shot him with an arrow," answered Fern as he cocked his head slightly, brow furled with confusion.

"How many times?"

Fern looked confidently and somewhat proud, holding his head high before answering the king.

"I shot the poor beast once."

"One arrow to kill a dragon? How is that possible?" He looked at Fern with the perfect blend of amazement and doubt.

Fern refused to break eye contact, recognizing Edinword's suspicion.

"I don't lie, Edinword. I forged the arrows myself. They're made from the Ulmeck Rock found deep within the caves of the Ulmeck Mountains."

"Those caves are infested with turgoyles and all manner of evil. Not even I have gone to that part of my kingdom. How is it that you obtained this Ulmeck Rock?"

"I travel to the caves and retrieve it myself." Fern stared as if he was reliving every harrowing moment, lost in the caves, fighting for his life against turgoyles.

The king looked at Fern with heightened suspicion and turned, signaling him to follow once more.

Fern snapped out of his dream-like state, but quickly became lost in thought about his conversation with the king. *Why so many questions? This king is a strange fellow. Call him by his name? Why? And now I'm being questioned about the dragon. What does he have in store for me?* Without realization, Fern was being led into the dungeon, deep within the belly of the fortress.

2

READY OR NOT

Fern was a cornered rabbit, nervous and guarded, as he became aware of his surroundings. Now behind the king, for there was no room to walk side by side in the narrowing corridors, he noticed the cells on either side of him. *This isn't good! What do I do? Should I run for it? No—no, keep your head Fern. Find the right moment. Don't do anything rash.*

Fern's paranoia rattled his mind as he peered into the dusty cold damp prison cells. Expecting to see chained men and women awaiting death, his eyes widened in their sockets as he witnessed creatures, groaning in anguish, glaring through steel bars of their tiny confines. Emaciated goblins, bound to each other, screeched gravelly in their language, and monstrous trolls shackled around their thick, pale-yellow necks and barely able to breathe, moaned as they scuffled on the cold stone floor. In one cell, a creature with the upper body of a man and the lower body of a horse lay on the floor with chains around each leg. *That must be a centaur*, thought Fern; another being he recognized from books that he read as a child, but never was able to meet. Until now.

The centaur wiped his mahogany, disheveled hair from his elongated face and looked up at Fern. Their eyes met. A feeling of pity immediately overwhelmed Fern's heart. *Oh, my dear friend, if only I could free you from this place.*

Each cell that Fern passed, Orcs, Griffins, Hobgoblins, or Giant spiders (just to name a few) bound by sturdy iron chains looked up at him with pleading in their eyes. It was not a dungeon, but a menagerie of mythical creatures, some of which Fern did not know existed.

Strutting like a peacock, the king continued leading Fern down claustrophobic passageways until they entered a large circular stone room. Flanking the two men were great iron doors, and beneath their feet was a white sandy floor.

Fern immediately noticed a mass of weapons. Scimitars, noticeably worn, and battle axes chipped at the edges, some with their handles splintered in two, stood propped against the curved walls. Swords in abundance, still bloodied from battle, and halberds decorated with unrecognizable body parts, packed several wooden racks.

Balconies above the iron doors, and five rows of stadium seating surrounded Fern. His eyes were the size of grapefruit as he stood like a block of ice, amazed by the size of the underground arena.

Soaking up the view, Fern suddenly realized that he was the only one left in the room. *How do I get myself into these messes?* he thought, shaking his head.

Suddenly he heard the king shout "Choose your weapon!" Fern snapped his head in the direction of the voice. Standing in a balcony to his right was Edinword.

"I'm confused, your Majesty," Fern responded, using the king's title again.

"Choose your weapon!" the king repeated.

Without another word, Fern, watching his back, side-stepped to the curved wall and grabbed a battle-axe. It was a weapon that he was familiar with and had used to ward off a troll or two back in his village.

"Let it begin!" shouted the king as he plopped down on a comfortable cushioned seat.

The iron door opposite the king eased open, shrieking like a banshee. Fern spun to face the door. With his battle-axe clinched tightly, he could only stand and wait. *What...is going...on?!* His anticipation was brief as thundering footfalls came echoing from the doorway. *This isn't right! I can't do this!*

Out galloped the centaur Fern had taken pity on, dressed in full armor and charging like a raging bull. Upright, it looked more horse than man as its pounding hooves tore through the sandy floor. A sword in its right hand and a shield in its left, the centaur attacked. There was no time for consideration. Fern rolled at the last possible moment, avoiding the sweeps aimed at his neck. *This is ridiculous! I'm not doing this!* Fern dashed towards the door, grasping its handle with his iron-grip, and jerked. There was no escape; the doors had been shut and bolted from the other side.

The centaur reared back, snorting. It whipped around for another charge. With nowhere to run, Fern stood his ground, twisting his feet into the sand. He swung the battle-axe as the centaur approached. Stabbing the air with its sword, the centaur leapt with ease over Fern's passing blade and landed behind him. A wave of pain filled Fern's body as his shoulder was struck by the centaur's blade. Blood spilled from the gaping wound, dotting the white sand like splashing paint. Fern winced and gritted his teeth. *So, that's how you want it!* His lips narrowed, brows scrunched together, and eyes glared in anger. Fern's retaliation was immediate. Swinging his battle-axe like an executioner, he struck the centaur's shield. The impact was fierce, and the centaur's shield flew from its arm like a frisbee. Edinword danced out of the way, as the spinning disk sliced through the air, barely dodging it. He began clapping emphatically at the excitement.

Stumbling back, the centaur swiftly regained its footing and charged once again.

"Don't make me kill you!" shouted Fern.

No response came as the sand kicked up into a dust storm, and the centaur gained speed. To the amazement of both the centaur and the king, Fern dropped his battle-axe.

"What are you doing, fool!" shouted Edinword.

A wild smile developed on the centaur's face as it swung its sword. Fern's head, rolling upon the ground, was the centaur's only thought.

Not this time, friend.

Like a skilled acrobat, Fern spun his body around, narrowly dodging the blade. He clinched the centaur's dark mahogany tail as it galloped past, pulling himself to a mount with a quick jerk of his muscular arms. Quickly grabbing the centaur's wrist, Fern cranked it behind its body. A sound like that of a horse's whinny echoed throughout the arena, and the centaur dropped its sword. Fern wrapped his right arm around the centaur's neck, and began to squeeze.

"Surrender!" shouted Fern.

No response came as the centaur tried its best to buck Fern from its back, but to no avail. Fern tightened his grip. The centaur's face was a beet as it gasped for air. Its eyes slowly rolled to the back of its head as its front legs buckled. Collapsing to the ground, the centaur fell unconscious. Fern released his hold, dismounted the fallen steed, and turned to face the king.

Clapping until his hands were red, Edinword stood and exclaimed, "Well done! Well done! Impressive! You have defeated my best warrior with relative ease. I must admit, I had my doubts about you, but you have proven yourself. Now we can trust one another."

"Trust one another?!" shouted Fern, forgetting his place. "Trust one another?! How can I trust you? You say to treat you as a friend, but you've deceived me, forcing me to fight a creature I've done no wrong to! I don't understand!"

"Calm yourself, Majestic!" commanded the king. "I have brought you here for good reason, and I had to test your skills. I could not go by your reputation alone. I had to see your abilities for myself, and only now am I satisfied. Not only are you an exceptional warrior, I find you an honorable man. Something I did not expect, given your lineage."

Fern slumped his head like a scolded child, sucking in a deep breath, "Your Majesty?"

"Edinword!" proclaimed the king.

"Yes of course...Edinword. Please, I'm sorely confused by this. Why'd you need to bring me here to test my skills, and what about the dragon that attacked my village? How is it you have a pet that can cause so much death and destruction?"

Huffing a slight chuckle, Edinword shook his head.

"Ah, yes...the dragon. That was Mallock's ignorant idea, to let you think that you had killed my personal dragon. Somehow, he thought it would bring you here indebted to me, but I cannot tame a dragon, Fern, no one can. That was, unfortunately, just another battle that you had to face. When I heard about it though, and how quickly you had vanquished the dragon, I hoped that I had found whom I was looking for, but I needed to be sure. So here you are."

Slightly less confused, Fern staggered as he glanced at the downed centaur. Strained agony gripped his body as slow drops of blood trickled from his wounded shoulder.

"What do you want from me?"

"Let's talk about this in a more comfortable setting," said Edinword with a sly grin.

He turned abruptly and exited through a small doorway in the back of the balcony. A few moments later, Edinword was standing in the doorway to the arena, motioning Fern to follow.

Fern stumbled forward as blood trailed behind him. His clothes were soaked in red and his strength was all but gone. Guards waiting at the dungeon entrance escorted them back through the corridors and up the spiral staircase to the throne room. As they entered, Fern was immediately engulfed with the aroma of the most delicious foods the kingdom had to offer. The array of smells imprisoned his pain for a moment, and his mouth began to drool.

Unbeknownst to Fern, Edinword's servants had been preparing a huge banquet in his honor while he battled a centaur down in the depths of the dungeons.

Four tables, arranged in a rectangle, stood in front of the dais. Each was set with the finest plateware, etched with the Loustofian Crest, and flanking its sides was silverware passed down by generations of the kings and queens of Loustof. In the center of the tables lay luxurious white silk runners that looked as fine as the king's robe.

"You will sit next to me," said the king. "But first, let's get you out of those peasant clothes and into something proper for a dinner such as this."

With a snap of his fingers, Edinword soon had multiple servants rushing forward to do his bidding. Dismissing all but one, a small plump man who waddled as he walked, he ordered the servant to escort Fern to the dressing chambers.

Located just outside the throne room was a well-lit space where rolls of fine fabrics lay against walls. In a corner, piles of chainmail and suits of armor were stacked like pancakes, while robes and royal garb hung neatly on racks. *Huh, I hope these clothes aren't the king's; they'll need to be fastened to me with rope and glue.* Edinword's husky figure should have been the least of Fern's concerns. Although, having your clothes fall to the ground in the middle of a banquet would worry most.

Soon after they entered, two more servants arrived to tend to Fern's injured shoulder, cleaning and wrapping the wound with quick, efficient movements. A handsome royal blue robe, similar to the King's, with a beautiful silver silken shirt and pair of finely sewn tan trousers were handed to him. He was shown to a small area behind wooden panels to change.

Finally, away from the eyes of strangers, Fern took a moment to breathe and assess his situation. Thoughts of the unconscious centaur suddenly flashed in his head. His remorse for the pitiful creature returned, and he wondered how it could have come to such an unfortunate fate. His trust in Edinword had never been shakier than it was at that moment, and Fern felt trapped and confused, still unsure of why he was brought to Loustof.

Fern pushed his foot into a well-fitted boot and stood up fully dressed. The outfit was a perfect fit, and his worries about having his clothes drop to the floor quickly vanished. A mirror on the back wall showed his reflection as he turned around. *I could get used to this.* Fern looked like a proper king, minus the crown. As he returned to the throne room, Edinword threw up his arms in amazement.

"Ah hah, now you look presentable! The guests will be arriving soon."

"Guests?" Fern asked, puzzled expression reemerging on his face.

"Yes, guests, all coming here in your honor." Edinword smiled full of guile. "Of course, they do not know it yet, but they will soon enough."

"I need a moment to process all this—and an explanation wouldn't be bad," Fern said, his face still a mask of anguish.

Edinword erupted in laughter, his plump belly jiggling with glee. "Everything will be revealed at dinner, Fern, all in good time." Mirth twinkled in the king's eye as he gave a quick wink.

"But, who are these guests?"

"They are all my loyal noblemen, lords and ladies of the kingdom. Now, please, no more questions."

Edinword motioned to a nearby servant who hustled forward and showed Fern to a seat. An opulent oak armchair, large enough for two, sat at the middle of the table facing the throne. Fern lowered down on its soft red velvet cushion, looking as awkward as a teenager.

All the chairs arranged around the tables were identical to Fern's, except one. The seat to his left, and obviously meant for the king, was identical to the throne. Edinword stood quietly atop the dais as the guests started to arrive.

A servant at the entrance called out their names.

"Sir Gerard and Lady Merrith of Glaisire!"

Another servant showed them to the table. Fern stared as they pompously pounced to their seats and sat down with their noses in the air. A man, wearing mostly green puffy clothing ruffled at the edges with white silk fabric, glanced at Fern, and with a haughty grunt whispered something to his wife that garnered a giggle. Her oversized, gaudy pink dress rustled as she peeked at Fern. Peering around her husband's shoulder, their eyes suddenly met. Realizing Fern's acknowledgment, she jerked her head forward, breaking eye contact, and nearly lost the giant brown wig balancing ever so precariously on her head. It teetered, but finally came to a halt, tilting like a three-legged dog.

As new guests arrived, all dressed in garish costume, their names were called and they were escorted to their seats. This went on for about an hour until all the chairs were filled except the king's. Fern sat motionless trying to avoid each contemptuous stare and dismissive gesture as the tables filled. One could only imagine his discomfort as he shifted in his chair.

Once all were present and seated, Mallock crept forth, slithering up the platform in front of Edinword.

"Noblemen, lords, and ladies of Loustof, rise in honor of your king as he approaches!"

Edinword rose from his throne, tall and proud and marching with conviction down the steps of the platform. His heavy foot falls shook the silver on the tables. The rattling noise cut through the silence like the edge of a knife. Everyone's eyes were fixated on Edinword, and they bowed as he passed saying, "your Majesty," until finally he sat in his chair.

Fern shook his head as he laughed quietly inside. *It doesn't happen often, but sometimes I'm happy to be a commoner.* His company was transparent, and their *act* of respect did not impress him.

Mallock swiveled to the king, and with a crooked nod said, "be seated."

Taking their seats, the guests began to talk amongst themselves. Fern could not help but overhear conversations of the arena battles and how fabulous it was to see new creatures fight to the death. He sat silently, chest tensed, and felt as if he was filling with steam, ready to burst like an overinflated balloon. *How could anyone truly find enjoyment from watching death?* Fern was nearly at his breaking point when suddenly, multiple doors swung open at the back of the room, and servants began bringing out a sumptuous feast.

The smell was almost too wonderful to bear. Suckling lard pigs and rare giant swamp fish from the Blue Marshes, cooked to perfection, rested peacefully on oval silver platters. Minced pies by the dozens stacked in wicker baskets, and skewered duck with mushrooms dripping in butter were placed only feet from Fern's watering mouth. Roast beef falling off the bone and the finest of fine wines capped off the feast.

The guests did not wait before they began digging in. Fern almost smiled at the sight of royalty plunging their plump, privileged faces into the feast like pigs feeding from a trough.

He waited until the chaos of the feeding frenzy died down before plating a leg of duck, three minced pies, and a large helping of roast beef for himself. Edinword grinned in satisfaction and poured Fern an ample amount of red wine into a handsome pewter goblet. Fern gave a half-hearted nod and rose the goblet in thanks.

Returning the toast, Edinword drank the entirety of his wine in one swift gulp, though some escaped his mouth, soaking into his beard. Fern chuckled as he ate his meal. Trying not to draw attention to himself, he made little eye contact and sat quietly.

As more wine was consumed, talks of who had more wealth in Loustof intensified. Edinword did not seem to care about his subjects, concentrating on his meal rather than joining conversations. Although Fern felt out of his element and was obviously uncomfortable with everyone around him, he thoroughly enjoyed the food.

After a long, filling supper and enough wine to fill a small pond came the desserts. Servants carried out multi-tiered cakes of all sizes and flavors. Neatly placed on silver pedestaled dishes, they were balanced perfectly. Next came ice cream made from mystic cow milk, followed by fruit pies filled with ice berries. Fern's taste buds bubbled in anticipation. Lastly, delectable truffles made by the most gifted chocolatiers in the land, stacked like pyramids on large square sheets of tin, were hoisted upon the table as servants cleared the tongue-licked dishes from the guests. The sweets and drink seemed endless.

Fern's eyes were larger than his stomach. Never had he experienced a feast as grand as this. In fact, he had never *heard* of a feast as grand as this. He could not help himself. Grasping his plate in one hand, he did not wait for the surrounding royal pigs to finish their gluttony. He was ashamed to admit it, but Fern joined in their rampage, swiping at least two of each dessert. Edinword watched, chuckling with his cheeks puffed with truffles.

By meal's end, everyone was jolly with wine and laughing with bellies full.

Silent throughout the meal, the king finally stood from his chair with a wine glass in hand.

Mallock crept from behind, and Fern suddenly realized that the counselor to the king sat separately, a good distance away, at a small unadorned wooden table.

"Attention, honored guests, King Edinword will now speak!"

Mallock slowly slumped back to his solitude and sat down, and for a moment, *only* a moment, mind you, Fern had pity for his sinister captor.

Edinword cleared his throat and glared at a giggling woman sitting at the table furthest from them. Who just so happened to be the "tilted hair lady," as Fern affectionately called her, the woman snapped to attention while her husband supported her wobbling wig. The king cleared his throat once more.

"I have called you here tonight for an announcement that must be brought forth to all. The kingdom is in great peril. I have been informed, as of last night, that my son and heir to the throne has been taken captive by an unknown beast that dwells in the catacombs beneath the Crags of Malice."

A pained expression was evident on Edinword's face, as the entire crowd drew a collective breath. The king soldiered on.

"I have already lost my dear wife to tragedy, but I cannot lose my son. I am in need of a warrior to go into the depths of the catacombs to bring him back and capture this unknown enemy."

The throne room was drenched in silence, guests turning their eyes away, and Fern was finally beginning to realize why he was brought to Loustof; his heart tried to clamber from his chest.

The king began to laugh as his audience shuffled nervously in their chairs.

"Hahaha, no, no, do not worry, my lords and noblemen, I do not ask you to rise to this challenge, for I have found my hero already, and he is here amongst us."

Everyone's eyes searched for the hero the king was referring to, eventually fixating on Fern.

"His name is Fern," the king announced, placing his hand on Fern's shoulder "Please, stand and greet your audience."

Fern hesitantly rose from his chair and bowed slightly to the crowd. *This is a dream, this is not happening,* he thought as he lowered back to his seat.

"Your Majesty," spoke Lord Michael of Higgshire from across the table.

Rushing forward once again was Mallock.

"Let it be known that Lord Michael of Higgshire wishes to address the king."

In a pompous tone, Lord Michael spoke. "Who is this hero, and what makes him qualified to save the prince and our kingdom? I have never heard of, nor seen him before, your Majesty." The brash man tossed a truffle into his mouth and glared at Fern as he loudly smacked his lips together before swallowing.

"He has proven himself to me. That's all you ever need to know," the king said in a commanding voice.

Lord Michael wiped bits of chocolate from his mouth and returned to his seat, flopping down like a fat seal. The thumping sound that followed shook the tables as he crossed his arms and mumbled under his breath.

"Your Majesty?" called another Lord from across the table.

Jumping from his seat, Mallock clambered over, panting like a dog.

"Let...it be known...that Lord Gabriel of Hamilton...wishes to address the king!" Mallock scurried back to his seat, wiping the sweat from his brow.

"Please, your Majesty, forgive Lord Michael's tone," spoke Lord Gabriel. "I'm sure he meant no disrespect, we would all like to know a little more about this hero that we have never heard of before."

"Very well," the king answered, now using a softer tone, feeling calmed by Lord Gabriel's show of respect. "He is Fern of the Village of Burdensville. He is their protector and blacksmith."

"A PEASANT!" exclaimed Lord Michael, jumping from his seat, beer belly jiggling like jelly.

"Yes, *a peasant*, Lord Michael. One more outburst like that and I will take you over my knee like the disobedient child you are and give you what for!"

The guests could be heard giggling under their breath as Lord Michael's face turned a deep shade of red. He lowered his head like a beaten puppy and sat back down.

Breathing a sigh and shaking his head, Edinword continued.

"He vanquished a dragon just this morning with a single arrow he forged from Ulmeck Rock, which he himself retrieved from the Ulmeck Mountains. Not only this, but he has also bested my most experienced warrior in front of my own eyes, all in a single day."

The crowd of nobles could only stare at Fern with complete awe.

The feast that Fern had just consumed began churning in his stomach as he squirmed uncomfortably in his chair. *This is maddening. Just let me go home.* Although Fern had heard enough, the king began to speak once more, "Is there anyone else who would like to address me in this matter? If so, let them speak now."

"Your Majesty, it is I, Lady Bradford of Rambsfield." A tall thin woman with a large glistening silver wig (though nowhere near the size of the tilted hair lady's wig) quickly stood from her chair, not giving Mallock the chance to announce her. "I was hoping you could elaborate on why your son was so far from Loustof, what manner of beast snatched him away, and how the prince was captured."

"MALLOCK! Come forth and give your account," shouted Edinword.

Fern's full attention was captured. Never did he expect Mallock could have anything to do with dangerous adventures, not this scraggly thin man with no muscle mass and a nasally tone. *This should be interesting.* Fern propped himself tall in his seat, watching intensely as Mallock shuffled his way towards the table.

Fern's ears were funnels as Mallock began his tale.

Apparently, the prince, whose name was finally revealed as Timal (which Fern thought was far from heroic) was sent on an errand by the King to the Crags of Malice to locate a rare gem. This gem, a blood red ruby, was said to hold great, unknown power, which garnered Edinword's attention. It was also told that an evil creature, one no one had ever laid eyes upon, guarded the gem.

Mallock, pawing at his pant leg like a nervous child in front of his classmates, revealed how the creature came during the night and murdered the sleeping soldiers sworn to protect the prince. Furthermore, and to Fern's complete suspicion, Mallock tried in vain to fight off the so-called invisible creature.

As the spindly man's eyes shifted from side to side, Fern had little doubt about the lies dripping from Mallock's mouth, though some parts of his story rang true. Mallock described how he saw the prince being carried through the mist, still alive, down into the catacombs. He spoke of how he escaped, accidentally falling into a deep cavern during his rescue attempt. Mallock claimed that by the time he had made it back to the surface, the battle had ended, and he was the only survivor.

Fern found it odd that he was the only one present who seemed to notice Mallock's pauses and twitchiness. He continuously heard *ooo's* and *ahh's* as Mallock spewed more deception at his audience. And the longer Mallock spoke, the more convincing his story became.

When asked about the creature's appearance, Mallock had little to no description. He swore that he did not even see a pair of eyes. It seemed to him as if it was merely part of the blowing wind.

After Mallock finished bragging about his hurried journey home where he battled trolls and goblins single-handedly (which were finally assumed to be lies), Edinword rose to his feet.

"Rise in respect!" commanded Mallock.

All stood and bowed. Edinword returned to his throne, and the crowd was allowed to mingle. All the noblemen, lords, and ladies (all but Lord Michael, who was too proud to talk to a peasant) came to Fern, bowed, and shook his hand, telling him how brave and courageous he must have been to face a dragon. They spoke to his loyalty, and what an honor it was for the king to choose him to save the prince.

The funny thing about this, thought Fern, was that he'd never accepted the quest in the first place. Edinword had never given him a choice. What was he to do? Did he want this? No. Well…maybe a little. It must be told that Fern Majestic was always itching for something more. He just never thought that "more" would involve such craziness.

The banquet was finally coming to an end as the last guests bowed to the king and departed the throne room. Fern suddenly found himself alone with only the guards and Edinword; not even Mallock was present. The king stood from his throne and came skipping towards Fern, happy as a lark.

"So, what are your thoughts? What say you? Do you accept this quest?"

Fern stood puzzled, fingers fidgeting by his sides, eyes squinting at Edinword.

"Well, what if…I don't? Do I have that choice?" asked Fern, not giving the king time to answer before launching into more questions. "And what would I gain from this? Most importantly, how do I defeat a creature I can't see?"

Fern plopped down in one of the armchairs, pushing his face into his open hands, not completely sure if he should have brought forth such questions.

The king shook his head, letting out a slight sigh before answering. Sitting down next to Fern, Edinword curved his arm around Fern's shoulders like a friend.

"First, of course, you have that choice, but the outcome resulting from that choice would not be to your liking. Second, you gain your good name back. Your family has been known as traitors to the crown for centuries. Third, you are the best warrior I have ever laid eyes upon. You have slain a dragon with a single arrow and bested my champion centaur in mere minutes. I have heard legend of other battles you have dealt with single-handedly and have no doubt about their validity."

The king paused for a moment, searching for encouraging words.

"How can you doubt yourself…with any foe you might come up against? I, for one, believe you will be victorious. Not only this, I will personally supply you with anything you need for your quest. What say you now?"

With a deep breath and heavy heart and knowing all too well that death or life of imprisonment forced to battle in Edinword's arena was the obvious outcome if he refused, Fern looked at the king and replied, "Edinword, I would deem it an honor to accept your quest."

"Excellent!" exclaimed the king. "We will ready your provisions in the early morning, for you start your quest tomorrow. Now, get some sleep." The king motioned to a guard to escort Fern to his room.

Fern entered the well-lit space, with thoughts of his upcoming adventure dancing in his mind, and barely noticed how spacious and grand his quarters were. He did, however, notice a portrait of a young man hanging on the wall, opposite an opulent four-poster bed. Candles scattered throughout the room lit the portrait well. The man was painted in fine royal clothes holding a magnificent sword with its hilt in the shape of a dragon. *I bet he never had to face anything like this.* Fern glanced at the painting as he stretched out on what would have been the most comfortable bed he had ever known if not for the sickness he felt in his gut. A combination of all the wonderful food and wine he had just consumed continued to churn in his stomach.

He had so many thoughts running wild in his head. He kept playing back the day, repeatedly, thinking of questions he now wished he had asked the king. *How did the queen die, and why are all those creatures locked in the dungeon?* He also thought about how sorry he felt for the giant he could not meet, due to being locked in a jail cart. Fern had so much to think about that the one question he had been pondering his entire life, about his family's past, never came forth.

Knowing there likely would be no time for answers, and that he might never return from the quest to find out, made his head feel as if it were in a vice. There was no hope for sleep that night.

3

LESSON LEARNED

The next morning, Fern was still lost in thought when a knock at the door interrupted him.

"Yes?"

The door creaked open and in slithered Mallock, his head held low, trying not to make eye contact.

"Excuse me, sir, but the king has requested your presence in the throne room."

The show of respect astonished Fern. He arose from his bed, fully dressed from the night before, and followed Mallock.

"Is it morning already?"

"Yes, it is four o'clock, to be precise, sir," Mallock replied.

Fern could tell that it pained Mallock to be so polite, and it was a new experience for him to receive any type of respect.

When Fern entered the throne room, he expected Edinword to be sitting atop his dais, but to his surprise, he greeted Fern at the door. Edinword slapped Fern on his back without a word and led him to five soldiers standing in formation. The fully armored guards stood proud as if they were ready for war, each armed with a sword and shield that carried the Loustofian crest.

"These will be your guards, my finest soldiers. They would give their lives to protect you and will aid you in your quest. I have all the provisions you will need packed and ready with your horses. You will leave after breakfast. Is there anything more you would request from me?"

"Yes," Fern said after a pause.

Edinword's head jerked up in surprise. "Well?" he asked, impatiently.

Fern thought for a moment before answering, "I would like to bring your giant, Garrick, on the quest with me."

Edinword looked a bit puzzled as he stroked his beard.

"Ah, yes, Garrick. Interesting request, but easily granted. I warn you though, he is as dumb as a rock. Now, let us eat!"

The breakfast consisted of giant eggs laid by squawk ducks raised inside the walls of Loustof. Freshly baked bread was sliced and placed in wicker baskets with small white ceramic bowls filled with butter and jellies. Mystic cow milk and freshly squeezed orange berry juice filled beautifully curved pitchers and was served in small crystal glasses. Platters piled high with fruit that Fern could not identify, nor felt like inquiring about, occupied the empty spaces of the table.

Although the breakfast was nearly as grand as the dinner the night before, there were two main differences: One was that it was only Edinword and Fern who attended, and the second was that it only lasted minutes. Edinword's anxiety was all too obvious as he shoveled food in his mouth, much of which slopped to the floor.

Immediately after breakfast, the king personally escorted Fern and his company to a set of stables. As they arrived, the sun started to peek over the horizon. Mallock could be seen standing outside next to the stables, and to his left stood Garrick.

Fern was getting his first look at the giant, and he was indeed enormous. It was like looking at a massive misshapen block of flesh, only slightly uglier. Not only was this giant extremely tall, but also extremely thick. His legs were wide as fully developed tree trunks, and his arms looked like two boulders joined at the elbow. He was a truly grotesque man with a protruding nose that sat crooked on his face. He had short brown disheveled hair covering the very top of his head, which was the size of a wine barrel. His small kind brown eyes, sitting lower than normal, were stationed unevenly below two large brown bushy eyebrows. He wore plain clothes the color of potato sacks that looked as if they had been hurriedly sewn together.

Amazing, thought Fern, *amazing!* His lower jaw weighed down with wonder.

"Good morning, your Majesty!" Garrick said with his deep baritone voice, awkwardly slouching from his massive weight with a hopeful grin upon his misshapen face.

The king looked at him with disdain.

"Good morning, Garrick. Now please, do not speak again. I have more important things to do than carry on a conversation with an ignorant creature such as yourself."

Mallock's face turned surprisingly bright, letting out a slight giggle as the king berated Garrick in front of everyone. Fern, on the other hand, who was usually the recipient of such insults, could not understand why Garrick deserved such treatment. Although the giant did seem dull-witted, his manners and demeanor seemed quite pleasant.

Garrick's hopefulness vanished from his face and his eyes turned away. Fern felt like giving Garrick a big hug right at that moment, if only he could reach his arms around him. His consoling thoughts were abruptly interrupted as Edinword suddenly turned to him.

"My servants traveled to your village last night and retrieved the Ulmeck Rock arrows for you to take on your quest. I must say, the people of Burdensville were more than willing to help my servants locate and raid your home. Do not be surprised if more of your belongings are missing when you return."

Edinword's apathetic attitude did not go unnoticed. Fern's face turned crimson and his muscles tensed. Trying to control himself, he grasped the sides of his trousers, squeezing them as he imagined strangling Edinword. The king continued, paying little attention to Fern.

"You will also find, strapped to your horse, chainmail armor worn by my fore-fathers, a sword forged by the dwarves of Dundire, a shield personally selected from my own armory, and, lastly, a bow crafted by the elves of Alkyle, given to me by King Dandowin himself. May they serve you well."

Fern examined each weapon, observing the masterful craftsmanship that each possessed. His anger for Edinword's previous lack of sympathy faded as he placed the weapons on his person.

Edinword raised his arms and turned to face the five soldiers. Watching as they stood erect with swords in hand, Fern felt a sense of awe. As a child of Loustof, there was no greater honor than becoming the king's guard. All placed a fist to their chests and stared forward.

"Hear me now, my loyal guards. From this moment on, you will serve and obey Fern of Burdensville; you will give your lives to protect him!"

In unison, the guards lifted their swords in the air and said, "By our lives, your Majesty!"

Fern waited for an introduction to his new companions...but waited in vain.

The soldiers bowed to Edinword and turned away, marching side by side to the stables. Although they wore helmets, concealing their faces, Fern could determine that all five soldiers were men.

Edinword suddenly snatched Fern by the arm and yanked him aside to the back of the stables.

"Fern, listen to me closely. Since the death of my beloved queen Amber, it has been only my son and me. You must go to the Crags of Malice and capture the beast that took him. Find it, and the gem, and bring them back to me. Do not return without either of them. Do you understand?"

Although Fern had questions, he felt the urgency of his mission, and merely nodded his head.

The king looked down, tapping the side of his crown, deep in thought, making sure he did not leave anything untold. His head jerked up, eyes wide.

"Ah, yes, I almost forgot. Mallock will be joining you. This you have no choice in, for he knows the way to the Crags better than anyone. He will be your guide. I have instructed that he obey your command, so you should have no troubles."

This revelation aggrieved Fern. *If things weren't bad enough, now I must deal with this lummox?* His contempt for his skulking captor could not easily be hidden, and Fern knew that even though Mallock would be under his command, trouble was bound to rear its ugly face.

"So, any last questions before you start your quest?"

"None," answered Fern in a single icy breath.

"Good, then mount up."

They walked back around to the front of the stables where everyone but Garrick was mounted on a horse. The giant was to walk alongside the company, for there was no horse large enough to bear his weight, a lesson he had learned the hard way when he was a teenager, already over eight feet tall. The poor beast he tried to mount was flattened like a pancake. Suffice it to say, Garrick never tried again.

With a deep breath, Fern marched to the remaining steed, and mounted. A beautiful creature it was. A shimmering black mane, brushed and trimmed, draped its neck, and a chocolate-brown coat covered its body. Provisions contained in fine leather saddlebags hung on its side. Fern grasped the horse's reins and looked down to Edinword.

The king, with a pleased expression beaming from his plump face, spoke, "I will not say this will be an easy journey, and I cannot ensure the safe return of everyone here, but I will say this is the most confident I have ever been since starting these quests. If everything goes well, I will see you again soon. Now, off you go!"

At that moment, Mallock lifted his arm and pointed to a dark distant mountain range.

"We go west!"

The road, only distinguishable by the slight indentation of the ground and winding like a snake, gave Fern little comfort. Trees were sparse and spread out on either side of the pathway. One could see the Crags of Malice in the far distance.

The sun was warming the air as the group started off. Forming a protective circle around Fern, Mallock lead as two soldiers traveled on either side and one trailed behind while Garrick followed, bounding in long strides on the company's right.

Fern sat astride his horse contemplating Edinword's curious speech. *Since starting these quests? Was he talking about the same quest we're on now, and how many more have there been?* It was all so confusing. Since the moment Fern had arrived in Loustof, he had been manipulated by a cunning king. *Will I survive this quest, he thought? And even if I'm victorious, what will happen to me when I return?*

Fern was driving himself mad dwelling on the unknown. He desperately needed to get out of his head.

"Garrick!" shouted Fern. "Won't you join me?" He gestured at his side, slapping the top of his thigh. Though, he felt foolish as he realized what he was doing. *Fern, you idiot! He's not a dog!*

With a confused look, Garrick turned his barrel-sized head, and with one swoop of his arms picked up the two guards and their horses and set them to the side.

"Yes, sir?"

Fern smiled and shook his head in amazement.

"So, um…Garrick…tell me about yourself."

Mallock turned and halted the company.

"Why do you want to converse with that grotesque excuse of a man? No one wants to listen to his ignorant mouth!"

Garrick dropped his head, looking up like an abused child as he pivoted on the heels of his boots to walk back to his original position. Before he could take the first step, Fern glared, burning holes through his hunched escort's eyes.

"Wait, Garrick. You stay here next to me. And, Mallock, you forget your place. The king has made me commander of this company, not you. You don't call halt, and you certainly have no authority over whom I speak with."

Fern could not believe his own audacity. Never had he spoken with such authority to anyone, let alone the counselor to the king of Loustof, but he was beyond tired of seeing Garrick mistreated.

Mallock's natural stoop became even lower as Fern rose high on his horse.

"Now, turn around and mind your own business."

"Yes, sir," Mallock said in a low contemptible voice, twisting his pencil-thin frame back around.

Fern looked up at Garrick again, who was trying to hide a smile without much success.

"So, Garrick, please, tell me about yourself."

Extremely happy to talk with someone, but uncertain about how to begin, Garrick hesitated.

"I not know how start, sir."

Fern smiled, white teeth catching Garrick's eyes.

"Well, friend, tell me how you came to be in Loustof."

Garrick's face came alive and his eyes twinkled like stars, hearing Fern refer to him as "friend." A smile that spanned from ear to ear lifted his cheeks, nearly clamping his eyes shut as his story began.

"Well, uh, my momma and papa was taken from home. I were only small baby. Prince brought us to kingdom. I not remember them much. They die in arena fighting. Soldiers raise me and teach me fight. I want be soldier someday, but I clumsy and break many stuff. The soldiers call me names. I become guard of gate, though!" Garrick's face was brimming with pride, and his massive chest puffed as he displayed a toothy smile.

"I'm sure you'll become a soldier someday, Garrick," reassured Fern.

"I not sure, sir. King says I dumb and forget things." The giant's posture drooped as his smiled vanished.

"I don't believe that, my friend. The king is only trying to correct you, teach you."

Fern's attempt at encouragement did not seem to work as Garrick shook his massive head in disbelief.

"I say to everyone that I sorry, and it only accidents."

"Besides the clumsiness and forgetfulness, is there any other reasons that the king and Mallock mistreat you?"

"They say I just dumb beast."

Garrick's head slumped to his chest, and his hand raised to his nose as he wiped it.

Fern looked up at the mighty giant as thoughts of living in Burdensville crept like an ominous shadow. *I understand you, friend, more than you know.*

"Maybe I is dumb, I not sure," said Garrick.

"I don't think you're dumb. Never let anyone decide what you are, that's your choice to make."

Tears formed in Garrick's eyes as he took his enormous hand and wiped his crooked nose again.

Mumbling like a grumpy old man, and shaking his head, Mallock listened to their conversation in relative silence.

After Garrick had finished adding a few details to his story, mostly of chores and odd jobs that he was responsible for, Fern began telling tales of his battles with dragons, goblins, forest trolls, and all sorts of creatures that had attacked his village, and how he was the only one willing to defend it.

Garrick, listening intently, suddenly asked a question.

"Sir, why you only one who fight?"

Looking away, Fern heaved a breath and sighed.

"Because Garrick, I'm expendable."

"Ex-pan-dah-bull? I sorry, sir, I no understand."

Fern smiled.

"It means no one cares if I die."

"Oooh. Uh, why?"

"You must understand, my friend, I'm a Majestic."

"A Majestic?"

"Yes, that is my last name. It means traitor in our kingdom. I have been treated like scum since before I can remember." Fern looked away again, misty eyed.

"I sorry, sir, but I knows how you feel."

Fern craned up at Garrick with a comforting grin as his eyes dried.

"I believe you do, my giant friend."

Garrick cocked his head and squinted at Fern.

"What *you* think of me?"

Fern was surprised by the question and took a moment before answering.

"Garrick...I think...I think you're magnificent!!"

A shade of bright pink painted the giant's cheeks, and a smile that could only be described as wide as an ogre's backside (for everyone knows they are massive) stretched across his face.

Mallock suddenly burst out laughing like a crazed hyena, almost falling off his horse, and Fern could not hold himself back.

"Mallock, I thought I told you to mind your own business!" Rage was burning in Fern's eyes.

Still laughing, though not as loud, Mallock said nothing, but due to his sudden outburst, the conversation came to an unfortunate end.

Fern began noticing the trees thickening around the company as the path narrowed, becoming rocky and uneven. Mallock, with a slight giggle remaining in his voice, spun on his horse to face Fern.

"Sir, I suggest we stop to eat. This is as good a place as any."

"Very well," replied Fern angrily. He commanded the company to halt and slid from his horse, landing firmly on the ground. Stretching his limbs, Fern observed how efficient the soldiers were as they prepared the site for their afternoon meal. Mallock, with his rabble-rousing stare, began to order Garrick to make the company's lunch.

"That's not necessary, we can prepare our own food," said Fern as he grabbed a loaf of bread from his saddlebag and tried to cease the giant's actions.

"Oh, no, please, sir, I enjoy!"

Garrick swiftly spun like a massive dancer, bounding into the thickening trees to the left of the path. A large circular indentation in the dirt was all that remained as he disappeared into the woods.

"Where's he going?" Fern exclaimed, a bit taken back.

"He went to fetch lunch, sir," Mallock replied, as if Fern should have known the answer to his own question.

The guards were in the midst of preparing a fire and unloading utensils when Garrick reappeared, almost as quickly as he had vanished, this time holding two dead deer over his shoulders. Fern was simply amazed.

How could he have tracked down and caught those deer so quickly, he wondered.

Looking up at Garrick, Fern politely asked him to lay the deer on the ground. Fern's intention was to clean and skin them himself, a skill obtained as a child that he proudly learned on his own. Garrick smirked and took out a two-handed sword (which looked like a dagger in his giant hand) from a sheath hanging on his side. He began to slice the deer in their bellies, spilling most of their intestines to the ground, and with one finger, scooped out the remaining innards. With his thumb and index finger, he pinched a deer's skin and ripped it clean off the body.

35

He looked at Fern with a smile and said, "No need."

As the venison cooked over the fire, the guards kept to themselves, talking and boasting about battles they had faced. Fern could overhear them speaking about the dungeon creatures, and how they wished the king would allow soldiers to fight in the arena. Mallock, sitting alone and mumbling to himself, barely gave his companions a glance. Garrick, on the other hand, sat legs crossed, rocking back and forth next to Fern, smiling like a daydreaming child.

Fern glanced up at Garrick, enjoying the giant's adolescent personality, and wondered what he was thinking.

"Can you answer a question for me, Garrick?"

"Only if I know answer, sir." Garrick giggled and smiled, proud of his wit.

Fern returned the grin with equal intensity.

"Do you know how the queen died?"

"Ah, yes, very sad, very sad," replied Garrick as his grin transformed into gloom. "It many years ago, before I born. Queen Amber took Prince Timal for picnic outside kingdom walls, king not know. They have meal, and hunting party of turgoyles came from forest and attack. Queen Amber killed," Garrick paused for a moment as a single tear danced down his lumpy face. "But Prince Timal able make back to Loustof with no hurt. Soon after, my family captured and put in dungeon."

"I see," said Fern. "but why so sad if you never knew her?"

Garrick tilted his head and grinned as if he was remembering a long-lost time of joy and comfort.

"Queen Amber known for love. She love everyone. I think she love me if she still alive."

Fern's longing for acceptance and companionship gripped his heart as he placed his hand on the giant's knee. The two men stared into the clear blue afternoon sky.

Sitting silently for a moment, Fern could hear Garrick's breathing. Deep sighs as loud as a dragon's growl emanated from his heaving chest, and Fern's compassion for the tender giant grew like a brother's love.

"Garrick, can you tell me more about the queen?" asked Fern with a gentle tone.

Garrick sniffled, as he easily sprang back from his doleful mood.

"Oh, yes, she very good lady. She very kind. She has baby one time, but king say baby die."

Fern's eyes strained, and his lower jaw dropped like a body in a noose. "The queen was pregnant and lost the child?!"

"Yes, sir, and Queen Amber not first queen, either. Queen Narminia was first queen, but she dies long time ago. I not know how."

Fern was astonished of how little he knew about the kingdom and its happenings. After all, Burdensville was not that far away.

Though, who would he have that could tell him such stories? The fat butcher who worked across the street, never once stepping foot in his direction, let alone speak to him? No? Or maybe the tailor who only spoke in one-word sentences? *Needles. Iron. Hangers.* No? How about the baker? She sure had a mouth that could span the kingdom, but somehow her gossip could never find Fern's ears. No...no one from his village ever spoke to Fern unless they were insulting him or ordering work.

Fern laughed at himself as he suddenly felt his stomach rumbling with hunger. Looking over at the fire, he watched with desiring eyes as the venison cooked to completion. The smells enticing him were shared by all.

"Garrick, how did you track those deer so quickly and kill them in just a matter of minutes?"

Garrick looked confused by the question as he scratched the center of his head.

"Oh, no, sir. I not kill them; they already dead. They lay on ground by fire in forest, but no one around, so I took them."

Fern knew this was not good news. Here they sat, in the open, with fire ablaze, cooking stolen meat, taken from who knew what.

Suddenly, out of the corner of Fern's eye he saw large figures swiftly approaching.

"Draw your weapons Garri—"

But before Fern could finish, five large and angry creatures with heads of horned bulls, massive hairy legs with hooves for feet, and the torsos of men came charging from the woods swinging battle axes over their heads. A blood curdling scream echoed into Fern's ears as a guard flew into the air.

"MINOTAURS" was the only word Fern could distinguish between the cries and yells as the flying soldier landed in the fire.

Garrick, already to his feet, massive swords in his hands, (made specifically for a giant) battled two minotaurs at once. The supposed warrior, Mallock, was nowhere to be seen. Fern, on the other hand, along with the surviving guards fought the remaining three.

Confident in his fighting skills, Fern engaged the largest. The minotaur charged with its horns down and ax raised, racing towards Fern like a runaway wagon. Fern, an agile leopard, vaulted to the side swinging his sword, slicing the minotaur's arm clean off its shoulder. The creature roared, stumbling in pain as blood spilled and spurted from its side. It fell face forward into the rocky path. Fern pounced onto the minotaur, plunging his sword through its back and deep into its heart. Meanwhile, Garrick had his two minotaurs by their legs, bashing them together as if they were rag dolls and tossing them aside. Dead as fallen tree limbs, the minotaurs bodies lay motionless on the ground.

Fern screamed, his voice cracking.

"GARRICK! Come help me with the others!"

By the time he arrived, two of the guards were lying face down in blood-soaked soil while the others were still battling the part-bull, part-man creatures. Garrick bolted, leaping onto the back of one of the remaining minotaurs. The scene was almost comical, like an elephant leaping on a cow. The impact crushed the minotaur, flattening it like a pancake, reminiscent of Garrick's first horseback lesson. The giant shoved his swords through the back of its head, splicing it into pieces. An explosion of red burst into the air as the bloodied mess added to the already graphic battlefield. Fern wasted little time, joining the other guards in finishing off the last minotaur. They quickly surrounded it. Managing to slice its right leg off, Fern kicked the minotaur to the ground. A guard ended its misery swiftly, chopping its head from its shoulders with a swift swing of his sword.

Mallock reappeared from around a tree soon after, shaking his head. Fern spotted him first.

"Where in the hell have you been?! Hiding no doubt," shouted Fern.

"Hiding?" Mallock exclaimed, shaking his greasy head emphatically. "I was not hiding. I was doing my part in the battle."

Fern nearly exploded with anger. His teeth chomped down and his arms tensed as he began to shout. "You were nowhere to be seen! You're a coward and a liar!" Fern raised his sword, threatening to relieve Mallock's head from his neck. Although idle, Fern's commanding voice made the threat seem quite convincing.

"No, sir, please!" Mallock's body began to shudder and his voice quivered as he pleaded for mercy. "I was in that tree throwing rocks at the beasts, trying to distract them, I swear. Please, no!"

Lowering his sword, Fern's face morphed into calm. "If you ever abandon a fight again, I give you my word, I'll not lower my sword until your head is rolling on the ground."

Mallock backed away, bowing as he spoke.

"Yes, sir, of course, sir, thank you, sir."

Fern's demeanor was rapidly changing, and a sudden feeling, as if his role as leader came naturally, overwhelmed him; his upper right arm began to burn. Fern grabbed it with his left hand and squeezed. Wincing slightly, he looked around to see if anyone was paying attention. The company, too busy to notice, were gathering the fallen.

The pain quickly diminished, and Fern turned to Garrick, motioning to him with a nod. The giant somehow understood, and lifted the slain guards from the ground, strapping them to their horses. Fern removed their helmets, finally getting his first introduction. Two men, high cheek-boned and plain faced with dark black hair that flowed down the horses' side stared blankly into the sky. *They look like they could be brothers,* thought Fern. The third, dark-skinned and striking, did not look as if he originated from Loustof, and Fern wondered what far off lands he might be from.

Fern quickly ran his hand over the soldiers' faces, sliding their eyelids shut. Steering the horses onto the path and pointing them in the direction of Loustof, Fern turned to the two remaining soldiers.

"Do you think they can find their way back?"

Both nodded "yes," but only one spoke.

"Of course, sir, these are Loustofian horses, born and bred, they will find their way home easily enough."

Fern dipped his head down and slapped the horses' hindquarters. The surviving company watched in silence as they trotted leisurely, eventually disappearing in the distance.

Fern turned only to find Garrick on his knees, sobbing into his massive palms, tears leaking through the giant's fingers. A puddle that could fill a wine barrel was quickly spreading upon the ground.

"Garrick, please get a hold of yourself. We need to make haste and leave this area at once." Fern spun around facing the two guards.

"Make ready our provisions."

Garrick slowly wrenched himself up, still holding his face in his hands. The loss of his fellow Loustofians was too much for the giant to bear, and the blame that he was feeling poured from his eyes like waterfalls. His blubbering ceased for a moment as he wiped ample amounts of drool and snot on his sleeve.

"I—I go b—back to where I d—do no m—more harm."

"What do you speak of? If it weren't for you, we would've all been killed! You've slain three minotaurs single-handedly!" replied Fern.

"B—But, sir, I t—took their food. If I—I leave food alone, king's guards st—still alive." Garrick began wailing uncontrollably. "I—I k-kill them!"

"That's right, sir!" Mallock piped in with a gleeful grin. "If it wasn't for that brainless buffoon, none of this would have happened!"

There was no containing Fern's anger. "SHUT YOUR MOUTH, MALLOCK!"

He marched briskly towards the weaselly man. Like steam emanating from boiling water, a heat rose from his tensed muscles. Mallock backed away with his eyes peeled open and his mouth quivering. Before he could retreat completely, Fern reached him. With a rapid backhanded smack to the face, Mallock fell backward hitting the ground like a falling oak.

"If it wasn't for you hiding like a yellow-bellied rat up in a tree, we might've stood a better chance! Besides, those deer weren't stolen from the minotaurs."

Pausing from his tears, Garrick questioned Fern.

"How you know that?"

Fern's face brimmed with confidence.

"Because minotaur's don't eat meat; they're known for eating vegetation. You stole someone's lunch, but I assure you, it wasn't theirs. So, you see, Garrick, this wasn't your fault."

Garrick wiped the tears from his eyes and nodded to Fern with a smile. Timidly standing from the ground with the imprint of Fern's hand plastered on his right cheek, Mallock quietly limped back to his horse and mounted. His contempt grew as large as Garrick as he sat astride his steed.

"He will see, they all will see," he mumbled.

Fern shook his head at his sulking guide. *I knew bringing him along would be nothing but trouble.*

Waiting for Fern's command, the guards sat patiently astride their horses. Fern motioned forward.

With Mallock still leading, one guard traveled to the left of Fern and one directly behind. Garrick, still on Fern's right, tears hanging in his eyes, sniffled as he shuffled forward, kicking the dust from under his flat feet. They all proceeded down the path, which was now surrounded by forest and painted in shadow.

For the first time, Fern turned to the guard on his left and spoke, "I'm sorry, but I don't know you or your fellow guard's name."

"Ah, yes, the king has never been very good at introductions," said the guard. "My name is Randal, and my companion behind us is named Phillip."

Phillip, listening to the conversation, bowed. Fern acknowledged him with a nod.

"Tell me, Randal, have you ever heard of minotaur's attacking like that, especially in such a large group? They're solitary creatures, from what I've been told."

"No, sir, I cannot say that I have, but it seemed they were fixated on killing my fellow guards and I."

Fern took in a deep breath and suddenly noticed the beauty of their surroundings.

"Randal, do you know what forest this is?"

"Of course, this is the Mystic Forest of Alkyle, but we are traveling in the land of elves simply called Alkyle."

Fern's eyes shot upward as the company traveled along the winding path. *Elves? How exciting.*

Tall, spiral-trunked, deciduous trees created a canopy over their heads, while small beams of sunlight barely made it through the openings of the luminous yellow leaves. Fern was mesmerized. Not only was he hoping to catch a glimpse of the land's inhabitants, he was also in awe of his surroundings. As his eyes lowered, he noticed massive white mushrooms the size of boulders planted on the sides of the path. They were edged in fluorescent blues, greens, and reds, glowing brilliantly. Hopping from mushroom to mushroom were hundreds of tiny neon green frogs the size of crickets. Beautiful crimson and violet ferns poked in and out of the dense underbrush on the forest floor, creating a spectacle of nature. Exotic birds, all in fluorescents, matching the edges of the mushrooms, sprang from the treetops as the group of travelers spooked them from their nests. Each bird sang a harsh song of warning as they faded into the sky. What could only be described as howling wolves, for there were none visible, sounded from deep within the forest. Water in the distance ran and calmed any pulse that traveled near. The noises of the forest played like a well-orchestrated symphony, making the thought of the recent battle seem like a distant memory.

Fern was so lost in the magic of the forest he barely noticed the figures surrounding his company. Only when one of them spoke did he truly regain his head.

"Ah, Mallock, we thought it was you. So, what have you for us today?"

It was a wood elf. He was tall and fair, dressed in a multitude of colors that matched perfectly with the surrounding foliage. Protruding from his long silver hair, which seemed to shimmer when touched by the light, were pointed ears. His face looked young, but somehow wise, a well-aged soul.

Fern looked around, finding that they were flanked on both sides by at least twenty more elves, all dressed in the same garb and armed with bows. *Just like I imagined they would look,* thought Fern as he twisted around smiling from ear to ear and wishing he had someone to share his awe with.

"I was wondering if I would see you this time," answered Mallock in a haughty tone.

"Young Mallock, you should know that no one goes through my forest without me knowing, and no one goes without paying a price," replied the elf with a smug smile. Fern sat quietly listening.

"Yes, yes, yes, I know you have eyes in every tree. The same speech you give me every time I pass through your little kingdom," His eyes rolled as he puffed a chortle through his pointed nose.

The elf laughed, arching his back and placing his hands above his hips.

"Mallock, I must say, you always seem to amuse me with your malcontent. Now, please show me what you brought for us today."

Mallock turned to his right and started digging blithely through one of the saddle bags.

"Ah, yes. Here it is."

He extracted his hand, revealing a beautiful sparkling white diamond the size of a grown man's fist.

"Compliments of King Edinword," said Mallock as he tossed the glittering stone to the elf.

"Ah, pure brilliance. Give my thanks to Edinword."

Pleased with his payment, the elf turned to leave.

"Excuse me, sir," Fern spoke, waving his arm, hand and fingers outstretched, to get the elf's attention.

Glaring with a friendly smile, he spun to meet Fern.

"Ah hah! Mallock, I am not used to anyone in your company with manners. Please speak, young sir." The elf leapt onto the back of Mallock's horse for a better look, landing softly with perfect balance. His acrobatic posture was natural, and Fern was immediately impressed.

42

Mallock turned suddenly to interrupt, "He is only a peasant, one of those Majestics."

Fern would have put Mallock in his place again, but he barely noticed him in the presence of their guest.

"A Majestic?" questioned the elf.

"Yes, my name is Fern Majestic. Can you please tell me your name, so I may address you properly?"

The elf smiled again and spoke proudly. "My name is Dandowin, and I am king of Alkyle and its surrounding forests. If you truly are a Majestic, then I am honored to give you and your company safe passage through my forest. Now go, for my party and I are already late for a prior engagement."

Fern's mouth dropped like a falling anvil, and his eyes stretched open. All his life, every time anyone heard his name, it had always resulted in shame. Never had anyone honored him for it. Before Fern could ask any questions, the elven king was down from Mallock's horse and striding back into the woods.

Almost out of sight, King Dandowin turned to speak one last time.

"Oh, yes, Mallock, tell your giant that the next time he decides to steal my men's midday meal, I will personally cut off that barrel-sized head of his."

With that, the elves disappeared amongst the trees.

Fern looked up at Garrick with a wide smile, smacking him on his back.

"See, my friend, I told you it was not the minotaur's lunch."

4

THE LAND OF VALOM

It was mid-afternoon on the third day, and Fern was becoming weary. They had been on the same path through the Mystic Forest of Alkyle without a sight or sound of anything larger than a sparrow.

There had not been much conversation between the companions, due to the hypnotic aura surrounding the forest, when suddenly the sound of rushing water broke the silence.

"Ah, finally, the river Dandowin!" exclaimed Mallock. "We have made it to the border of Alkyle and the land of Valom beyond."

"Valom? The land of the centaur?" asked Fern, twinkling in his eyes and breathing heavily. To be able to see these lands for himself was indeed thrilling. And, yes, Fern had read many good books about the centaurs. He felt as if he knew them well and held a special place in his heart for them, even if one did try to kill him.

"Yes, and we would be wise to watch our backs, for the centaurs are on high alert ever since their strongest warrior, Galeon, was abducted. Luckily for us, they do not know who the abductor was," Mallock said with a grin and menacing stare.

Fern felt sick to his stomach now knowing who the centaur in the dungeons of Loustof was. Everyone throughout the lands knew how gentle these creatures were, and that they liked to be left alone. Fern cringed, understanding that centaurs would never harm anyone unless provoked. Though, he also realized Edinword didn't seem to empathize with anyone, let alone fair creatures beyond his own kingdom. Angering Fern beyond control, he began to shout.

"How could the king do this?! Centaurs are peaceful creatures! How could anyone be so arrogant as to think that he can enter someone else's land and just take what he pleases?!"

Forgetting his own strength, Fern clenched the reins of his horse, nearly wringing them in two.

Without turning, trying to conceal his glee, Mallock spoke with unconvincing restraint. "Sir, with all due respect, I suggest you hold your tongue. The king would not take kindly to your insulting words."

"Don't worry, Mallock, I won't give you the pleasure. I'll say it to the king's face, if ever I return from this quest."

Fern, feeling like giving the king a piece of his mind, knew how Edinword devalued life. He was nearly positive that if he returned without both the prince and the gem, Edinword would end *his life* before he could say a word. Not only this, and he might not admit it, but Fern was enjoying the excitement of being on an adventure outside his own village.

The rushing water of The River Dandowin flowed wide and swift between the two lands. The noise of the crashing current along the banks drew Fern's mind from his thoughts of vengeance.

"How will we cross?" he asked, agitation still in his voice.

"There is a shallow section two miles downstream that will be easy enough for the horses to manage," answered Mallock.

"Let's be quick, night will be upon us soon."

"Excuse me, sir," said Garrick. "I bear you across river. There no need travel downstream."

Mallock sprang around on his horse at once, "Sir, I would not trust this dumb beast to bear us across! He will drown us all!"

"Garrick," replied Fern. "Take Mallock and his horse across first, and if you accidently drop them, save the horse."

Randal and Phillip burst out with laughter as Garrick hoisted a sullen-faced Mallock, and his horse, over his shoulder. The gentle giant had a calming effect, as the horse showed no fear.

Garrick plunged into the river. The water, slightly above his belt, rushed around him like he was a planted boulder jetting from the river bottom. He waded through successfully, placing Mallock and his horse gently on the bank. Garrick carefully waded back and reached for Fern.

"No, I shall go last. Take Randal and Phillip, I'll wait for you here."

"You boss, sir," replied Garrick, smiling from cheek to cheek.

The growing comfort that Garrick showed was not only new to Fern, but something he had been longing for his entire life. *So, this is how it feels*, he thought as he watched the giant step from the river, soaked to the bone.

Garrick hooked his large arms under the guards' horses and lifted them with ease upon his shoulders. Randal and Phillip, with eyes frozen open, held tightly to the reigns as they tried to keep their balance. It was apparent that the two Loustofian guards trusted the giant about as far as they could throw him, but they were loyal to their king, and did not argue with Fern's command.

Fern waited patiently, wondering what sort of creatures they might come across in a land that had amassed his curiosity since reading about it as a child. *I wish I had some parchment or something that I could record all my adventures on. I wonder if we'll see any centaurs.* Fern was anxious, to say the least. Thoughts of meeting, and even talking, to a centaur (one that wasn't trying to kill him, of course), was making him crazed with excitement.

Garrick was finally back and standing beside Fern, his giant arms stretched out.

"Hold on, sir," said Garrick as he drew a deep breath.

There was no worry in Fern's mind as he rode through the river astride his horse and atop Garrick's shoulder. Garrick hummed a soft melody in a surprisingly gentle voice as he avoided logs and other debris that swam through the cool water. Enjoying the experience more than he realized, Fern was saddened when it came to an end.

Once upon dry land, Garrick rung his clothes out the best he could, and the five remaining companions traveled on.

Noticing how drastically different the landscape was, Fern took a mental picture of everything he could, from the smallest of insects to the chalky white boulders in the distance.

Vast meadows of tall vibrant green grass as far as the eye could see covered the Land of Valom. When the wind blew, it seemed as if the entire ground moved back and forth like a swaying ocean. The path was easy to discern, because it was the only thing devoid of the verdant waves.

Fern suddenly spotted what he thought was a giant jackrabbit the size of a mountain goat leap in the air.

"Garrick, did you see that?" exclaimed Fern with his outstretched finger pointing in the direction the rabbit landed.

"Uh, oh, yeah, that is Spring Rabbit. They only here for couple weeks. They have babies and die. Babies lay underground and get big and come out next year."

Fern shook his head in wonderment. *I hope I live through this...if only for the memories.*

As the company carried on, many more creatures came into the open to greet them. Some large, like the Junk Fox, a red and white bear-sized animal that scavenged for anything worth eating. They were harmless to most, and only eat meat if it's been rotting in the sun for days. On the smaller spectrum, and one Fern will soon want to forget, was the snot weasel. It was the size of a common ferret, but its hair was pitch black and grew so long that it dragged the ground, hiding its feet. Of course, that was not the reason Fern wanted nothing to do with the creature; the name is the indicator. On the animal's face were two tiny red beady eyes that sat directly on top of a nose that was far too large for its head. From that nose, poured out a thick, green, revolting liquid that smelled as if ten skunks had died on top of a pile of dog feces. Suffice it to say, the group steered clear of any Snot Weasels. Numerous brightly colored bugs, some large as bullfrogs, leapt from the grasses like trout from a stream. One in particular, the Silver Slate Fly, was shaped like an oval disk, and when it flew in the air it would reflect the sunlight, which would send a blinding beam from time to time directly into Fern's eyes. *Blasted bugs, am I the only one that this is happening to?*

As they traversed the path through Valom, Randal and Phillip began to converse more with Fern, and even Garrick joined in. Mallock, of course, remained silent. Fern learned that Randal and Phillip had been best friends from childhood, and that Phillip had even married one of Randal's sisters (making Phillip Randal's brother-in-law). He also learned that both became guards for the king on the very same day. They told Fern how they had vowed to Randal's sister that one would not come back without the other. Fern promised them both he would do everything in his power to help them keep that vow.

Garrick was giddy being allowed to engage, skipping alongside the group like a toddler on the first day of preschool. Constantly baring his crooked teeth as he smiled, the giant beamed with joy, telling everyone of how happy he was to have friends. Fern looked up at Garrick with a jubilant smile of his own.

"I feel the same, my friend," said Fern as the merriment of conversation and excitement of discovery gave way to nightfall.

Mallock suddenly halted.

"Is there anything the matter?" shouted Fern from behind.

"No, but I think we should stop for the night; I am weary from being on this blasted horse all day."

"Very well, let's stop and set up camp," replied Fern. "Oh, and Garrick?" Fern gently placed his hand on the giant's forearm.

"Yes, sir?"

"*I'll* get dinner."

"Uh course, sir," Garrick said, blushing.

Randal and Phillip stood guard as they gathered enough material to start a fire. The task was difficult, given the absence of trees, and the fire needed to be confined to a small area in the middle of the path so as not to spread, because one needs a wildfire as much as a cancerous tumor.

Fern was content preparing dinner, and despite the difficulty, a fire was set with a nice blaze dancing in the darkness by the time he brought over a pot full of vegetable stew. Placing it on a large flat stone lying in the center of the blaze, Fern ordered Mallock to stir. He noticed the lack of eye contact his skulking companion gave him as he brought some salted swamp fish over to Garrick. Glancing in Mallock's direction, Fern could still see the imprint of his hand upon their guide's cheek. A feeling of guilt engulfed him, and he stepped over to Mallock.

Fern's outstretched reconciling hand made Mallock recoil.

"Let's let bygones be bygones," said Fern with a hopeful grin.

Mallock finally looked up at Fern with hatred burning in his eyes.

"I will let nothing be nothing," replied Mallock, hissing like a snake that had been backed into a corner. "You are as important to me as that overgrown monstrosity you call your friend. You both will get what's coming to you."

"What's that supposed to mean?" snapped Fern, standing tall and intimidating with broad shoulders and strong chest tensed. Mallock turned his eyes away and shrank low in his stoop.

"Never mind, just leave me be."

Fern shook his head, still feeling slightly guilty, and walked over to Garrick with two salted swap fish and a pewter bowl of stew. Garrick smiled, cheeks bulging full of fish and vegetables. Fern sat next to him on the soft grass that had been pressed down by Garrick's massive boots. A bug, the twinkling twirler (similar to a firefly, but much larger), sprang from the grass, glowing constantly as it spun in the air, decorating the night sky.

Fern and Garrick enjoyed small talk about the beauty of Valom and what other creatures they might discover when out from the darkness, chest pounding and labored breath, Phillip stumbled through the tall fescue.

"Sir, I hear voices in the distance. They seem to be getting closer."

Fern sat up, wide-eyed, and listened. A sudden breeze picked up and the grass began to sway violently. Clouds covering the moonlight made it almost impossible to see.

"I think I hear them," said Fern, his heart racing. "Centaurs?"

"I believe so," answered Phillip. "What's our course of action?"

"If it's centaurs, I suggest we put down our weapons. There's no reason to provoke them and start a fight, but keep our arms close. Garrick, can you see anything in the distance?"

"No, sir, I tall, but eyesight not good. I hear them, they not speak our language."

It must be centaurs, thought Fern. *They have their own language, as well as knowing man's tongue.*

The voices grew louder, and to Fern's disgust, it was a speech he was all too familiar with.

"Arm yourselves!" whispered Fern. "These are not centaurs we hear, but turgoyles, and they are close. I can smell the foul maggots. And by the sound of it, they outnumber us by many!"

A few things about turgoyles: if one has never seen a turgoyle, they are fortunate indeed. They live mostly in mountain ranges, carving holes, and deep winding caverns where they can dwell away from the sunlight. They are a species of creatures that have small wings that have devolved throughout the years. The appendages are mostly useless, though some turgoyles can still catch air for short distances. Their sense of smell is as keen as a bloodhounds', and their large, rigid pointed ears that protrude from the sides of their heads like sails can hear movement from a great distance away. Their faces are putrid, pale, and green with a slime covered resin that emits a smell that can wilt the most fragrant flower. They have a nose that jets from between their sunken cheeks, long and curved. Their eyes are only slits and show only dark blackness. One last thing about these evil creatures, and without a doubt the most important, is the resin. It is the most potent poison in Harth. If ingested or taken into the bloodstream of any being, that being will walk the earth mindless, aimless, and hopeless until it rots into the ground.

Fern knew all about the creatures that now surrounded his company in the darkness; his dealings with the dull-witted turgoyles were all too memorable. Often, they would come in the night to pillage the town of Burdensville, and Fern would be the people's sole savior. His hatred for the turgoyles was strong, and the sport of killing them became pleasurable.

Suddenly, what sounded like thundering drums started to shake the ground and screams of agony filled the air. Clinks and clanks clashing against metal could be heard all around them. For what seemed like hours, Fern and his group stood peering into the darkness ready at any moment to see the pale green faces rushing in from the grass...but they never came. Sudden silence took over.

"Lower your weapons," came a deep commanding voice from the dark.

Before they could do so, out galloped a centaur from the tall grass in front of Fern and his companions. Ten more surrounded their camp in full armor, holding both shield and sword.

The leader stood nearly eight feet tall from head to hoof. His hair color was indiscernible in the dark, and he had a helmet upon his head covering his face. Long, flowing hair graced his chin as it blew in the breeze.

Fern commanded everyone to lower their weapons, but he could not be in awe of the creature that he was so anxious to meet. The centaur's presence was far from welcoming.

"Do you command dis group?" A deep accented voice bounded from the centaur as it looked down at Fern.

"I do," said Fern as he soaked in the centaur's inflection, thoroughly enjoying its sound.

"And were does disgusting creatures we just slaughtered part of your company?"

"No, they were not," Fern said adamantly, standing firm.

"Den state your name."

Fern looked up at the centaur, realizing how closely he resembled his arena opponent from the dungeons of Loustof.

"My name is Fern Majestic."

A low grumbling noise like the sound from a pack of snarling wolves emerged as the centaurs stomped their right front hooves into the grass.

"Majesteek? Dis not possible. Dee last Majesteek died over dree undred moons ago. Ow is it dat you came by dis name?"

"It was given to me by my parents when I was born," answered Fern, with great intent of finally having questions answered.

"I see, and where do you originate?"

"I come from the village of Burdensville in the kingdom of Loustof. Now, please, tell me, does my name bring pleasure or pain to your ears?

"Ah, young Majesteek, dat is a very strange question. Pleasure of course!" answered the centaur as his demeanor suddenly became hospitable.

Fern's face stretched into surprise. "Well then, first, tell me your name, and then, can you explain to me why I've been treated like a traitor by my own kind my entire life, but as soon as I enter other lands I'm treated so kindly?"

The centaur stepped forward, vigorously stamping his hooves, and answered, "My name is Reagal, Captain of dee guard to dee land of Valom. I am not sure why you av been named a traitor by your own kind, but I do know dat dee name Majesteek as been eld in igh regard in our lands, and in uder lands of fair creatures, for undreds of years. Your ancestors fought alongside mine, against tyranny dat as fallen upon our lands in times past. You are not an ordinary man, my young Majesteek, you come from an extensive line of great people. It is a pity dat you should find dis out only now." The centaur bowed to Fern as he finished.

Fern's eyes teared as his heart lifted by the unexpected praise. Even Mallock sat surprised with his mouth agape.

"Tell me, Majesteek, what brings you to our land?"

Fern answered without hesitation. "I've been sent on a quest by King Edinword to find his son, Prince Timal. He has been taken by a creature unknown to us. It holds him in the catacombs beneath the Crags of Malice."

"A creature you say. Der is all manner of dark beasts dat lurk in dee catacombs benead does mountains, but all are known to us." Reagal looked intrigued by this information as his eyes gave a slight squint. "Tell me, what does dis creature look like?"

"I haven't seen him myself. My...companion—" He wrinkled his nose in controlled contempt at the word. "—Mallock is the only one to have survived his attack, and even he did not get a good look at the creature."

"I see, dough it is strange dat I av never urd of any unknown creature," said Reagal as he glared towards the slumping Mallock.

Regaining the centaur's attention with a clearing of his throat, Fern continued.

"There is also a gem that I'm supposed to retrieve, lost within the catacombs."

"A gem you say, tell me more, please, for it is dee first I av urd of it as well."

Mallock suddenly interrupted, "I think you have divulged enough information to this beast. The king will not be pleased!"

Fern growled as he stared at Mallock. "Hold your tongue, Mallock, and watch your manners. No one asked your opinion." Fern bowed to Reagal, "I apologize for my companion, he will not interrupt again, unless he wants me to follow through with the promise that I made him two days past."

Mallock huffed as he turned away, mumbling in the darkness.

"Fern Majesteek, I av a request to ask of you," said Reagal. "Will you please wait for my return? I know you are in a urry, and time is of dee essence, but it is still night, and will be too dangerous to travel. Wait for me to return, I will be no later den sunrise."

"Of course," replied Fern.

"Excellent!" Reagal exclaimed. "I will leave alf of my company wid you tonight to guard you while you sleep. Der will be no need for you to stand wid dim. Enjoy dee night, my friend, and I will see you in dee morning."

Reagal choose a select few for watch-duty, and galloped, pounding the earth in haste, into the darkness with his remaining company.

Laying wide awake, unable to find comfort, Fern analyzed the conversation he had with Reagal. *Finally, I might find out where I come from, but I can't believe...I can't believe this!* Fern was having an arduous time coming to grips with the fact that his name was held in such high regard and wondered, more than ever, why his name was synonymous with that of a traitor in the kingdom of Loustof. The weight of questions and intrigue finally began to close his eyes, and after a few hours, he finally dozed off into an unsteady slumber.

In the morning, as promised, Reagal came galloping back to camp. Fern and company were all packed and ready to continue their quest.

"Good morning, my young Majesteek." Reagal said, approaching Fern. "I av just come from my king, and av made im aware of your presence in our land. Ee is most pleased to discover your line as not been broken, and requests your company on your return journey. I av also been granted my request to join you on your mission, if you will allow it."

Staring into Fern's eyes, Reagal's anticipation was unwavering. His body quivered as his hooves tapped the ground.

"What great news! Of course! It'd be a great honor to have you in my company!" Fern sprung up on his horse, gripping the reins tight.

"Dee honor is all mine!" replied Reagal in a voice that sounded almost like a whinny.

Fern could hear Mallock whisper under his breath, "Great, that's all we need, one more savage beast to deal with."

Ignoring him with every restraint he could muster, Fern finally came to an understanding that no amount of reprimand was going to change Mallock's malcontented soul.

Fern introduced the rest of the company to Reagal. Garrick was extremely polite, bowing and nearly knocking the centaur onto his backside with his barrel head, saying it was an honor to meet him. Randal and Phillip, on the other hand, seemed distant towards the centaur. Though, Fern chalked that up to Edinword's terrible influence.

And Fern did not forget that the centaur, Galeon, held captive down in the dungeons of Loustof, would need to be revealed, nor did he intend to keep it a secret from Reagal forever. He just didn't know how to tell him.

Commanding the rest of his company back to his king with the message that Fern Majestic would grace him with his presence on his return journey, Reagal trotted to Fern's side.

The company set out once again. It being morning, and the sun fully risen, Fern could get a good look at the Captain of the Guard. He truly represented his name. He stood tall with his back held rigid and his armored chest held high as he trotted gracefully next to Fern. The hair on his body, chestnut brown, gleamed in the morning light, smooth and well-maintained. He held his helmet in his left arm, exposing his face, which resembled a human's, but slightly elongated. Shimmering black hair that covered his full head, hanging long past his shoulders, danced in the breezy morning air. Running directly over his spine, and hidden from view, was a long black mane that traveled all the way down his back and out the bottom of his armor. Long silky hair that flowed off his chin to his chest, and matched the color of his head, swayed back in forth with every trot. It was tied at the tip with a small golden chain, which carried a golden pendant in the shape of an ornate star.

This pendant caught Fern's attention. "Excuse me, Reagal, what does that star represent?"

"Ah, yes! Reagal replied. "Dis is dee symbol of my king and dee land of Valom. For King Soleece (spelled S-O-L-A-C-E) is a Star Reader."

"A Star Reader?"

"Yes. My king and dee kings before im were all Star Readers, a skill dat as been passed from generation to generation. Ee can read dee stars to predict dee future. Of course, it is not always dat accurate," whinnied Reagal.

"Please explain," Fern said, fixated on every word.

"Do not misunderstand me, young Majesteek, my king is great, and so are is abilities, but take last night for example. Ee sent us knowing der were going to be visitors in our land, but mistook you for a company of fairies from dee Blue Marshes. Not only dat, ee did not foresee dee turgoyle war party in is readings. Derfore, you can imagine my surprise when we came upon dim last night, and den running into you and your company. I can say dat we might av mistaken you and your ooman companions for one of dee fair folk in dee dark of night, but your giant friend is far from being a fairy."

Garrick looked at Reagal with a big, ugly, toothy grin as Fern started to laugh.

"Tell me, Reagal, what land are we traveling to?" asked Fern.

"Are you telling me you do not know dee way yourself?" Confusion stretched itself across Reagal's face.

Fern gave a puff of embarrassed laughter. "No, I'm afraid not. Mallock's our guide. He's been to the Crag Mountains numerous times I've been told, but he doesn't like to speak with me. He thinks I'm a traitor and unworthy to converse with. You have to remember, Reagal, I'm not well thought of in my own land."

"Understood," Reagal replied. "And, to answer your question, we will be traveling nord to Dundire and dee land of dee dwarves. Now, can you please answer dis: why, if you are considered a traitor in dee kingdom of Loustof, as dee king made you commander of dis quest?"

"I've been asking that question myself for the last three days," replied Fern.

Travel was smooth for the most part, though Garrick did stumble from time to time, nearly crushing Fern once. As the midafternoon sun rose high in the sky, Fern and company found themselves at a "T" in the path, with north to the right and south turning left. Fern commanded the company to halt, noticing his guides intent.

"Mallock, are we veering off the path?"

"Yes, if we wish to make the trip in good time, we must continue to head west."

"I must disagree, young sir," Reagal said looking at Mallock. "Dee road to Dundire is much less dangerous, and aldough longer, it will save us unnecessary troubles dat would delay us furder."

Ignoring Reagal completely, Mallock directed his attention to Fern.

"You must remember, the king has made me guide of this quest, not some wandering beast that came along uninvited. I have made many quests through this part of the world, and I assure you that this is the quickest way to the Crags of Malice. Time is of the essence, we must make great haste! The prince's life might depend on it!"

Fern's forehead crinkled with strain. *Timal could be starving to death in some cold, dank cave. Should I trust Reagal? Though, Mallock supposedly knows the way. I can't believe I'm going to do this.* Although it pained Fern to do so, he reluctantly agreed with Mallock. The company veered off the path and continued west.

The long green grass gradually vanished and turned to jagged rocky ground, making it difficult for the horses to traverse. Sparse vegetation was to be found, and the land was no longer flat. Instead, it climbed to steep rock cliffs, then down, and back up again, for what seemed like miles. Fern was quickly beginning to rethink his decision to trust Mallock.

The air became stagnant and stale. Random animal bones were scattered along the path, and a stench of death made Fern feel more than nervous.

"Mallock! How much longer are we going to be on these accursed cliffs?" yelled Fern.

"Not much longer. Please be patient."

Any respect that Mallock had for Fern had long been absent, and the sulking guide was not about to put on an act, even for his king's sake.

The group became scattered throughout the rocky cliffs, trying to maneuver their horses without tumbling off. The only one managing, to everyone's surprise (given that the horses were having so much trouble), was Reagal, who seemed to leap from rock to rock with great ease. Garrick, on the other hand, was having the most difficulties. Not being on a horse, he kept turning his ankles with each step, causing him to bellow in pain. With every agonizing twist, the reverberating noise from the giant's mouth would shake rock loose, causing small avalanches to come tumbling down from the cliffs, ricocheting off the ground and hitting the company.

Mallock, annoyed by the falling debris, would crank his head and snarl at poor Garrick without saying a word. Fern noticed this, but was pleased that Mallock, finally able to contain his insults, kept quiet. Though, Fern was fairly convinced that the smack across the face had plenty to do with Mallock's newfound restraint.

When Mallock was a good distance from Fern, Reagal came leaping towards him.

"I tried to warn you, my young Majesteek. The way is treacherous. Dis is dee land of dee Stone trolls. Dae are dimwitted creatures dat feed on dee very stones we travel upon, and dae do not like visitors stepping on der food. Dae will be difficult to spot because dae look like boulders. I suggest we steer clear of dim, if at all possible."

This time, Fern had no problem agreeing with Reagal.

Hours dragged past, and they remained on the jagged cliffs, when suddenly from behind a loud *crack* was heard. Large saw-toothed rocks began tumbling down from one of the ledges.

"Trolls!" shouted Phillip, pointing to the cliff.

Fern spotted three enormous Stone Trolls, only distinguishable from the rocks by the movement they made.

"Watch out, Phillip!" called Randal, grabbing his reins and forcing his horse to the right.

A boulder the size of a horse-drawn carriage flew over Phillip's head, striking a cliff and sending fragments of large rock crashing down directly above him. Phillip was struck on the crown of his head, denting his helmet as he was sent flying from his horse before crashing down between two large boulders.

Fern observed the trolls as they yelped, bubbling with joy, slapping their large, gray, cold hands together as they saw Phillip disappear. The heads of these grotesque creatures were rather insignificant compared to the rest of their body. Their small brown eyes were squinty, and they had only two small round openings in the middle of their face for a nose. The mouths were wide with square, stone-like teeth. No ears of any kind were visible, and Fern wondered how they could hear. Their bodies were squat, but large and wide. They were no taller than a full-grown man, but their feet were the size of Garrick's. Their bulky, uneven arms and large plump hands lifted another boulder from the ground.

"Leave at once! I will fetch young Philleep!" shouted Reagal.

Everyone but Randal raced to escape the trolls.

Randal leapt from his horse, running as fast as his legs could carry him, and made a valiant dash to his fallen companion. Fern swung back, astonished at how agile Randal's movements were, given his cumbersome armor.

"Leave now, young Randal!" shouted Reagal once more, trying to dodge the falling rock. "You as well, young Majesteek!"

Randal was nearly to Phillip when another boulder was sent hurtling from one of the troll's hands directly towards him. Before Randal could react, the boulder smashed into his body. A blood-curdling scream escaped the loyal guard's mouth, and the sound of splintering bones echoed as Randal was crushed against the rock cliff.

With shaking joints and panicked movements, the two unmanned horses tried as they could to outmaneuver the trolls' attack, but the avalanche of rock falling from above overwhelmed them. The trolls' skill was apparent, and there was no escaping the constant barrage of stone missiles.

While the trolls were celebrating their success, Reagal was able to make his way to the unconscious Phillip. He leapt down, grabbing the wounded guard just below the ribs and hoisted him over his shoulder.

Fern, Mallock, and Garrick were finally off the cliffs and on level ground when Reagal came galloping up.

"Where is Randal?" questioned Fern, seeing only Phillip upon the centaur's shoulder. Reagal's head dropped and his posture sank.

"I am sorry, my young Majesteek. I was unable to save young Randal."

Silence consumed the group as they mourned Randal's death. Garrick's knees buckled as he hit the ground, lifting his hands to cover his face. Fern's confusion over the giant's attachment to his fellow Loustofians mounted. *How can he have such strong feelings for the ones who have treated him so badly?*

Reagal placed Phillip upon the ground, slowly and gently, making sure his head was supported. He reached into a saddle bag and pulled out a scrunched-up ball of green plant-like material. Kneeling, Reagal skillfully tended to Phillip's wounded head. He suddenly looked up at Fern.

"Young Majesteek, do you av any bandages?"

Fern, remembering that he saw medical supplies in one of his saddlebags, frantically searched. The guilt of breaking the promise he made to both Phillip and Randal came crashing down like boulders as he reached deeper into the bags. *Snap out of this, Fern, stop blaming yourself. Phillip is still alive and wounded; you must keep him safe.*

Finally locating the supplies, Fern pulled out a roll of tan leather bandages. As he raced to Reagal, he desperately tried to think of a compassionate way to break the news to Phillip that his best friend, and brother-in-law, was now dead.

Phillip, still unconscious on the ground, took shallow breaths as Fern handed Reagal the bandages. The centaur quickly wrapped Phillip's head and stood, finally able to wipe the sweat from his brow.

"It is severe, but ee will survive," Reagal said, looking down at Fern. "We must find a safe place to camp for dee night, far from ere. If we run afoul of any more creatures, young Philleep will surely perish."

Fern nodded his head, sighing, and turned to Mallock. "You must lead us clear of this place, somewhere where we can set up camp in relative safety."

"There is a place just a few miles away that will do nicely," replied Mallock in an unempathetic voice.

Garrick placed Phillip gently on Reagal's back, and the company traveled onward following Mallock's lead. Garrick walked next to Reagal holding Phillip's body, preventing jarring from any uneven road.

Luckily for the dwindling group, the ground soon became level. But good fortune veiled itself as sparse, low, beige grass that shot up from the ground like sharp toothpicks dotted every inch of their path. The horses had to step gingerly around each blade to avoid being stabbed. Again, Garrick took the brunt of punishment, having gargantuan feet. Every so often, one of the blades would puncture his boot, just far enough through the thick sole to poke his foot.

The trees that sprouted from the landscape were not of the deciduous variety so prevalent in the Mystic Forest of Alkyle, these trees were evergreens. Suddenly, Fern noticed dead needles from the tree branches falling to the ground. They fell with great heft, as if they each weighed fifty pounds. Fern quickly realized that what he first thought to be grass was, in fact, pine needles.

Fern kicked his horse and swiftly trotted towards Reagal.

"Tell me, Reagal, do you happen to know what type of trees these are?"

"Of course. Dae are Iron Pines. Dae are a major source of weld for my people. Dee dwarves of Dundire pay handsomely for der wood. It as been known to be strong as many metals."

"Amazing!" exclaimed Fern as he looked up to see the towering treetops.

"Yes, dat dae are. Dee trees keep dee dwarves, and my people, in very good relations."

Garrick stood by, listening intently, and Fern noticed a look of wonderment on the giant's face.

"Garrick, do you have any thoughts to share?"

The giant smiled, and the bright pink color that Fern had become so accustomed to seeing returned to his cheeks.

"I just think. I always want to meet dwarves. I so big, and they so small. I think it funny."

Fern chuckled.

"Everything's small to you, my giant friend."

Time seemed to drag, even though the enjoyment of conversation continued. The nagging worry of Mallock's trustworthiness gnawed on Fern's mind. Not only this, darkness was approaching, and no one had eaten anything since breakfast.

"Mallock," Fern called out in a calm friendly voice, trying to cut the tension between the two. "I thought you said this place was only a few miles away? It has been nearly two hours and we have yet to stop."

"It is further than I remembered."

Fern could hear Mallock mumbling under his breath again and started to wonder if he really knew where he was going. *Could it be that he was merely boasting about the many quests he had completed through these lands*, thought Fern? When he nearly convinced himself of this, Mallock shouted.

"Here we are! The Ruins of Liffland! This will serve as a nice camping place for the night."

An incomplete palace of sorts, now succumbing to decay, appeared against the setting sun. Surrounded by steps, a wide circular building crumbling from age and made up of beautiful bluestone cast a luminous glow on the ground. At the top of the steps were many arched doorways, some still unfinished, with stacked stone, dust covered and chipped and waiting to be hoisted into place. Large pillars made of white granite and sculpted into spirals lay in large pieces on the ground, and a copper dome ceiling sat tilted on crumbling supports. Small black rodents called tickners were the only wildlife spotted, scurrying about under the debris like little thieves.

Camp and dinner were prepared swiftly in the center of the ruins. Escorting the two remaining horses to a downed pillar, Mallock secured them for the night. Phillip was still unconscious, and Fern and Reagal placed him near the campfire to keep him warm. Garrick took a seat next to Phillip, plopping his plump bottom on the ground and shaking the unstable ruins. Quiet grasped the night. Garrick gently laid his enormous hand on Phillip's chest, and began to sing.

Lay my son of Loustof
Down upon your head
Lay my son of Loustof
Nothing you shall dread

Dream the dream of heroes
Dream the dream of men
Dream the dream of soldiers
For soon your wounds will mend

Battles we have faced
Times of war we've seen
Many men have died
On battlefields of green

Soaked in blood the victory
Peaceful times are near
Celebrate the Kingdom
With women, wine, and cheer

Lay my son of Loustof
Down upon your head
Lay my son of Loustof
Nothing you shall dread

Dream the dream of heroes
Dream the dream of men
Dream the dream of soldiers
For soon your wounds will mend

Fern and Reagal sat next to Garrick as he sang softer and softer until it became nothing but a hum. Marveling at the giant's voice, Fern could not understand how he could sing so perfectly given his imperfect speech. He began to see that there was much more to Garrick than anyone could have guessed.

Reagal interrupted Fern's thoughts with a question for the giant minstrel.

"Tell me, large man, where did you ear such a song?"

Garrick lifted his hand from Phillip's chest and scratched his scruffy head.

"Oh, that song from soldiers. They sing after battle. Sometime they sing after king's quests."

Fern suddenly jerked his head to the side.

"Quests?" he asked, freezing his movements.

"Yes, king sent prince on many quests to search new creatures for arena battles."

Without warning, Garrick stretched his gigantic arms in the air and yawned, sending a shock wave through the pine trees. Hundreds, if not thousands, of needles could be heard plunging into the ground as Garrick slumped to his side and immediately fell asleep. Fern, disappointed at having no time for further interrogation, nudged Garrick to wake him. The giant was a rock, snoring like a sawing log. Laughing, both Fern and Reagal shook their heads in amazement.

Mallock was separated from the company, sleeping with his back turned while Fern and Reagal stayed awake, standing guard. Sitting on a fallen pillar, Fern watched Reagal peering into the darkness.

"What do you know of this place?" he suddenly asked.

"Dis was once dee palace of dee Elves of Liffland. Dae ruled dis land, before anding it down to my ancestors, nearly a millennium ago. The centaurs gave many treasures for our kingdom, and it was renamed dee land of Valom, after dee first king of dee centaurs."

"I did not realize we were still in Valom."

"Oh, yes, our kingdom is vast."

"It's a pity the palace was never completed and left to ruins."

"Oh, no, we did not let it crumble to dee ground. Der was a great battle ear, once upon a time. A battle between elves and dee great turgoyle lord, Orgle, who dwelled in dee catacombs benead dee Crags of Malice. Is kin still occupy does evil mountains. Dee elves came out victorious in dat battle, but not widout great loss. Dee elven prince, Galindrin, lost is life dat day. Dee elves eventually moved to dee east into Alkyle, now ruling der. Der king, Dandowin, and our king are great allies and friends."

"Ah, yes, King Dandowin. I've met him on my journey to your land. But, unfortunately, I wasn't able to speak with him as much as I'd like."

"Dat is no surprise, ee is always in a urry. Dat is dee way of elves, I'm afraid."

Voices from beyond the ruins suddenly crept from the pines.

"Turgoyles!" whispered Fern.

"Yes, dae av been tracking us for some time now," replied Reagal calmly. "I av smelled der stench since mid-afternoon when we entered dee land of dee Stone Trolls. Dae av been keeping out of dee sunlight lurking in dee shadows, but do not worry, my young Majesteek, dae will not attack us ear. Dis place is cursed to dim; dae will not step foot on it. Wid any luck, by morning, we will av full sun, and dae will av crawled back to dee caves from where dae came."

"Let's hope so, Reagal, for Phillip's sake."

Fern peered into the darkness and pondered for a moment.

"Reagal, I hate to trouble you with more questions, but there's something I've wanted to know my entire life. Could you please tell me what you know about my ancestors?"

"I will tell you what I know, but I'm afraid it might not be enough to satisfy you."

Fern, still looking up at Reagal, spoke with a slight smile, and laughed inside his head at his dreamy thoughts. "Do not worry Reagal, I'll be satisfied with any news you can give." Fern slid down to the stone floor and leaned against the pillar to get comfortable.

Reagal nodded his head and began to speak. "Dee name Majesteek comes from dee men of dee nord called dee Land of dee Drakes. Dae ruled der, coexisting wid dragons dat lived in the mountainous regions igh above der kingdom. Dae were a great race of people, each strong as ten men, even dee women were stronger than normal men. Dae were great builders of our world. Dae constructed a mighty kingdom, and were wise, ruling in a fair and just manner. But dae were deceived by a friend. I am not sure ow, but ee killed dee igh ruler of dee Majesteeks and took over dee land of dee nord. Ee waged war on all dee surrounding lands; is motive is still unknown to us. It was your kin dat escaped is rule and elped my ancestors finally defeat im. Dee Majesteeks revolted and drove the evil man into dee Ulmeck Mountains, never to be seen again. Dee Majesteeks tried reclaiming der lands to dee nord, but it was overrun by turgoyles. Many of dim died fighting, and dee few who remained settled in dee farmlands outside of Loustof. We urd an army of turgoyles, sent to erase dee name of Majesteek, killed dee last ones, but dat was over tree undred moons ago. Your parents must av idden you from dim, before dae died." As Reagal finished speaking, he looked down at Fern, grasping the star pendant in his hand.

"Thank you, Reagal," seemed to be the only words Fern could muster as his mind flooded with visions of what could have been.

"My pleasure," exclaimed Reagal.

Getting much more information than he expected, Fern sat silent in the darkness. *If the Majestic's were such great people, then why were they considered traitors to The Kingdom of Loustof?*

The sounds of Phillip coughing and moaning interrupted Fern's thoughts. Garrick sprung from his short slumber, wide-eyed, and rushed over to the horses to get a leather pouch of water as Mallock, awake, stood back watching.

"Here sir drink, drink," Garrick said as he placed the nipple of the pouch to Phillip's mouth and held it up at an angle.

Phillip took a large swig of lukewarm water and looked around in a daze as he grabbed his head with both hands..

"W—Where am I, what happened?"

Fern walked over and knelt by Phillip's side. "You are in the Land of Valom at the Ruins of Liffland. Stone Trolls attacked us, and you were knocked unconscious. Captain Reagal saved your life."

Without acknowledging Reagal, Phillip scanned the camp, cranking his head in every direction. "Where is Randal?"

Reagal stepped forward, chest heaving and head low. "I am sorry, Philleep, but ee was killed by dee trolls."

Phillip's eyes grew wide. "No...no...no, he can't...he can't be dead! He cannot! Where is he! WHERE IS HE!"

"Please, Phillip, you must understand, he is gone...he is dead," Fern answered softly.

"How could you take me from him?!" cried Phillip. "Where is he?!"

"Sir, he dead," said Garrick.

"I know, dumb beast! Where is his body?!"

Phillip tried standing, but his head ached severely from the recent trauma, and he stumbled to the ground, pounding his fists into the earth. Two black tickners scurried from the ruins, frightened by the noise from Phillip's rage. He rolled to his side, sorrow gripping his head. Fern tried catching him from his fall as Garrick backed away, hurt by Phillip's outburst. Helping him to his feet, Fern could feel the warmth from Phillip's skin. Heat like a fully loaded furnace rose from Phillip's body. He was on fire with fever, and Fern knew that Phillip was not in his right mind.

"Randal is crushed beneath a great rock in the land of the Stone Trolls. There's no way to recover him. I'm sorry," said Fern. "Now please, settle your mind; a fever has taken hold of you."

Reagal nodded his head as he came closer.

"Dee young Majesteek is correct. Please, Philleep, you must take rest; your wound is severe." Reagal placed a hand on Phillip's shoulder.

The Loustofian guard recoiled at the touch, shrugging the hand from his body and stumbling back. "Do not lay a finger on me, you filthy, disgusting mongrel!"

Phillip suddenly swung around, pulling the sword from Fern's sheath and staggering with surprising speed into the darkness.

"NO!" screamed Fern.

Fern dashed after him, Reagal and Garrick on his heels.

"Wait!" shouted Reagal, halting them in their tracks. "We cannot go charging into dee darkness, my eyesight is keen, but not even I can see does dirty little turgoyles in dee black of night. Dae will turn us all into mindless lost souls before we find our companion."

Fern looked at Reagal, scrunching his face and fighting the guilt that was overwhelming him.

"But...I made a promise to see them both back alive, and Randal has...has, and now Phillip...he's mad with fever. How can I not go after him?"

Mallock suddenly appeared from behind.

"If I might, sir," he said calmly with no expression on his boney face. "You cannot hold yourself responsible for the king's guard's and their actions. They knew what risks they were putting themselves into. We must keep the task at hand as the priority. Rescuing Prince Timal is our main objective here, let us not lose sight of that." Mallock turned around and sat on the top step just below one of the unfinished doorways.

Fern shook his head at Mallock's show of concern, or lack thereof, and started into the darkness. Reagal quickly grabbed his shoulder, stopping him.

"Maybe dee young sir of Loustof is correct. Der is no telling where Philleep ran off to."

Fern looked up at Reagal with his brows held tightly together.

"I know where he's heading. He'll not leave his brother to rot under that boulder. He's returning to the land of the Stone Trolls."

"Den it is even more dangerous to follow. Turgoyles in dee dark is not an easy obstacle to avoid, but trying to steer clear of stone trolls as well will certainly get everyone eer killed."

Garrick stood stone-faced, as Fern finally sat down in submission, head in his hands. *I must think of the remaining group...I must.* Mallock, unbelievably, lay curled in a ball, snoring like a train, fast asleep.

5

REVELATIONS

The morning came, and a low cloud cover darkened the sky, matching the company's mood. There had been no sign of Phillip during the night, and a small ceremony in Randal's honor was held at dawn. Solemn faces and heavy sighs were all that accompanied the dwindling group as they gathered their remaining provisions.

Fern and Mallock mounted their horses, and Fern twisted around on his saddle, looking back one last time at the boulders in the distance, guilt mounting like sand in an hourglass. *I wish I could've done better. I'm sorry.* They set out, leaving the Land of Valom behind.

The landscape was again changing as they entered the Blue Marshes. The ground became soaked with clear blue water, and the only thing that could be considered dry were small islands of thick mossy earth scattered throughout the land. Weeping willows that sprang up from the wet ground made the marshes look surprisingly pleasant. Though, their long whip-like branches with silver leaves hung down as if they were mourning with Fern and company.

A dense fog quickly blanketed every corner of the marshes, making it painfully difficult to see further than a few yards in any direction. Garrick was miserable having to walk through the mushy wet ground in his boots, but the horses seemed content with the cool water gracing their hooves. Reagal, however, was still saddened by the events that transpired the night before and could find little comfort.

For hours, the companions trudged through the marsh without a word. The fog started to thin, and after a while, their mood started to ease a bit. Garrick acclimated to his soaked feet and even started humming a catchy tune that Reagal found himself trotting along to. Fern couldn't help but smile at the sight of it, even with his heavy heart. Mallock's persona never changed, sulky and discontent as ever. But despite Mallock's dreary personality, something about the marshes was enchanting. The large willows that inhabited the land had small narrow leaves in an alluring shade of glimmering silver. There was no wind to speak of, but the trees still seemed to dance as if a cool breeze tickled their hanging branches, and the leaves vibrated with joy. Patches of turquoise algae floated on the surface of the watery ground, pushed away with every step. Small silver fish the size of a toddler's pinky, and quite often mistaken for fallen willow leaves, swam spastically trying to avoid Fern and his companions.

Fern noticed a swamp fish jet out of a deep pool in the distance. Its silvery shade of blue and full plump body made it almost unrecognizable compared to its salted grey counterpart. The translucent fins lining its spine opened as it twisted in the air and plunged back into the pool of water.

Being reminded of the salted fish, Fern was beginning to get hungry. He was about to halt the company when he suddenly noticed a bright light glowing through the fog and spreading all around them.

"*Reagal,*" called a soft voice that seemed to echo throughout the marshes. All four companions screeched to a halt and searched through the light, squinting their eyes to see where the voice was coming from. Suddenly, they heard it again. "*Reagal.*"

This time, Reagal answered. "Yes, who calls my name?"

"It is I, Lillia."

Suddenly, a beautiful woman hovering above the marshes appeared. She was translucent, floating towards the centaur like a mesmerizing ghost. Blue shimmering hair, swaying like silk ribbon in a breeze, touched her heels as she gently stopped in front of Reagal. Her thin frame, dressed in a white gown that hung just slightly shorter than her hair, curved elegantly as she remained hovering just above the water. She was the pure essence of beauty. Her eyes, like pale blue diamonds, sparkled. Fern was immediately taken by her. His mouth was frozen open, and he could not peel his eyes away. Thoughts of everything beautiful he had ever seen came racing through his mind; none compared. *Should I...should I introduce myself?* Lillia glanced at Fern with a shy smile, and for a moment, Fern swore she could read his thoughts.

"I have come to fetch you, Captain Reagal," she said as she looked away from Fern. "Your King requests your presence at once." Her voice, soft and sweet, entered Fern's ears, and his knees began to shake as she suddenly turned to him. "He has requested yours as well, young sir."

Fern stood silent, still mesmerized and captivated by her eyes.

"We av not yet finished our quest, Lillia," Reagal said, speaking to her as a friend.

"Yes, I know, Captain Reagal, but King Solace says it is urgent and asks you to return with great speed."

A look of confidence beamed from Reagal's face as he spun to Fern.

"My young Majesteek, we must leave and return to Valom, to my king. Ee would not ask it of us if it was not of dee foremost importance."

Fern, needing a few moments to think, dropped his eyes. *What should I do? The Prince is in great peril, and I've given my word to Edinword. But, on the other hand, I would have the chance to speak with Lillia. She's so, so...Fern, snap out of this! Think about the prince. Who will save him if not you? Mallock? He can barely pee without wetting the front of his pants. No, you mustn't deviate from your mission. You gave a promise. Keep it!*

Fern's face winced with conflict, but finally, he spoke, "I'm sorry, Reagal, I've made a vow to King Edinword, and I can't break it. I *must* finish this quest. We're the only hope for the prince. Please understand."

Reagal looked down, shaking his head slightly.

"I do understand, you are a man of great honor. I shall tell King Soleece, but please, urry to im when you complete your quest. I am sorry, but I must go. Tread carefully, my friend. I wish to meet you again very soon. Farewell."

With those parting words, Reagal and Lillia vanished into the fog.

Fern sat astride his horse staring into the misty air of the marshes, nearly forgetting about his hunger. *I hope to see him again. And Lillia! A fairy of the marshes!* Fern shuddered, and a feeling of anxiety overwhelmed him. Everything seemed to be happening so quickly. Since that fateful day in his village until now: Fern had witnessed the death of four men by creatures he had never seen before; watched a soldier run desperately to a sure death; fought one centaur and befriended another; and a few moments ago, met a fairy of such great beauty he could not get her off his mind, all in a matter of days. Not only this, he had learned so much about his family's past (questions that he had been wondering his entire life) it was nearly too much to bear. One can surely sympathize, if ever they had to face such moments.

Rumbling in Garrick's giant belly abruptly interrupted the panic in Fern's mind.

"When we eat, sir?"

"Yes...yes...I'm sorry Garrick, we'll stop at once."

The group, now down to only three, sat on one of the mossy islands to have lunch. It was a surprisingly bouncy and smooth surface the texture of rubber. To Fern and Garrick's astonishment, Mallock sat relatively close. Fern credited the absence of Reagal for the man's sudden affection.

With questions still in his mind, he peered over to his cowering guide.

"Mallock, I know we don't see things eye to eye, and that you think me a mere peasant and traitor, but it doesn't mean we can't converse with one another and be cordial."

"What would you have to say that would interest me?" Mallock asked with his usual rude tone.

"I thought maybe you could answer a few questions I have," replied Fern. "For instance, why do you call me a traitor when I've never betrayed the king?"

"Because that is what the king has declared. That all with the name of Majestic are traitors to the crown of Loustof." Again, Mallock spoke as if Fern should have known the answer.

"How is that possible? The king said the name of Majestic has been known as traitor for centuries," said Fern. "How could he have been the one to declare it?"

"How should I know? Leave me be!"

Turning to Garrick, Fern shook his head and rolled his eyes.

"So, Garrick, what can you tell me of this matter?"

"I sorry, sir, I not know of your family or what king do."

Fern sighed and returned to his lunch. He sat thinking of Lillia, and why King Solace needed Reagal so urgently. *I wonder why my presence was necessary? If only I could have gone! I would've taken Garrick with me and left Mallock to save Timal. After all, according to his boastings, he's a great warrior.* Fern started to laugh quietly to himself. His thoughts consumed him for the remainder of the day.

Night came like a swift pain.

"We must leave this land quickly," announced Mallock. "Once the sun sets, the marshes will become an inhospitable place to dwell."

"What do you speak of?" asked Fern, kicking his heels to move his horse next to Mallock's.

"Can't you just listen without so many questions?" snapped Mallock.

Fern took a heavy breath and sighed as he and his horse lagged back.

"I can't win with that guy, can I?" asked Fern as he looked up to Garrick with a toothy grin.

"Mallock just loyal to king, sir. He want impress him very much, but he never can. I think he just sad man."

Fern sat astride his horse staring at Garrick with a gleam in his eye.

"You know, my friend, you are quite the giant."

Pink cheeks and crooked teeth appeared on Garrick's face.

"You know, sir, I know why we leave fast from this place," he said as he looked up at the darkening sky.

"You do?" asked Fern.

"Yes, sir. You want know?"

"Of course, please."

"Well, it because of fairy magic."

"Fairy magic?"

"Yes, sir, fairy put spell over marshes. If get caught after nightfall, you fall asleep for very, very long time. When wake up, you forget who you is."

Suddenly Mallock piped up.

"Ah, yes, we are nearly there!"

"What? The Crag Mountains are just beyond the Marshes?" asked Fern.

"Yes," answered Mallock. "I told you I knew where I was going, and taking a straight westerly path would be the quickest way. You cannot rely on what wandering beasts discovered in the night will say."

"Be that as it may, Mallock, we sacrificed two good soldiers for that shortcut."

Fern stared at Mallock with some hope for sympathy. He would get none.

"The king knew the sacrifices that needed to be made to save his son, and I have already told you that the guards knew it as well," replied Mallock. "They were honored to die for their king, and will be celebrated as heroes when we return."

"Look, sir," Garrick said pointing to the ground. "It's drier."

"Ah, yes, we must be out of the marshes," said Fern. "Mallock, how much farther to the foot of the mountains?"

"Not much, we should find the path shortly."

Fern couldn't help but hear Mallock mumbling under his breath again. Though, Mallock probably wasn't trying to hide his distaste with much effort.

"Patience, patience, why can't this traitor understand patience?"

Fern laughed uncontrollably at Mallock's lack of patience and suddenly noticed the ground was completely dry and devoid of trees. Grass became scarce and brown, and the sun had almost set as silhouettes of rocks and boulders started to dot the darkness. The clouds parted and the moon shone bright, lighting up the night sky. Large black rat bats (named so due to their size and the long hairless tail that trailed behind them) swooped inches above the company's heads, gulping down tiny insects that were invisible to the naked eye.

The mountains, now before them, seemed to stretch on both sides as far as the eye could see. Fern looked skyward, amazed at the size of the Crags. Their peeks were sharp and jetted through mist that hovered ominously in wisps. A stench that penetrated the company's nasal passages burned, making their eyes water. Death was not seen, but it could be felt in every direction as frigid air penetrated their bones. Even the horses were vibrating with shivers.

The closer they came to the foot of the mountain, the less vegetation they saw, until eventually there was none. It was a harsh, barren land.

Garrick walked close to Fern, humming another tune he learned as a child. The hum, about giant yellow sea turtles that swam freely amongst the waves, was pleasant to Fern's ears. Garrick's voice continued to amaze Fern as the hum eventually transformed into a full-fledged song.

Yellow is the turtles
Blue is the sea
Yellow is the turtles
Free as can be
Waves crashing down
Rough and white
Yellow turtles swim
All through the night

Mallock spun with a jerk to face Garrick, his teeth clinched like a bear trap, and a look that could pierce one's heart haunted the poor giant.

"Will you please stop that annoying racket!" whispered Mallock. "This is an evil place with evil beasts lurking around every crack and crevice. What are you trying to do, call them to us?!"

Fern winced, knowing Mallock was correct.

"I'm sorry, my friend, but Mallock's right. We need to be as silent as possible. I've heard stories about this place, and wouldn't want to meet the creatures that inhabit these lands, especially in the dark."

"Sorry, sir," whispered Garrick.

If one hasn't guessed by now, Fern Majestic, although isolated most of his life, knew many a thing about the lands they were traveling. Having no friends or even souls to speak to, Fern had ample time for reading.

Mallock suddenly raised his hand to get Fern's attention. Pointing to the ground, he had found the path they were looking for. The three men veered onto a narrow trail, now traveling single file.

Noticing a shadowy figure move across the path a distance in front of them, Fern was reminded about the turgoyles that had been tracking his group, though, the creeping silhouette seemed too tall to be a turgoyle.

"Mallock, did you see that?" whispered Fern.

"See what?"

"Something just ran across the path up ahead."

"I saw nothing," he said, squinting his eyes as he held his hand above his brow and peered into the darkness.

Fern was positive he saw something, but Mallock shrugged his shoulders and carried on. They had traveled through the darkness for an hour without another sight or sound of anything when Mallock halted the company.

Still speaking in a whisper, he pointed to the ground.

"This is where the path ends. We must continue on foot up the mountain to the base of the Crags. The entrance to the catacombs is still half a night's journey from here. Take what provisions we have from your horse."

"But what about the return journey, and our horses? They'll surely be gone by the time we return, or killed by some wandering beast," said Fern, his brows tightening.

"Do not worry about the horses, Garrick is staying. He will guard them for us."

"What? Why?" asked Fern.

"He is too large for the catacombs. They were tunneled by turgoyles *for* turgoyles, not twelve-foot giants," explained Mallock as he shook his head, irritated that he had to explain everything to Fern.

Fern nodded, slightly red faced, and turned to Garrick, "I'm sorry, my friend, you must remain with the horses."

Looking down, worry covering every inch of his misshapen face, Garrick began to shiver.

"How long you be gone, sir?"

"Not sure, but we'll try to be as fast as possible," Fern said, grabbing Garrick's forearm and trying to reassure his giant friend. "I must warn you, though, we've been tracked by turgoyles since the land of the Stone Trolls. I don't think they'd bother a giant, but you must watch your back; there are other creatures in this land far more dangerous than those wretched turgoyles. Please be safe."

"Not worry bout me...my friend. Just save prince, I be fine."

Garrick eased his enormous, trembling hand on the top of Fern's head.

"Garrick, you're a good man, and you've become my friend. If I don't make it back from this, I want you to remember that."

Fern placed his hand on top of Garrick's.

"Thank you, sir."

"Pathetic," said Mallock, shaking his head. "Let's be off. We are wasting precious time."

"Yes, of course," said Fern, taking Garrick's massive hand from his head. "Goodbye."

The two men turned from the giant and began their ascent up the steep mountain. Jagged rock protruded outward in every direction like the horns of a dragon. Mallock climbed with ease, knowing every hand grab and foot hold, as if he had scaled the rock wall a million times. Falling a distance behind, Fern was shocked at how quickly his spindly guide crawled up the mountainside. Mallock was as comfortable as a spider in its web.

Fern looked back to see Garrick still standing by the horses, looking more like a dwarf than a giant. Not realizing how fast they were climbing, he was soon out of sight.

A fog quickly settled beneath them, making it impossible to see the ground below. Mallock, now yards away, continued to gain distance as Fern repeatedly asked him to slow down. But, of course, the skulking spider pretended not to hear, eventually disappearing from Fern's sight.

"Mallock!" shouted Fern in a harsh whisper.

"Do not worry, I have reached the top of a cliff!"

Fern suddenly noticed Mallock's pale face peering over the rock.

Hanging his scrawny arm over the ledge like a limp noodle, Mallock grabbed Fern's hand to hoist him up. His cold, clammy skin made Fern's senses crawl, and a sinister feeling suddenly grabbed him by the heart.

Releasing Mallock's soft grip, Fern's eyes scanned his position. An enormous, level landing cut from the mountainside sat in solitude. A cavern opening, covered in thick spider webs, gaped at Fern, and an icy cold chill ran up his spine.

"Is this the entrance to the catacombs?"

"No," answered Mallock. "This is the cavern I fell into when I was trying to save the prince."

"Why are we here?" Fern scrunched his face again in confusion.

"I saw the gem the king wishes for when I fell in," replied Mallock adamantly. "but, unfortunately, I could not retrieve it."

"Why?" Suspicion colored Fern's tone, and Mallock became defensive.

"Because, fool, I was attacked by giant glass spiders and had to escape. I barely made it out alive." Mallock's eyes shifted from side to side as he spoke. "I am not a skilled warrior like you. Now go in and retrieve the gem for the king. You gave your word."

"Don't you think the prince is more important than this gem? Shouldn't we try to save him first and worry about this afterward?" Fern was biding his time as he tried to determine what was up Mallock's sleeve.

"This gem holds great power and will help us defeat the creature that took Prince Timal. We must find it first!" Mallock's voice tightened with anxiety.

"But you told me the creature is the one that guards this gem."

"Well, then, what's the problem? If this is where the gem is, then the creature must be holding Prince Timal here as well."

Using whatever deductive skills he had, Fern scrutinized Mallock's every word. He stood rooted to the spot for a moment wondering what was really in the cavern.

"Well? Are you going or not?"

Fern's chest heaved.

"Fine, Mallock, I'll go, but if you try anything foolish, I'll follow through with that promise I made to you. Mark my words, your head will be detached from your neck before you blink an eye."

"I swear to you, I do not lie," Mallock exclaimed with conviction.

Looking back at Mallock one last time, Fern took his sword from its scabbard. He cautiously proceeded down into the cavern, hacking down the unbelievably thick spider webs hanging from the rocky surface. The wide strands spun around his blade like cotton candy. Frustration swelled in Fern's chest, and anger reared its putrid face as he scraped his sword along the cavern walls. His cursing echoed like a congregation speaking in tongues.

Pacing the ground just outside the entrance, Mallock waited anxiously. His palms were sweating, and his heart thundered inside his concave chest. Repeatedly, he would glance at the entrance speaking to himself.

Hurry, hurry! I will show them! I will show them all!

Inside the cavern, Fern stumbled in the dark as the ground began to take a steep downward course. He bent down, placing his hand on the stone floor, and began combing the ground. Touching what he thought was a stick, he picked it up. He tore a piece of his shirt from underneath his chainmail and wrapped it around the makeshift torch. Pulling a flint rock from the pack strapped to his belt, he struck the rock on the steel of his sword. A bright flame engulfed the cloth, illuminating the cave.

Fern was slightly bewildered, realizing what he held in his hand. What was first thought to be a stick turned out to be a human arm bone. Fern shook his head in disgust. *Maybe I should have lit a torch before stepping into an unknown cave*, he laughed.

As he shuffled down deeper into the cavern, Fern could only wonder if the bone he held belonged to the missing prince, and if so, would he find the rest of him alive?

More bones decorated the floor, although none looked human, and sticky spider webs hung from every opening, crevice, and crack, making it difficult to maneuver quickly.

Fern was not far into the cave when he noticed a misshapen crimson stone the size of a large strawberry on the ground encircled in a ring of red light. He approached it cautiously, expecting to see some great beast hiding in the darkness. As he came closer, he noticed the ruby was attached to a golden chain and devoid of dust or debris.

Odd, Fern thought, looking down at the red ruby. *Why would it be hung on a necklace? And how it shines! And where is this beast Mallock was talking about? Where are the inhabitants of this cave?*

As he bent down and gingerly plucked the ruby from the ground and placed it in his pocket, his torch went out. Fern laughed at himself for hiding a perfectly useful source of light, and immediately drew the gemstone back into the open, attaching the chain around his neck.

His search for Timal continued, but Fern's path abruptly ended. He was now standing at the back of the cave.

Turning to try another course, Fern spun around. The glowing yellow eyes of more than a dozen Glass Spiders froze him to the cavern floor. The hideous creatures stood four feet from the ground clicking the ends of their long, jointed legs on the hard, rocky surface. They were completely transparent, and Fern could see their hearts in the center of their abdomen, beating rapidly. A dozen eyes in the middle of their heads and long fangs that dripped poison decorated their clear face.

They lunged from every direction. Fern began to swing his sword, quickly striking down numerous spiders. Climbing the ceiling of the cavern, the spindly-legged creatures flanked the rear while innumerable others attacked Fern from the front. A strange gurgling noise, reminiscent of a starving belly, resonated from the spiders. *Are they speaking to one another?* The creatures were intelligent. Fern could recognize the sounds as language, and the spiders were strategizing their moves.

As Fern defended himself, one managed to scamper on his back, knocking him to the ground. The giant arachnid immediately began wrapping web tightly around his ankles, spinning it like yarn. Fern dropped his sword for only a moment trying to tear the silky substance from his legs, but the second his weapon fell from his hand, a spider was upon it, kicking it from Fern's reach. Free from his sticky bindings, Fern booted the transparent beast to its side and punted it across the floor just in time to see countless more heading his way.

A sudden sharp pain shot through Fern's back as a spider sunk its fangs deep between his shoulder blades. He quickly spun around, knocking the spider to the ground and shoved his sword through its chitin-encrusted underbelly. Pain swiftly coursed through Fern's veins, scattering like lightning. The stone around his neck grew brighter and the spiders were blinded by the luminous glow. Fern maneuvered himself against the cavern wall, reaching for his sword. Grasping it in his hand, he swung, slicing the spiders down one at a time, but there was no respite. More continued to appear, crawling from narrow openings scattered throughout the cavern walls.

Fern forced his way through the oncoming horde, legs flailing, arms punching, and sword swinging. He was clear! He ran for the entrance as fast as he could, trying to gain some distance between himself and the spiders. He grabbed the elven bow Edinword had given him at the onset of his quest and took out one of his Ulmeck Rock arrows. Pulling back his bowstring, he released. The arrow soared through the tunnel, hitting its intended target. Flying clean through the spider's body, the arrow impaled another directly behind it.

Fern continued shooting the spiders down with unerring accuracy until he had exhausted his ammunition. His shoulders slumped as he noticed more spiders still approaching. Knowing it would only be a matter of time before he was overwhelmed, Fern contemplated his options. He looked down at the gem, trying to figure out what power it might hold and how he could use it, but it just hung around his neck giving off the same dim glow.

Spiders were nearly upon him when he did the only thing he could think of. Using his immense strength, Fern grasped a large boulder from the ground. Arms bulging and chest heaving, he hurled it at the cavern ceiling with a roar of colossal effort. Large stones and fragments of rock began to rain down as the cave collapsed onto the approaching horde. Most of the creatures were killed, crushed beneath the fallen rocks, but Fern could hear the gurgling screeches of countless more trying to claw their way through. He was certain it would only hold them off for so long.

They must have other tunnels out, he thought.

Adrenaline fueled his exhausted body, as Fern remembered his wound. Reaching to his back, he examined its severity. To his amazement, the spider had bitten through his chainmail, but did not pierce his flesh. Fern could have sworn it broke the skin. He felt the pain, and even felt the venom pulsing its way into his muscles, yet he felt no effect from it. There was no time to be puzzled. He had to search for the prince, and he still had the creature to worry about.

Fern scoured the rest of the cavern as quickly as he could, killing the occasional spider, but there was no Prince Timal. He decided to head back to the surface before more glass spiders found him. As he came to the entrance of the cavern, webbing as thick as harp strings covered his escape. He took his sword and began to hack into the stiff, fibrous strands, but it was layers upon layers thick and not easily cut through. Suddenly hearing Mallock pleading for help, though he could not see him, Fern called out.

"What's wrong?!"

"Please, please help me! There are turgoyles coming from the catacombs, I cannot protect myself from them." Mallock's voice sounded truly frightened, free of feigning an ulterior motive.

Fern could hear the yells and screams of turgoyles approaching.

"I'm sorry, Mallock! I can't cut through this barrier so quickly! I'm trying my best! Just—just hold on!" Fern continued to hack at the webbing with every ounce of strength in his body.

Finally managing to cut a hole through the side of the opening just large enough to fit his arm through, Mallock came running forward out of breath.

"Did you find the gem?"

"Yes!"

"Please, hand it to me! They are almost upon me! It's my only hope at survival!"

Without thinking, Fern took the gem from around his neck and handed it to Mallock.

"Thank you!"

Fern could hear the clanking of metal and the yells of turgoyles dancing outside the cavern. He hoped he would be in time to save Mallock. Even though he could not stand him, pity for his pathetic guide had grown in Fern, and he did not want to see him die, at least not under his watch.

Fern continued hacking and slicing the webbing until finally he broke through. The scene greeting him brought him up short, to say the least.

Mallock stood with the gem around his neck, an army of grinning turgoyles behind him. Looking at Fern, Mallock laughed, his ratty goatee stretched around his crooked smile. "I suggest you drop your weapons. As you can see, you are extremely outnumbered. Even with your strength and fighting skills, there is no way you can win."

Fern stared, bewildered by the turn of events. He knew Mallock was a conniving weasel, and betraying him was no surprise, but never did he think Mallock would be in league with the turgoyles.

Fern stood facing Mallock, chest heaving, and arms fatigued from hacking and fighting. He swayed on his feet from side to side in his exhaustion, sweat dripping into his eyes. Despite his lack of strength, Fern was not about to drop his weapons. His arms hung heavy at his sides as thoughts bombarded his mind. *How could it come to this? How could I let it?! How could this man get the better of me? I've come so far...for what?* Fern trembled with anger.

Swallowing the rising lump in his throat, he spoke. "I—" Hoarseness strangled his vocal cords. He swallowed and tried again. "I will surrender my weapons, but before I do, you must answer my questions."

"Very well, traitor, ask your questions! You will be dead soon enough, anyway."

"What about the king? If you go back without Prince Timal or myself, he'll surely suspect something," Fern said, clenching his sword in his weak hand.

"No wonder you and that ignorant giant are such good friends," Mallock said, grinning. "You are just as dumb as he is. The king is the one who ordered you killed. He wanted you dead as soon as you found the gem and captured that imaginary beast for his stupid arena battles."

"Imaginary? Then what about Prince Timal? Where is he?"

"I killed him in his sleep, along with his idiot guards."

"Why? Why kill the prince?"

Mallock's wild smile widened, and his eyes even more so, brimming with maddened glee. "Because...I am the bastard son of the king! I have been living in the shadow of Prince Timal my entire life. My father killed my servant mother, trying to hide his sin, but could not bring himself to kill me. Instead, I was made the stinking counselor to the king. Nobody knows who I am, but now, now that Timal is dead, he will have no one but me to take his throne when he is gone!"

"So you made up the story about the beast...but what about the gem?" asked Fern.

"The king's gem. He would give it to Prince Timal every time he sent us on these blasted quests for new beasts that he could watch being slaughtered in those ignorant arena battles. I took the gem from Timal's neck as he slept, hiding his lifeless body in the caverns for the spiders to consume, right after I slipped a knife in his heart. The king would believe he was kidnapped by the beast, and I would play the hero as I brought back his precious gem. Unfortunately, I lost the blasted rock when I fell into that cavern. I was chased out by those disgusting glass spiders before I could retrieve it."

"What's so important about the gem, what power does it hold?"

"Only the king and Prince Timal knew that, they did not divulge its power to anyone. But it holds value to them, which means it holds value to me." Mallock answered.

"So, you made this entire story up?"

"Yes. I knew the king's lust for those dumb beasts, and I knew he would send Prince Timal on another one of these stupid quests to capture the unknown creature, especially if he thought it was a rare one no one had ever seen before," Mallock laughed. "But now that I have the gem back, I will return to Loustof and tell the king you were not able to save his son, and that you killed the beast. He will see how valuable I have become when I return his precious gem to him."

"You're a fool, Mallock, the king will see through your plot and surely kill you."

"I think not, you do not know how convincing I can be, traitor! He will not kill me. After all, I am his son."

"I can't understand why the king is in league with the turgoyles. Aren't they the ones who killed the queen?" Fern said, asking it more to himself than to Mallock.

"That is a question I cannot answer," he replied. "Now, lay your sword down. The turgoyles want you alive...for now, that is." The menacing smile returned to Mallock's face. "Now, surrender your weapons!"

Without warning, Fern leapt towards Mallock, swinging his sword like a mad man. The skulking weasel spun, squealing like a stuck pig, and ran spastically, barely dodging Fern's blow.

Swarming him like buzzards on a corpse, the turgoyles attacked Fern. Fern was a crazed lunatic, slaughtering them by the dozens until he was finally overrun by their sheer numbers. Piling on his back, the turgoyles pressed Fern to the ground. Fern, unable to move and barely breathing, struggled to free himself, though there was no use.

A large turgoyle the size of a man with working wings fluttered over to Fern as he gasped for air.

"Shackle the putrid rat's arms behind its back!" the bulky turgoyle commanded in a gurgling voice, raspy and choking.

They jerked Fern to his knees, stomping down on the backs of his calves as they cranked and twisted his arms behind him. Binding his hands with thick, scratchy rope and spitting in his face, they yelled profanities in their language as they kicked his ribs with joy.

"You're lucky, little tenderloin, my lord wants you alive, or else I would disembowel you and gnaw on your intestines one succulent link at a time right before your piggy eyes." He clamped his serrated teeth together in a few quick clicks as thick yellow drool splashed Fern's cheek.

Fern gave no response as he hung his head. The leader ordered the few remaining turgoyles to march forward, dragging Fern along. *Stay strong Fern, stay strong. Keep your head, think!*

80

Meanwhile, Mallock crawled down to Garrick and the horses. As the giant watched Mallock's spidery appendages release the last holds of rock and slink down to the ground alone, he scrunched his face in confusion.

"Sir, where my friend and prince?" asked Garrick, worry accompanying his uncertainty.

"The beast has killed them both, now let's go!" Mallock said, impatiently.

Garrick looked up at the mountain then back at Mallock. The giant clenched his fists and turned. His large arms stretched upward, his hands opened, and his plump fingers clung to the face of the mountain. To Mallock's puzzlement, Garrick began to climb.

"What are you doing? Come down here at once!" commanded Mallock.

"I find my friend," sniffled Garrick.

Suddenly, the rock grasped in Garrick's hand fractured from his enormous weight, breaking from its position. The giant flopped to the ground, causing dust and dirt to lift into the air. Mallock chuckled.

"I told you...he is dead. I saw the glass spiders devour him with my own eyes. Besides, there is no way *you* could make it up that mountain. Now, let's go before something else decides to attack me."

Garrick stood up slowly with tears dripping from his eyes. He looked up at the mountain one last time, hoping to see Fern smiling down at him...and saw nothing.

6

BARELY ALIVE

The horde of turgoyles marched sluggishly along a hidden path winding around the mountain. Fern, cut and bruised, felt like a fool and could not believe how manipulated he had been by both Edinword and Mallock. He felt ashamed as he was poked and prodded by the turgoyles. *If I live...never again. You must be smarter than this, Fern.*

The path that hugged the side of the mountain was narrow and steep, but the turgoyles footing was solid and accurate as they strode the edge with confidence. They took immense joy in dangling Fern's body over the side just to see him scramble, his arms flailing in the misty air trying to grasp something solid. Raspy, choking laughs, echoing throughout the mountainous crags, plagued Fern's ears. *Just drop me already, you torturous monsters!*

Thoughts of the fairy maiden, Lillia, sprung in Fern's mind as death became a desirable concept. *I wonder if I'm ever going to see her again? Not if you die, Fern; pull yourself together! This can't be the end!* Reagal and Garrick also drifted into his thoughts as a sharp jagged rock ripped through his pant leg and entered his thigh. Fern grunted as his body contorted and strained from the unexpected pain. Unfortunately, this did not go unnoticed, garnering the attention from one of his captors.

"Shut your maggoty mouth, rubbish rat, or I'll give you a real reason to squeal like a stuck pig!" The raspy-voiced turgoyle slurped a large gooey chunk of saliva into the back of his throat that combined with nasal mucus. Arching his head, he jerked forward, hocking the juicy mixture onto Fern's face. Splatting his cheek, the chunky green phlegm dripped and rolled, touching Fern's lips before it stretched to the ground. Fern wiped it clean as best he could, giving no reaction or response. He didn't feel up to more torture or torment at the moment.

Sudden visions of Randal and Phillip captured Fern's mind, spinning like tops in his head. Fern became angry with himself, disappointed in his failures. *Come on you bloody fool...think! Try to get out of this mess! Think! You have let enough people down! THINK!*

The turgoyle leader suddenly halted his scraggly band of miscreants, and Fern came to his senses on his knees. His trousers were shredded and his legs were striped with blood and surface wounds. The pain throbbed like a thousand bee stings. Fern stared, teeth grinding and eyes peeled open.

Shaking his head in disbelief, Fern viewed the catacombs beneath the Crags of Malice. They were not just tunnels bored into the base of a mountain, like the Ulmecks south of his village, this was a turgoyle fortress. Walls of jagged rock piled fifty feet high, a small mountain range of its own, formed an expansive barrier around wide circular tunnels. Turgoyles, stationed at the top and armed with bows, aimed at the halted rabble. A prodigious iron gate was the only entrance, and two giant Mountain Trocks, barefoot, dressed in beige woven tunics, and gripping mammoth spiked maces, guarded it. Their stout, nine-foot frames slumped lazily as they stood guard, glaring at Fern's captors. The two hairless beasts yawned in unison, drooling as they did, protruding lower jaws hanging open and distorted yellow teeth clearly visible. To Fern's bewilderment, one of the trocks stretched its tongue up and over its large broad nose to its bulbous, bald head and began to stroke its crown. Even more astonishing to Fern was that the unusually long tongue was covered in thick, brown fur and was the only hair visible on its entire body.

The gates did not immediately open as the turgoyle leader approached the entrance. A small, skinny turgoyle Fern had not noticed came scurrying from around the giant Mountain Trock standing to the right of the entrance. It carried no weapon and was dressed in a tan, torn potato sack that hung down past its knees. To hold its fashionable ensemble together was a tattered tangle of rope.

"State your business!" it said rapidly in a high-pitched, raspy voice, teetering back and forth on its heels with hands clasped together behind its back.

"We're the turgoyles of the Ulmeck Mountains, and we've a gift from Lord Ratlarp to present to Lord Orgle the Ninth," replied the large turgoyle leader.

"And who might you be?" asked the little pale green monstrosity.

"I'm Stragurt, general to Lord Ratlarp's army. Now, grant us entry, sweet morsel, before I skewer your pint-sized body on a stake and enjoy your putrid meat for my lunch."

"Wait here," said the tiny turgoyle, not fazed by Stragurt's threat.

Easily squeezing through the bars on the entrance gate, it disappeared into the darkness of the catacombs. The tiny turgoyle reappeared a few minutes later and commanded the trocks to open the gate.

"Stand back!" said the little turgoyle to Stragurt. "The Lord Orgle will meet with you here."

"What's the meaning of this, spineless barf maggot?" Stragurt yelled in anger. "Are we not welcome?"

"Be patient, General Stragurt, the lord'll treat with you shortly." The small turgoyle turned and scurried out of sight.

Fern gripped the ground with his bloodied knees trying to catch sight of anything of note. *I can't see a blasted thing! If only those disgusting monsters would move.* Fern craned his neck around his puckish green captors, looking through the bars of the gate. *I'll not survive if they take me inside this place.*

A few moments passed when a loud horn blared from the catacombs. Out marched a horde of turgoyles that dwarfed Stragurt's company tenfold. Armed with gleaming long swords and large diamond shaped shields, they tread in perfect formation. Their weapons did not give the impression that they were made by turgoyle hands. Finely crafted steel made up the blades, and thick speckled leather strapping that Fern recognized as Mystic cowhide from his homeland of Loustof wrapped the hilts.

Fern was positive that he had seen these weapons before. In fact, he was their maker. Nearly one year to the day a stranger dressed in a hooded cloak entered his workshop demanding swords and shields customized with the leather adornments. He paid handsomely, providing all materials, so Fern never questioned him. *Was that Mallock? No, he was built like a man, not some skulking weasel. Who then?* Suddenly the ranks parted.

In the front of the army stood a large turgoyle, heavily armored in platemail and holding a two-handed sword with a hilt made of finely crafted gold in the shape of a dragon. His chest plate had etchings of dragon's eyes, peering and menacing. The turgoyle's face was scarred as if he had been tied to a horse-drawn carriage and dragged along a gravel road for miles. He had one massive jagged tooth protruding from his lower lip that was green with mold and mildew. He was tremendous in width, even taller than Stragurt. A crown made of bone and rock, giving him a kingly appearance, sat upon his slimy head.

"Ah, Lord Orgle, it's an honor to see you again," Stragurt said in a submissive tone. "I come bearing a gift from Lord Ratlarp."

"Why does Lord Ratlarp send me a gift, rotting pile of troll dung?" Lord Orgle asked, speaking in a low bellowing tone that sounded like a drum.

"Beg your pardon sire, but he wants your allegiance."

"Ah, so that wingless, rancid excuse for a turgoyle has war on his mind, does he?" Lord Orgle smiled, revealing the rest of his yellow-green teeth, catching his bone crown as it slipped from his head.

"It's King Edinword who has war on his mind. He's asked for my Lord's help, and he's promised him a great turgoyle army."

"Yes, King Edinword is a very ambitious man. But what does he need this army for?"

Fern kept his head down, but took in every word.

"I've not been informed of all the details, my lord."

"HAHA, your king does not trust you, you lowly maggot, but I'll need to know what we'll be going to war for before I can give my allegiance to that gutless glob of mutton you call a lord."

"Yes, yes, of course, sire. Lord Ratlarp wants you to meet with him in our kingdom."

"HAH! *Your* kingdom? It's Edinword's kingdom, he just allows you to dwell there, ignorant moron!"

"It won't be that way for long my lord!" Stragurt smiled.

"So, Lord Ratlarp thinks he's power enough to defeat Edinword? Interesting." Orgle scratched the side of his head, knocking his crown down in front of his eyes.

"No, my Lord, it'll not be necessary to defeat Edinword. Lord Ratlarp will explain everything when you meet with him. Now, please accept our gift."

"What gift could that insignificant excuse for a turgoyle possibly offer me?" Lord Orgle replied, snarling as he straightened his crown again.

"It is one of those turgoyle-killing Majestics."

"WHAT?" shouted Orgle. "King Edinword declared all those turgoyle-murdering-scum as traitors to the kingdom of Loustof, and promised me they'd been erased from this world...years ago! Where's it? Where's this scum?"

Stragurt walked over to Fern, grasping him by the collar. Spinning Fern around, he placed his crusty black leather boot between Fern's shoulder blades, grinding him to the ground at Lord Orgle's feet.

"Here is the scum!" Stragurt said as he kicked Fern in the ribs.

Fern gave them no satisfaction. Instead of showing pain, he stood to his feet looking Lord Orgle in the eyes.

Stragurt took a club from one of the turgoyle's hands, swinging it into the back of Fern's legs. The sound that followed was that of shattering glass. Crushing pain shot through Fern's body. He gritted his teeth, but he made no sound as he collapsed to his knees.

"Yes, I can see that you are strong like your rancid ancestors, but don't worry, we'll break you!" Lord Orgle circled Fern. "Tell me, Majestic, how'd you stay hidden these years?"

Fern remained silent, blood trickling from his legs onto the dry, dusty ground. Stragurt struck him in the back with the club, knocking him flat. Placing a foot on his face, he pressed into the soil, twisting Fern's cheek on the gravelly earth. Fern bit down hard. *Show these beasts no pain! They will get no satisfaction at my expense! Damn them!*

"Answer the lord's questions and your death will be quick and painless. Otherwise, we'll make you beg for it, maggot!" exclaimed Stragurt as he bounced his foot off Fern's head.

Fern forced himself to his knees once more and turned to spit blood from his mouth as more dripped from his chin. Gravel was embedded in Fern's cheek, and he growled as he looked at his enemy.

"Hah! Very well," proclaimed Lord Orgle. "You'll suffer more than you know. This is not the first Majestic I've had in my possession, but it looks like it'll be the last. Bring out my whip!"

A turgoyle peeled from the ranks and ran to do the lord's bidding.

Fern looked up at Orgle, determination burning his eyes. "I'll answer...your questions...if you'll answer...mine." Fern spat more blood from his mouth as Stragurt raised his club.

"No, wait!" Lord Orgle commanded. "Let him speak, this might be amusing."

Stragurt lowered his weapon, curling his lips and snarling in disappointment.

Fern tried his best to speak through the pain, taking a breath every few words.

"How's it...that Edinword...could declare...the Majestics...as traitors? The declaration was...made hundreds...of years ago."

Lord Orgle loosened a bellowing laugh, spraying thick green saliva into the air.

"King Edinword has been the king of Loustof for over two hundred years, ignorant fool! He claims to be an Ager, a line of men said to live thousands of years. Like your kind, they were supposed to be extinct. Though, he apparently is the last one."

"Why would he be...in league...with your kind? You're the ones who...who murdered his wife." Fern could barely keep his head up as he spoke.

"He paid Lord Ratlarp well to have her slaughtered," Orgle said, his yellow-green teeth crunching together as he smiled.

"W—Why?" This time, it was shock that splintered Fern's voice.

"How should I know? I'm not the one he paid to have her murdered!"

Fern could sense the impatience building in the turgoyle lord, but he needed to ask one last question.

"B—But...why does he...he...hate my kind...so much?"

Hoping to finally get an answer, Fern nearly collapsed to the ground.

"I don't know, nor do I care, but what I can—"

An arrow suddenly shot through the darkness, striking Stragurt in the back of the head. The general fell face forward in a dead heap next to Fern, dust kicking in his eyes.

"TO ARMS! TO ARMS!" shouted Lord Orgle.

As quickly as the arrow punctured Stragurt's head, an army of centaurs came charging from the darkness like a tidal wave. Orgle and his army retreated inside the fortress, scattering from their perfect formation like dust in the wind. The iron gates slammed shut behind them.

The two mountain trocks rushed forward, swinging their massive clubs and sending centaurs flying left and right. Stragurt's turgoyles fought hysterically upon seeing their leader's lifeless body lying on the ground. They charged, springing up on the centaurs' backs, axes hacking into them.

The centaurs, strong as iron shields, bucked the miserable creatures from their backs with quick twerks and thrusts. Flailing spastically, the turgoyles writhed as the centaurs trampled them into the ground. Their screeching yelps of agonizing pain gave Fern little comfort as he shimmied his way clear of falling corpses and pounding hooves.

Blood ran like growing streams and was soon unavoidable. Fern lay drenched in the thick dark liquid, fingers tickling his bonds, unable to free his wrists.

Horns inside the fortress were sounding like calls from dying cattle. The loud reverberating force bounded from within as turgoyles manning the walls fired their arrows down on the centaurs. The gates reopened and out poured turgoyles astride the backs of gargantuan warthogs armored with platemail. The massive tide of enemies would soon overwhelm the centaurs.

Fern, in the meantime, wounded and bleeding, maneuvered through the ferocity of battle. Getting to his feet, he shuffled behind a boulder and out of sight. There he sat soaked in blood trying to pull his hands free from the thick rope; there was no use.

As fortune had it, Fern managed to yank his arms underneath himself and bring them to the front of his body. At least now he was able to fight. Hobbling back onto the battlefield, he used his restrained hands to snatch up a sword from a fallen centaur. Wobbling like a three-legged dog, and barely able to hold his weapon, Fern found the strength to slay a few turgoyles within his reach, though he could see the reality of the situation. *We're losing, there's just too many of them.* Watching the centaurs being overrun, Fern raised his sword. A turgoyle on hogback charged him. Fern stood his ground, planting his tired feet in the dry soil. His arms were jelly as his sword became an anvil.

"Come and get me, you piece of filth," shouted Fern.

The turgoyle raised its ax and Fern fell to one knee, bringing his sword across his body. But before the two weapons could make their fateful greeting, Fern felt himself become weightless as he was lifted into the air. He watched the turgoyle as a spear emerged from its chest.

"Hang in der, my young Majesteek!"

It was Reagal! Fern nearly cried in both joy and amazement as he tried to smile.

"Thank you, my friend!" Fern shouted as he held onto the centaur's back. "But there's no use, we are being overrun!"

"Av faith; we av allies approaching."

Reagal pointed into the inky blackness. Fern looked and saw elves rushing into the turgoyle horde. The skilled warriors struck them down like fish in a barrel. Elves armed with bows could be seen in the distance releasing flocks of arrows into the air. Fern caught a glimpse of King Dandowin in brilliant royal armor astride a beautiful white steed racing towards one of the mountain trocks. Its throat sliced open as the elven king galloped past.

Moving swiftly away from the fight, Reagal gained speed.

"No! Take me back, Reagal! I need to help!" Fern pleaded to his rescuer as he coughed up blood. "I can't flee from a battle that's been caused by my stupidity!"

"Trust me, dis battle is more ours den yours, and King Dandowin's most of all. I need to get you far away from ear, for you do not av dee strengd to last much longer."

Fern knew deep in his heart he would not stand a chance if he remained. With pained eyes, he shook his head in compliance.

The battle raged on as Reagal galloped away on swift hooves. Fern was barely able to hold on to the centaur's back, grasping the dark mane with weak hands. Leaping over rock and gaping crevasses, Reagal never faulted. Fern, however, bounced like corn popping over a fire.

The sun began to rise, and Fern could feel the warmth on his face. He was badly wounded and unable to hold his head up for long, sliding in and out of consciousness. Flashes of Garrick's face came into his mind as he continued to bounce up and down on the centaur's back. Fern could only wonder what lies Mallock told the giant and hoped no harm would come to Garrick.

Time passed like the ripples of a cool river, slowly healing Fern's wounds. Reagal was at a trot as Fern lifted his head to view their surroundings.

"Where are we going?" he asked.

Seeing Fern awake, Reagal's face was one of shock.

"We are on dee road to Dundire and dee land of dee dwarves," replied Reagal as he grunted, realizing Fern's hands were still bound with thick rope. "I need to get you some aid, but first, let me free you from does bonds."

Reagal spun his torso around and sliced through the ropes with a small dagger. "We will arrive at dee dwarves stronghold in about an hour. Try and rest, my young Majesteek; you av ad a rough night."

"But, Reagal, how'd you know about my capture?"

Fern was still barely conscious as he tried to sit up. Grinning at his efforts, Reagal watched Fern slump back down, nearly falling to the ground.

"Please, my friend, rest. All questions will be answered when we arrive in Dundire."

The rhythm of Reagal's quicktime trot lulled Fern into an easy slumber, and dreams quickly entered his subconscious mind.

He was home in his workshop when Lillia suddenly appeared in front of him. She spoke, but did not move her full, supple lips. He could hear her in his mind... no, it was more of a feeling. She communicated with him, telling him to be strong. It was real, so real. She vanished. A dragon, black and hideous...Garrick!"

"Garrick!" shouted Fern, as he awoke.

Startled, Reagal's hooves hopped from the ground as Fern sat up slowly and rubbed his sleep-encrusted eyes.

"Bad dream?"

"What? Oh...not sure, I just remember being in my workshop when Li—"

Fern abruptly stopped himself as his cheeks went pink. He wasn't ready to share his feelings just yet with his newfound friend.

"I saw...just a shadow, it was nothing. Where are we?" asked Fern, trying to change the subject, "We are approaching dee ome of dee dwarves. You av been sleeping for some time, we are nearly to dee gates of Dundire."

A quaint village built at the base of a mountain met Fern's eyes. *Not another mountain range*, he thought, but these were nothing like the evil Crags that were all too vivid in his mind.

They were lush with forests. Beautiful blue pines and firs grew up its face, and the very peak was covered in snow. Healthy, green trimmed lawns surrounding handsomely-built homes of stacked stone, and straw roofs, sat at their base along a winding pea gravel path. Running swift, a sparkling river twisted and turned around the lovely curvature of nature.

Fern could hear birds chirping along the rushing water, which made music of its own.

As Reagal trotted along the village road, dwarven men and women peered out of their doors and windows to see who was coming. Noticing the shutters moving on the upper levels, Fern watched as dwarven children peeked out to get a look at the strangers traveling through their quiet little town.

Waving as he passed, Fern couldn't help but smile as the children ducked out of sight. Though he could swear that a few were playing a game of peek-a-boo.

Reagal's trot quickened as they came closer to the gates. The fifty-foot walls surrounding Dundire were not piles of rock like the Crags of Malice. They were expertly quarried rectangular-shaped stones laced with gold and intricately placed to fit perfectly together. Gigantic seventy-foot-tall watchtowers were built into the walls, placed every one-hundred yards or so, and were capped with solid gold stones larger than Garrick. Two towers flanked the sides of the gate, which was made from solid steel and stood as high as the walls. Symbols Fern did not recognize were beautifully sculpted into the steel and made of pure gold that were even more intricately designed than the palace doors of Loustof.

If there was such a thing as arrogant architecture, Dundire was it.

No guards stood watch at the gate as Reagal and Fern approached. Instead, the gates began to open on their own, operated mechanically from within. Sounds of metal cranking and cogs smoothly rolling together could be heard as the gate came to a stop. Never seeing anything so advanced, Fern marveled at its construction. *How? How is this even possible? I must learn this craft! Simply amazing!* The dwarves were the true engineers of their time.

Four stout bearded men, no taller than a ten-year-old child and no older than thirty, dressed in armor met them as they entered.

Not plain chainmail or platemail was worn, but the most detailed shining steel Fern had ever laid eyes upon. Opulent and adorned with golden details, it shone like polished silver glistening in the afternoon sun.

One of the dwarves stepped forward, bowing slightly, and spoke in a deep, masculine voice.

"Reagal, son of Solace, King Ardin is expecting you."

"*Son* of Solace? You're the prince?" Fern asked, amazement lifting his voice.

"Yes, my friend, it is not someding I parade around as, I dink it preferable to be a umble creature. It serves me better."

Fern dipped his head at Reagal with considerable respect.

"Reagal, I'd like to walk on my own two feet to meet King Ardin."

Trying to muster up enough strength to get down from the centaur's back, Fern sat up.

"Yes, of course, but are you sure you av dee strengd?"

Fern answered, laughing as he spoke. "No, but I'll give it all I've got."

Fern slid to the ground, limbs still like jelly, and stood. Wobbling and weak, he could feel his legs were going to buckle.

"Reagal, can I use your back to hold myself up?" asked Fern with a shade of humiliation.

"Of course, my young Majesteek. Der is no shame in dat."

Reagal, grinned, noticing Fern's blushed cheeks, and he was astounded Fern could even stand. The punishment the man had withstood would have killed most humans, but Fern's wounds were nearly healed completely.

Fern placed his hand on Reagal's back as the dwarves led the pair through the courtyard of Dundire. A large, floral white granite fountain was the first marvel to catch Fern's eye. In the middle of the fountain was a graceful sculpture in the shape of a rearing unicorn. Circling its base were jade sculptures of dwarven women holding golden fish in their hands that spouted crystal-clear water into a large circular pool. Small blue fish with long thin fins jetting from their sides swam in zig-zag patterns as the water from the fountain splashed playfully upon the surface.

Surrounding the courtyard was a sprawling city comprised of the same handsomely built homes they had seen lining the pea gravel path, only these homes were much larger.

As they exited the courtyard, an enormous set of stables, largely constructed of tree trunks, shaped and stripped of bark stood tall with high-pitched, slate-tiled roofs. Inside the stables, to Fern's amazement, were unicorns. He nearly fainted at the sight of them. They were beautifully white, purer than freshly fallen snow, with shining silver manes that reflected the light coming through the trees. A golden spiraled horn sat perfectly on their forehead, and deep blue eyes that seemed to pierce the soul, decorated their faces. Fern was speechless as the majestic creatures shook their heads, manes flowing like wisps of clouds on a windy sky. Their nay was musical and mesmerizing. *Never in my wildest dreams did I ever think I'd see unicorns. Somebody please pinch me!* Fern shuddered in pure ecstasy.

Having to be forcefully pried from the unicorns' gaze, Fern suddenly found himself standing at the base of stone stairs leading to the mountain entrance. A dwarf raised his arm and pointed. His pudgy index finger stretched in the direction of a set of golden doors. Huffing and puffing, the dwarven guides brought their knees to their chests as they climbed the large steps. *These are funny folk*, thought Fern. *So short, yet they build for normal-sized men.*

As they reached the top, Fern was surprised to see the large doors unadorned; they were merely polished with two silver handles. Heaving and straining, sweat dripping down their foreheads, the dwarves pulled the doors open with a grunt. They signaled Fern and Reagal to enter. The doors closed behind them with a thud.

Inside the mountain, towering as tall as redwood trees, were giant greenstone pillars. White jagged accents within the stone scattered like veins from bloodshot eyes. The monstrous stanchions seemed to carry the weight of the entire mountain as they lined a sprawling room. In between them lay a twenty-foot wide red velvet carpet framed in golden fur that led to a platform at the back wall.

As Reagal and Fern strolled closer, they could see a short, stout man sitting on a golden throne speaking with a centaur standing to his right. Staring at the approaching guests, the centaur suddenly leapt from the platform, trotting with quick hooves to greet them.

"Ah, my son, welcome! And, young Majesteek, you look in need of medical aid," he said, suddenly turning to Fern. "Come ford and meet King Ardin. He will call for is nurses to eal does wounds for you."

Fern immediately knew this centaur to be King Solace.

"Thank you, your Majesty," he said with a bow.

"Ah, no, please! No Majesteek will call me 'your Majesty'! We are friends, my young sir, you will call me Soleece, noding more."

The king of centaurs looked on Fern with a massive smile.

Fern could immediately see the resemblance; of course, King Solace looked much older than Reagal, though no crown adorned his head.

King Ardin, on the other hand, a typical dwarf, had broad shoulders and a large chest. His full beard, that was white with age and grew down to his belly, flopped about as he popped up and down and came into view. He was dressed like royalty, ostentatiously in Fern's opinion, wearing a green cape that draped the floor. His shirt was green silk, adorned with golden buttons down the middle designed like small battle shields. He wore brown trousers laced with gold leaf, and a black leather belt with a gold buckle that supported an ivory horn that hung by a long silver chain next to his right leg. His boots shone like silver steel and had sharp, long spikes that stuck out from the toe. He wore a crown so magnificently designed that only dwarves could have crafted it. It was pure gold with silver accents, and each peak of the crown was adorned with a red ruby. Green emeralds decorated the front, while diamonds bordered its base.

"OI! Where is this Majestic that I've heard so much about?" King Ardin barked in a low but friendly voice as he came hopping to a stop. "Oi, me boy, you look like you have been trampled on by these two centaurs!" He dropped his head back and let out a deep bellowing laugh. "Come, let's get those wounds treated, then we can talk."

King Ardin was nothing like his clothes might have suggested. He *was* boisterous, of course, but he was also a jolly man who constantly smiled and smacked his belly.

Suddenly lifting the ivory horn from his belt, he blew as he winked at Fern. Two dwarven women, slightly shorter than Ardin, came scurrying out of a doorway from behind one of the large pillars. It was then Fern noticed: lining the walls behind the massive columns were numerous doors leading to various parts of the mountain.

The dwarven women were plump with rosy cheeks. They waddled to Fern, grabbing his hands and pulled him toward one of the doorways. Fern could barely tell the women apart. Their faces were young and pretty, and both had braided hair the color of chestnuts that hung down in front of their ample chests. Deep brown eyes looked at Fern with great kindness and sat perfectly below thin brows.

Entering a room that looked like a large healing facility, Fern was overwhelmed with hundreds of beds fitted with clean white linen lining the walls on either side. *What are they expecting, a war? Do they already know Edinword's intentions?*

No windows were present; only candles lit on bedside tables gave light. The women showed Fern to a bed and began to treat and bandage his wounds. Gentle were their touches and soft was their skin as they dressed Fern's injuries. Moments later, another dwarven woman came in the room holding a cup of blue liquid and politely asked Fern to drink. He sipped it at first, not sure of what it was. The women began to laugh, reassuring him it was not poison. Finishing the strange concoction, Fern found it tasted quite pleasant.

"What was that?" he asked.

"Don't worry, sir, it was medicine produced by the fairies of the Blue Marshes. It has great healing power and will have you feeling well by morning. Now, get some rest."

Fern, of course, wanted to rejoin Reagal and the two kings. He was dying to know everything that had happened, *and* tell them what he had found out. The dwarven women reassured Fern that King Ardin wanted him to rest before speaking with him, but Fern was anxious and stood from the bed before the women were able to fasten the final bandage. Four surprisingly powerful hands gripped Fern by the seat of his pants and yanked him back in bed. Wide-eyed with shock, Fern shook his head and submitted to the dwarven women with a smile. *Never underestimate anyone, Fern.*

Almost relieved, Fern lay down on the bed, which was a bit too small for his body, and fell asleep immediately. He quickly became lost in dreams. Images of a child running from home to home begging for scraps of food...memories of the townsfolk pelting him with rotting fruit and screaming traitor rang inside his mind...then darkness, and again...Lillia, tall and slender standing in front of Fern, staring into his eyes with her mouth still. He could feel her thoughts. They walked in the moonlight, their hands together in a loving grasp. It was real, so real. What was she trying to say? She spoke...

Suddenly, Fern woke, popping up with sweat dripping down his forehead, his feet dangling off the end of the bed. He wiped the moisture from his brow and surprisingly found that he was feeling refreshed with very little pain, only slight soreness as he looked around the medical chambers. A nurse came in shortly after carrying a new set of clothes.

"Ah, sir, I see you are feeling better."

"Yes, much better, thank you," Fern said with a sleepy grin.

"Well, then, you must change. It is breakfast, and you have company waiting for you in the great hall. I will be back in a few minutes to escort you to your guests."

Fern quickly changed into a white, puffy, long-sleeved shirt and some simple brown trousers. Appearing shortly after, a nurse entered the room. She escorted Fern by the hand into the great dwarven hall of Dundire. When they entered, Fern was immediately greeted by a large gold circular table set with beautiful gold plating. In fact, everything but the napkins and the food seemed to be made of gold.

Speaking of food...Oooh, the dwarves. Fern never witnessed so much protein on one table. Roast pigs on platters of gold, apples stuffed in their mouths and corkscrewed tails blackened thoroughly, giant edged-backed eagle eggs plucked from nests high within the pines of Dundire, boiled medium, and laid in bowls of—what else—GOLD! T-bone steaks from home-raised Granite Cattle, slopped with thick brown gravy, were stacked on platters and placed in the center of the table. Cheeses of every shade of yellow and orange, shape and size, and thickness and texture, covered in white cloth, were crammed in-between the meats. There were multiple varieties of fish, from the very small to the very large. Yellow liquid that tasted like honey, but not quite as thick, filled golden pitchers sitting sporadically where space was available. Although the breakfast was neither as grand or well-prepared as the feast in Loustof, the aromas were just as enticing. Fern's mouth watered, and his stomach grumbled like Garrick's. *Now I see how these people become so plump, not to mention strong, if this is their usual breakfast,* thought Fern, huffing a small chuckle as he finally noticed his company, some hidden by the stacks of food.

Fern could see King Ardin, well...actually...only the top of his crown, sitting at the table behind a tall pile of baked fish. To Ardin's left sat Reagal, and to his right was King Solace. Both centaurs sat on plush purple velvet pillows.

This company Fern expected, but he did not expect to see King Dandowin of the elves proudly sitting across from King Ardin, overlooking a stack of steaks. And nearly knocking Fern to his backside was the fairy maiden, Lillia. She sat tall, but humble, on Dandowin's right.

Fern's skin shuddered, and his heart drummed at the sight of her. His dreams of the beautiful fairy were in the forefront of his mind.

"Oi! Me young Majestic! Please come join the celebration! After all, it's in your honor," King Ardin thundered, motioning him to a chair between Reagal and Lillia.

Fern snapped back into reality as he walked awkwardly to his seat.

"I trust you healed well, young sir?" Lillia said, peering into Fern's eyes as he gingerly plopped down, hands shaking and knees knocking.

Having trouble speaking, Fern mumbled, "Um...ye—yes, yes, thank you!"

A laugh erupted like a volcano from King Ardin as chunks of fish flew from his mouth. Food tumbled off platters, and the pitchers of drink wobbled precariously as the jolly dwarf slapped the tabletop.

"Don't worry lad," bellowed the dwarven king as more partially chewed fish shot across the table. "I could barely speak at the sight of her as well."

King Solace patted Ardin on his back.

"My friend, when av you ever *barely* been able to speak?"

Fern's cheeks blushed a rosy pink as everyone began to laugh.

Side-eyeing Lillia, Fern immediately noticed her hair. Locks that had been blue when he first met her, were now platinum blonde. Lillia noticed Fern's confusion as he stared at her.

"Is there something wrong, sir?"

"Oh, no, no, of course not, I was just wondering about your hair."

Fern blushed a darker pink, rolling his eyes at himself, when he realized what he had just said.

"My hair, sir?" questioned Lillia, now with her own confused expression.

"Yes, I'm sorry...um...I just remembered it being...blue." His pink hue sharpened with every word.

"Oh, yes, this is my true hair color, the water from the marshes reflects on my locks, giving them their blue tint," Lillia said, now blushing as well.

King Dandowin looked at both with an odd expression. "Yes, well...we can talk about the magic of fairies' hair at a later date, but for now, I suggest we get to the importance of this meeting."

"Oi, yes, King Dandowin is a very serious fellow," King Ardin said with a crooked grin. "So, Dandowin, my old friend, fill us in on this mighty battle that you had with those miserable turgoyles."

Fern snapped out of his hypnosis and listened intently as King Dandowin told his account.

"Well, to be honest, there is not much to tell, but I will say what I can."

If the dwarves are known for their gold, and food, one must be aware of elves and their exaggeration.

To put it mildly, Dandowin broke out in story.

With great detail, he spoke of Fern, crawling and clawing, bloodied and barely alive, out into battle, crushing turgoyles by the dozens with his last ounce of strength. *Not exactly the way I remember it*, thought Fern as he caught Lillia staring at him.

Though, Dandowin was just getting started.

The elven king gushed about Reagal stampeding his way through the hordes and slicing three trocks' heads from their bodies with a single swing of his sword (it was only one) before scooping Fern from the ground and galloping away to Dundire.

As Dandowin hit his stride, boasting of his elven army began.

Plowing through the turgoyle masses like battering rams through terrycloth, they pushed the turgoyles back into their fortress.

But wait...Dandowin's crowing was amping up.

Standing from the table and shouting, he roared how they fought until the break of dawn without respite, and just when they thought they were on the brink of victory...

The elven king, out of breath, paused as he looked around the table.

"They have something I never thought would be possible. Never in all my years could I have imagined..."

King Dandowin sat looking down at the table.

"Blast it, man! Tell us what you're talking about!" King Ardin howled.

"Very well." He looked up, scanning his company. "They have a dragon."

"What?!" King Solace asked.

"They have a tamed dragon under their control. It attacked us just as we were breaching their walls. We had to retreat. Never have I had to utter those words in battle, but I had no choice. The dragon was killing my men, and yours, with ease."

King Dandowin was out of breath, his chest heaving for air.

The table fell silent. Fern sat unable to eat a single bite of his breakfast knowing *he* could defeat a dragon. *If only I had my arrows. Should I tell them? No, that would sound arrogant.*

King Ardin finally broke the silence.

"Not much to tell, huh? You are a silly fellow, my friend, but answer me this: how could those ignorant turgoyles learn how to tame dragons? Their brains are the size of a pea!"

An epiphany slammed into Fern like a hammer. *King Edinword! He had to be the one who tamed this dragon, and the dragon that attacked my village! He lied about everything!* Fern could stay silent no longer.

"My Lords and Lady, I have some troubling news to tell you."

Fern steadily rose from his seat to address his company. Trying to recall every element and minuscule detail, Fern relived his story in words.

King Solace and Reagal grasped each other by the arm as they listened to the account about Galeon's battle with Fern in the dungeon arena. They thanked Fern profusely for sparing his life. Of course, Fern could only apologize for not telling them sooner.

Astonished to discover that everyone knew about Edinword being an Ager, and ruling the kingdom of Loustof for hundreds of years, Fern was surprised to see the company's shared shock when he finally revealed his knowledge of the Loustofian king's involvement with the turgoyles.

Letting them ponder their thoughts for a moment, Fern eventually broke the silence with a question.

"King Dandowin, please tell me, did you kill the turgoyle lord, Orgle?"

Everyone came to their senses as King Dandowin shook his head in disappointment. "I am afraid not. The coward ran back behind his walls when he saw us coming."

"Then Edinword will know I'm still alive."

"Yes, that I am sure of," answered Dandowin. "Lord Orgle has already sent out messengers, no doubt, to Edinword and his filthy turgoyle cousin down in the Ulmeck Mountains."

Ah, the turgoyle lords are cousins, thought Fern. "Who do you think Edinword is plotting against?"

King Ardin, bouncing from his seat and rocking the table, shouted, "Oi, with both turgoyle armies, and a dragon or two on his side...it sounds to me that he plans on waging war with us all." King Ardin's face became stern and his eyes seethed with rage.

Reagal calmly stood from the table.

"Der is no time to waste, my lords and lady, we must gader our forces and march on dee land of Loustof. We must not let im bring war to our lands."

"Sit, my son. Remember dee fate of Galeon, we cannot be too asty. Dis calls for great planning. You must remember dat King Edinword knows is plans av been revealed to us, and you must also remember dat ee is old and wise. Ee will be expecting an attack. We must dink dis drough clearly, and I must look to dee stars."

King Solace spoke with such tranquility that it did not seem there was much to worry about.

Fern watched Lillia's dress flow to the ground as she stood from her chair.

"We fairies are not warriors, we are healers, but we will aid you in whatever ways we can. We have seen dark days before. We must stand strong against the evils of the world. I will go to the Blue Marshes and prepare my kind for the coming events. I will return soon to give you what news I have." Lillia turned to Fern, her long yellow locks waving hypnotically. "Will you escort me out, sir?"

"Yes, of course!" Fern replied, nearly jumping from his chair and knocking over a pitcher of the honey drink.

Feeling foolish once more, he grabbed a napkin from the table and bent down to clean his mess.

"Oi, silly boy! Leave it be! My dogs will clean that up in no time." Ardin placed his index and middle fingers from his right hand into his mouth and blew. An ear-piercing squealing whistle reverberated throughout the hall. Four lazy hounds with tails wagging and ears flopping came hobbling from under the table, unbeknownst to the company until that very moment. Waddling with their short stout legs, reminiscent of their master's, they slowly lapped the sweet liquid from the floor.

Smiling, Fern turned to walk away, and Lillia took him by the hand. The touch of her skin was as smooth as silk and gave Fern a warm feeling that filled his entire body, calming his rapidly-beating heart. If anyone would have asked him, Fern would have sworn that he had known Lillia for years. The connection was mysterious.

Fern stared at her, trying to build up enough courage to speak as they strolled to the entrance doors.

Plucking a vial of bluish liquid from a pocket of her dress, she handed it to Fern.

"Please, take this on your quest, it is the same medicine that you drank when you first arrived. May it serve you well in time of need."

Fern accepted the gift and bowed politely.

"Lillia, it was an honor meeting you; I truly hope to see you again very soon."

Trying not to stumble over his tongue, it took every ounce of wit to finish that sentence.

Lillia looked over at Fern and smiled, curtsying as she spoke. "It was an honor meeting you as well, my fair Majestic, and it would be an even greater honor to see you again. Farewell, sir."

Fern's eyes bulged as Lillia's supple lips kissed his cheek. The fairy maiden swept away like a spirit, leaving Fern standing on wobbly knees.

He walked back to the circular table with an uncontrollable smile spanning his beet-red complexion.

King Ardin looked at Fern, slapping his belly with both hands and bellowed a laugh.

"Here we sit talking about turgoyles, wars, and dragons, and the young Majestic has love on his mind! Oi, to be young!"

Fern's expression sobered, and he apologized for his behavior.

"Do not worry, me boy, even 'King Serious' Dandowin has had that look before. Isn't that right, my pointy-eared friend?"

King Ardin's belly began to jiggle as more laughter came pouring out, and King Solace and Reagal could be seen smiling as they shook their heads in unison.

"I am sorry to break up the gaiety, but do you not think we should be taking this matter a bit more seriously?" King Dandowin said sternly, brows furled.

"Yes, yes, yes, it is a serious matter, my friend, but we must not forget to live," King Ardin replied.

"That might be so, but to live, we must defeat this evil that has arisen. If Edinword amasses two turgoyle armies and his own army, those alone would be a formidable foe, but adding dragons into the equation gives him an advantage too powerful to overcome."

"I can defeat the dragons."

Everyone at the table immediately fell silent, stone faced, and turned to Fern.

Dandowin smirked, tilting his head and swiping his shimmering hair from his face.

"I know you are a great warrior and have the strength of ten men, but to defeat dragons single-handedly is a gift I can say...is quite impossible."

"I told you I defeated the dragon Edinword ordered to attack my village."

King Ardin interrupted Fern. "Yes, me boy, but to be lucky twice is not likely."

"I don't want to sound arrogant, my Lords, but I wasn't lucky. I've found something that can penetrate the dragon's hide with ease...the rock that comes from the Ulmeck Mountains. I've used them to forge arrows, but, unfortunately, they were all lost in the cavern at the Crag Mountains while I was fighting off glass spiders."

"Well, then, let's go retrieve these arrows from this cavern," King Ardin said.

"I'm afraid that would be impossible, sire, the cavern roof has collapsed, burying the arrows under tons of rock and stone. The only way is to travel back into the Ulmeck Mountains and retrieve more rock to forge more arrows."

Dandowin spoke as he sprang from his seat.

"The turgoyles will be swarming all over those mountains, and if Lord Orgle's army is on its way, it will be an impossible task!"

"Yes, and King Edinword knows of these arrows. He will surely set turgoyles on close watch," King Ardin added.

"Dae will spot you before you get close," said King Solace.

"This isn't true," Fern replied with confidence. "I've been going to those mountains undetected for years by using an abandoned turgoyle tunnel. It's not been occupied for decades; they've forgotten about it altogether."

"Dat might be so," Reagal replied, after sitting silent for some time. "But you must travel drough dee kingdom of Loustof to get der. King Edinword knows you're alive, ee will av patrols at every corner looking for you."

Fern sat contemplating all options. He glanced up at Reagal and the three Kings with determination in his eyes.

"We have no choice!" he said. "I must try! As King Dandowin has already stated, if Edinword attacks us with his army and two armies of turgoyles, victory will not easily be won, but if he attacks with dragons as well, victory is hopeless."

The company simmered in silence once again. Moments went by before Reagal stood, eyeing his father as he spoke.

"I will travel wid dee young Majesteek. If we need to make a quick retreat, I can bear him away wid great aste."

Fern nodded with a grateful grin.

"Yes, dis is true," said King Solace. "And I shall go to Valom and prepare my warriors. We will gader ere at Dundire, for it is dee strongest of all our lands."

"Yes, this is true also," King Ardin said with considerable pride. He stood from his seat with his chest inflated, though still shorter than the rest. "And I shall ready my great dwarven army."

King Ardin clenched a gravy-moistened steak, cramming it into his mouth, barely chewing, before gulping it down with a swig of the honey drink.

"Very well," announced King Dandowin, handing a napkin to king Ardin as he shook his head in disgust. "I will return to Alkyle and ready my forces there. We will be back before the sun rises on the second day. Lord Reagal and young Majestic, may all the luck in this fair world be yours. Farewell, my friends."

"Fare thee well!" all said at once.

The company stood and departed from the great hall to prepare for the upcoming war.

7

JOURNEY TO THE ULMECK MOUNTAINS

King Ardin escorted Reagal and Fern to a large room where every provision they might need was piled high in numerous jumbled heaps. *What a mess! These dwarves are brilliant engineers, but when it comes to cleanliness they come up...short.*

After rummaging through the mountainous clutter, Fern and Reagal gathered as much as they could carry and crammed Reagal's saddlebags full. The dwarven king came to Fern, slapping a sturdy hand on his back.

"OI! I am truly sorry, me boy. With the imminent war, I cannot spare a unicorn. I am sad to tell you this, but you must continue on foot."

"Don't worry, sire, you have done more for me than I could've hoped for. Thank you for your hospitality. Besides, my legs could use a good workout."

King Ardin chuckled and walked with them to the gates of Dundire.

"Me boys, we will await you for ten days. It will take Edinword at least that long to gather his forces. If you have not returned by then, we will march to war. Make haste and be watchful. I send my hopes and prayers with you both. Good journey!"

King Ardin turned and bounced back to his great hall.

It was midday, and moods were hopeful when they set out. Reagal, being accommodating, tried to convince Fern to ride on his back. Fern was not having it.

"No, my friend. We'll need your full strength if a quick escape is required."

"Yes, I suppose you are correct, young Majesteek, but our travel will be sluggish."

"I appreciate your inadvertent insult Reagal," smiled Fern, slyly.

The remark nearly stopped Reagal in his tracks. The centaur cleared his throat and smiled sheepishly.

"I am terribly sorry, I meant no slander. I was merely stating dat well...dat, um..."

Fern's smile grew the more Reagal stumbled on his words, and he truly enjoyed his friend's awkwardness.

"Reagal, my friend, what path do we take? I hope we don't have to travel through the Crag Mountains again," interrupted Fern, giving Reagal a reason to climb from the hole he dug.

"Of course not, you av lost your bearings." Reagal smiled clearing his throat again. "The Crag Mountains are furder west; we must travel soudeast to Loustof."

Fern eased out a breath.

"Well then, what road will suit us best?

"Dee road drough Eardingland will be dee quickest." Reagal replied.

"Earthingland? Isn't that where the minotaur's roam?"

Fern's heart sank as he suddenly remembered the battle outside the mystic forest of Alkyle.

"Yes, dae inabit dat land. It borders dee nordern region of Alkyle. It is mostly dense forest, which should make it easy for us to keep out of sight. We also will not need to worry about turgoyles. Dae do not dare enter dat land. Dee minotaur's kill dim on sight," Reagal said, grinning. "It should take no longer den dree days to make it drough dee forest, if we do not run into any trouble, but once we enter Loustof..." Reagal shook his head. "Dat will be a different story."

"How do you mean?"

"We will be entering at dee most nordwesterly part of Loustof, which means we will av to travel straight drough to dee soud. You know as well as I dat Loustof will be on igh alert looking for you," replied Reagal.

"I know...I know, but luckily they don't know which way I'm coming from," Fern said with hope brightening his words.

"We need all dee luck we can get, young Majesteek."

The two companions "sluggishly" walked through the land of Dundire, noticing little villages bustling with dwarves. As they traveled further, they came upon human settlements, and Fern was astounded to see how admirably the two races flourished together.

Up to that moment, he had no inkling that humans had anything to do with dwarves, and what surprised him more were the reactions Reagal received...they were friendly.

Men would wave and smile, greeting the pair as they passed businesses and quaint little homes. Handshakes and swats on the back came frequently and without warrant. *This is how it should be.* Fern strolled lively, nearly dancing as he did, uncontrollable smile plastered brightly on his face.

Fern admired the landscape. Although much the same as it was at the base of the mountains, now there were no mountains.

Little streams cut through pine forests, and every now and then Fern or Reagal would spot a Wade Deer bounding away, startled by their approach. The deer were called such because they rarely left the rivers, wading in the waters feeding on any plant life they could find. Very strange ornamental trees called squat-bodies, because of their short, rounded trunks and fat oval leaves, were planted throughout the villages. One could usually find them in front of businesses or churches paired with vibrant rose-like flowers called beautics, usually planted to give a burst of bright red color. Riverstone wells, dotted alongside the path, provided fresh drinking water.

Granite cattle, a thick-skulled beast with short legs, were grazing in fenced areas, tended by the locals, and squawk ducks that Fern recognized from the farms in Burdensville waddled freely throughout the villages.

If one has ever walked the countryside passing farms and quaint little homes, and likes such things, then they can imagine the aromas wafting in the air. Bouquets of cattle pies, chicken feathers, duck down, pigs—wait, maybe not the pigs, horses, fresh stacked hay, and baked goods cooling on window sills. Those were the fragrances tickling Fern's and Reagal's senses, and they smelled of comfort.

It was quite pleasant walking through Dundire, so much so that Fern found himself thinking that if ever he had the chance, he would love to live there. With all the wonderous nature surrounding Fern, Lillia swirled amongst his thoughts. He never seemed to truly get her off his mind.

An unexpected vision suddenly came without mercy: Lillia lying injured upon a battlefield, a shadow of death hanging above her.

Fern wondered if he would ever see her again. His head plummeted from its recent oblivious joy down to his chest, attracting Reagal's attention.

"My young Majesteek, are you feeling well?"

"Oh yes, I...I was just wondering about Lillia."

Fern's face flushed as he did not mean to speak out loud.

"She is quite unforgettable," said Reagal, smiling. "I av known er my entire life; she as been visiting my land since she was a little fairling. We av become great friends."

Fern looked concerned.

"I'm sorry, I had no idea. I didn't mean to intrude."

The centaur chuckled.

"Oh, you misunderstand. She is like my sister and friend, noding more."

"Glad to hear," Fern said as his brows unfurled. "I was also wondering though… who is she?"

"Ow do you mean?"

"Well…I mean, what position does she hold in her kingdom? Is she their queen or leader of some sort?"

"Ah, I understand. She is neider," said Reagal. "In dee Blue Marshes, where dee fairies rule, der is no leader of any kind. Dae live a free life, caring for one anoder, all bound to different tasks given to dim at bird. Lillia is merely der ambassador."

Fern stared forward lost in thought for a moment.

"Has there ever been a fairy who has left the Blue Marshes…to live in a different land, I mean?"

"Yes, given dee right reasons."

The corner of Fern's mouth curved up in a grin as he thought of sweeping Lillia off her feet. Daydreams flooded his mind when, without provocation, he suddenly remembered a question he had been meaning to ask.

"Reagal, why did King Solace need you so urgently when we were traveling through the Blue Marshes?"

Realization lit the centaur's face. The subject was meant to be revealed in Dundire, and it completely slipped Reagal's mind.

"I apologize my friend. I did not mean to leave you in dee dark."

Fern smiled.

"Oh, no worries, Reagal. It didn't occur to me until now."

"Well den, do you remember dee night in Valom when we first met?" Fern quickly nodded. "My troops and I battled a large group of turgoyles just before we spotted you and your company. We slaughtered most of dim in dat fight, but my men captured two survivors. We took dim back wid us to find out what mischief dae were up to, and why dae were in our land, but I did not remain to find dee

answers. I spoke wid my fader requesting to join you on your quest, and immediately left. After my departure, my fader interrogated dee turgoyles wid severe
means and discovered dae were part of Stragurt's army. More importantly, ee found
out der lord sent dim der to capture you. Oh, yes...and I must say, my fader's star
readings were correct. Der was a group of fairies traveling drough our land dat
night after all. Dae ad passed us while we were fighting dee turgoyles. Lillia was
in dat group. Dee fairies were traveling to see my fader about troubles dae were
having wid dee Stone Trolls entering der land. When my fader found out about
dee plot, ee sent Lillia to come and retrieve us boad. You can imagine ow upset my
fader was when I returned widout you. Ee immediately gadered up our strongest
warriors. I led dim as quickly as I could to aid you." Reagal suddenly opened his
eyes wide. "Ah, yes, and I nearly forgot! Dandowin was der wid my fader. He was
telling im about a giant who stole is men's lunch when I came galloping up to tell
im about your presence in our land. Ee told my fader ee ad met you on is way to
der meeting and dat you almost made im late."

Fern could not believe how fortunate he had been. If he had not met Reagal
that night, he surely would be dead, and Edinword's plot to wage war would never
have been revealed.

The two continued along the winding path through Dundire without much
conversation. They both seemed to enjoy the scenery and were content to walk in
silence. The beautiful pines lining the path kept Fern's attention.

As wide as Fern's workshop, these trees were home to many creatures. Fern
watched as Parachute Squirrels leapt from branch to branch, and quickly found
the reason for their name. As strong as the trees trunk wood was, the branches that
grew from them were a different story. As each squirrel landed, the thick branches
from which they grasped, snapped like thin twigs sending the little red-furred
creatures plummeting to the ground. However, before the squirrels could fall any
distance, a pouch of skin upon their backs caught the air, opening like a parachute.
Suffice it to say, they all landed safely at the base of the pine before scurrying off.
Why do they even climb these trees at all, wondered Fern with a laugh.

The forest had no underbrush due to the abundant number of needles covering the ground, and Fern could see deep into the woods. He spotted a pack of
Bluntvolks, wolf-like creatures with blunt snouts and long grey fur.

The creatures stopped for a moment to observe Fern and Reagal. Light breaking through the treetops struck the eyes of the Bluntvolks, making them glow red

like shining dots of blood.

"Um, Reagal, I think we have company."

Fern pointed to the deepest part of the woods.

"No worries, young Majesteek, dae only eat dee insects dat live benead dee pine needles. Dae do not attack our kind."

"Well that's definitely good to know," sighed Fern.

The sun began to set as they approached a small village. Cozy homes of stone and wood lined the path on both sides, and short metal posts holding flaming torches every few yards lit the way. They came to a sign attached to a large 'squat-body' tree that read "Hindsville."

An inn called the Dwarf Dagger greeted them as they strolled into town. Large windows with inviting glowing yellow lights emanated onto green hedges that were planted along the side of the inn. Muffled voices of boisterous townsfolk could be heard singing from within.

"Should we stay here for the night?" asked Fern.

"I'm not sure. As friendly as it sounds, do you dink dae will be able to accommodate my kind?" Reagal asked smiling.

Fern felt foolish that he had not thought of that.

"Well, we can go in and see."

Fern opened a large wooden door. Creaking hinges alluded to their presence as they both walked inside. Reagal, ducking nearly a foot to clear the doorway, immediately caught the whiff of freshly brewed ale.

"Ah, my kind of place! We should get a drink before calling it a night. It will elp me sleep soundly!" Reagal slapped his armored gut and smiled as he peered into a large open dining area.

Hanging throughout were brightly-lit candle chandeliers, and on the back wall was a bar where humans and dwarfs sat drinking and laughing. Customers filled the dining area sitting on small round stools placed around numerous rectangular wooden tables. They were singing a dwarven song of friendship that Fern, unfortunately, could not understand, though, he wasn't quite sure if it was because of the language or because of the beer.

A check-in counter stood to Fern's left.

Given the name of the inn, Fern expected to be greeted by a dwarf as they entered, but instead, there was a tall thin man with a full black beard standing behind the counter; he cleared his throat. "Welcome to the Dwarf Dagger, masters!

Do you need a room for the night?"

"Yes, as a matter of fact, we do, but we're wondering if you could accommodate us both?" asked Fern.

"Of course. You can lay a feather mattress on the floor for the centaur, if that'll suffice?" said the man, looking up to Reagal.

"Yes, dat would be just fine. Dank you, my good man!" Reagal leaned his head down in a slight bow.

The bearded man led them down a long, dimly-lit hallway to their room. Turning to Reagal in an apologetic manner, he spoke.

"We've no seating to accommodate you in our dining facilities."

"No worries, sir, I can stand."

The man's face brightened with relief.

"Superior, don't hesitate to let us know if we can do anything to make your stay with us more comfortable. Have a good night!"

The innkeeper handed Fern a key, spun on his heels, and briskly walked away.

"Well, young Majesteek, what say we go get a drink!"

"Shouldn't we at least see our accommodations before we go? Those saddle bags must be cumbersome. Wouldn't you like to relieve yourself of them first?"

"Yes, yes, good dinking. Den we go!"

They entered the room, which was plain and rather large with hardwood floors and two windows positioned in the wall on the opposite side from the door. There were two simple metal framed beds to the left, covered in simple white linen with a white down blanket. Fern pushed one of the beds to the far side of the room and took the mattress, flopping it on the floor. Dust puffed into the air, entering Fern's nostrils and causing him to sneeze violently. His head jerked forward as he covered his mouth with his right hand.

"Bless you, my young Majesteek, and dank you for preparing my sleeping quarters." Reagal unstrapped his saddlebags and laid them next to his mattress. "Now let's get dat drink."

Fern huffed a chuckle and followed Reagal, locking the door behind him. Both walked swiftly to the dining room and watched as three patrons stepped away from their table and exited the inn. Fern and Reagal quickly claimed their spot, and Fern sat down on a stool. Reagal scooted the remaining seats to the side and stood looking for a waiter.

A dwarven man, shorter than most, came waddling by carrying a round tray stacked with empty jugs. Froth dripping from the rims left a stream of beer trailing from behind him.

Reagal tapped his front hooves on the wooden floor and waved his hand. "My good fellow, my good fellow."

The little red bearded dwarf spun around, splashing a bald man in the eye with the sudsy white foam. Sitting adjacent to Fern and Reagal, the burly man snorted loudly, slamming his fat hands down on the surface of his table. The friendly singing that attracted Fern into the inn abruptly stopped, sending a shockwave of silence throughout the tavern.

"Blast it, Merkle! What in lands sakes are you trying to do, blind me?"

He snatched a dirty white towel hanging from the dwarf's black leather belt to wipe his eyes, knocking the tray from Merkle's hands. Jugs shattered, and spent beer splashed Fern's trousers.

"Oh, so sorry, sir!" replied Merkle as he knelt to clean up the mess.

"No worries," said Fern as he dropped down to help, Reagal right behind him.

The burly man's face scrunched as he threw the balled-up towel down on the floor next to Fern.

"Why help that fool? He can clean that disastrous mess himself. Come, my good men, join me for a drink."

He must be from Loustof, thought Fern as he glared with gritted teeth at the man.

Fern was oblivious to the fact that his face was steaming like a brewer's vat, red as a beet, and his posture threatening. Laying his hand on Fern's shoulder, Reagal squeezed slightly to ease the tension. The burly man's eyes bulged, and his face shone with terror as he quickly spun back around in his seat.

Realizing his anger, Fern slowly calmed himself. His muscles shrank to normal size and the veins, pulsing through his forehead, subsided. Taking a deep relaxing breath, he looked at the dwarf and smiled.

"I apologize, that was uncalled for. No one should be treated like that."

"I do thank you, sir," whispered Merkle, glancing side-eyed at the back of the burly man's polished bald head. "but that's Mr. Barflow, he's the proprietor of this establishment."

"Owner or not, no one as dee right to abuse anoder," said Reagal as he gave a quick nod to Fern. "Now, my friend, ow about a drink!"

"Oh, of course, sirs. What's your pleasure?"

Merkle had his tray above his shoulder, piled high with broken mugs, and a wide closed smile planted on his bearded face.

Fern gave Reagal an indecisive look.

"Well, den, it looks as if it is up to me!"

The Centaurian prince glanced towards the bar. Stone and mirrors stared back. Dozens of mugs lay on their rims against the back counter, and barrels of ale, lager, and stout, tapped and ready for enjoyment and positioned on their sides, were stacked carefully on a long wooden cart.

Reagal studied Fern's face, scrutinizing it as if he was searching for some deep dark secret, when suddenly his eyes popped opened.

"Yes, yes, my young Majesteek, you are most definitely a lager man. I would bet my life on it! As for me, my good Merkle, I am, and always will be, a stout man!"

Fern shook his head, tittering as he did.

Hobbling quickly, tray balancing on his fat fingers, Merkle raced to the bar. Reagal, down on all fours, slowly came to a seated position on the wooden floor.

"I must let you know, my young Majesteek, dwarven beer is good, but it lacks strengd compared to what I am used to."

Mr. Barflow huffed a large grunt, jostling, as he spun around in his chair to face Reagal.

"Excuse me, sir, but my brew is the finest brew in any pub or tavern that you or your ill-tempered friend will ever come across. That I can assure you. Besides, I am no dwarf!"

Fern gave Reagal a lightning fast wink, and with a deep growl and brows furled, he glanced at Mr. Barflow. The owner of the Dwarven Dagger shuddered in his seat as Fern stared with a menacing snarl.

"Uh, uh...well then. You fine men enjoy y-your evening. I-I have...um, uh... some business to attend to, yes, business."

The bald, fat Mr. Barflow hopped from his seat and shuffled, weaving around numerous patrons, knocking down stools, until he reached a wooden door with a sign reading: Mr. Barflow: Owner, Connoisseur, Brewmaster. He quickly spun with a scowl and entered, slamming the door behind him. Fern and Reagal bellowed a laugh.

"Ah, my young Majesteek, who is dee ill-tempered now?"

As the two friends continue to laugh, Merkle came waddling up with a pair of large quart-sized jugs, froth slowly billowing down the sides.

"Here it is sirs! The best brew this side of Dundire Mountains. Enjoy!"

Merkle's plump cheeks raised as he revealed three missing teeth and a gold cap on his upper right front tooth. He carefully placed the jugs in front of their intended consumers, and Reagal reached in a pocket of his shirt, extracting a silver coin and tossed it to the dwarf. Merkle grasped it in midair, clamping down tightly.

"Thank you, sirs, let me know when you need another."

"Oh, der will be only one drink tonight, my good man. We will need our eds in dee morning."

"Well, sirs, if that be the case, I must warn you. This brew is potent."

A thin man two tables from Fern and Reagal stole Merkle's attention as boisterous singing began again. The song, a dwarven tune, uplifted Fern's spirit, and after a few sips of his lager, the young blacksmith found himself pounding his feet to the beat and singing along with Reagal in tow.

Brew, brew
Drink it through
Take it slow and keep it true
Drink long
Drink strong
Drink until the break of dawn
Drink for me
Drink for you
Drink for everyone you knew
Get on up
Keep your feet
Dance around the quiet street
Laugh out loud
Slap your knees
Have another if you please
Find your home
Find your door
Open before you hit the floor
Crawl to bed
Lay your head
Close your eyes and dream instead
Come the morning

FERN MAJESTIC AND THE FALL OF A DRAGON

Tomorrow night
Start again to your delight

As the song ended, Fern and Reagal gulped their last swallows of beer, slamming their jugs on the table, laughing hysterically.

"M-My y-y-young Majesteek, d-dis breeew i-is m-much st-stronger den, den I expected. I dink m-my ed i-is spinning."

"Y-Yes, Reagaaal, I think your h-head is sp-spinning too."

The two companions froze for just a moment and looked at each other before bursting into uncontrollable laughter.

"Reagal, Reagal, w-we must take con-control."

Reagal, up on all fours, and tapping his hooves to another dwarvish tune, straightened his face.

"Yes, you are right, my young Majesteek. I-I, we, we must."

Frozen again, Fern and Reagal suddenly exploded into crazed laughter. Jumping from the floor, Fern danced like a wild gypsy while Reagal trotted around him clapping his hands in the air.

The inn was alive, and the merriment abundant. Hours flew, and the two friends danced and sang as the floors shook and the chandeliers swayed. Fern would never forget that night, though, whether he remembers it entirely, remains a mystery.

Waking on a table, groggy and head aching, Fern lay with his face planted in a pool of drool. He wiped the side of his mouth with his sleeve and stretched his eyes open.

Decorated in unconscious men, women, and dwarves, the room felt cold and dark, and besides a sea of snoring, the dining area was quiet.

Fern scanned his surroundings. The chandeliers were extinguished, and stools and tables were strewn about from the merriment that Fern was desperately trying to remember clearly. His eyes came to a halt and focused on Reagal, who was standing in the darkness, eyes squinted, peering through a window.

The moonlight shone bright, and stars could be seen twinkling in the midnight hour. The Centaurian prince breathed a heavy sigh as the moonlight cast a large shadow upon the floor.

"Dere will be a day when I will read does stars, my young Majesteek." Reagal turned, looking stern yet pathetic. "I will lead my people. It will be upon my shoulders to lead dim, to lead dim right."

113

"You'll be great, my friend. I've no doubt."

Reagal grinned and shook his head as he knelt on all fours.

"I cannot disappoint im…I cannot."

"Disappoint who?"

"My fader. Ee is counting on me. I must not let im down."

"There's no way you'll let him down, you'll be everything he hopes for, and more. I have no doubts."

Reagal sighed again, dropping his head, chest heaving.

"You do not understand. If I fail im…it will…it…wi—"

Fern staggered over to Reagal, catching his balance as he placed his hand on the centaurs armored back.

"You worry needlessly, my friend. Your father adores you. I could see it in his face."

"Ee olds me to igh expectations, and I must not fail im."

"Correct me if I'm wrong, but is there something deeper you want to share with me? If you need an ear, I have two."

Peering around to meet his friend's solemn expression, Fern's half drunken smile curved high and nearly closed his bloodshot eyes.

"Dank you, it is just…there is so much." Reagal looked away.

"Please, my friend, I won't judge."

The tall Centaurian prince, turning his head, could see his tipsy friend's sincerity.

"It is my broder. Ee as made my fader do someding ee as never ad to do before."

"You have a brother?"

"Yes, an older steed. Ee is impertinent, and ee as given my fader much trouble, defies im every chance ee gets." Reagal paused, and to Fern's surprise, a faint grin developed upon the centaur's face. "Dough, as amusing as is insolence is at times, my fader finds no umor in it. Ee as banished my broder from our kingdom, along with many like-minded centaurs; it as never appened before."

Fern interceded loudly, eyes popping. "Your father banished him, just because he was disrespectful?!"

"No, my young Majesteek, it was more dan just dat. My broder did not believe in dee stars as my fader taught, nor did ee agree on dee manner at which my fader ruled. Ee wanted dee drone, ee wanted to be king of our land, and ee wanted it now. Ee was ambitious and unruly, but ee was my broder, and I loved im. I did not want im to leave our kingdom. I tried to reason wid my fader, but ee would not listen. I miss my broder greatly."

"So, now *you* are in line to be king?"

"Yes, and my fader could not bear it if I fail im like my broder as. I must old myself to is standards, and I must obey is command at all costs."

Fern could almost see the weight upon Reagal's shoulders as the centaur fought to keep his posture in the moonlight.

Still seeming quite tall, Reagal suddenly turned to Fern.

"Tell me about *your* life."

"I'm afraid that that's a very boring story, my friend," said Fern, his face downtrodden as he looked up at the ceiling.

"Even so, I would like to ear it. Tell me about your childood. Oo raised you?" asked Reagal, staring with great curiosity.

"Very well, if you must know, I raised myself. I don't really remember how I even came to the town of Burdensville. I just remember running from home to home as a little boy begging for food. Most of the people ignored me, but some of the older women would throw me scraps from time to time. I mostly found food in the garbage."

Fern's eyes dropped as a sadness took over his face. The memories of the poor little starving boy who was once Fern danced devilishly in his mind. The cramping pain of hunger could still be felt these many years later. He sighed.

"I slept in the stables with the horses; in the winter I'd go to the blacksmith workshop to warm by the fires. When I was old enough, I started making weapons out of stone and sticks to hunt with. That was a wonderful time for me; I was finally able to eat on a regular basis."

Fern's face brightened slightly, remembering the forests and sunny spring days where he foraged for food.

"When I was older, the old man who owned the blacksmith shop took pity on me. He took me in and fed me. He became the only friend I've ever had in the village. His name was Edgar Jacobs, the closest thing I had to a father. He became my mentor and taught me everything I know about blacksmithing. He left me his shop when he died."

Fern looked down again, his eyes began to well up with tears, but he did not cry.

"If it is not too painful, might I ask ow ee died?" asked Reagal, his expression heartfelt.

"I...I...well...he, he just died."

Fern's eyes shifted, and his glare landed to the floor. Reagal did not press for further explanation.

"When he passed away, I nearly died from despair. It was about that time when dragons and other beasts started attacking my village. It helped me keep my mind off Edgar's death; it saved my life, really. That's also the time I discovered the use for Ulmeck Rock. I'd stumbled upon a deserted turgoyle tunnel one day when I was hunting. I followed it, out of curiosity, and it led me to the base of the Ulmeck Mountains where I found the rock. I took some back with me and experimented on it, making all sorts of tools. The tools I forged from it were the strongest I'd ever made, so when the dragons started attacking my village, I crafted the arrows to defeat the destructive creatures."

Fern spoke confidently about his craftsmanship.

"Though, even I was surprised when they fell from the sky after being struck by the arrows."

Fern stopped talking and stared at the ceiling as if he was watching the fire breathing beasts falling from the sky.

"Ow did you come to know your own name?" asked Reagal.

"I have an inscription tattooed on my right arm."

Fern pulled up the sleeve of his shirt to show Reagal. It read:

You are Fernand Majestic,
the son of a great people.
May they rise again through your life,
and may you lead them to prosperity
once more.

Fern pulled his sleeve back over his arm and laid down.

Huffing a large sigh, he cleared his throat.

"It burns sometimes, not quite sure why. Anyway, my entire life I thought that whoever carved this inscription into my arm had to be the craziest person in this world, and that if I ever met them, I would show them the same life of misery and pain they've caused me, but now...now with all that I've learned...I'm not sure what to think."

Fern stood, still staring at the ceiling.

Reagal breathed lightly and spoke.

"My dear Majesteek, your family put all der ope in you! You *will* rise, and you *will* be dee salvation of your people. You must look to ope, for you are strong and brave. I am honored to know you, and I am honored to call you my friend."

Fern turned to Reagal with a sleepy smile.

"Reagal, I'm grateful for your friendship, and your company, and I hope you are right."

The two companions sat in the dark pondering the conversation that sobered their bodies. Reagal finally stood.

"My dear friend, we must catch a few hours of sleep if we expect to av strengd tomorrow."

Fern nodded slowly, and both strolled from the dining area and down the hall to their room. Unlocking the door and easing it open so as not to make noise, Fern entered first. He plopped down on the bed, and a cloud of dust rose around him before settling back on the blanket. Ducking through the doorway, Reagal walked slowly to his mattress, hooves clicking on the wooden floor, and laid down.

They both put their heads on comfy feather pillows and drifted off to sleep.

As one might guess, Fern soon found himself emerged in dreams of Lillia. Side by side, they strolled. Beautiful green meadows decorated with fragrant pink flowers surrounded them as they shared memories about their childhood and dreams that each held for their lives. They grasped each other's hands and embraced. Their minds were one. Dancing as birds chirped in a clear blue sky, their hearts sang. Fern's and Lillia's bond was growing strong, and their love was real, so real.

Fern awoke, staring at the dark ceiling. Crickets chirped, and the air was stale. His eyes clamped shut as he dozed off again.

The morning came quickly, like it always does, and the two companions gathered their gear, ate a light breakfast, and paid the innkeeper for a night's stay.

Only a few miles stood between them and the borders of Earthingland.

Rising fast, the sun beamed down upon Fern's shoulders. The heat was pleasant and had both companions feeling refreshed from their excessive behavior the night before. *Another morning, another adventure*, thought Fern as they found the path.

Fern and Reagal shared small talk as the birds began to whistle *good morning*.

Noticing the forests becoming dense, mixing with large deciduous trees, Fern realized they were close.

"Ah, yes, ear it is!" announced Reagal, Fern's hunch confirmed.

There in the middle of the path grew an enormous oak tree, reaching nearly five hundred feet into the sky. Carved in its bark, in whimsical letters, read: *Welcome to Earthingland, entering is optional.* Fern gave a quizzical look, scrunching his brows.

"I must warn you, dese are untamed lands we are entering. Dee inabitants can be dangerous if provoked, so we must be vigilant."

Fern gave a hesitant nod, and both proceeded past the giant oak tree and into the wilds of Earthingland.

Although it was only midmorning, the dense forest made it seem like dusk. It was nothing like the woods of Alkyle or the pine forests of Dundire; it seemed unbroken and gloomy. The foliage was scant, and the underbrush was nonexistent. The trees were so close together that Fern could not see more than a few feet into the forest. This did not give him a sense of security. *If anything decides to attack us, we'll have little warning or none at all.*

Large thick brown vines slithered around every tree. On occasion, Fern would mistake them for giant serpents. *They almost look alive. I would hate to meet a snake that big!* The branches of the trees jetted from their thorny trunks high above Fern's and Reagal's heads and twisted and tangled, interwinding with each other. The forest was unified. Thick brown crumbling leaves grew from the branches and were as large as a dinner plate. They would fall from time to time, gliding down like parachutes, one even landing on Fern's head. He reached up grabbing it only to have it crumble into thousands of tiny specks, filling his hair with an itchy dust. *Nice one, Fern.*

"Reagal, how long will we be traveling through this murky forest?" asked Fern as he frantically combed through his hair, a brown cloud hovering above him.

"Dis forest is called dee Witless Woods, and unfortunately we will be traveling drough it until we reach dee borders of Loustof."

"The Witless Woods? Why on harth is it called that?" asked Fern as the dust settled on his shoulders.

"Oh, yes, it is a funny story, my friend. Dee dwarves named it dat because it is so dense. But dae claim dae gave it its name because of dee untamed beasts dat dwell ear. I know oderwise."

Fern smiled as his head tilted upwards, eyes surveying the tangle of thick gray tree limbs.

Tiny yellow twinkling eyes dotted the treetops, and every so often, Fern could spot a fluffy tail or two of some unknown creature, dangling for a moment before disappearing back among the branches. The Witless Woods was a place of mystery, dark and foreboding. *I wonder if these creatures have ever seen the likes of me before?* Hoping to catch a glimpse of something amazing, Fern's thoughts wandered. *Maybe I will see something never discovered before. Wouldn't that be grand!* His adventurous mind swirled with thoughts of new species and enchanted sprites.

Could anyone blame him? After all, he had never set foot out of Edinword's lands until that fateful day when the king sent him on his quest. No, Fern was justified in his giddiness, and although his errand was dire, he was having the time of his life.

The day stretched long, and Reagal found himself sluggish and weary. Fern, on the other hand, was still enjoying his new surroundings, even if they were gloomy, when Reagal suddenly piped up.

"So, my young Majesteek, maybe you would like to ear a story or two?"

Fern shook his head emphatically, and the tales began. Speaking, not boasting, of course, Reagal told about turgoyle battles he had fought, and the near-death experiences he had faced. Though, Fern reminded him of their most recent battle at the Crags of Malice, and how if it were not for Reagal, it would have been a "sudden" death experience. The two friends began to hoot with laughter.

Thunderous blubbering quickly drowned out their chuckles, and in the distance, they could see a large figure sitting in the middle of the path with its hands covering its face, crying uncontrollably. The deep bellows of sadness trembled down the path, and Fern could feel vibrations crawl up his legs. Reagal came to an immediate halt.

"My young Majesteek, we must be very cautious! Dat is a giant! I av never eard of one being in dis part of dee world, and I am not sure if we should go any furder."

Reagal's quiet voice trembled.

"We've no other options," whispered Fern. "We can't venture into the woods, we'll surely get lost, and I'll not go back. I must get to the Ulmeck Mountains."

The immediacy in Fern's voice was loud and clear, and Reagal knew that there was no convincing him otherwise.

"Very well den, we must face dis giant and ope it does not kill us boad."

Reagal began to advance, creeping lightly, like a lioness stalking its prey, and Fern was on the tips of his toes. As they both inched forward, the giant suddenly stood up. He was mountainous. Wide and tall, his silhouette blocked the path. Shining yellow eyes stared towards them, and Fern could not tell if the giant was armed, for it was still too dark in the dense forest.

They froze in their footsteps, as the giant suddenly spoke.

"Who there?" it said in a frightened, shaky tone.

Fern was stunned as he immediately recognized the giant's voice. It was Garrick.

"Garrick! How...how did you get here?"

Fern burst out running like he had hot coals under his feet, kicking up the dirt behind him.

"Sir, is you? But Mallock say you dead."

Garrick was dumbstruck as he picked Fern up in his arms, nearly crushing him. Gripping Fern's torso, Garrick squeezed the air from his lungs.

"I so happy you not dead, my friend!" he said, finally letting Fern down.

Fern was laughing, mouth open wide as he relearned how to breathe.

Finally reaching them, Reagal bellowed with pleasure. "Garreeck? It is good to see you again. Ow did you appen to come to dis place?"

"It too horrible to speak, sirs, too horrible!" replied Garrick, nearly starting to cry again.

"Please try, my friend," Fern asked, patting Garrick on his back, trying to sooth the giant's emotions.

Garrick nodded and wiped the tears from his eyes as a drip of snot fell from his nose, splashing upon the dry ground.

"Prince Timal alive, and he kill Mallock, and I...I..." The words caught in his throat. "I help him!"

The giant's head fell back, and his mouth cranked open. His crooked teeth protruded from his lower jaw as he burst into tears once again.

Fern's face dropped.

"How's that possible? Mallock said he put a knife in his heart!" Fern stood motionless. "Garrick, you must pull yourself together and tell me the entire story."

Garrick wiped his face and tried slowing his breathing as a lump the size of a watermelon lodged in his throat.

"Sir, Mallock come down from mountain and say you and Prince Timal kill by beast. I sorry, I believe him."

"He deceived me as well, my friend, you have no reason to be sorry. Please, continue."

Fern was shaking with anxiety.

"Well, we start back to Loustof, it third day on road, someone jump on path in front of me and Mallock. I saw that it prince. He order me grab Mallock. I not know what I do, so I obey. Before Mallock have time to run, I grab him. Prince Timal took my swords and tell me take necklace off Mallock's neck and give to him. I obey him, he my prince, and I obey him."

Garrick sat in silence, eyes filled to the brim with salty liquid, and Fern spoke gently with sympathy in his voice.

"Please, Garrick, I know this is difficult, but you must tell us everything."

"Prince Timal cut head from body," Garrick's lower lip quivered as he spoke, "while he still in my arms!"

He could not control it any longer. His eyes burst into a sprinkler, wailing like a newborn baby, watering the ground with a downpour of tears.

Fern stood next to him patting him on the back in complete shock as he became drenched by Garrick's thunderstorm of emotion.

"Garrick, you didn't know what he was going to do. Please, you must believe me, this was not your fault. Mallock brought this on himself."

Fern repeated those words, trying to console his giant friend.

"Ow did you end up all dee way out ear?" asked Reagal.

Garrick looked up and wiped the tears and snot from his face, the lump in his throat bouncing like a ball. "I r-ran, I r-ran, I-I ran, I r-ran! I—I—It d-dark, I h-hit tr-trees, b-but I n-not stop, I j-just r-ran!" Garrick plopped down on the ground again.

"I know you are distraught, but you must pull yourself together. We are traveling to the Ulmeck Mountains. We could use your help, if you are willing," Fern smiled up at the giant.

"Y-Yes, c-course, but p-p-please not m-make me go back t-to king and p-p-prince!"

"Don't worry, you will stay with me from now on."

Fern patted Garrick on the back gently, giving him a reassuring grin. Smiling with relief, Garrick stood as a long strand of snot hung from his nose. The thick green rope of goo snapped and clung to a tree branch, swinging wildly in the air.

"We must continue at once, my young Majesteek, we av limited time."

Fern agreed, and the company of three proceeded through the Witless Woods.

After a while of walking in silence, Fern turned to Garrick and noticed he was reasonably calm. The giant had a goofy grin on his face, and his uneven eyes studied the trees. He carried his arms close to his sides, but they swung back and forth as if he was marching in formation. Thinking the time was right, Fern asked him some questions.

"Garrick, could you tell me what you know about King Edinword and Prince Timal?"

Fern prayed he wouldn't burst into tears again. Surprisingly, Garrick seemed giddy and ready to talk.

"Oh, I tell about Prince first. He more interesting than king. He always stay young. I never see him grow. I never seen him as baby neither. He always same. Mallock and prince go on many quests that king want. They bring many creatures to dungeons for battles."

"How often would this happen?" asked Fern, Reagal stepping close, listening fiercely.

"Oh, every month. Sometime two times. King always want dungeons full. He get very mad if cells empty."

"I would like to know more about the prince, Garrick. You say he never aged?"

"Oh, yeah, I know he never get old, cause of Mallock."

"What do you mean?"

"I remember me and Mallock. We grow up together, Timal, never get older, but Mallock do. Mallock always have questions for king, but king say 'shut up, you little vagabond.'"

Garrick's impression of Edinword was impressive, and Fern chuckled under his breath as Garrick continued.

"I never know what king talk about. He say many words I not understand."

"I'm a little confused, my friend. How was Mallock in the kingdom as a child?"

"Ooooh, there many talk that say Mallock king's son, but king always say that people dumb like me and make stupid lies."

Wait a second, if both are Edinword's sons, they must both be agers. Why would they grow at such different rates? Fern couldn't understand it and began to wonder if Mallock was in fact Edinword's son. *Maybe Edinword was manipulating Mallock as well.* Fern suddenly noticed Garrick staring at him. The giant wanted more questions.

"What about the arena battles, can you tell me about those?"

Garrick bounced with glee as he smiled wide.

"I not know much about fights, I can't fit in dungeon. It good for me, say king, cause he say I never leave there if I small like you. Though, I know of centaur like

Reagal. He king's favorite champion. He never lose battle, cept against you, sir. King say he keep him til he die in fights."

Reagal's eyes nearly popped from their sockets. The desperation and anger in his face was evident to anyone watching, and the thoughts of freeing Galeon from the depths of Loustof battled with his duties given by his father.

"Tell me Garreek, does your king treat is prisoners well?"

A tightness in Reagal's chest labored his breathing, and Fern noticed the centaur's hand gripping tightly around the hilt of his sword.

"I know he feed the centaur good. He say he want him have strength to fight."

By Valom's star, keep im safe. I will come for im if I survive dis journey...if my fader allows it, prayed Reagal.

Garrick, relieved from his woes, announced how wonderful it was to find his friends.

The funny thing about giants, they never stay sad for long. Their naivety is that of a child, and their spirit lacks no bounds.

Fern could never wipe the smile from his face when Garrick was happy.

Merry by the conversation's end, which was several hours later, given the fact that the giant was doing most of the talking, the company's spirits were high. Garrick, and his large floppy feet, cracked the dry ground as he skipped like a playful fawn.

The forest was becoming eerily dark, and the sun was nearly set. Rumbling as if a thunderstorm loomed overhead, Garrick's stomach vibrated, catching his friends' attention.

Deciding to make camp for the night, they ate dinner quickly while Fern filled Garrick in on all that had happened to him and Reagal since parting at the foot of the Crag Mountains. Astonished, and taking gasping breaths every few seconds, Garrick sat, legs crossed, in complete bewilderment.

"I not believe king can do so bad stuff. Poor, poor prince Timal. I feel so sorry for him, and Mallock bad, very bad man."

Garrick shook his barrel of a head, losing all guilt for Mallock's death.

The company split guard duty throughout the night, with Reagal taking first watch, letting Garrick take the last. They figured he needed rest first, above all else.

Garrick's spirit was completely refreshed as the morning came without incident. Just before dawn, he woke Fern, who was lost in dreams of Lillia again. Reagal was already awake preparing their morning meal of salted fish and dried berries. The three of them ate a quick breakfast, packed their gear, and headed off towards Loustof.

Things were quiet for the most part, and the sun started to rise, giving the forest a luminescent glow. According to Reagal, they still had two more days in the Witless Woods.

Their pace was steady, but slower than Reagal would have liked, which he made sure to voice from time to time.

"Sir, I have idea." Garrick said suddenly, looking at Reagal.

"And what might dat be my friend."

"I carry young sir on my shoulder. He not weigh much, and I not slow down."

"A great suggestion," Reagal said, turning towards Fern with a sly grin. "What say you?"

Fern looked at his friends and rolled his eyes as he shook his head.

"Well, I'm obviously too slow for you both, so what choice do I have? Garrick put me on your shoulder."

Fern, slightly annoyed, lifted his arms. Garrick wrapped one hand around Fern's waist and hoisted him to his right shoulder. Swinging his legs in front of the giant's chest, Fern balanced himself as he laid his hand on Garrick's neck.

Fern, like a child on a swing, kicked his feet as Reagal looked up.

"You see, my young Majesteek; you av already risen to great ights. I am becoming as good a star reader as my fader."

Reagal burst into laughter.

"Yes, Reagal, but this is not exactly what I had in mind," snapped Fern, crossing his arms and giving his companions a pouty frown.

"Don't feel bad, sir," said Garrick. "It not your fault you born small with short legs."

Reagal pulled his head back and burst out a deep bellowing laugh that made it difficult for Fern to feel anything but happy.

With the centaur being so light on his hooves and Garrick with his long strides, Fern realized how much faster they were moving through the forest. He felt a little foolish for making a big deal of what turned out to be the right thing to do.

Now with the pace quickened, the mood of the three companions became light, and conversation was abundant. So much so that they lost track of time and became lazy in their vigilance.

A good knock on the head would have served them right as a figure abruptly interrupted them, walking out of the thick forest blocking their path.

"HALT!" it said in a harsh voice with a raised hand.

The company was startled. Fern leapt down from Garrick's shoulder and drew his sword without hesitation.

"Please, lower your weapons. I have not come to start a fight. I would only like to ask questions of you," it said trilling its r's as it spoke.

Standing in front of them was a minotaur, eight feet tall and carrying a battle-ax strapped to its back. Its bull face was stern, and its large open nostrils flexed as it breathed. It had two sharp horns projecting from its head that curved forward, sharp and foreboding. Its hair was jet black and dusty. Dull orange and red beads decorated braids that hung sporadically from its body. A short-sleeved dark-brown leather shirt covered its upper torso while it wore no trousers to hide its hairy legs.

The minotaur stamped the ground, whipping its long dusty tail in the air to shoo flies away. Fern glared at the creature in wonderment, and he smiled as another mystical being could be filed in his memory. The list was growing long.

"I have been looking for my brother and four of his companions. They left my company nearly ten days ago. Have you seen them?"

Minotaurs! He must be talking about the ones that attacked us in the Mystic Forest of Alkyle, thought Fern.

Reagal tilted his head, eyeballing Fern and trying his best to make him understand his thoughts. *Please my friend, say noding of is broder or is friends, say noding!* Fern understood completely, but he was not about to let this minotaur continue searching in vain.

"I am sorry, but—"

Reagal suddenly interrupted, sighing and shaking his head gallingly.

"You must realize, Minotaur, dat attacking us would serve you ill. You are outnumbered and outskilled. You must listen widout asteful reactions, for you are not going to like what we av to say. Dis is young Fern Majesteek; I know you av eard of is race before, der kind as elped yours in times past. I also know dat your kind owes im as much gratitude as mine, for dee deeds of is forefaders, so please ear im out. Den you can react as you wish."

The minotaur nodded his head in compliance as hanging beads swaying with his movements mesmerized Garrick.

Fern's recap was brief, telling how the minotaurs attacked his camp and killed three of his companions, and how he reacted the only way he thought possible. He spoke of how perplexed he was over the attack, and that he never would have harmed them otherwise.

"I truly am sorry," said Fern, Garrick standing back scratching his bottom and snorting loudly as he still stared at the swaying beads.

Reagal suddenly interceded.

"I must say, Minotaur, when ee revealed dis story to me, ee told it in a very regrettable manner. Dae sincerely did not want to arm your people. Please understand dat."

Glancing at the three of them, stiff, and not knowing what to say, the minotaur turned his back. His breathing became heavy as he began mumbling to himself in an unrecognizable language.

He suddenly spun around, startling Garrick.

"I undeřstand," he said. "but I am veřy confused about many a thing." His head hung low in anguish over the death of his brother. "Please, tell me, did he suffeř?"

"Your brother...no, no, he did not," replied Fern, unsure of what to say.

"Is der any reason you know of dat would av given dim cause to attack my friends and der companions?" asked Reagal.

"Yes," replied the minotaur quickly. "My břotheř and I, and ouř fouř companions, weře řeturning fřom a meeting with the elves of Alkyle about the abduction of one of ouř finest wařřiořs named Xařion. He was taken by soldieřs fřom an unknown kingdom. We met a hooded man on the path. He knew of ouř meeting with the elves and told us that soldieřs fřom the kingdom of Loustof took Xařion. He said he saw them coming down the path a few miles behind us. When we asked him how he knew about the abduction, he told us he witnessed it fiřst hand, and that he, too, was going to see the elves about this situation. He seemed quite convincing. My břotheř told me to go back to the elves to wařn them of this thřeat, that they would deal with the soldieřs themselves. I was supposed to meet them back in ouř land if I did not find them on the řoad."

Fern now understood. *The minotaurs must have overheard the soldiers talking about the battles in the arena when they were sitting around the campfire. That is what made them attack without question.*

"Tell me, Minotaur, did you get a good look at dis ooded man?" asked Reagal.

"Fiřstly, my name is not Minotauř, it is Dominance, but you may řefeř to me as Dom, and no, unfořtunately, I did not. I did not even get his name. I left befoře my brother was finished speaking with him."

Reagal apologized for his rudeness.

"I am sincerely sorry, my friend, my ead was somewhere else."

Dom gave him an unconvincing nod.

"Can you please answer questions of mine?" he asked. "Why have you entered my land, and what is the purpose of your quest?"

He was still visibly distraught from the news of his brother's death, but handled it with considerable dignity, standing tall and steadfast shedding no tears.

Fern looked at Reagal, and Reagal nodded while Garrick still stood by quietly, though now swaying along with Dom's beads.

"Very well, Dom, we will tell you everything," said Fern.

He proceeded to divulge the entire story, from the first day in Loustof until that day. Dom stood for a moment after hearing their tale.

"I now understand," he said suddenly.

Dom walked back and forth, pacing the ground with heavy hoof steps, before finally speaking again.

"We minotaur's are solitary creatures and do not keep company, unless it is at the utmost importance. I seek justice for my brother's death, and I believe your quest requires my attendance. I wish to join you in your mission. I am a skilled warrior, and I can move unseen with great stealth. Will you have me?"

Dom stood with an unwavering stare as Fern and Reagal looked at each other, nodding simultaneously.

"Good," said Dom as he gave what Fern thought could be a slight smile.

"I know a much faster way through the Feral Forest," said Dom abruptly.

"The Feral Forest?" questioned Fern.

"Yes, that is its name," replied Dom in a puzzled voice as his eyes scanned the surrounding trees.

Fern turned to Reagal with a confused expression. Reagal shrugged his shoulders.

"I am sorry, my young Majesteek, I av never dought it necessary to speak to dee inabitants of dis land to obtain dee proper name for dese woods."

"Is it safe to travel into the forest?" Fern asked Dom.

"With me as your guide, absolutely!"

His confidence was resounding.

Fern looked up to Reagal with an inquisitive stare.

"Do not worry," whispered Reagal. "Minotaurs might be brash creatures, but dae usually are not deceptive."

"Usually?" questioned Fern eyebrows slanted in worry.

"I dink we should trust im, if dis short cut ee says is true, it will save us valuable time."

"Very well," said Fern turning to Dom, hesitation in his voice. "Lead on."

The company turned right veering off the path and followed Dom into the forest. Large trees, some with protruding thorns that were not easily seen, taunted and poked Fern and Garrick in their arms and legs as they tried to maneuver through the wood. Reagal, like Dom, easily weaved his way around each puncturing attack that the trees possessed.

Dead rotting leaves covered the forest floor, and the only life to be seen, besides themselves, were thousands of tiny flies that hovered around their faces and crawled in and out of every crevice of their bodies. The torturous insects were unrelenting. Fern scratched, swatted, smacked, and shook frantically trying to rid himself of the irritation. It was nearly maddening for all but Dom who paid little attention to the minuscule pests.

They had been traveling for an hour or so when Garrick's stomach announced he was getting hungry. The deep rumbling that reverberated from his giant belly was something no one could ignore, even the annoying flies would back away at the sound of it.

Insisting they not stop, Dom told them there was an opening in the woods, not far from where they were, and it would be a better place to have their midday meal. Fern and Reagal agreed, and Garrick looked on, grabbing his gut with both hands trying to calm the constant ache as they continued to traverse the Feral Forest.

It was so difficult to navigate through the dense thicket that Fern kept questioning how it could be a quicker way. Dom assured him that he was leading them straight, and that the previous path they were on would have led them up and around to the northernmost part of his land. Not only were they saving time traveling through the forest, he said, but they would cut off half of their trip through Loustof as well.

Come on Dom, don't disappoint me. I don't need more surprises. Fern couldn't help but think of his last guide's deception and wondered if he was making the same mistake.

When they finally made it to the opening, the sun could be seen overhead. It was a welcoming sight as warmth touched their skin and the beaming rays of sun seeped into their bodies.

The company walked deeper into the clearing and immediately noticed large holes, in no particular pattern, scattered all over the ground. Tall strands of brown grass grew around the gaping holes, and large dirt encrusted stones that looked like they had been recently dug up, lay scattered throughout the clearing.

"Dom, what are these holes for?" asked Fern.

"Not sure," Dom said quickly.

Fern looked at Reagal, shaking his head, suspicion mounting, when Garrick tapped Fern upon his shoulder.

"Pardon me, sir, but I starving," said Garrick as another loud rumble scared the flies away.

"Of course, my friend, let's eat." Fern's suspicion faded slightly as his mind became busy preparing the midday meal of more salted fish and some small beige mushrooms that were found on the edge of the clearing.

They all sat down to have lunch. Dom, silent with his legs crossed and head down, chose to distance himself from the company as he sat some feet away. Fern, Reagal, and Garrick let him have his space, thinking he needed time to mourn the loss of his brother. Meanwhile, Fern wanted to hear about Lillia, asking Reagal to tell him all he knew. Garrick was content, as well, listening to the stories.

Reagal spoke about their childhood together, and how Lillia would ride on his back as a little fairling. Though, he slightly regretted telling the fact that he would buck her off from time to time. Laughing at the sight of Fern's confounded face, Reagal quickly explained to him that fairies do not hit the ground; they float.

Reagal could see Fern's eyes brighten and fill with interest as he spoke of Lillia's kind and caring nature, and how she would care for the woodland creatures that wandered into her lands, some lost and injured. Of course, Fern realized, long before now, that Lillia was much more than a pretty face. His feelings for her grew the more Reagal revealed. Though Fern became saddened as he learned how upset Lillia was that Galeon (the centaur from the arena battle) had been captured. Reagal explained that Galeon grew up with Lillia as well.

The conversation suddenly caught Dom's attention. He stood and stomped over to Reagal, interrupting him.

"You have had one of your own taken?" asked Dom.

"Yes, I av. In fact, ee is very close to me," replied Reagal.

"Who took him?"

"Dee same soldiers who took your kind, I'm afraid."

Dom spun away with an examining look on his face and turned to Fern.

"I am afraid we should be on ouř way," he said with sudden urgency.

It was evident to all that something was troubling him deeply.

"My friend, if you need to speak with me about your brother, I'll do what I can to relieve you of your pain." Fern winced, his face a picture of grief. "I feel indebted to you for your loss. I wish I would've known who the king was, and whom he sent with me on my quest. If I'd only known, I would never have kept company with them, I swear to you."

Dom searched Fern's eyes, took a deep breath, and then spoke.

"I am sořřy; I should have neveř come with you. I have deceived you."

"Wh—What are you talking about?" Fern asked, fear welling up inside him.

"We weře told by the hooded man that you might třy to deceive us with gřandiose tales. I was hoping that you weře lying, that you had only captuřed my brother instead of killed him, like the soldieřs captuřed Xařion, but I see now that he is třuly gone, and it was not you who deceived me."

Dominance stood staring at the ground, chest heaving, as he suddenly raised his head.

"I must leave you now, foř I do not belong heře. Please do not třy to convince me otheřwise. I have made up my mind."

Turning to leave, he stopped and looked at Reagal.

"Befoře I go, I must wařn you: we weře told that if we captuřed any of youř gřoup, we weře to břing you to this cleařing. I do not know what plans the hooded man had in stoře for you, but it looks like he has left this place. I suggest you go as well."

"You can't just leave us here!" shouted Fern. "We don't know our way out!"

Dominance turned with a sad grin.

"Let this be řetřibution for the killing of my břotheř."

He sprinted into the woods and was out of sight before anyone could react.

"This can't be happening! Can we trust no one?" Fern screamed in anger, muscles tensed as he ran his hands through his auburn hair.

"Please, my young Majesteek, dis will get us nowhere. We must remain calm and try to get our bearings," Reagal said, though, just as panicked as Fern.

Garrick sat in the center of the clearing, legs crossed, looking up in the sky.

Something was circling them.

"Sirs...Sirs...Sirs!" Garrick yelled, trying to get their attention, but Fern and Reagal were too busy trying to figure out which direction to follow.

"SIRS!" Garrick yelled, his powerful voice making the leaves rustle, finally garnering a response.

"What is it?" Fern replied, startled by Garrick's sudden outburst.

The giant said nothing, he just sat motionless pointing his plump index finger to the sky. Fern and Reagal slowly arched their heads back. *Dragon*, thought Fern! Reagal suddenly burst out roaring in joy!

"Soma!" he yelled. "Soma!"

"Soma, who's Soma?" asked Fern, flabbergasted.

"She is my chamrosh. I av ad er since I was a young steed. Ah, my fader is brilliant! Ee must av seen our plight in dee stars and sent er for us. She can lead us out of dis place."

Reagal let out a loud whistle and the chamrosh swooped down landing gracefully next to him. It was a beautiful creature, with the body of a canine and the head and wings of a bird. She nuzzled Reagal as he patted her on the head.

"Faele silumni, faele silumni," Reagal said, to the puzzlement of both Fern and Garrick.

"What did you just say to it?"

"Dat was dee language of my people, and 'it' is a girl. I merely told er 'good animal.'" Reagal continued to pet Soma down her back. "Come meet er. She is docile to my friends."

Fern and Garrick walked over and stroked Soma down her spine. Her furry back arched.

Her head resembled a golden eagle, with beautiful brown feathers that grew down to her shoulder blades. She nuzzled Fern's legs and squawked joyfully as he scratched her chin. She spread her wings, which spanned nearly twelve feet and were covered in the same brown feathers as her head. Her body, a light gold, mirrored that of a long slender dog, and was trailed by a long tail that had a tuft of hair at the tip. She was extremely friendly, rubbing her body against Fern and sitting on Garrick's foot. The attention thrilled Garrick as he slapped his hands together with glee. Though the thunderous clap made Soma jump slightly, she gave the giant a cocked headed inquisitive look before determining that he was harmless.

"Soma was a gift from dee fairies to my fader, who den gave er to me. I av ad er since she was a mere pup. She is a good and faidful friend."

Fern shook his head, though worry still painted his face.

"This is all well and good, my friend, but do you not think we should leave before we get caught in another mess? I doubt your father can send help every time we find ourselves is trouble. Remember, Dom told us the hooded man had plans for us here; I don't want to wait around for those plans to appear," Fern said, anxious to leave.

"You are right, we must not let my fader's gift go to waste," replied Reagal. "Let's be off!"

Leading the group with Soma by his side, Reagal spoke in the centaurian dialect. Fern thoroughly enjoyed listening to him give the chamrosh commands in the strange language, even though he couldn't understand a word. All he knew was that she was leading them out of the Feral Forest, and that was good enough for him.

Keen to her surroundings, her eyesight was equal to her hearing and could detect the slightest movement. Multiple times she halted the company as large shadows darted passed in the close distance. Fern could never discern what the shadows were, but he had a strong feeling they were better left alone.

Night started to fall, and they still had not made it out of the dense woods. Garrick's hunger never seemed to leave him, and he was begging to eat.

"Reagal, we must stop for the night. I can barely see, and Garrick's stomach is rumbling like thunder," grumbled Fern.

"Yes, of course, let's set up camp," replied Reagal as he halted Soma. "We will be able to rest easy, my friends. Soma will stand watch tonight. Er eyes are keen and er sense of smell even more so. She will not let anyding close widout alerting us."

By the time they had set up camp and ate their dinner, night had fallen, settling like a thick barrier over their eyes. They all huddled together for warmth and protection and fell asleep with ease, trusting Soma to keep watch.

It had not been long when Fern awoke in the darkness.

"Get up, my young Majesteek!" Reagal demanded in an urgent whisper as he shook Fern's shoulder.

Fern leapt to his feet. His sight was immediately engulfed by the pitch black. "What is it?" he asked.

Reagal's voice was trembling with both fear and anger. "Soma as been taken!"

"Taken? By whom?"

"I'm not sure."

"Garrick, did you hear anything?" whispered Fern as he lit a torch.

There was no answer. Fern swung the torch around, flame flickering and nearly dying. Garrick was gone.

"What is going on?" Fern asked in a panic. "Reagal, why did you wake? Did you hear something?"

"No, I felt someding brush against my leg. I dought it was Soma, but den, I awoke, and found she was missing. I tried calling for er, but eard no response," replied Reagal.

"Tracks, tracks, look for tracks," said Fern.

He held the torch close to the ground. What they saw nearly took their breaths away. On the forest floor were two large gaping holes only five feet from where they stood.

"By Valom's Star!" said Reagal.

"What's going on?!" asked Fern.

"I dink I know what we're dealing wid, but I am not altogeder sure." Reagal's voice was still shaking.

"Reagal, will you please give me a straight answer," snapped Fern, completely befuddled.

"Do you remember dee oles at dee clearing?" asked Reagal. Fern nodded. "It crossed my mind den, but I did not dink it was possible. When I was a young colt, my fader would tell a nightmarish tale to scare me from going into unknown forests. Ee told of a large umanoid creature covered in shaggy white air wid dee face of a bear dat dwelled underground. Ee said dae were savage unters dat only unt at night, pulling der victims from dee surface as dae sleep. Dae were called... Quaggods." (spelled Q-U-A-G-G-O-T-H).

"It can't be," Fern replied. "I've read about those in children's tales; they're just myths. Anyway, how could they grab Garrick without us hearing anything? He's a twelve-foot giant."

"My fader said dae are extremely quiet and very strong. Ee said most victims don't even wake up from der sleep until dee quaggods have dim deep in der lairs," Reagal spoke with a quiet sadness.

"If this is true, we must go down and save our friends at once," Fern said, nearly at a yell.

"If we go down to save our companions, I am afraid we will not be coming out alive." Reagal paused for a moment as he stared at Fern. "We av a more important task. If we do not go to dee Ulmeck Mountains to retrieve dee rock, dousands of innocents may die."

Fern found it difficult to believe that Reagal would consider leaving his friends.

"I won't abandon Garrick and leave him to die. He is my friend, and I'm willing to sacrifice my life to save his. Either follow me or I go alone."

Fern grabbed his gear, and with his torch in hand, slid down into the cavernous hole.

Reagal paced around the edge looking down watching as the light from Fern's torch quickly began to fade. *Dis Majesteek is a stubborn one, but I must say, dee loyalty to friends is commendable.* Conflict in the centaur's head swirled. *What would my fader say... ee would say not a word. Ee would look to me to make dee right decision. Ahh, ear goes noding.* A large breath entered his lungs. Reagal leapt down into the darkness.

Deep in the hole, Fern's torch allowed him to see enormous drag marks, which he quickly realized were made by Garrick's giant body. He studied the indentations, holding his torch low. The ground shook. A loud pounding of hooves grew loud, and Fern swung around to see Reagal swiftly approaching. He gave a slight nod of gratitude and smiled. *I knew he would come.* Pointing out the indentations, the friends' followed its path into the darkness.

The underground passage was massive, nearly ten feet in height, making it easy, even for Reagal, to stand fully upright. It was carved out of the ground with expert precision. No tree roots or jagged rocks were protruding from the walls, and even the ground under their feet was level and easily traversed.

"Reagal, how long ago were you awakened?" asked Fern.

"Mere seconds before alerting you."

"Good, that means they can't be too far ahead."

Fern increased his speed to a run, lowering his torch towards the ground. As they followed the tracks through the tunnel, Reagal puffed out growling sighs. *I ope dee young Majesteek as not lost respect for me*, he thought. He sighed once more before speaking.

"Please do not dink badly of me. I would not forsake my friends if it weren't of significant importance. I was looking to dee greater good."

Reagal galloped beside Fern, worries mounting.

"I understand," replied Fern releasing a sigh of his own. "but friends are hard to come by, and for me...they are the greater good."

Increasing his speed once more, Fern tried to catch whatever snatched Garrick and Soma.

Silhouettes stretching up the tunnel walls came into view. Appearing in the distance were five shadows; four were the same, one was massive. Fern drew his sword.

Reagal raced ahead of him, yelling, "I will attack dim, you free our companions. We will need der help."

Reagal galloped forward at full speed, Fern racing behind him. They could see Garrick's body in the distance lying limp on the ground wrapped in large tree roots. Sprawled on top was Soma, bound and motionless.

The quaggoths turned and attacked at the sight of the charging centaur. Reagal caught one of the beasts off guard, slicing him in the back, causing the quaggoth to release a searing roar that shook the ground. Running to Garrick's side, Fern guarded his friend's body. The giant was bleeding from the head and lying on his back unconscious.

"Reagal, we are on our own," yelled Fern.

Fern immediately leapt onto Garrick's belly to take the high ground. Soma's limp body lay strapped tightly in roots constricting her breathing. Fern had to act fast. As he began to hack away at the thick bonds, Reagal was surrounded. Fern watched as four quaggoths pounced towards him.

Standing seven feet tall with bear-like faces, they attacked Reagal. The centaurian prince avoided their long razor-sharp claws projecting out from their dirt-encrusted paws like swords, curved and strong.

Fern roared, getting the attention of one of the quaggoths. It immediately sprung upward, grabbing the ceiling of the tunnel with its blade-like nails and flung itself towards Fern. Gaining momentum as it flew feet first, it slammed into him. Having no time to react, Fern was pummeled to the ground. The impact felt as if he had been hit with a large sledgehammer. The wind was knocked from his lungs as he rolled like a barrel.

Before the quaggoth could sink its claws into him, Fern made it to his feet. He was shaken and heaving for air, but otherwise unharmed.

Meanwhile, Reagal had the other three to contend with. Darting around them with relative ease, Reagal realized the creatures were nothing like the great warriors his father had warned him about. They were sluggish and did not seem to know how to deal with moving targets.

Fern, on the other hand, had just felt the strength they possessed. The quaggoths were a force to be reckoned with, and if they were to get a hold of either Fern or Reagal, they would stand little chance of escape.

With his sword drawn, Fern was ready as another quaggoth attacked. *Come on, you hairy monster. Let's see how skilled you are.* The quaggoth tromped its hairy feet clumsily, slashing its clawed hands in the air. Fern spun to the side, chopping its arms off with one swift swing of his sword. The quaggoth screamed in agony as it hit the ground writhing in pain as blood gushed from its severed limbs. Squirming and flailing its legs in the air, the pitiful creature flopped around like a worm in the sun. The excruciating wails and moans echoed, and the remaining quaggoths ran into the darkness with loud thudding foot falls.

Fern and Reagal stood wide eyed, shocked by their retreat. Reagal slowly galloped towards the fallen quaggoth and thrust his sword into the its chest, ending its misery.

They quickly sprinted to their unconscious friends and began hacking at the thick tree roots that bound them. Finally freed, they attempted to revive them.

Fern suddenly remembered the blue potion given to him by Lillia. Taking the bottled liquid from a bag strapped around his waist, he poured a few drops into Soma and Garrick's mouths. Within moments, both were regaining consciousness.

"Sirs, how you get here?" asked Garrick with groggy confusion.

"You know where you are?" asked Fern.

"I woke, hairy creatures drag me down in tunnel. I thought I dreaming. I hear speaking, but I not understand what they saying."

"Why did dae knock you unconscious, did you struggle?" asked Reagal.

"No, not first. I thought I dreaming, until they start speak our language. They meet turgoyle down here. They say they take me to Ulmeck Mountains and come back for you. That when I knew I not dreaming. I try break free from roots, but I bound too tight. So I start yell, hope you hear me. That when turgoyle hit me over head with club. I not remember after that."

Garrick hoisted himself up, rubbing his head and gritting his teeth. Soma shook like a wet dog and was back to her usual affection in no time.

"What luck!" Reagal said suddenly, his face lighting up like a torch.

"Luck? You call this luck? The turgoyles know where we are," Fern said, astonished by Reagal's comment.

"Yes, dae know where we are, but now we av a straight pad to follow. Dink, if dese creatures could drag Garrick and Soma to dee mountains and av time to come back to get us, dat means we must be close, and since dae already know where we are, der is no use going back to dee surface. We can follow dis tunnel, retrieve dee Ulmeck Rock, and make it back to Dundire wid time to spare," Reagal was bursting with hope.

"But this tunnel will be swarming with turgoyles, and we still don't know if those creatures went back to get reinforcements, or worse, to warn the turgoyle horde at the Ulmeck Mountains," said Fern, emphatically.

"True, but we will be attacked regardless, at least down ear we know which direction to go," replied Reagal.

"That might be correct, if in fact this tunnel doesn't fork off in a thousand different directions," replied Fern continuing to argue.

"You av forgotten, we av Soma. I will tell er to follow dee quaggods scent, she can lead us to dee base of dee mountain."

Soma stretched her wings and hopped slightly off the ground.

Fern sighed and looked at Reagal.

"What about Garrick? He is twelve feet tall. He can't even stand up in this place."

Quickly replying, Garrick began to squat down.

"No worry bout me, I crouch."

Garrick shuffled to his feet as he finished bending his knees and arching his torso forward.

"Tah-dah," he said grinning with accomplishment.

"Very well," Fern said, finally conceding. "But I suggest we stay vigilant this time. We've been way too reckless thus far."

"Agreed!" replied Reagal triumphantly.

Quickly speaking to Soma, Reagal gave her a command to follow the quag-goths scent.

With eyes focused, she lowered her head to the ground. Walking at a good pace, they followed Soma as she led them through the tunnel. Fern left his torch fully lit, knowing that turgoyles could spot them easily in the dark regardless.

Quite often the tunnel would split off in two or three directions, and Soma would lift her head and sniff the air. It would not take long for her to catch the scent again, lower her head to the ground, and continue forward. This went on for hours, and time was slipping away from the group. No sign of anything living was seen or even sensed, and Fern was wondering where the tunnel was leading them.

"Reagal, I thought you said we were close. We've been stumbling in the dark for what seems like days. How much longer can this take?"

Fern was truly beginning to worry. They were miles underground, and no one knew the exit. Was it day...was it night? Time was lost, and their torch was nearly extinguished.

Reagal must've been wrong. Had Garrick misheard the turgoyle? Is there another band of quaggoths on their way? These questions plagued Fern as his head pounded like a drum and the torch flickered. The flame was quickly dying.

Soma never skipped a beat and never seemed to tire. Garrick, on the other hand, was getting hungry again. His stomach sounded even louder underground, and Fern was becoming agitated.

"Here, Garrick, eat this."

He handed the giant a large piece of salted fish. Garrick reluctantly accepted it, being tired of the same food day in and day out, but his hunger was insatiable, and he gobbled it up in one bite. A giant-sized belch followed that shook dirt and rock from the tunnel ceiling coating everyone in a layer of filth.

"Oh, I sorry, my friends."

Garrick blushed as he slapped his forehead in shame.

Fern found himself smiling once again at his giant friend's childish behavior.

Soma's head suddenly jerked up and her eyes fixated on something ahead in the darkness. Ordering a hurried pace, Reagal and Soma took a significant lead. Within moments, they were barely visible. Fern's torch suddenly went out. Pitch black was the darkness.

"Reagal," whispered Fern as Garrick grabbed his shoulder in terror.

"Do not fear, my young Majesteek, we are ere. Der is a bend in dee tunnel only a few yards in front of you. Come quickly."

Fern shuffled his feet, sliding his hand along the passage wall with Garrick still grasping his shoulder. When the tunnel took an abrupt turn, they could see a dim light coming from around the bend.

Soma stopped and stood erect staring forward. Reagal put his hand up, halting Fern and Garrick.

"I ear turgoyles," he whispered.

"Yes, it sounds like there could be quite a few of them," said Fern "What should we do?"

"I av a plan," said Reagal. "I will send Soma out to get der attention, opefully dae will not come after er all at once. She will lead dim to us. We will stand around dis bend in dee tunnel." Reagal turned to Garrick, "Garrick, you will grab dim when dae come in sight. Do not esitate."

"What I do after I grab them?" asked Garrick.

"Break them in two!" whispered Fern.

Reagal nodded in agreement with a sly grin.

Fern dropped his extinguished torch and they quickly prepared themselves. Reagal sent Soma walking around the bend into the open. The chamrosh looked in the direction of the turgoyles and made a low squawking noise to get their attention.

"What was that?"

"Look over there!"

"Go get it, slime bucket!"

"What is it? Does it bite?"

"How should I know, maggot vomit, just go get it."

Soma stood staring at them cocking her head. One of the turgoyles started to approach. Soma crouched down, shaking the back end of her body playfully. She hopped backwards, leading the turgoyle around the corner.

"Stop moving, you goofy-looking peacock, and come here!" yelled the turgoyle.

The other turgoyles stood back tittering as Soma jumped around its outreached hands.

As soon as the turgoyle turned the bend, Garrick grabbed him with surprising speed and snapped his body like a toothpick.

Soma pranced back out into the open.

"Whas going on here?" screeched the commanding turgoyle with a hissing lisp. "Garble! Garble!"

He turned and pointed to three turgoyles with his gangly green index finger.

"You tree, come wiss me!"

They started to jog slowly towards Soma as she bounced backwards, leading them to Garrick's giant hands. All four turned the corner at once. Garrick managed to grab three of the turgoyles, crushing them with his mighty grip, but the commander dodged his grasp.

"ALERT!" he yelled.

Fern swung his sword, taking the turgoyle's head. Unfortunately, he was not quick enough. Ten more turgoyles came running around the bend.

Garrick immediately grabbed two turgoyles, throwing them against the tunnel wall, breaking every bone in their bodies while Reagal reared up with his powerful hooves bounding down on another one as he thrust his sword into its back.

Hovering above three more, Soma pecked their heads as they tried to strike her with their clubs. Their wings fluttered as they struggled to catch air, but Soma squawked loudly staying just outside their reach. Fern leapt into the middle of them, stabbing a turgoyle in the chest. Swinging their clubs, they missed wildly spinning out of control.

"Soma, go help your master, I can handle these idiots!" shouted Fern.

Garrick suddenly came crouching from behind, grabbing the turgoyles around their waists. He chucked them with unimaginable force, sending them barreling into the turgoyles attacking Reagal. They fell like a mass of dead flesh. With a few thrusts of his sword, Reagal quickly finished them off as they lay on the ground.

The few remaining turgoyles fled, scrambling to get away, but Garrick's reach and gargantuan mitts proved too impossible to escape. Grasping the squealing creatures in his hands, Garrick slammed them together. Green goo squirting from between his fingers, splashing his companions from head to toe.

Fern grinned and shook his head, astonished at his friend's abilities.

"It sure is nice to have a giant on our side," he said as he grabbed a handful of the slimy substance from his hair.

Garrick smiled wide and blushed as he wiped his hands on his pants.

"Check for wounds," warned Fern. "If we get this resin in our veins we are done for!"

Fern pulled a pouch of water from his belt and cloth from his pocket.

After everyone cleaned themselves thoroughly, the group gathered and walked around the bend in the tunnel. To their relief, they saw a set of stairs leading upward.

8

TRUTH REVEALED

As Fern peered up the stairwell lit with torches, no exit could be seen. Extremely steep and narrow, the stairs looked as if they had been dug with bare hands. The compressed dirt steps were uneven and unleveled. Curved walls on either side were infested with twisting tree roots, and hundreds of creepy-crawly insects scurried about, making the walls look as if they were moving. *This must be the work of those lazy, filthy turgoyles. Only they could construct such a monstrosity*, thought Fern as he turned and looked to Garrick.

"I'm not sure you'll be able to make it up."

Garrick got to his hands and knees like a giant bear. Clearing the ceiling with room to spare, he smiled with satisfaction. But as soon as he took the first step, his broad shoulders wedged into the narrow stairwell. He could go no further.

"What shall we do?" asked Reagal as Garrick shimmied his way out.

"You both must stay here. If these stairs lead to the mountains, I'll be swift, for I know them like the back of my hand, and I'll be able to keep out of sight well enough."

"Very well, but you must take Soma," insisted Reagal. "I will instruct er to fly above you and keep watch. She can signal you if anyding approaches. If you need er just whistle and she will fly down to you. Please, be careful."

Fern gave a quick nod and started up the stairs.

Torches spaced every few yards, hanging in tangles of roots, lit the way sufficiently. The crude steps crumbled and collapsed with every footfall. Glancing towards the top, Fern could see no exit; they were deeper than anyone could have imagined. Fern shook his head in disbelief as he turned back to look at his feathered companion.

Soma was close behind, wagging her tail and seemingly oblivious to the danger that awaited them at the surface. *At least someone is enjoying this.*

Fern's legs began to tire as sweat drenched his hair and poured down his face. Soma's giddiness had faded, and her tail dragged. Muscles ached and bones creaked as the two trudged further up the stairs. To Fern's everlasting joy, he glanced up and saw a faint glow. *Oh, please tell me that's the exit.* His pace quickened with his newfound hope, and Soma stayed on his heels.

Finally reaching the top, which simply opened to the ground above, Fern sighed a breath of relief, but something puzzled him. *How many days have passed? I can't believe it's still night. Did we really travel that fast?* His confusion was the least of his worries. Fern needed to concentrate, for there was no telling where the turgoyles could be hiding.

Now out of the tunnels, and beyond the dense forests of Earthingland, Fern could see his surroundings clearly. The stars shone brightly, twinkling like diamonds in a sea of midnight blue. The moon, full and luminescent, looked down upon Fern, smiling like a father to his son. It was magnificent, and Fern realized how truly precious the sights of Harth were. *It's a pity the filthy creatures of the world taint such beauty.*

The last thing Fern wanted to do was alert turgoyles to his presence, so creeping like a thief in the night, he traveled close to Soma, watching her every move for any reaction that might indicate his enemy was near. Luckily, there was none.

Soma suddenly spread her wings and lifted into the air, rising above the treetops and leaving Fern alone. The sky was clear and the light of the moon cast Soma's shadow as she circled above.

Studying the landscape, Fern looked around to see if he recognized where he was. *Unbelievable! I know this place!* The forest he found himself in was the very same that he hunted in as a child. It was not particularly large or dense, but it lined the base of the Ulmeck Mountains; what's more, he stood just a few hundred yards from the old abandoned turgoyle tunnel.

The mountains stood before him like an executioner, threatening and evil. Their summits rose into the sky and resembled dragon's teeth. The sharp menacing peaks cut into the night sky like massive daggers.

A constant rumbling of jagged stone tumbled from cliffs, crashing upon the ground like bombs and shattering into razor-sharp fragments.

Fern knew the hazards all too well. He also knew that the outer shell of the Ulmecks was young and fragile, and the stone he would be searching for could only be found at its base, deep inside the caverns.

Traveling quickly, Fern was well aware that the longer he stayed in the open, the better chance he had to be spotted or struck by falling rock. Thankfully, he was not far from a cavern where he could find plenty of stone. Remembering every turn and path, Fern easily weaved his way towards the mountain.

Though his stealth was impressive, Fern couldn't believe the quiet; there wasn't a sight or sound of a turgoyle anywhere. Fern found himself at a loss. *This makes no sense. The flightless little cretins should be swarming this area.*

Realizing he had not seen Soma's shadow in a while, Fern searched the skies. She was nowhere to be seen. Dropping his head, Fern stared into the forest.

Prominent dark oaks inhabiting the little woods spread out leaving little cover. Small boulders and low-lying shrubs were also scattered throughout the ground, and small black rat bats, swooping down with their long hairless tails in the moonlight, could be seen displaying their acrobatic skills as they caught insects for their late-night meal.

With still no sign of Soma, Fern made his way to the far east side of the mountains. Recognizing two large oaks that twisted together at the trunks, Fern knew he was close to the cave. A rocky outcrop just beyond the tree line blocked Fern's view to the mouth of the cavern. Large boulders scattered below the mountain gave sufficient cover, and Fern knew that any number of enemies could be hiding amongst them. Although, normally, he would see a few turgoyles patrolling this area out in the open, there were none that night. *This could be a trap, Fern; watch yourself.*

Quickly and quietly, he bounded from boulder to boulder staying out of sight. Implausibly, there were still no turgoyles. He slowly entered the cave with feather-soft footsteps. The silence was as cold and stiff as death. Darkness took over, but Fern knew the cavern well. The ceiling was high, and the walls jagged. Piles of stone, broken free from violent earthquakes, lay scattered upon the ground. The Ulmeck Rock was plentiful. Fern took two large burlap sacks (provided from Dundire) and filled them to capacity. He was pleased with his find, but the absence of turgoyles continued to nag him. What could have happened to them, he thought. Then it suddenly came crashing down like a bolt of lightning. *They have marched to war!*

I must get back to Reagal and Garrick!

Fern spun around to run, but was suddenly frozen in his tracks by an agonizing scream coming from deep within the cavern. It sounded human. Fern knew someone was suffering, but he had to go. Racing back towards the tunnel stairs, he heard it again, a scream even more agonizing than the one before. It echoed through the mountains, burning Fern's ears. *What must I do? Do I have time? No, I must go.* He couldn't stand the sound, but he was determined to get the Ulmeck Rock to Dundire. The screams became more frequent as he continued to race towards the stairs. *How can I leave someone to suffer?* Fern could bear it no longer. He quickly turned around and sprinted as fast as he could back to the cavern, hoping he would be in time. Placing the bulging sacks of rock outside the cave, he drew his sword and entered.

Dawn broke, and the sun started to bleed light over the horizon, helping to light his way as he walked further into the cave. The silhouette of a large creature holding a whip in its right hand started to appear as Fern crept slowly behind it.

As he came closer, he could see it was an enormous ogre. Fern knew whoever was being tortured did not have long to live, for ogres eat humans.

This ogre was hideous and pale white, long black hair growing out of every crevice of its body. Its head was abnormally large with massive flaps of skin that looked like elephant ears hanging from the sides of its face. It stood ten feet from the ground and wore nothing but an old, tattered tunic. Its immense forearms snapped its whip, causing dust from the ground to kick up, spinning like a dust devil. Fern scrunched his nose as the putrid smell of rotting cheese reached his nostrils, nearly incinerating his nose hairs. *If the whip doesn't kill his captive, the stench will finish the job.*

Fern could not see the ogre's face or the poor soul it was torturing. Crouching quietly, Fern waited for his chance to attack. As the ogre raised its arm to snap the whip, Fern charged like a raging bull. He leapt toward the cavern wall, kicking off its jagged surface, throwing his body forward, and landing on the ogre's shoulders. Aiming his sword down, he plunged. Fern's arms vibrated like a jackhammer as the sword ricocheted off the beast's skull. The blade snapped back, grazing Fern's leg and slicing into his calf. Tensing his muscles, Fern roared in pain. Blood poured down the monster's face and into its eyes.

The ogre reached up, grabbed Fern by his gushing leg, and tossed him against the cavern wall, knocking the wind from him. A splash of blood spritzed across the floor, looking very much like an abstract painting as the ogre snapped its whip blindly, somehow finding his left arm. A burning sensation shot through Fern's bicep and into his shoulder, gnawing deep. Blood began to spill from the wound. The pain spread like lightning through a cloud, but it did not deter Fern from his attack. He charged, dodging the ogre's fierce lunging punch and sunk his sword into its stomach. Roaring like a lion, the ogre dropped to its knees; Fern's blood was still dripping down its face.

Driving his sword deep into the ogre's chest, Fern thrust his blade through its pulsing heart. The ogre's eyes went still, and one last vomitus breath puffed into the air as it flopped dead to the ground in a pool of blood.

Standing and exhausted, Fern surveyed the aftermath. He ripped a piece of cloth from the lower leg of his trousers and wrapped the wound on his shoulder as tightly as he could.

His strength was spent as he hobbled over to a figure in the dark. On the cavern wall was a man bound by iron chains. His slumped head and hanging dirt-encrusted hair hid his face. Ripped clothes, shredded from the ogre's whip, and blood dripping like a leaky faucet decorated his body as Fern reached him.

"My friend, are you still alive?"

The gravely injured man tried to speak, but only mumbles escaped his bloody, cracked lips. Fern quickly pulled out the vial of healing potion, only a small amount swirling at the bottom, and propped the man's head back. The sight of his face immediately made Fern drop the vial. Quickly catching the potion before it shattered to the ground, Fern stumbled back in disbelief.

"P-p-please help m-me," the man mumbled.

Is this...but...but how?

Fern rattled his head and regained his composure. He stomped forward, brows furled, and grasped the prisoner's hair. Fern jerked the man's head back with little sympathy and gave him a drop of the potion.

"King Edinword?" asked Fern, still not sure if he was really seeing what he was seeing.

"Please...l-let me down...from this w-wall," begged the king.

Fern stood silent trying to get a grip on what was happening. *Did the turgoyles betray him? Why wouldn't they just kill him?* Fern's confusion was a roadblock.

"P-Please, Fern Majestic..." King Edinword said, starting to feel the effects of the potion as he regained some of his strength.

Hearing his name coming from the king's lips angered Fern, boiling his blood and thawing him from his shock. He lifted the other man's head to look at him.

"You are lucky I don't kill you while you hang from this wall!"

Fern clinched his fingers around his sword.

"Please...please, let me down, and I will explain everything."

"No!" shouted Fern. "You'll answer my questions, and only if I'm satisfied will I decide whether to release you."

"Of course, of course, I owe you that."

"You owe me much more."

"Please...ask your questions."

"Very well." Fern's voice quivered as he spoke, hoping he might finally receive the answers he had desired his entire life. "Tell me, *king*, why have you declared the name of Majestic as traitor?" Fern's anxiety overflowed, causing his entire body to shake.

"I did not declare your name as traitor, it was Timal."

"What...why?"

"I do not know, and I have never cared to ask. It was never my concern."

Fern growled at Edinword's lack of empathy.

"But how could Timal declare it? It's been known for hundreds of years. I know he's your son, but he can't be that old."

"I will tell you everything if you give me the chance."

"Very well. Tell me, *king*, and don't try to deceive me. If I catch the least whiff of treachery, I'll slice your throat!" He raised his sword to Edinword's neck.

"No need for intimidation, Fern. I have no reason to lie to you...not now. I have already lost everything," replied the king. "Where should I start?" Edinword thought for a moment, his eyes circling. "I was betrayed by Timal. He is the one who chained me to this wall, and he is the one controlling the turgoyle armies."

"The prince?" asked Fern, taking every word with a grain of salt.

"He is not the prince, he never was. He is a powerful man with a powerful weapon."

"You aren't making any sense, and you're trying my patience."

"I am telling you the truth," replied Edinword quickly. "Please, listen to the entirety of my tale, and at the end you can decide whether I deserve death." Fern nodded, peering into the king's eyes.

"Timal came to me when I had just become king of Loustof. He was a traveler from the far north. He claimed to be thousands of years old and told me he wielded great power. He promised me great wealth, said he could make me the most powerful king in the world. The only thing I had to do was name him counselor to the king. I was young and naïve, so I agreed. Soon after, he approached me with an idea of building an arena in the depths of the dungeons. It was an intriguing concept, so I had it built. Timal would go to other lands and capture the most ferocious beasts to battle in the arena. I was amazed how he could capture these animals, sometimes single-handedly. It was proof to me that he indeed had great power. My kingdom became powerful like he had promised. The arena battles attracted nobility and royalty. They paid handsomely to come and watch the creatures fight to the death. I, myself, fell in love with the excitement of it. It consumed me and became the only joy in my life, but that joy changed when I met my first wife, Narminia.

"When we married, all my attention fell from the arena battles and went to her. Timal seemed furious over this. Narminia and I soon started talking about having a baby. She wanted a boy, someone to take the throne when I was gone. Narminia and Timal both knew I was an Ager and thought our son would be able to hold the kingdom for hundreds of years after my death."

Fern held his hand up, shaking it vigorously. "What does you being an Ager matter?"

"You must understand, that unless my wife is an Ager, my children will be no different from anyone else's. In other words, my son or daughter will live a normal life span."

That's why Mallock aged normally, thought Fern.

King Edinword continued. "Unfortunately, Narminia never became pregnant. She died from an illness years later. I was so distraught from her passing that I desperately needed to relieve my pain, so my attention quickly returned to the arena. Meanwhile, my kingdom became vast and strong just as Timal had said. I had to do nothing. He came to me one day and told me of a dream he had, of Timal and myself ruling the world side by side as father and son. After telling me of this dream and assuring me it was an omen, he convinced me to start calling him my son and to name him the prince. By this time, I had become great friends with Timal, he was like my brother, so it was easy for me to do. After a few hundred years of calling him Prince Timal, no one ever questioned him as my son.

"Later, I met a woman named Amber, a kind and gentle noble lady from the northern part of my kingdom. We quickly fell in love. We were married, and soon after she became pregnant. Timal was furious and threatened to kill the queen and my unborn child. I could not understand his anger. I tried to calm him, but his rage was unconquerable. I resisted his madness as long as I could until my wife gave birth to a son. I was so frightened Timal would have him killed that I gave my only son to a servant woman and claimed that he died at birth. And even though I promised Amber that I would get rid of Timal, she never forgave my cowardice. I told her once he was gone, we could raise our son as the proper prince. Unfortunately, the queen was too impatient; she tried to murder Timal in his sleep. She came to me the night of the attempted murder and confessed." Edinword looked away as if he remembered the scene all too vividly. The terror in his eyes read like a book. A deep sigh rustled from his mouth and he slowly shook his head. "Amber knelt by my bedside, tears in her eyes. She could barely speak as she confessed to stabbing Timal in his heart as he slept. I did not know what to think. My wife, whom I loved dearly, had just killed someone she thought was my son. I was devastated that Timal was dead, my attachment to him was strong, even with his threats on my son's life."

Fern shook his head. *This king is crazier than I thought.*

"The next morning," continued Edinword. "I was in my throne room grieving the loss of Timal when he walked in without a scratch. My wife fainted, as I nearly did. I ran and put my arms around him in joy. He did not respond. The look in his eyes was murderous; it was never the same between us after that. A few weeks passed, but my wife remained in a constant state of paranoia. She swore Timal was going to have her killed. I tried to reassure her I would not let that happen, but she did not have faith in me, and rightfully so. She left the palace one afternoon for a picnic in the fields just outside the walls of Loustof. My guards came running to me hours later saying she had been attacked by turgoyles and killed. I had no idea Timal could have been the one behind the attack. After all, it was turgoyles the guards reported seeing."

Fern's brows furled as another wave of anger burst from his mouth. "You found out he killed your wife and you did nothing?"

"No, of course not! I would have done everything in my power to have him answer for the murder of the queen," defended Edinword, putting his hands up to his face. "but I did not discover this until Timal was chaining me to this wall. I swear to you!" Edinword, balled his hands into fists and slammed against the cavern wall. "I became so depressed after her death that I started to ignore my own son. I even resolved to the idea that he wasn't really mine at all. I fell deep into the arenas again, the excitement of battle made my blood run cold and kept my mind dull to all happiness, no matter who's."

Edinword paused and hung his head. Memories of his wife's smiling face flashed in his mind, and a vision of a small child with shimmering black hair bounced in his head. Darkness clouded his thoughts as the happy memories died. New visions came forth, and death was among them. His wives' bodies lay side by side upon the ground along with his son.

Fern showed no pity as he barked, "Continue!"

"Yes, yes..." a single tear dripped from Edinword's eye, crawling down his cheek reaching his chin and hanging in solitude before plunging to the ground. The king opened his mouth, no words came out.

"Continue!" shouted Fern.

Edinword breathed a heavy sigh, his thoughts trying to collect themselves. "Timal...Timal would go out and supply my addiction with new beasts for the battles every few weeks." Edinword's eyes strained as he concentrated his memories into words. "I was standing at the gates one day when he was bringing in a giant he had captured for the arena. Timal was knocked off his horse as it tried to escape. This is when I first saw the source of his power. As he fell, a red ruby attached to a golden chain hanging from his neck came flying out of his shirt. He quickly leapt to the ground, grabbing it and placing it back around his neck just as the giant stomped on him with its great foot, crushing him into the dirt. Something of that magnitude would have killed a normal man, but Timal stood up from it like it was nothing. I knew at once that it was the gem that gave him his power."

Fern interrupted again. "But what about the true prince. Who was he?" Of course, Fern had a good notion, but he wanted to hear it from Edinword's mouth.

King Edinword paused for a moment. Fern could see he was holding back tears. "Yes, my true son...you knew him." Tears started to flow from the king's eyes as he spoke. "The true Prince of Loustof was...Mallock." He paused for a moment to regain his composure and noticed no shock on Fern's face. Edinword cleared his throat. "Timal killed him on his way home from the Crags of Malice. That was another piece of information he shared with me as he bound me to this wall. Timal thought I had sent Mallock to the Crag Mountains to have him killed."

The king glanced at Fern, tears still flowing down his cheeks. "I loved my son, but I felt powerless against Timal. He ran everything in Loustof. I was merely his puppet. Only after I thought Timal was dead did I search for a warrior to go to the Crag Mountains. That is when I found you. I wanted the gem; the beast was just a bonus for my arena."

"There was no beast, the story was a farce," said Fern. "Mallock devised the entire thing himself, just to kill Timal. He would have succeeded, but you did not tell him what power the gem possessed. You kept that secret for yourself."

The king's eyes squinted in confusion as he spoke, "How do you mean?"

"Mallock stabbed Timal in his heart as he slept. Unfortunately, he did not take the gem from around his neck beforehand," said Fern, now in complete understanding.

King Edinword dropped his head, sobbing onto the ground.

"You brought all of this upon yourself," said Fern. "Your greed and hunger for power has lost you everything."

Fern stared at Edinword for a moment, trying to digest everything he had just learned, and suddenly remembered something.

"If it was Timal who controlled the turgoyles, how was it they knew we would be at the Crags of Malice, and why was Mallock with them?"

"I can only assume Timal had recruited Mallock unbeknownst to me. Timal was extremely manipulative, and Mallock was equally naïve."

"But Mallock said you ordered my murder," replied Fern.

King Edinword's head dropped, shaking as dried clumps of dirt fell from his hair.

"I am ashamed to admit...but I did give that order. Of course, it was not meant for Mallock to carry out. I gave the order to my guards. I was going to have you killed once the beast was captured and the ruby found."

Fern stared at the king, laughing silently in his mind, realizing the events that had to take place for him to be standing there.

"So, you never intended for me to save Timal?" asked Fern, smirking, knowing the answer.

"No, I believed he was dead. So much time had passed, and he had yet to return home. I thought he finally came across a beast he could not defeat. And to be honest, I was extremely relieved. I had all I could take from his iron fist, and my love for him was gone. I truly felt free." Edinword cracked a faint smile and puffed out a deep sigh.

"Edinword, you still haven't told me why Timal has brought you here."

Edinword looked at Fern with dread in his eyes. "When Timal returned to

Loustof, he did not come alone; he was accompanied by a massive turgoyle army. He brought me here soon after and chained me to this wall to be tortured by one of the beasts from my own dungeon. He said I should pay for my treachery against him."

The king paused briefly. "Fern Majestic, Timal knows you exist; he has been tracking you since you entered Alkyle. I have told him everything I know about you through torture and threat of death. He fears you and wants you dead. I do not know why your name is so dangerous to him, but he will not stop until he finds you. I must also warn you, he has taken control of Loustof and has command of my soldiers, led by his great turgoyle army. He has also taken my throne, and he...he has dragons!"

"Yes, I know he has a dragon," Fern said quickly.

"No, you do not understand, he has *many* dragons! He can speak with them! He controls them! You must listen: the gem he holds around his neck is not limited to just healing, it has power far beyond any of us. He has become unstoppable!" The king trembled with fear.

"What do you know about his plans? Who does he want to wage war with?"

"His hate for this world runs deep. I am unsure what his dark past holds, but I know that he will attack every corner of every land until nothing good in this world remains. I am afraid there is no stopping him, and I am the one to blame for this." Edinword looked up to an unsympathetic Fern.

"Stop your self-pitying and tell me, does he know about the Ulmeck Rock?"

"No, it was a question he never asked, so I did not think to tell him."

"Where does he plan to attack first?"

"I do not know. Did you expect him to tell me everything? Now, please, I have answered enough of your questions; decide what you will with me." Edinword hung from the shackles, wrists bloodied and bruised. His head had given up the fight to stay upright, and the once proud king, bound and shamed, cried softly on his knees.

Fern glared at Edinword with disdain. "My pity for you is slight, but I have decided to spare your life." Fern's breathing jetted from his nostrils as his chest heaved. "The punishment of living with the weight of your sins is more severe than any death I could bestow upon you."

He swung his sword and broke the chains. Edinword crumbled to the ground, blubbering into the dirt.

Knowing there was no more time to waste, Fern drank the last drop of his blue healing potion and ran for the entrance.

Shining bright, the sun was directly above Fern as he exited the cavern. Time was of the essence and he raced toward the tunnel. He grabbed the sacks of Ulmeck Rock and looked to the sky. Soma was nowhere in sight. Knowing there was no time to search, Fern quickly flung the sacks across his back and began racing towards the quaggoth tunnel.

The returning path seemed never ending as he swiftly made his way past boulder and tree. He finally found the opening to the stairs and began the descent into the deep earth. Thoughts were running through his mind as he hurried to rejoin Reagal and Garrick. *So Timal's the mastermind behind this mess. Though I wonder...can I trust anything from that serpent king? He seemed genuine enough... but still.*

The stairs seemed to stretch further than Fern remembered. It was taking too long, and he was beginning to worry. *I hope my companions fared well. I can't wait to tell them all I've learned.* Fern was hoping he would see Soma with them as he came to the bottom of the stairs. What he saw instead brought him up short.

At the bottom lay the remnants of a great battle. Turgoyles and quaggoths scattered across the tunnel floor, all dead. Blood ran like small rivers as Fern made his way around the corpses, searching the ground for his friends. Severed heads and other body parts separated from their owners were difficult to avoid as Fern stumbled over them. The stench was overbearing, and Fern gagged, clamping his mouth closed so as not to vomit.

His anger was mounting as he argued with himself. *Damn you, Fern, you shouldn't have left them! They were your friends. You should've known!*

Fern suddenly noticed Reagal's saddle bag poking out from under three large quaggoth bodies. He raced over holding his breath as he pushed the corpses away. Reagal's body was absent. *Oh, thank the stars! But where can they be?* Fern's search was exhausting. Corpse after corpse he searched for any sign of his friend's whereabouts. High, low, and deep within the tunnels he traveled. Fern was confused, though relieved, as the bodies of Reagal and Garrick were not amongst the dead, but they were nowhere to be found. He could only hope they made it out alive and weren't captured by the enemy.

Observing light shining through small holes in the tunnel ceiling, Fern noticed a distinct set of footprints leading away from the battle. *They have to be Garrick's,* he thought. Next to Garrick's were a set of horse tracks, obviously Reagal's. Fern could not understand why they would have run back through the tunnels. There were no other tracks, and he knew that they would not have left him unless the circumstances were dire, and of course they were.

Fern was suddenly faced with the decision of whether to go back to the surface or trace his friend's tracks deep into the tunnels. Just when his frustration grew to its breaking point, Fern noticed a shadow coming from around the bend in the tunnel ahead. He drew his sword, expecting to see a turgoyle or quaggoth, but poking her head around the corner was Soma.

"Soma!" exclaimed Fern, his face beaming.

Soma trotted to Fern wagging her tail.

"Lead me to Reagal, girl."

She cocked her head and grabbed Fern by his chainmail shirt, pulling him toward the stairs. Fern resisted.

"No, we must go and find Reagal!"

Soma squawked loudly and jerked her powerful beak, pulling him towards the stairs once more. Fern was having a grim time understanding why Soma wanted him to desert his friends.

"Soma, please! We need to find Garrick and Reagal! NOW!"

Soma flapped up into the air and started pecking Fern on his head. Landing behind him, she pushed Fern towards the opening of the stairs. It took a moment, but Fern finally realized Reagal must have commanded Soma to do this.

"Okay, okay, Soma, you win. I'll follow you," said Fern, shaking his head.

Soma led the way, never slowing down. The urgency in her body language began to worry Fern.

Bright daylight greeted them as they reached the surface and stepped onto the ground. The Ulmeck Mountains could be seen clearly, standing tall and black as midnight, even in the light of day.

Soma walked swiftly, making it difficult for Fern to keep up. Of course, his lagging injuries and the fact that he had almost a ton of Ulmeck Rock over his shoulder did not help matters.

Fern knew every tree and stone as they entered the forest heading towards the village of Burdensville. He explored the woods extensively as a child, sometimes living there for days in the summertime. Given its small size, the forest was never given a name, though Fern affectionately called it 'The Majestic's Kitchen' due to the fact that it was his primary source of food.

Fern continued to follow Soma, watching her pounce from tree to tree. Realizing exactly where she was going, Fern began to take the lead. The abandoned turgoyle tunnel was just a few hundred yards away. *That's how they escaped*, thought Fern. *It must connect somewhere underground.*

As they approached, to Fern's surprise, Reagal and Garrick could be seen standing at the opening. Fern ran, still carrying the sacks filled with Ulmeck Rock, overjoyed his friends were alive and well, but as he came closer he could see Reagal was not standing at all. He lay propped up against a tree while Garrick held a blood-soaked cloth to his side. Reagal's eyes were closed when Fern reached him.

"Garrick, what happened?!"

"We attacked in tunnel. Turgoyles and hairy tunnel bears by dozens came at us from stairs. We fight hard, but poor Reagal bad hurt. One of tunnel bears cut him with claws. I try help," sniffled Garrick as he tried to hold back his emotions. "We go back to tunnel in fear of enemies come from surface. We meet Soma in tunnel and follow her here."

Garrick looked exhausted, but otherwise unharmed.

"Sir, you have blue medicine?" he asked, slight hope in his eyes.

With dread, Fern shook his head.

"What we do?" Garrick asked, quivering as he pressed the cloth firmly against Reagal's wound, blood covering his giant hands.

"We must try to get to my blacksmith shop. I have bandages and medical supplies there. We're not that far away."

The thoughts of Edinword and all that Fern witnessed in the cave quickly vanished from his mind as Reagal's face slowly turned pale.

"Can you carry him?"

"Yes, but we hurry. He been bleeding for long time, he stop moving."

"Follow me!" said Fern as he raced through the forest as fast as his legs could carry him. *Come on, Fern, you can do this!*

Although he told Garrick his village was close, it would be nearly an hour before they would reach the doors of his workshop.

Even carrying the sacks of Ulmeck Rock did not slow Fern down. Garrick stayed on his heels while trying to keep the cloth pressed firmly against Reagal's wound; blood trailed behind them as they dodged trees and boulders.

Time seemed to drag as it always does in dire situations, and Fern and Garrick pushed their stamina to its limits, neither of them stopping.

Soma stayed above the trees, closely watching. As the village came in sight, she flew down squawking frantically. Fern came to a sudden halt with Garrick nearly plowing into the back of him.

"Garrick, wait!" whispered Fern, trying to get a good vantage point to survey the village. "Damnit!" Fern grimaced.

Armed soldiers from Loustof patrolled the roads coming in and out of Burdensville.

"What we do?!" whispered Garrick.

"Let me think for a moment."

Soma began squawking loudly. Fern watched as she dive-bombed the soldiers and led them away from the roads.

"Here's our chance!" said Fern.

They both sprinted, trying to keep out of sight as much as possible until they reached his workshop, but Fern was suddenly overcome with a strange urge to go north towards the fortress of Loustof. It was as if a magnet was pulling his entire body. Fern turned uncontrollably. He could barely think straight as his body dragged him north. Abruptly interrupting Fern from his trance was Garrick.

"I give you Reagal," Garrick said, handing the wounded centaur to Fern. "I not fit inside."

Fern's sudden urge to go north vanished as quickly as it came, and he hoisted Reagal upon his back and entered his workshop. There was a large worktable in the center of the main welding room.

Rushing to the table, Fern used his arm as a bulldozer, knocking everything to the floor. He gently placed Reagal on the hardwood surface and hurried to a low-lying cabinet in the back corner of the room just below a window. Slinging the door open, he grabbed a handful of bandages and ointment. Garrick had successfully stopped the bleeding and Fern was able to get a better look at the wound.

Five long, deep gashes stretched across the entire side of Reagal's body. *Oh no, this is worse than I could've imagined. I'll do my best my friend!* Fern cleaned the wounds thoroughly, sweating profusely as the stress grew. He knew that if they did not get help soon, Reagal would surely die. Rubbing the ointment on the centaur's side, Fern dressed the wound, wrapping it tightly. He stood in his workshop looking at Reagal's limp body. Before recent events, Fern was hoping he might be able to forge the arrows in his workshop. After all, he had everything he needed, and it would be so much easier carrying arrows than a ton of rock.

But with Reagal so badly wounded and the soldiers guarding the roads, he did not know if it was possible.

Garrick stood watch outside while Soma kept the soldiers busy, flying above them and occasionally pecking them on their heads and enticing them to give chase.

Propping open the front door with the wooden stool, Fern slowly emerged dragging Reagal on a clean apron. As smoothly and gently as he could, Fern cleared the threshold. He signaled to Garrick to come closer.

"We must get Reagal some help. I have done what I can, but I'm afraid it's not enough. We must head back to the Blue Marshes to the fairies. They're the only chance he has."

"But you need get rock to Dundire," Garrick said, taking Reagal from the apron as gently as a giant could.

"My friend, I will tell you what I told Reagal: I will not forsake either of you for any cause." Fern spoke with heartfelt emotion, and Garrick pulled the grown man into his chest to give him a giant hug.

"Friend, I know you say I be with you always, but I not forsake master Reagal too. I take him to marshes, and you deliver rock to Dundire." Garrick spoke with a surprisingly commanding tone.

"Garrick," said Fern. "You are much wiser than you give yourself credit. I will concede to your will. Head due west, and do not stop for anyone. I have absolute faith in you, and I will see both of you again."

Soma's frantic cawing suddenly interrupted him. Fern and Garrick could see an entire platoon of soldiers marching down the main road of Burdensville.

"Go!" Fern whispered in a harsh tone.

Garrick nodded, did an about face, and darted west towards the Blue Marshes; Soma was soaring above them.

Fern grabbed the sacks of Ulmeck Rock and dodged out of sight from the oncoming soldiers.

9

FINALLY, THEY MEET

Fern observed the soldiers entering his workshop as he escaped their view behind a cluster of elms; the underbrush of holly-berry bushes surrounding the trees kept him hidden well.

Hearing the crashes and cracks of his belongings being destroyed, Fern watched in anger. A few moments later, he could see the men running from his home as it caught fire. The blaze grew quickly as the soldiers stood mesmerized by the flickering flames and billowing smoke. Watching the only home he had ever known burn to the ground saddened Fern's heart.

The heat became intense and the soldiers retreated, leaving the fiery workshop unattended. Fern snuck from the bushes out into the open. Quickly, he ran to his inferno of a home, though there was no saving a single belonging. Fern could not get within thirty feet before the heat was unbearable.

A flood of memories smashed into him like waves, nearly knocking him from his feet. Memories of comfort, security, and any joy he had ever known were disappearing in a heap of fire right before his eyes. It was the only escape from the world that insulted and mistreated him, and it was being scorched from his life.

His home snapped and popped as red-orange flames danced hypnotically into the sky. Fern slumped back on his rear, head between his knees. *If I live through what is coming, where will I find a place to lay my head, where will be my escape now?* Fern cleared his eyes and stood to his feet. *Snap out of this, Fern! There are more important things to worry about!* Taking three deep breaths, he shook the self-pity from his mind. He had a task to complete, and if anything, his resolve was that much stronger.

With all hope of forging the arrows in his workshop obliterated, he turned and headed northwest to Dundire.

Stopping dead in his tracks, Fern suddenly realized he did not know where he was going without Reagal to guide him.

Even if I was still with them, Reagal is near death and would be unable to help. If I travel back through the tunnels, it would just lead me to the middle of the Feral Forest. Without Soma, I would never find my way out, thought Fern. His mind pounded, and he knew only one thing for certain: Dundire was to the northwest.

Needing a horse, or some faster means of travel, Fern suddenly had a revelation.

Galeon! The centaur from the arena battle. He must still be locked down in the dungeon. If only I could release him. He must know these lands as well as Reagal.

"But how could I accomplish such a feat?" said Fern aloud. "It's nearly an eight-hour trek on foot to the gates. But what choice do I have?"

His mind was made up. Filled with new purpose, Fern kept out of sight as he ran into the woods along the path Mallock had taken when he first brought Fern to Loustof. Watching as a small group of soldiers marched up and down a byroad, Fern shook his head as they seemed oblivious to anything around them. They kicked their legs high in the air singing a cadence about victory of war.

Knowing the gates of Loustof were shut and heavily guarded once the sun set, Fern had little time to waste. Already past midday, he realized he needed to reach the walls by nightfall if he was going to have any chance of getting inside.

As Fern traveled further in Loustof's direction, the urge that briefly controlled him in Burdensville suddenly crept upon him like a sickness. It quickly grew into a quiet whisper echoing in his head. He could not discern the voice, and began to question his sanity. *What's happening to me? Am I going mad?* Fern could not pull away.

He traveled through the woods remarkably silent, despite the heavy sacks of rock across his back. Not even the crows flying through the trees paid him any attention. Taking momentary breaks for a bit of crusty bread and a swig or two of water, the feeling that had him would not let him rest.

Keeping out of sight of anything living, he finally saw walls in the distance. Fern was surprised at the absence of turgoyles marching along the road or scouting the woods. He was even more surprised to see the gates wide open and unguarded as he approached. *No one is expecting me to be so close to the enemy*, he thought.

Fern intensely watched for any sign of soldiers or turgoyles and stayed hidden by the surrounding forest. Half an hour went by without a sight or sound coming from within the walls. He crept closer, trying to peer inside.

Dodging behind one of the giant entrance doors, Fern peeked around. To his amazement, the fortress seemed empty. Not even a servant could be seen scurrying through the streets. The wealthiest kingdom on Harth was a ghost town.

Fern could view the magnificent palace doors from where he stood. Slowly, with silent footsteps, he walked to them. He drew his sword, expecting at any moment to be ambushed by turgoyles. But like the Ulmeck Mountains, nothing appeared. The silence was eerie, like the dead of night when one sees only shadows and feels only shivers.

Fern came to the steps leading to the entrance. Climbing to the top, he carefully cracked the doors open to a slit and peeked in. The soldiers who once lined the walls, were absent, and the doors at the end of the hall stood wide open. Fern was puzzled at the ease of his intrusion.

Why would Timal leave a kingdom so unguarded, thought Fern. *Even if they had marched to war, it would not make sense to abandon a stronghold such as Loustof.*

Fern walked cautiously to the spiral staircases that led down to the dungeons, but the voice inside his head suddenly became stronger. It was pulling him to its will. Fern could not control his own movements, and he quickly realized he was walking away from the staircases and through an unfamiliar hallway.

Gold-framed portraits of royal men and women lined the walls. *Must be past kings and queens*, thought Fern. The urge abruptly released him from its grip, and the writing upon his arm began to burn. As he opened his eyes from the wincing pain, he found himself standing in front of a set of arched doors.

Solid, silver, and intricately carved with brass hinges and iron pulls, the doors looked like something Fern might have imagined coming from the elves kingdom, or maybe even fairy-made. He grasped the handles with palms sweating, and slowly opened the doors.

A large rust-colored slate courtyard in the center of the palace greeted him as he cautiously stepped forward. There was no time to look around as Fern immediately noticed a colossal emerald green dragon bound to the stone ground by large black chains. The dragon was thirty feet long and nearly as wide. A long, thick tail adorned with pointed finned scales wrapped around the side of its body as its tip flickered from side to side. Its head lay between its enormous front feet armed with razor sharp talons. Its face was elongated, and its mouth curved down like a beak. Fern could see pointed teeth protruding from its lower jaw and black horns crowning its head as they curved back towards its neck. Its body inflated with every inhale and was armored in large thick scales that shone with great brilliance. The dragon lay with its eyes shut, breathing heavily in a low grumble.

Standing as stiff as steel, his eyes bulging and heart pounding, Fern held his breath. He had no means of slaying the dragon, and decided, quickly, that he should retreat. As Fern lifted his right leg to leave, the dragon opened its eyes. Deep blue with a slit of black stared directly at Fern, and it spoke.

"Ah, so it is true. There is one of you who remains." it said with a deep voice echoing in Fern's mind.

Fern stood paralyzed.

"So, Majestic, you followed my call," the dragon said, trying to lift his head from the ground only to be stopped by the chains that bound him.

Fern was speechless. He had no idea dragons could speak. The strange thing, Fern thought, was the dragon did not even move its mouth.

"I am surprised by your silence; I would think you would have several questions for me."

Fern slid his sword back in its scabbard and studied the dragon for a moment, making sure it was real and that he was not going mad. *Is my mind playing tricks on me? A talking dragon? Well, I guess the polite thing to do would be to respond.*

Fern took one step forward cocking his head and rubbed his eyes.

"How do you know who I am?" Fern finally asked.

"I do not know who you are, I only know what you are," replied the dragon.

"How are you speaking to me? I can't see your mouth move, and I don't hear the words, yet I know what you're saying." Fern stood, frozen once more, still not sure if he was of clear mind or if he was under some sort of illusion.

"We dragons call it transference. We do not speak in the traditional sense. We communicate through our emotions, and we are able to transfer them from mind to mind. We can translate those emotions into words and read each other's thoughts. You have that ability as well. If you have been paying attention, Majestic, your mouth has remained still, the same as mine."

Fern watched the dragon contort its face as it struggled with the chains.

"Who are you?" asked Fern.

"My name is Paliden, and I am an ancient dragon who has lived many lifetimes. I was even there when your kind was created; I was a part of your making."

"What do you speak of?" asked Fern, so intrigued he cleared all worry about haste from his mind and sat to listen.

"The race of Majestics are thousands upon thousands of years old, same as dragons. Your kind was a race of pure-hearted people. They ruled their land in peace for a millennium, but an evil arose that threatened that peace. The Majestics came to the dragons in need of help. We took it upon ourselves to grant them a gift that has never been given to humankind, and thus, a new race of Majestics was born."

"What was this gift?" asked Fern, not giving Paliden a chance to finish his thoughts.

"We dragons are magical beings; we have the power to infuse our blood with any living creature we choose. Our blood, when given willingly, can give any creature powers beyond that of normality."

"How can this be accomplished?"

"It is quite simple. A dragon must give her or his life for whatever creature deemed worthy, and that creature must then drink its blood before the dragon draws its last breath. I was the one who struck the first dragon down. I was there when your kind was reborn," exclaimed Paliden. "This is why you can communicate with me, and why you have the strength of ten men. It is also the reason why you heal so quickly. All these powers are because you have dragon's blood flowing through your veins."

Fern sat in a daze. "So, what you're saying is that whoever drinks the blood of a dragon can obtain these powers?"

"No, on the contrary. Only creatures that drink the blood of a dragon given to them *willingly* will receive such power, and everyone born from them will retain that gift, *but* if any creature drinks the blood of a dragon taken by force, they will live a life cursed for thousands of years plagued with an unquenchable thirst for dragon blood, until they no longer walk the earth."

Fern sat staring at the dragon in complete bewilderment.

"Why haven't you called to me before, and why now?"

"I heard that your kind was hunted down and murdered some years ago, so I did not know there were any of you left. I only found out you had survived this very morning. I overheard some guards talking about a plan to hunt you down. A human by the name of Timal has been behind the murder of your kind. He thought he knew where you were headed, and most likely would have caught you if I had not called you to me."

"You were not captured by Timal?"

"Not exactly" replied Paliden with an embarrassed look on his green face, though turning slightly yellow. "I was landing in a meadow to feed on some sheep and was caught in a trap. You would think a dragon as ancient and wise as I would know better."

"Then you have seen Timal?" asked Fern.

"No, I have not, but I have heard him. He can communicate with dragons. I could hear them as they flew overhead. He was riding atop one of my kind. I am not sure how he obtained this power, it has not been bestowed on any other human, and he is no Majestic."

"How can you be sure?"

"All dragons are connected through the blood that runs through our veins, we can sense each other from a great distance and call to one another if close," answered Paliden. "I felt your presence when I found out about your existence, but I could not sense this Timal, even when he was supposedly here at the palace. If he had our blood running through his veins, I would know it. The power must come from another source."

"He carries a jewel around his neck that I'm told holds great power," said Fern. "I've worn it myself; it saved my life when I was bitten by a glass spider at the Crags of Malice, but I don't know what other power it possesses."

"How did it save your life?" questioned Paliden, tilting his head with a suspicious look.

"I had no wound from the bite," replied Fern. "It's as if the fangs never penetrated my flesh, yet I felt the pain and even felt the burning sensation of the venom as it coursed through my body. I know my healing ability is swift, and I can endure more than mortal men, but this was beyond any power I've ever had. I also know Timal has been stabbed in the heart twice while wearing the gem, and both times walked away without a scratch."

"Thousands of years I have lived, but never have I heard of a stone that held such power," Paliden replied with severe concern on his face. "You must find a way to free me and fly north with me to my kin. I must warn them of this threat before more fall slave to this Timal."

Fern sat lost in thought for only a moment, shook his head as if he was arguing with himself, and turned to Paliden.

"Very well, I'll find a way to set you free, but I can't go with you," replied Fern.

Noticed when he first entered the courtyard, Fern studied the three padlocks clasped to hooks embedded in the stone that bound the dragon to the ground.

"I'll need the keys to free you, but I don't know where to begin to look."

Fern suddenly screamed in frustration. He knew he had already spent far too much time listening to Paliden, and he could not get the thought of Reagal's lifeless body out of his mind.

"You must do what you think is right," replied Paliden, looking at Fern with surprising understanding.

Night had already fallen as Fern ran back through the doors and through the numerous hallways until he reached the hidden door that led to the spiral staircases. Fern's chest filled, stretching his shirt, and he released a breath of relief as the hidden door stood wide open. *Finally, a little bit of luck!*

Clank!

Fern spun around in the darkened hall to see what made the sudden noise. His eyes squinted as he peered through the shadows but saw nothing. Shaking his head, he turned back to the staircase.

Disregarding the fact that there might be soldiers or turgoyles guarding the dungeons, Fern raced down the center staircase and to the iron door that led to the cells. He immediately noticed a silver ring of pewter keys hanging on the wall next to the door. He grabbed them and ran back up the staircase and out to the courtyard.

Quickly sprinting over to the first padlock, Fern slid to his knees and began trying the keys. Just when Fern believed his luck was changing for the better, none of the keys seemed to fit the locks.

Fern pounded the ground in anger, cracking the stone floor. Looking to the dragon, Fern's eyes saddened and brows slanted outward as he apologized.

"I'm sorry, Paliden, I can't waste any more time. I'll try my best to set you free if ever I return."

Fern could not wait for a response. Spinning around with keys in hand, he bolted as fast as he could down the spiral staircase to the dungeon door. Fern began fitting each key into the lock until one turned the tumblers and unlocked the door. In he ran searching for Galeon, but there they were, poor souls locked in cells, no telling how long they had suffered, and under what pain of torture.

Some standing, hands wrapped around the bars of their doors shaking hysterically, pleaded to Fern. Tears filled their eyes, begging to be set free. Fern's body shook as he fought his emotions. He wanted to release them all; even the foulest of creatures should be put out of their misery and not left to rot in a dungeon cell.

Fern's heart cramped, but knowing he had no time to release the pitiful creatures, he tried to erase the guilt from his mind. The next cell would not let that happen. A minotaur, tall and black with colored beads hanging from braids throughout its body, stared through the steel bars. His face was emaciated, and his frame had dwindled to half its original size, though still intimidating. Fern, for a moment, thought it was Dominance from Earthingland. But no, it couldn't be...then he remembered. *This is Xarion, the one Dom spoke of.* Fern had to try. He began to fit the first key into the locked cell door.

Without warning, the minotaur rushed forward, horns down. With an unbelievable pounding force, he rammed his head into the door.

"I will kill eveřy last Loustofian I see. Yes, yes, open this dooř, you sack of řancid, maggot-infested dog meat, so I can show youř Loustofian face what Xařion of Eařthingland can třuly do."

Fern dropped the keys from the impact and jumped back, startled. He could see the madness burning in the minotaur's eyes. Fern knew that letting Xarion loose, at least at this moment, would surely be a bad idea. Shaking his head, Fern moved away from the cell and continued his search for Galeon. *Well, I gave it a try.*

Fern approached the cell, and huddled in a corner lay a centaur with shackles around each leg.

"Galeon!" shouted Fern.

The centaur immediately raised his head and looked towards the door.

"That is your name, isn't it?"

"Yes, dat is my name," replied the centaur as he looked inquisitively at Fern. "You are dee one I fought in dee arena."

Galeon stood, eyes squinted and chin to his chest while Fern found the key to unlock his cell door.

"Yes, that was me, but I don't have time to explain everything now. You must trust me; I've been sent by one of your own. His name is Reagal, the son of King Solace. We must make great haste, for he is wounded, and Timal has raged war on this world. I must reach Dundire before it is too late. Will you bear me?" Fern ran forward sliding upon his knees by the centaur's shackled ankles.

"My broder? Ow badly is ee wounded?" asked Galeon, the last cuff finally off.

Fern stood shocked from this revelation. Head shaking again, and eyes half closed, he answered.

"Severely, I'm afraid, but one of my companions is taking him to the fairies of the Blue Marshes as we speak."

Fern waited for a response as he stared at the centaur with his eyes wide open. Galeon stood quietly.

"Please, it is imperative we leave as soon as we can," begged Fern. "Tell me, how's your strength?"

"My strengd is fine, dee king as fed me well to keep my fighting ability at its prime, but ow do you plan on getting past dee guards of Loustof, and ow did you get down ere widout an army of soldiers after you?" Galeon trotted in place feeling the relief of his discarded bindings.

"I'll explain everything on the way. Now please, will you bear me to Dundire?" Fern's body shook with anticipation.

"No, I will not," answered Galeon bluntly. "But I dank you for my release."

Fern stood stiff as a board, with his eyes bulging and mouth agape.

"Please trust me, Galeon, I'm not trying to deceive you! I need—"

"I do not know you, derefore I cannot trust you. Now, take your leave from me, I must go to attend to my broder, if you are indeed trudful." Galeon galloped past, erupting from the cell floor and cloaking Fern in a cloud of dust.

Standing alone in the cell, silent and dirty, shaking his head without pause, Fern was at a complete loss. His head snapped still, and he suddenly darted through the doorway, running and yelling for Galeon's return.

His effort was all for naught. The centaur was far faster and already out of sight. There was only one option now: find the key to Paliden's chains and convince the green dragon to carry Fern to Dundire.

Tearing down the dungeon corridors, Fern searched for the elusive keys. Though, why would they be in the dungeon? So up the spiral staircase he climbed, leaping like a professional hurdler, until his feet touched the soft plush runner.

The halls were dark, and the doors were shut and locked, making the chance of finding *anything* less and less likely. But Fern had his strength. So...door after door flung from its hinges with swift front kicks.

The palace was filled with shadows and strange noises, making Fern continuously feel as if he were being followed. And on numerous occasions, he thought he saw the silhouette of a man dart from sight. Though curious, but having no time, Fern ignored his feelings and continued his room-by-room search.

Without any luck, he decided to return to the throne room. Fern could feel Paliden sensing his emotions as he entered. Trying his best to smother the intrusion, he ransacked Edinword's pride and joy. By the time Fern was finish with the room, it was unrecognizable. Tables had been overturned, chairs scattered, vases shattered, curtains torn to shreds, and the king's own throne tossed through a stain glass window.

With the keys still absent, Fern was nearly ready to relinquish his plight. Suddenly it dawned on him: *they might be in Timal's quarters!*

All Fern had to do now was find them.

Almost immediately, he remembered the room he had stayed in his first night at Loustof.

The portrait on the wall! Was that Timal? The thought intrigued Fern as he entered. The framed portrait hung by a wire above a darkened stone fireplace, though Fern did not remember the fireplace.

No details were visible, due to the darkness of night, and there were no candles lit. The room looked as if it had not been stayed in since Fern had last been there.

He found a candle sitting on a bedside table and lit it quickly. Searching the room for the keys was essential, but as he came to the portrait, he held the candle high to get a better look. Fern quickly noticed a sword in the man's hand. It looked identical to Lord Orgle's. *This must be Timal, they share the same sword.*

But he was nothing like Fern had imagined. His appearance was quite pleasant. He had long golden blond hair and piercing blue eyes. His face was thin and as young as Fern's. High cheekbones and a square jaw gave him a chiseled look, and he stood tall holding the sword in his hand.

The portrait mesmerized Fern. Eyes fixated and mind frozen, he stared. And the longer he did, the older the face seemed to become.

Fern quickly regained his head and resumed looking for the keys. After a thorough search, he found nothing. Discouraged and annoyed over wasted time, he ran back to the dungeons for one last attempt. *Why does everything have to be so difficult? Please, just let me find them.*

Through the cell blocks he bounded until he finally arrived at the arena doors. In he walked, realizing his failure. The sandy floor was still blood-soaked from his battle with Galeon, and the only thing besides the red stains were the weapons upon the racks. As he was turning to leave, Fern noticed a black, two-handed battle ax at his feet. It was the same ax he'd used to fight Galeon. *Huh, I wonder.*

Fern bent over to examine the weapon. Grasping it by the handle, he dashed to the courtyard. Luckily for Fern, his skills at being a blacksmith were paying off. Knowing the precise spot to strike the locks, he raised the ax. His hands gripped firmly upon the handle, and his forearm muscles tensed.

"Close your eyes, Paliden," he informed the dragon.

Fern brought the blade down with uncanny accuracy, striking the lock at its weakest point. Shattering like glass, Fern broke the chains one by one.

The massive green dragon rose to his feet and spread his wings (which seemed to reach twenty feet in both directions), stretching with a roar. His size was immense, and the wind from the flap of his wings nearly knocked Fern on his backside.

"Ah hah! Thank you. Now, please come with me to my kin, they will know how to handle a threat of this magnitude."

Paliden rose into the air for a moment before landing gently on the court-yard floor.

"I'm sorry, Paliden, but I must get to Dundire as quickly as possible. Please take me there! I have allies who can defeat Timal, if only I could bring them this Ulmeck Rock," pleaded Fern, hope rekindling in his eyes.

"And what do you plan on doing with that Ulmeck Rock, might I ask? Kill dragons?"

"What choice do I have? They are on Timal's side, and they plan to take over this world."

"No, you are wrong, they are under Timal's control through no will of their own, I assure you of that," Paliden said with confidence. "Now, please trust me as you wanted your friend Galeon to trust you. After all, you have known me longer than you have known him," he said with a smile.

Fern stood questioning every decision he had made. Realizing that his instincts had not been kind to him, and going against his better judgment, he nodded his head.

"Very well, I'll go with you, but you must promise me that you'll take me to Dundire as soon as you've spoken with your kin."

"I give you my word," replied Paliden with a wink. "Now, climb on my neck... and hold on."

Fern threw the sacks of Ulmeck Rock over his back and did as he was told.

Paliden lifted into the air, his mighty wings flapping like a hurricane sending the dirt from the courtyard swirling into dust devils. In seconds, they were hundreds of feet from the ground, soaring through the night sky.

If one has ever had an experience so dazzling, so mesmerizing, so incredible that it consumes all conversations for years to come and never leaves the mind, then that is what Fern would achieve this night.

His eyes sparkled as Paliden reached the clouds. Oceans of misty white flowed around them like liquid silk. The sensation as it touched Fern's skin was magic. It enveloped them, kissing Fern's face like tiny snowflakes. The frigid moisture soothed his wounds as Paliden burst through the wisps of clouds like a fish from a pool.

"So, Majestic, how does it feel to be a dragon?" laughed Paliden.

Fern could not respond. His face was mystified in utter awe.

Treetops and mountain peaks desperately reached for Paliden's underbelly, but never could quite attain such heights. And Fern was an eagle as he spread his arms and opened his eyes. *I'm flying on a dragon!*

His mind exploded as millions of stars captured him. Never had he seen such brilliance. Like sparkling crystals. No, diamonds. No...There was no comparison.

And the moon...It was alive and massive, a face smiling at Fern, bright and luminescent. The heavens had never seemed so real, and Fern felt free.

Lifting his heart, the emotion surged through his body like electricity. It shot from his fingertips like beams of light, and Fern felt as if he was a ball of fire exploding in the sky.

As the stars began to fall, taunting Fern to make a wish, his mind ran wild. *But what could be dreamed greater than this*, he thought, brimming with unbridled joy. He wanted more, and the pounding in his chest did not want to let go.

Unfortunately, everything must come to an end, and Paliden began his descent.

As they dropped beneath the clouds, Fern began to see thousands of lights dotting the ground. Twinkling like fireflies, he could only wonder if they were campfires of his allies stopping for the night before marching to war. *But wait, it must be too soon. Has it been ten days? Maybe we were in those blasted tunnels longer than I thought.*

Crossing his mind that it could be Timal and his army of turgoyles on their way to attack the dwarves, or some other unfortunate souls, made Fern's skin shudder.

A sudden change in altitude forced Fern to gasp for air as Paliden dipped towards the ground. To Fern's surprise, the landscape was littered in tens of thousands of lights. *More campfires? Why so far north? Who could it be?*

"Paliden, what's going on?" asked Fern.

"Let's fly down to get a better look," he answered.

The green dragon pulled his wings close to his body and dove towards the ground. It took all of Fern's strength to hold on to the sacks of Ulmeck Rock with one hand and Paliden's horn with the other.

Down they plummeted, faster and faster, cutting through the air like a knife. The wind whipped Fern in the face, forcing his eyes shut. He felt like he was going to lose consciousness but could not seem to communicate to Paliden. *Why can't he hear my thoughts? Slow down, slow down!* Just when he thought he was blacking out, the dragon landed with a thunderous boom. Fern opened his eyes only to realize that his vision was blurred and his hearing was muffled. The force of the descent temporarily disabled his senses.

The feeling of weightlessness took over his body. He was being lifted from Paliden's neck. He hit the ground like a bag of sand.

Almost the moment he touched the earth a great force shoved him down on his chest. He could feel his arms being forced behind his back and could begin to hear muffled screaming. His eyes began to clear, and he could see numerous short figures stomping their feet as they surrounded him.

Binding his wrists and ankles with iron shackles, they stood with their wide, pungent feet upon his back. Fern's hearing and eyesight were nearly back to normal as he witnessed massive red dragons in the distance, hovering above an equally massive army.

Legions of turgoyles spread in every direction. Crude wooden structures that served as army headquarters broke up the landscape. Stables of giant warthogs wallowing in mud and snorting with pure delight could be seen surrounded by their caretakers. Turgoyle commanders barked at their troops to fall in line as they attempted to gather them into platoons. Trocks, armed with clubs, strolled through the ranks curling their lips as they slapped turgoyles to the ground. Chaos ruled the campsite while the commanders tried to control the hoards as they swung their weapons wildly at the bullying trocks. The noise was deafening.

Fern lay on the ground in disbelief that he was once again in the custody of the enemy. Swinging around under the feet of two large turgoyles, he winced as sharp jagged rocks tried to force their way through his shirt and into his chest.

Where's Paliden? Fern searched the sky, cranking his head to get a better look, but the green dragon was nowhere in sight.

Staying silent, not wanting to provoke his enemy, Fern closed his eyes. Suddenly, the noise from the army died down. The horde parted, and a tall figure approached Fern.

Dressed in black and wearing a long cape dragging on the ground behind him, stood a man, stopping no more than two feet in front of Fern. Fern arched his neck like a turtle.

"Pick him up," said the man calmly.

The turgoyles took their feet from Fern's back and jerked him off the ground. Fern winced in pain, growling low.

"Now, now, let us be gentle with our prize," said the man.

An evil menacing smile developed on his face as he chuckled and brought his teeth together like a trap.

Fern was now face to face with the false prince.

Their height was nearly equal, as was their build. Timal looked Fern over before speaking, walking casually around him, eyes moving up in down, scanning his opponent. Fern could feel his glare like beams of light burning into his skin.

"So, we finally meet," spoke Timal in a delicate, friendly tone as he halted in front of Fern, looking directly into his eyes. "You were a very difficult little tadpole to locate; I have been searching for you for years. Who would have thought you were living in my own kingdom? Your parents were smarter than I realized, knowing I would never expect you to be so close. The ironic thing is, they actually did me a service hiding you so well."

Fern stood listening silently.

Timal walked slowly around Fern again, holding his hands behind his back as he spoke.

"You must have many questions for me, goofy child." Timal stopped in front of Fern, placing a cold clammy hand upon his shoulder. "Please ask, if you wish."

"Why would you humor me?"

"Why not, my naive boy?" answered Timal. "After all, you are no threat to me, you never have been."

"What have you done with Paliden?"

Timal chuckled before answering, "Nothing," he said.

Fern looked like a bug under glass. He had no idea how he was going to escape the new mess he was in, and now he had the reason for his troubles standing face to face ready to spout words that had to be taken with a grain of salt. He was not about to be deceived again, not if he could help it.

"What do you want from me?" asked Fern.

"I want everything from you, silly fool!" answered Timal as he smiled wildly.

"But you'll get nothing," answered Fern quickly.

Timal laughed quietly and circled Fern like a vulture.

"You're a funny little thing, aren't you? But we shall see," he said.

"Who are you?"

"Ah hah, finally, a good question!" exclaimed Timal. "I am the creator of your people."

"What?!" shouted Fern in true disbelief.

"I am the dragon who gave the Majestics my blood nearly two thousand years ago." Timal tilted his head down slightly as his eyes rose to meet Fern's.

"What are you talking about? You're a human."

"Yes, yes, difficult to believe, I know. I, myself, was in denial for nearly a thousand years. Until I happened upon an old text written by that very same Majestic I was so willing to give my blood to. I read about the blood of a dragon and the effects it would have if given to a human, something that I did not fully understand before." Timal crossed his arms and began to pace back and forth. "I learned the magic behind the ritual, but I could not understand how a mortal man came by this information. Not even we dragons knew the truth behind the magic. I was told and taught by our most revered and ancient dragon, Deity. He was said to hold all knowledge of dragon power, and not even he knew of this. We were deceived by the Majestic, who somehow knew the effects that would be placed on me if I willingly gave my blood to a human. I was a young and naïve dragon. I thought I was bestowing great power to a great people, but they were no better than any other power-hungry men of this world. I was punished, to walk this land for the rest of my days as a human, never again able to fly with my brothers or congregate with my fellow dragons." Timal abruptly stopped, staring in Fern's eyes like a crazed lunatic. "Your kind has cursed me, and I have vowed to hunt down every last one of you for the misery you have caused me."

Fern looked completely dazed, wobbling his head like a drunkard.

"I don't understand...how'd you become human?"

"Pay attention, silly boy! The ritual I performed with the Majestic was tainted by his lack of purity!" shouted Timal as he pounced like a falcon, grabbing Fern by the arms and shaking him vigorously. "Little did I know there was no such thing as a human who is pure of heart. What I later discovered in that text, was if I gave my blood to an impure being, I would transform into that being for eternity and become banished from the dragon empire. My rage at finding this information was greater than this world could bear, but it gave me new purpose in my cursed life. I was determined to rid this world of your putrescent race. I had a challenging time though, I must admit. By the time I came across this knowledge, your people had become vast and powerful. I had to be cunning. I befriended the new king of the Majestics, as I did Edinword, and destroyed his kingdom. I have spent the last thousand years hunting the Majestics down, and now...I have the last one," Timal flashed a devilish smile as his eyes lit up with glee.

"Why not kill me and be done with it then!"

"You—are—funny!! That will come, boy, of course it will! But first, *you* will help me destroy your allies," answered Timal.

"You'll get nothing from me." Fern held his head in defiance.

"I have more power than you could ever conceive of. You will give me everything, and you will do it without even realizing it. Like most, you underestimate my abilities," said Timal in an unbelievably calm voice.

"No, it's you who underestimates me," he said, standing his ground like a twig in a tornado.

"We shall see."

Timal's nonchalant demeanor frustrated Fern.

"Why do you want them dead anyway? You already have me!" he shouted angrily, spit flying from his lips.

"Your allies have been a thorn in my side, ever since my pursuit of the Majestics begun. They have aided your kind, trying to stop my ambitions. For that, they will suffer the same fate as you," replied Timal. He turned to take his leave, but suddenly squinted his eyes as he glanced back at Fern.

"Straggle, Doth! Bring him closer!!"

The two turgoyles dragged Fern to Timal. Fern's sleeve had been shredded from the fall and revealed the inscription upon his arm. Timal studied the writing for a moment and shook his head grinning.

"Now I understand," he responded, laughing hysterically as he walked away.

"Wait!" shouted Fern. "What do you understand?"

Timal quickened his pace with a little hop in his step.

"Stop!"

Timal halted and turned towards Fern.

"Yeeesss?" he said sarcastically as an arrogant child.

"Why take Loustof? Edinword was no enemy of yours," shouted Fern.

Timal smiled, puffing a laugh.

"It is simple, your allies cost me my previous kingdom, and I needed a new one to build my army. For you see, I do not forget easily, and everyone will pay for what they have done to me. Now, I must go, there will be no more questions.

Fern clenched his fists, screaming, as Timal strolled away. "YOU WILL GET NOTHING FROM ME, NOTHING!!!"

10

REUNION

A large group of heavily-armed turgoyles surrounded Fern. Surprisingly, they did not taunt or torture him; they merely stood guard, making sure he did not escape. Uncomfortable with his hands shackled behind his back, Fern tucked his feet and legs under his arms as he plopped to the ground. The turgoyles did not give him a second look as he sat, elbows on his knees, staring into the sky.

Fern's thoughts consumed him, much like they had in recent times. *Why is Timal having such difficulty finding my allies*, he thought. *After all, he has dragons that can scour the lands from the sky.*

Fern craned his neck as a shooting star dazzled from above. Its tail trailed for miles, sending sparks of light dancing like fireworks. The spellbinding display showed once again that even in the darkest of times one kind find beauty. But Fern could not see such things, for his thoughts were consuming. *Have I done it again...could I be so dull witted...again?*

Fern could not believe the betrayal he had faced from so many: first Edinword and Mallock, then Dominance of the minotaurs, and now Paliden. He began to wonder if anyone was truly on his side. *Bite your tongue, Fern...have you forgotten already? Garrick and Reagal would never betray you, that I'm sure of.*

The turgoyles surrounding Fern suddenly tossed some of their slop at his feet.

"E-Eat, phlegm w-w-wad, our m-master w-wants y-y-you a-alive, and f-fat," said a stuttering hunched-backed turgoyle as it danced around Fern, flailing its bloodied club in his face.

A combination of maggot-riddled meat and mashed corn steamed on the ground between Fern's boots. Ignoring the offering, he sat quietly in hopes he would discover a way out of his nightmare.

He kicked the slop away as the stench became too much.

"Eat this garbage yourself," said Fern under his breath.

Fern shook his head in disgust as a small group pounced on the pile of rotten mush and began to argue and fight.

A large grotesquely obese turgoyle waddled like a duck into the middle of the ruckus. Pulling one of the instigators by its scrawny wings, the plump turgoyle chucked the squealing creature into the air. Fern watched as it flew overhead, slamming into a stacked pile of firewood. The remaining rabble scattered like flies as the fat turgoyle flopped down, crossing its legs Indian-style, and began stuffing its round, resin-dripping cheeks full of the rancid slop.

As Fern sat observing his ignorant captors throughout the night, Timal never returned to question him. Finding it curious, though not dwelling on it, Fern sat studying the shackles around his wrists.

"They w-won't come off e-e-easily, p-p-pig," said the stuttering turgoyle as he caught Fern testing his bonds. "W-Where would you g-g-go anyways? Our m-master w-w-w-would b-be on y-you b-b-before you could t-take y-your first st-st-step.

Fern spun around with his back to the turgoyle, trying his best to ignore it, and realizing there was no escaping his shackles, he laid upon the barren ground to sleep.

"Yeah, y-yeah, that's r-right, l-l-little p-piggy, y-you go t-to s-s-sleep. In the m-m-m-morning everything w-will be b-b-better."

The turgoyles burst out laughing, smacking the back of the sarcastic stutterer.

As usual, Fern paid no attention to them and tried his best to find a comfortable position to sleep, curling into a ball.

Sudden commotion made him spin back around.

Turgoyles dragged numerous creatures into a clearing, each one being yanked by a tattered length of rope bound tightly around their necks. Fern watched in horror as they practiced their fighting skills on the smaller and weaker beings. Snotlings (which were no more than miniature versions of goblins), dark green and pointy eared, and tiny bearded men called Wood Gnomes were given weapons and told to defend themselves as the turgoyles easily overpowered them. Helpless and mortified, Fern was forced to hear their screams as they were being slaughtered mercilessly. *This is evil at its worst! If only...damn these creatures! They best not let me free.*

Dragons flying overhead every couple of hours landed just beyond Fern's sight. Fern, trying to get the visions of butchered gnomes out of his head, watched as the dragons took off again in different directions. *They must be searching for them*, thought Fern. *But how can my allies stay hidden?*

As dawn crept, and the pink hue showed itself over the horizon, Fern still sat surrounded by the turgoyle guards. Though, now huddled under large squares of leather (to hide from the rising sun). The stretched shelters were held at an angle by spears thrust into the ground.

Finding small comfort as the sun warmed his face, Fern laid upon his back, shackled hands behind his head. Dragons continued flying above him, and Fern concentrated, trying to read their thoughts.

This ability was new to him, and he could not seem to get the hang of it. Each attempt left his head scrambled. Too many voices bounced in his mind like popping corn that he could not distinguish between them. Of course, the dead bodies of gnomes and hobgoblins surrounding him only made matters worse. Fern was exhausted, and he soon found his eyelids heavy. A sudden sleep took hold, and Fern was lost in dreams, though Lillia was not amongst them.

Timal stood in blackness, staring...just staring. Reagal, bound and bloodied... and Garrick, eyes still. The visions were haunting.

Fern woke in a drenching sweat. Night engulfed him. *What? I slept all day?*

Still groggy eyed, he scanned his surroundings. To his dismay, he still sat shackled amongst Timal's army. Massive fires rose into the night sky, and spastic dancing circled Fern as songs sprang up from the chaotic hordes. Fern had no recourse but to listen to the tunes of pillage and slaughter. Sickened by the sheer idiocy of it all, Fern lay on his back trying to hum a song that he heard Garrick sing to Phillip in the ruins of Liffland.

> *Lay my son of Loustof*
> *Down upon your head*
> *Lay my son of Loustof*
> *Nothing you shall—*

Suddenly, a voice echoed in his mind. *Stand*, it said. Fern stood almost at once, his hand above his brow shading his eyes from the campfire's light as he squinted and searched his surroundings. The guards jumped at his sudden movement, their small scrawny wings spread and weapons raised. Fern saw a flash of light come from the sky, and within moments there was a ring of fire engulfing the guards. They burned like the evil that stung their souls, and their screams were music of justification.

Without warning, Fern felt himself being lifted from the ground, feet dangling. He looked up to see the hard-scaled belly of a green dragon.

"Paliden!" shouted Fern. "Where have you been?"

"Let me get you far from here and I will tell you everything," he answered.

Paliden's wings wrapped around the wind, pushing it down with each powerful flap. Flying swiftly, he successfully dodged the barrage of arrows fired from the turgoyle army. Turgoyles cursed as they chucked spears and stones into the air. Fern grinned as they were soon beyond the army's reach.

The moon was bright with a smile of its own, and Fern was once again enjoying the view. Though, it must be told that his comfort was far from ideal, for Paliden's talons dug deep into Fern's shoulders like knives.

Fern was a rag doll, swaying limp from Paliden's grip as they made their way over rivers and mountains. Flying above clouds whenever possible to keep out of sight, Fern noticed a familiar scene as he stared down between his dancing feet. Flying above the dense forests of Earthingland, Paliden began his descent. Fern's skin crawled at the sight of the clearing. It was the sameFern had visited the day Dominance deserted him and his companions. A feeling of dread gripped him.

"I think we will be safe here, at least for the moment," said Paliden as he gently planted Fern on the ground next to a quaggoth hole.

Barely having time to collapse his wings and land, Paliden was bombarded with questions.

"What happened to you? Why did you abandon me? Where did you go? Why did you give me to Timal?"

"I did not give you to him," spoke Paliden in defense. "I was shot by a black arrow that nearly pierced my heart," Paliden grasped a wound on his chest, showing Fern. "I nearly crash-landed in the middle of the turgoyle army. I was just able to regain flight before we hit the ground. You fell from my neck. I tried grabbing you and nearly had you in my grip, but you slipped from my hand and landed amongst the turgoyle horde. I had no choice but to fly away. I am sorry. Now, please hold still while I release you from your bonds." He looked to Fern for forgiveness as he struck the shackles with his talon.

Fern stared at Paliden and shook his head as he rubbed his wrists. "I suppose, you had no choice; you did what you had to...but why did you wait for so long to come and rescue me?"

"For one, I had an arrow in me, and two, I needed to wait for nightfall," replied Paliden. "There were too many dragons around as well. I would have stood little chance at a quick escape. I needed to wait until they were gone and the turgoyles were preoccupied before attempting any rescue."

"What do we do now? Those disgusting turgoyles have the Ulmeck rock."

"We must find your friends, for mine are now under Timal's command," said Paliden.

"What about your kin to the north?"

"They were the ones you saw flying to and from the turgoyle camp. I saw them when I was planning your rescue. There is no use trying to convince them to follow us. Timal must have them under some sort of spell," replied Paliden. "Our only hope is to locate your allies and attack Timal's forces," he added.

"I've no idea where they could be. If Timal can't find them with an army in the sky, how do you expect me to be able to locate them?"

"What about your friends in the Blue Marshes? Maybe they know where they are hiding."

"You're right. If Reagal has survived, he'll surely know where the centaurs go in times of desperation. You must fly me there as soon as you can." Fern paused for a moment and then jerked his head up, eyes straining and jaw clenched. "Wait...how did you know about my friends in the Blue Marshes?" he asked, slightly suspicious.

"I read your thoughts when you were speaking with Galeon in the dungeons of Loustof," replied Paliden. "Please, trust me," he said, looking Fern in the eyes.

"Of course...of course." Fern took a deep breath before letting out a long exhausting sigh. "I hope you can forgive my lack of trust, but I have been betrayed by so many in such a short amount of time that my faith in people has taken its toll."

"Yes, I can understand, but I am not people, I am a dragon," answered Paliden winking at Fern.

Fern nodded with a smile as he leapt onto the dragon's neck.

"I can take you to the borders of the Blue Marshes, but I cannot enter there," said Paliden.

"Why not?"

"That place has a powerful magic around it cast by the Blue Dragons of that land."

"Blue Dragons?" Fern asked with a curious look.

"Yes, the Blue Dragons of the Marshes. They claim to be the oldest of all dragons and superior to my kind. They are usually seen in the form of fairies."

"What!!" shouted Fern. "Are you telling me the fairies of the Blue Marshes are dragons?"

"Yes, they take the form of beautiful fairies. They are friendly to your kind, and your allies, but they believe my kind are less than worthy. They have cast a barrier over their land impenetrable to my kin and me. It is old magic, a kind that even I am unfamiliar with," replied Paliden. "Though the magic of the Blue Marshes, I have heard, causes your kind to become disoriented, sleepy."

Fern could not pay attention to Paliden's warning; he sat completely shocked at finding out Lillia was possibly a dragon. *It's impossible...she can't...she can't be... can she?* Fern's mind boggled over visions of Lillia as a scaly dragon. Focusing his eyes, he cocked his head as a question blocked his horrible thoughts.

"Why do the fairies need protection from your kind?" he finally asked.

"They call themselves pacifists and healers and think of us as violent and unhinged. We believe that one must be strong, and sometimes a show of aggression is necessary to prevent further catastrophe. Would you not agree?"

"I'm not sure of anything right now, Paliden. I've so many questions dancing around in my head that I can't think clearly," replied Fern, still bewildered by this new discovery.

"I realize your dilemma, Fern Majestic, and understand you will need time to absorb this latest information, but I must insist on something."

"What would you ask of me?" questioned Fern.

"You must not speak of me if you find your companions; they will cast judgment on you for keeping my company."

"I shall not lie to my friends, Paliden," replied Fern quickly.

"I am not asking you to," he said in rapid defense. "But you must understand we dragons have been falsely accused of being dangerous, just as the Majestics were falsely accused of being traitors. They do not know who we really are, and being quite familiar with fairies, I do not believe they will understand why you have been keeping company with my kind. Please trust me, it is better to not mention my existence at all."

Understanding how Paliden felt, Fern thought for a moment and nodded. After all, he had lived his entire life with the same affliction.

Paliden spread his wings and lifted into the air, rising above the treetops, and headed toward the Blue Marshes. It wasn't long before Fern noticed the wetlands forming below them. He could see the heads of the blue-tinted weeping willows poking up out of the fog as Paliden descended. They landed softly just outside the Blue Marsh's border in The Land of Valom.

"Where will we meet when I find my companions?" asked Fern.

"I will find you," replied Paliden. "Now, go with great haste." He motioned to Fern with a slight nod of his head.

"But how will you explain yourself to my companions if you find me?"

"Your memory fails you. Have you forgotten already? You have dragon blood in your veins, Fern Majestic; I will be able to communicate from a distance. They will never know I am near. Now please, no more delays." Paliden gave Fern a wink and a shove, sending him on his way.

Disappearing from sight like a ghostly vision, Fern faded into the fog. As he tromped through the wet ground, he could not shake the thought from his mind of Lillia as a dragon, wondering if Reagal knew this information, and if so, why he would keep it from him.

Fern wandered through the marshes, aimlessly, hoping to stumble upon tracks left by Garrick, but there was no sign of anything on the spongy ground. *I wonder if they even made it this far. What if I'm searching in vain. What if Reagal is...no...no Fern...don't let yourself think such thoughts, they must be somewhere around here.*

Searching for what seemed like hours, Fern dashed from tree to tree calling out his companion's names. Poking and prodding on and around every spongy island for some sort of entrance to the fairy's kingdom, Fern found himself at a loss. Not a single clue to their whereabouts was found. *Come on Fern, what are you missing? It's Garrick for goodness sake, he had to have left a trail.*

Every soggy step led deeper into the marshes, and Fern began to feel it. There was magic in the air, and it was not friendly. Shivers of frigid coldness shot through his bones. Fern's eyes circled inside his face. *Where am I?* He was becoming hopelessly lost in the fog; everything looked the same. He could not tell where he had searched and where he had not. The marshes started to close in on him like a box. It was shrinking and becoming dark with night.

He escaped to an island where two giant willows grew. Fern sat in between them trying to gain his bearings. The fog grew thick like syrup and hung low around Fern; it was a comforting blanket. The air was pleasant and warm. Fern sat in the darkness looking nowhere. A great tiredness came over him. His eyes closed as he uncontrollably laid to his back. The spongy surface was his bed, and the tufts of soft fluffy moss was his pillow.

Fern had not paid attention to Paliden's word of caution, but a dream of Garrick suddenly appeared in his sleeping mind; a dream of warning. "*Wake, sir, you not find us if you sleep. You not find you, if you sleep. WAKE UP, FERN MAJESTIC!!*"

He suddenly leapt to his feet, slapping himself upon his cheeks. Before realizing what was happening, Fern found himself lying on his back again, eyelids as heavy as stone, dozing off. *Get up, Fern, get up!*

He swung his head trying to shake free of the enchantment. Staring at the two willows, a sudden idea sprang into his mind. As insane as one might find it, Fern began slamming himself between the trees. Back in forth he ran, knocking the willows with such great force that soon neither one had leaves left on their branches. But he did not stop his constant jolting. A smile formed on Fern's face as he rattled his brains; his sleepiness was slowly fading. *It's working!*

Without warrant, a barrier swelled between Fern and the trees like a stone wall. His vision was blurred from the constant slamming that he could not determine what had stopped him from his attempt to stay awake. As Fern's eyes began to focus, he could see Garrick's big ugly face staring back at him.

"Sir, whatchya doin?" asked Garrick, looking at Fern in bewilderment, though grinning from ear to ear.

"GARRICK!" yelled Fern. "I've found you!"

Garrick let out a giant snort of laughter. "My friend, I think I who found you."

Fern wobbled and swayed like gelatin as his head slowly regained its equilibrium.

"Where's Reagal?" asked Fern as a picture of worry stretched across his face. "Is he well, is he alive?!"

"Yes, yes, you not worry sir, Master Reagal safe with fairies of marshes. I come fetch you for them."

"But how did they know I was here?"

"Beg pardon, but how someone not know you here?" Garrick asked still smiling.

Fern looked at Garrick and dissolved into laughter. "I guess you're right; I was making quite the racket, wasn't I? I only wish I would've thought of this earlier,"

Fern began to laugh again. "Please, Garrick, take me to Reagal," he said after clearing his eyes of happy tears.

Garrick shook his head and picked Fern up like he was weightless, placed him on his shoulder, and ran through the marshes until they reached a row of willows. The trees created a long curtain of hanging branches, making it impossible to see beyond them. Garrick counted his footsteps as he walked sideways along the row of trees and stopped on the count of twelve. Parting the branches, he walked through. Just beyond the wavy wooden curtains, bright sunlight shone down onto a massive patch of dry land bordered as far as the eye could see by giant willows that cast the same hanging branch-like barrier. The fairy kingdom was made up of bright pink flowered meadows and lush green carpeted rolling hills. Birds sang sweet songs of spring, and trees sprouting fresh, large, green, star-shaped leaves gladly stood planted, shooting up tall through the clean air. A crystal-clear river ran swiftly through the middle of the land as pink and blue fish, resembling trout, leapt into the shimmering morning sunlight. Hundreds of purple dragonflies hovered over the flowers as Garrick found a pebble stone path dividing the meadows in two. Staring in awe, Fern could not understand how he could have missed such a place, and wondered even more how he missed the sunrise.

"Garrick, are we far from Reagal?" asked Fern.

"Not far, fairy's palace very close," he answered.

"How'd you find this place?"

"I not," answered Garrick. "fairies find me and take me here."

"What about Soma, did she come with you?"

"No, she flew once we enter marshes. I not see her since."

"Are the dwarves and centaurs here? And what of Dandowin and his elves?" asked Fern.

"I not seen them. We only be here short time," replied Garrick. "How *you* get to us so soon, and where rock?"

"I'll have to explain that at a later time, my friend, it's a long story. First, get me to Reagal. We must find out where the centaurs might be hiding."

"Hiding?"

"I will explain soon enough. Now please, hurry."

Garrick nodded and quickened his pace. As they ran over the path, Fern noticed exotic creatures darting out of sight, most of which he had never seen before. One, he later found out to be a Sun Bear, had massive legs attached to a gigantic bear-like body covered in an amber-yellow fur. There were three-legged creatures as well, known as Turning Wheels. They were small elvish beings that traveled by doing what looked like a cartwheel, but with extreme speed. Flying creatures zoomed into the trees as Garrick swiftly ran by. Giant Moon Wisps, which were no more than large beetles, and Flare Flies that were so brightly colored in orange and red they seemed to be set on fire as they flew by. It was a true sight to behold. Fern was so enchanted by the magic of the fairy kingdom that he nearly fell off Garrick's shoulder. Many times, he had to catch himself before hitting the ground.

Tall singular blades of grass with a ball of purple fluff resembling a dandelion capitulum swayed in a soft cool breeze, and Fern would slide his hand across them as Garrick hustled by. Large stones spotted in the fields began to move as the two came closer. Fern caught a glimpse of little stick-like legs protruding from underneath the stones as they moved further into the fields. He couldn't tell if the stones themselves were alive or if some creature used them as a protective shell of some sort.

Fern soon noticed the path begin to widen and Garrick began slowing his pace to a walk.

"We here!"

Fern looked around but saw absolutely nothing other than the landscape that had followed them to their current position.

"Where?" asked Fern turning his head from side to side.

Suddenly, Garrick let out an amazing roar, bursting several of the purple fluff grasses into the air sending twirling seeds to the ground. Fern fell from the giant's shoulder, hitting the path with a thud. Almost at once a fairy appeared in front of them both.

"Ah, Garrick, very good, you have found him," said the fairy as he reached out his hand and helped Fern to his feet.

Fern was surprised to hear a masculine voice coming from what he thought was a female. At closer review, Fern felt foolish, noticing the fairy had a square jaw and broad shoulders. His hair was long and dark blond while two green eyes graced his face. He was dressed in a glistening blue gown and secured around his waist was a silver belt.

"Greetings, Fern Majestic, my name is Lorew. I will lead you to your companion."

"Reagal? Is he going to be okay?" asked Fern without responding to Lorew's introduction.

"Yes, yes, you will not need to worry, he is conscious and healing as we speak," replied Lorew, forgiving Fern his rudeness. "Follow me, please."

Lorew turned and vanished from Fern's sight. Without hesitation or question, Garrick walked forward. Lorew suddenly reappeared in front of them. Fern was amazed to see they were now standing inside a beautiful palace. *We must have walked through an invisible barrier*, he thought. *Unbelievable!*

More to Fern's amazement was the palace itself. Lined in silver, the walls climbed to meet a cathedral ceiling made of glass that let the sun shine through. The palace was one gigantic room with no beams or columns to support its weight. Fern knew it must be magic holding the structure together. *Simply fantastic! And I thought the dwarves knew how to build.* Fern's face was a pure sight of wonder. His eyes darted in every direction so as not to miss a single experience.

Fairies gathered in groups throughout the palace. Some were seated on plush white pillows while others stood deep in conversation. Though, they would still take a moment to great Fern as he passed.

Noticing numerous translucent spheres filled with multi-colored mist floating in midair just above his head, Fern's neck arched like a crescent moon. Sumptuous trees bearing plump red fruit were planted in the floor which was no more than a lush layer of green grass. The trees freeform patterns gave the entire area a sweet succulent smell. Exotic birds in bright brilliant colors flew freely above the fruit trees but wouldn't stay still long enough for Fern to study them. Sun Bears, lay by the feet of fairies, lounging on large feather pillows, snoring softly in a deep slumber. Fern uncontrollably shook his head. *Now I've seen everything. This is utterly fantastic!*

"Garrick, can you believe this place?" asked Fern, eyes wide open.

"Yah, it nice," replied Garrick as he skipped alongside his friend.

Lorew led them down to the far end of the palace. Fern kept looking around trying to spot Reagal. To his surprise, he saw him lying down on a large feather pillow dressed in a white long-sleeved silk shirt and bandaged on his side, looking quite well.

"Reagal!" shouted Fern. "It's so good to see you, my friend!"

Fern, wrapping his strong arms around his friend's torso, squeezed him tight. Reagal gasped in a low whinny.

"I'm sorry, I nearly forgot you're still on the mend. I'm just so happy to see you!" Fern said, grinning from ear to ear.

"No apologies necessary, I am just as pleased to see *you* are still alive."

Fern suddenly turned to Garrick and wrapped his arms as far around him as he could. Garrick's eyes sprang open, cheeks turning pink, not understanding the sudden cause for emotion.

"Garrick, you're an amazing friend. I must commend you for everything you've done. Without you, we would never have made it this far. I thank you from the bottom of my heart. You're a hero."

The smile on Garrick's face spanned a mile as he turned a dark beet red.

"Now, we've so much to talk about," exclaimed Fern.

Just then Fern felt a soft touch upon his shoulder.

"My fair Majestic, I am pleased to see you have made it to our home unscathed."

Fern spun around to see Lillia standing before him, as beautiful as ever.

"Lillia!" blurted Fern.

Without realizing what he was doing, he grabbed her around her waist, lifting her clear off the ground, her bare feet dangling. Fern pulled her close with a loving embrace, hugging her gently.

"It is *so* good to see you!" said Fern as he released his grip. He could see Lillia's face turn a beautiful shade of pink. Reagal and Garrick smiled behind them.

"I do not mean to interrupt your reunion," said Lillia. "But we have important news to share with you and your group. Please, come with me, we have prepared some food you and your company can dine on as we share our information." Lillia turned as she finished speaking and led the three companions to an oval dining table.

Seated around the table were three fairies, two of which were male, and one female nearly as stunning as Lillia. Plated in front of every seat was a porcelain platter of fresh fruit and vegetables, accompanied by a glass of pure honey mead. Lillia took her seat. Fern sat next to her followed by Reagal, who lay on a pillow. Garrick, sitting on three pillows, was provided with an oval table of his own, piled high with the same fruit and vegetables as the others, and a large jug of honey mead.

"Good day, my friends, I am Forona, next to me is Gathriel, and to his left is Reannthane. We are here to share some unsettling news that has been discovered only this morning: A green dragon has been spotted just outside the borders of our land. We also have been told a human was seen speaking with the dragon just before he flew out of sight." Forona paused for a moment, her eyes fixating on Fern.

Not believing they had unknowingly been spotted, Fern knew at once his hosts were aware he was the human in question. He also knew it would be no use in trying to keep his relationship with Paliden a secret. Fern stood from his seat.

"I was the human seen with the dragon," said Fern, to the astonishment of Reagal and Garrick as they shifted suddenly, looking wide-eyed. Garrick even choked on a piece of his meal as his shock lodged a large chunk of fruit in his throat.

"He's saved my life and brought me here to you. I owe him much." Fern stood, back rigid, and unsympathetic. Garrick began to choke. Reagal calmly walked to his giant friend, and with one solid smack to Garrick's upper back, the bit of food dislodged from his throat. Fern still stood as Reagal slowly took his seat. Forona smiled and cleared her throat.

"No need to stand, Fern Majestic. Please, sit, and tell us how you came by this dragon," she asked. Fern complied and slowly sat back down.

"I met him as I was attempting to free Galeon from the dungeons of Loustof." Reagal nearly jumped up from his pillow.

"Galeon? Was ee alive?" shouted Reagal as his eyes stared down at Fern.

"Yes. I told him where you'd been taken and that you were badly injured. He left immediately to find you. To be honest, I was expecting to see him here," replied Fern, turning back to Forona. "The dragon was also a prisoner of Loustof, chained to a courtyard and left for dead. I freed him, and he flew me north to his kin."

His next words were stopped by a chorus of gasps.

"You were taken to his kin?" asked all three of the fairies at once.

With a quizzical look on his face he answered, "No, we never made it that far. We were struck down by an arrow, and I fell from his back, landing amongst the turgoyle army. They are gathering to a northern region of our world, between Dundire and the Land of the Drakes."

"How did you escape?" asked Forona.

"It was the green dragon who rescued me. He put his own life at risk for mine. He's not what you think."

"I doubt that is so, Fern Majestic. Dragons are known for their deception. We are sure his motives are for his gain, not yours," replied Forona.

"I mean no disrespect to you or your kind," said Fern looking toward Lillia. "But he has shown me no deception. I don't know what's happened in the past between the fairies and dragons, but he's saved my life, and I owe him my trust."

The three fairies turned to each other and spoke in a soft whisper for a moment before turning back to face Fern.

"Very well, Fern Majestic," spoke Forona. "We shall allow this dragon to remain close to our borders, but please heed our warning. We know dragons better than most; they are cunning and evil creatures that feed off the kindness of fair beings, such as yourself. You must not let this dragon, who has remained nameless, twist your thoughts against your loyal friends."

Fern could see the wisdom in Forona's eyes. He nodded his head in response.

Reagal suddenly spoke as the three fairies stood to take their leave. "I do not mean to trouble you, my good friends, but I am in deep worry for my broder."

Forona smiled gently and replied before Reagal was finished speaking. "Forget your worries, Prince of Valom, we have already dispatched a search party for Galeon. If he is near, we shall find him and bring him to you."

Everyone but Fern stood, bowed to one another and took their leave from the oval table.

"Wait, please! There is more that needs discussing. We have not spoken about the imminent war." Fern could not understand why this had not come up in their meeting, or how they could leave without a word on the matter.

Forona turned and looked Fern in the eyes, indifference plastered on her face. "I am sorry, Fern Majestic, we fairies are healers, we do not concern ourselves with war."

Fern turned and looked at Lillia, whose head hung low as to not make eye contact with him. Standing in shock, Fern's eyes sprung open, mouth slack-jawed, as the fairies departed from their company. Lillia trailed behind the three fairies, looking back at Fern as she walked away.

Fern swiftly turned to Reagal and Garrick. "Is this truly happening? How can they sit idly by and do nothing? They must understand that if this evil is left unchecked, it'll destroy our entire world, including this land." Still believing Edinword was behind the war Reagal and Garrick had no idea it was Timal Fern was referring to.

Reagal put his hand on Fern's shoulder with downcast eyes. "It is dee way of dee fairies. It as always been, and will always be."

Fern looked up, a sly expression etched on his face. "I've heard otherwise."

Reagal, bewildered by his response, quickly defended. "I av known dee fairies my entire life, which is considerable, and never av dae faltered from der beliefs. Whomever you av received dis knowledge from, I assure you it is misinformation."

"This might be," said Fern. "But I must speak to Lillia, I've an important question to ask her about her people. Plus, I need to convince her to persuade the fairies to join our fight. If what I've heard is true, we can't defeat this evil without their help."

Turning from Reagal, Fern could see Garrick sleeping on the floor with his head lying on a pillow. The giant's uproarious snores and excessive drooling made him smile. Reagal suddenly leapt in front of Fern, blocking his way.

"Please, tell me about my broder before you seek Lillia. I must know everyding," pleaded Reagal, unblinking.

"Of course, Reagal, forgive me. I've had so much weighing on my mind, but I'm afraid there's not much more I can tell. I went to Loustof with the intentions of rescuing your brother and having him carry me to Dundire. Unfortunately, he did not trust me, and when he heard of your injuries, he left without warning. I wish I had more to say. I've so much to ask you, and I promise I'll divulge everything that's happened to me since our last company, but first I *must* try to speak with Lillia."

Fern sprinted around Reagal and through the great hall of the fairies. Seeing Reannthane talking to another fairy in front of a beautiful fountain just inside the opening of a corridor, Fern approached speaking in a polite manner.

"Excuse me, I apologize for the interruption, but could you tell me where I can find Lillia?" asked Fern wide-eyed and unwavering.

"Certainly, I can take you to her chambers."

Reannthane bowed to the other fairy and escorted Fern through the corridor passed the fountain and up a winding staircase to a silver wooden door.

"Lillia is within," said Reannthane as he bowed and departed back down the staircase.

Fern gently knocked. "Enter," came a soft voice.

Opening the door, Fern observed Lillia sitting on a cushioned wooden stool in front of an ornate white washed dressing mirror, combing her long shimmering hair. The sun was beginning to set, and light shone through a window cast a glorious glow around her silhouette. It took a moment for Fern to catch his breath.

Lillia looked at him and smiled. "I did not expect to see you again this evening."

"I must speak with you," Fern said adamantly.

"Of course, Fern," replied Lillia with a brooding expression coming over her face.

Fern was taken aback at the sound of Lillia referring to him by merely his first name. Inhaling a deep breath, he finally managed to speak again. "Lillia, I don't mean to trouble you, and I'd never do anything to offend you, but I must ask a question that's been weighing on my mind."

Fern waited for a response, but Lillia remained quiet, watching him as he paced the wooden floor of her room. Fern sighed.

"I've heard that the fairies of the Blue Marshes are...dragons." Fern stopped and looked directly at Lillia. "Is this true?"

"No," answered Lillia in a calm voice. "It is true, however, that some of us can transform into blue dragons whenever we fear our lives are in danger." Lillia stood from her stool as she finished speaking and walked over to a large bed, covered in silver silk linen, and sat down. Raising her hand Lillia motioned to Fern to sit beside her. Immobilized and bug-eyed, Fern stood like a statue. Lillia smiled at the sight of him frozen in place.

"Do not worry, my Fern, as I said, we are not violent people; I will not bite. Come, sit."

Fern hesitantly walked towards the bed, still wide-eyed, and sat down next to her. Gently grasping Fern by the hand, Lillia caressed it as she peered lovingly into his eyes. Fern felt as if he had entered her soul; she was kind and caring, and somehow, he knew that he could trust her.

"Am I correct in assuming you felt a connection with me when we first met?" she asked.

Fern, slightly taken aback, wanted to shout out the answer: *of course!*

Instead, all he could do was nod yes.

"We are very similar, Fern," said Lillia with a slight smile. "So similar that we have shared dreams."

Fern couldn't quite understand what Lillia meant.

"Yes, my Fern, you have seen me in your dreams, as I have seen you in mine. It is a bond that each fairy gives to another."

Fern finally spoke, "To any other?"

Lillia's face gleamed, and she smiled from ear to ear.

"No, my Fern, only *one* other." She stared into Fern's eyes intensely. "I know you, Fern Majestic, and you know me. We have kept close in our dreams."

Fern took a large gulp, his blood pumped rapidly to his heart as it thundered from his chest, and he shook his head in realization.

"Yes, I...I understand, but why not tell me of this magic before now?"

"My Fern, we do not have control over our dreams. I knew not, and only after we met at Dundire did I realize what we shared was real. As I sat at your bedside in the—"

"What? You were there in the medical chambers?" exclaimed Fern baffled, having no idea or memory of this revelation.

Lillia's face blushed as she answered.

"Yes, my Fern, I only left your side when the kings called me to their council."

Fern, head uncontrollably shaking from side to side, remembered every dream, and finally understood why his feelings were so strong for the woman that sat next to him. *That is why they felt so real...they were!* Fern suddenly peered into Lillia's eyes.

"But how can *we* be connected so closely? I'm human, and you're fairy."

Lillia gave Fern a soothing look of comfort.

"You share a trait that all fairies of the Blue Marshes share. Like you, we too have dragon blood running through our veins. That is what connects us. The Elders of our kind were the creators of this magic, and the creators of every dragon in this world." Lillia could see the shock form on Fern's face as she continued. "The dragons you know today were once fairies of this land, but they could not control the power bestowed upon them and were cast out of the fairy kingdom. The power consumed them, permanently transforming them into their dragon forms."

Fern sat in astonishment trying to digest this news. His body began to quiver as his mind felt like a time bomb ready at any second to explode.

"But how's it possible to transform into a dragon?" Fern blurted suddenly.

"Firstly, there are only a few remaining in this world who can, and secondly, I am not one of those fairies," replied Lillia. "It is a power that has been passed down to the elders of our race nearly ten thousand years ago when the first fair folk came to be. The power is something we no longer want, and it will die with its possessors."

Fern stared for a moment searching for the correct words.

"I still can't understand why your kind refuses to help us in these times of war. They must understand our world is in jeopardy."

Lillia sighed and began to speak softly. "You must understand, we fairies have lived in peace for two thousand years. The last time we saw war, our kind was nearly extinguished from this world. The elders swore to never again lay hand on sword or shield. They cast a powerful barrier over our world that has kept our land safe. We will aid you and your allies with our magic of healing, but I am afraid that is all we can do."

Fern stood from the bed and paced the floor, footsteps heavy and chest heaving. Suddenly, he stopped and looked at Lillia. "Where can I find these elders you speak of?" Pleading was bursting from his eyes. "Please, Lillia, I must try!"

Lillia sighed deeply. "My dear Fern, they will not concede to your will. You must believe me, it will be a waste of your time." She stood from her bed and approached Fern, taking him by the hand again. Fern explored her eyes.

"I do believe you, Lillia, but it's worth a try."

Lillia dropped her head and slowly released his hand. "Very well," she said. "Follow me."

Lillia led Fern out of her room and down the staircase into the main palace. Fairies still stood throughout, conversing about gardening and potion making, oblivious to the happenings outside their own kingdom. Fern could only listen and shake his head in disbelief as he followed, until they arrived at a set of transparent glass double doors at the back of the palace, darkness behind them. Lillia turned to Fern.

"I must leave you here," she said.

Fern could see the sullenness in her eyes as she turned to walk away. As much as he wanted to go to her, he could not let it stop him from his goal.

With no handles of any kind, Fern pushed the doors open and walked inside. He stepped into oddity. Large with no windows, the room's only light that shone was from hovering flames suspended in the air above ten white Birchwood chairs positioned in a circle. In each chair sat an ancient fairy. Their thin bodies were garbed in dark blue robes with their eyes closed and their heads down. Their hair, which was bright white, hung in front of their faces, concealing them from Fern's eyes. Fern stood frozen in place once more. Suddenly, without movement, the fairies spoke in unison.

"Fern Majestic, we know why you have come. We know of Timal, and of Paliden." Their voices echoed as they spoke. "You have come seeking our help, which we will not grant."

"But why?" shouted Fern out of pure frustration.

"Fern Majestic, understand this: we fairies are the heart of this world. If we vanish, darkness will consume every corner of every land. We cannot let that happen. Our sun is a dying crippled star, and we are its life force. Without the fairies this world will be no more."

"But that'll happen regardless, if you sit idly and do nothing!" shouted Fern.

"You must help us destroy Timal and his armies! You must transform into the blue dragons."

"You are brave and strong, as all Majestics before you. You will face and defeat these enemies without out our help," replied the Elders.

Fern clenched his fists, trying to contain his anger. Lillia spoke correctly; there was no convincing them.

"If you will not help us, then please, tell me, is it possible for a Majestic to transform? I have dragons blood coursing through my veins...can you teach *me?*"

Fern, wanly expression on his face, waited for their response. Moments went by when suddenly they spoke.

"Tell us, do you have a pure heart?"

Fern thought to himself, not quite understanding the question.

"No," he answered. "I don't claim to be pure. I'm human and have made many mistakes in my life."

"Do you consider yourself strong in will and courage?"

"I believe myself a humble man, and don't care to boast of such things."

"And do you believe yourself to be a good and loyal friend?"

"Yes, that's something that I can say without a doubt," answered Fern, assured and eyes concentrated. "I have very few friends and would give my life for theirs."

The elders sat quietly.

Time lingered as Fern waited for them to speak. His impatience became overwhelming.

"Please, you must help us. I'm begging you!" shouted Fern.

Without warning, the elders levitated from their chairs and started spinning in a circle. Their blue robes lifted showing no bodies as a beautiful blue light started to appear in the center of the fairies. Fern felt himself being pulled into the light. He lifted into the air, suspended, and was engulfed by the luminous glow. He could feel his heart beating rapidly as the light was drawn within his body. Slowly, he descended back to the floor; he felt... nothing.

"Now GO!" shouted the fairies as they slowly lowered back into their chairs.

"But, I don't understand," replied Fern. "What has just happened?"

"GO!" shouted the fairies once more.

Fern slowly walked towards the exit. His confusion was at its height. He opened the glass doors and stopped, ready to plead his case one last time, but was astonished, turning around to see an empty chamber. The floating flames suddenly vanished and pure darkness was the only thing left in the room.

As Fern turned back and entered the main palace, he stood looking towards the floor trying to sense a change in his body.

"My young Majesteek."

Fern looked up to see Reagal standing in front of him with Garrick by his side. Reagal could see the troubled look on Fern's face.

"What appened?" asked Reagal.

"I'm not quite sure."

"Well, did you receive dee answers you sought?"

"No, not exactly," replied Fern. "I'm afraid we'll get no help from the fairies."

Reagal placed his hand on Fern's shoulder. "Fear not, young Majesteek, we will find a way," he said with surprising optimism.

"I truly hope so," said Fern as he lowered his head again. "I truly hope so."

Fern filled his two friends in on all that had happened to him from the moment Garrick left with Reagal upon his back until their reunion at the Blue Marshes. Reagal, usually stoic, shed a tear for his brother, and Garrick, easy to emotional fits, stood expressionless after hearing everything. Fern was somewhat puzzled by their roll reversals.

"I always want to fly on dragon," said Garrick suddenly.

Truly falling in love with his giant friend, Fern was a kite flying high in a summer breeze. Garrick's child-like personality was intoxicating. Fern found himself smiling at the mere sight of him. Looking up at the mighty giant, Fern's face beamed radiance.

"My friend, I swear to you, if I ever see Paliden again, and he allows it, you'll be the first to take a ride." Fern suddenly became stern and the smile on his face faded. "My friends, it's time to get to business. As you now know, our allies have gone missing. Timal is on the hunt as we speak, but we must locate them before he does. Reagal, you must know of where your father might go in times of danger."

Reagal shook his head. "I am afraid we av no secret iding place; we av never ad need of one."

"Then I'm at a loss," replied Fern.

Reagal turned to Garrick. "Garrick, my friend, in what direction did Soma fly when she left?"

Garrick's eyes rolled upward as he thought to himself. "Umm...let think, let think," he said. "Yes, northwest."

"Are you sure?"

"Without doubt."

"Well den, we av our direction," Reagal said with a smirk.

"But how is your strength?" asked Fern.

"Do not worry, I av enough strengd for all."

"Very well," said Fern. "We'll get an early start tomorrow morning."

11

INTO THE TUNNELS

Morning came quickly, and Fern found himself preparing for another journey with an uncertain end. The fairies supplied them with every necessity, and each member of the company was given a vial of healing potion. Lillia met them at the palace doors before their departure. She gave Reagal and Garrick a hug before turning to Fern. Grabbing him by the hand, she pulled him away from the others.

"My dear Fern, you must not leave this place with disdain in your heart. The Elders have bestowed a great gift upon you. The help you sought has been given. You must learn how to control this gift, for it is a power that most cannot. I fear for you." Lillia strained her eyes as she stared into Fern's. "My heart is yours, if you will have it. Please be safe. Someday you can return to me, but for now we will be joined in our dreams." She leaned in and kissed Fern on his cheek.

Fern could not find words as he stared, heart aching, and wondered as she walked away. *I'm falling in love with her*, he thought, *how is this possible? Through dreams? How can it be real?* Fern's mind suddenly shifted. *And how can I use this power, if indeed it was given? What power? Can I transform? These fairies are a strange bunch.*

Fern had felt no change since the incident with the Elders and found himself lost in thought pondering these questions. Of course, how could he truly concentrate on anything with Lillia constantly on his mind?

Fern rejoined Reagal and Garrick, and they all proceeded out the palace doors. They were met outside by Lorew.

195

"Ah, good morning my friends!" he said as he came bounding towards them in long elegant strides. "I will escort you to the borders of our land. After all, it would not be wise to come all this way just to end up sleeping in our marshes for months, now would it?" He let out a bellowing laugh. Though, asking Fern to join in Lorew's joviality at that moment was like trying to get a turgoyle to take a bath. So instead, Fern simply nodded his head to Lorew as he signaled Reagal and Garrick to follow.

The morning was sunny and cool, and the air crisp as the company made its way down the pebble stone pathway to the willow branches that separated the fairy kingdom from the marshes. Not much was spoken between the companions during their travel to the barrier, and the silence continued until they reached the border of Valom. Once there, Fern turned to Lorew and thanked him for the hospitality, and Reagal and Garrick did the same. They all said their farewells, and Lorew departed back into the marshes.

As the three stepped onto the land of Valom, Fern was half expecting to hear Paliden's voice echoing in his head. Instead, he heard Reagal.

"It seems Soma has flown nordwest, which would lead us to dee eastern part of Dundire. Do you av any idea where our allies could be iding?"

"Your guess is about as good as mine," replied Fern.

"But why they not in mountain, dragons can't see through stone. Timal no find them there," piped Garrick.

"No, Garrick, Timal was confident about his search efforts. He's desperate to locate them and has thoroughly searched each land and kingdom without success. They must be hiding in an unknown location. That I'm sure of," replied Fern.

Garrick suddenly looked away from Fern and placed his large hand upon Reagal's back. The gentle giant noticed the brooding look on the centaur's face.

"What matter, friend?"

Reagal patted Garrick, stretching his arm, barely reaching Garrick's shoulder with his hand.

"Dank you, for your concern, but I received no word on my broder. I fear for is life."

"He's a valiant warrior and a strong centaur; this I know firsthand," Fern said with a smile. "I'm sure he's made it to a safe place."

Reagal looked at Fern and nodded in thanks for his reassurance.

No need for instruction, Fern was already atop Garrick's shoulder as they proceeded through Valom towards the Land of the Stone Trolls. Noticing the looks on his companions' faces, Reagal assured them both it was the only way to the road north that led to Dundire.

Fern, with the best view, scanned the landscape around them and looked to the sky. His thoughts were on Paliden, and he wondered why he had not heard from him. *Why did Paliden tell me the fairies were dragons, when in fact the dragons were the ones who were once fairies?* Fern was determined to get answers, if ever he met Paliden again.

Noticing Fern continually watch the skies, Reagal asked a question.

"My friend, do you search for our enemy...or peraps you search for your dragon friend?" The word *dragon* caught Garrick's attention and he jumped, twisting in the air in excitement.

"Oh, I can't wait ride on dragon!" he shouted.

Fern was again smiling wide as he answered Reagal's question.

"I was searching for both, to be honest. Paliden promised me he would contact me once I left the marshes, but I've not heard from him, and Timal's dragons must still be searching for our allies, if they've not located them already, of course."

Fern looked down from the sky and turned to Reagal. "Tell me, my friend, I've been wondering about your brother ever since I learned of his capture in Valom. How was he taken?"

Reagal's face turned doleful. Fern immediately responded.

"I didn't mean to upset you."

Reagal, shaking his head, turned to Fern. "Do not worry, my emotions for my broder av been strained far before is capture by dee Loustofian soldiers."

Fern stared in wonderment as Reagal continued.

"Galeon is my older broder, and ee as always been far from typical. Is jealousy of me and atred to is king av led im to is current situation. Ee was captured as ee was leaving our land. Ee did not old the same ideals as my fader and I, and swore to us dat ee would prove imself a better leader of our kind. As you know, ee and a group of likeminded centaurs were banished from dee land of Valom by my fader, someding dat as never appened. Dee soldiers of Loustof, who were unknown to us at dee time, killed all but one of my broder's followers. Dat lone survivor crawled back to my fader mortally wounded and revealed to im of my broder's fate just before is dead. I wanted desperately to lead a search party for im, but was ordered by my king to do noding. I will regret dat decision for dee rest of my life." Reagal's head dropped to his chest once more as he let out a deep sigh. Fern was at a loss for words.

Garrick suddenly stopped.

"Uh oh. Look, friends," Garrick said as he pointed forward.

Before them was the land of the Stone Trolls. Suddenly, the memory of Randal's and Phillip's fate was all too fresh in their minds.

They looked at each other as if they knew what the other was thinking as they proceeded forward cautiously. The cliffs were more treacherous than Fern remembered, and not being on a horse made travel slow and difficult. Garrick, again, was wincing in pain with every step as his ankles continued to turn in abnormal directions. Reagal led the way with great ease, making sure they steered clear of any trolls. They were no more than a hundred yards in when Reagal spotted a shadow moving slowly against a large boulder.

"My young Majesteek—"

"I see it, my friend."

"What you see?" asked Garrick.

"Look, there," said Fern pointing towards an outcrop of rock.

The shadow crept, hugging the boulder, and then disappeared. A low moaning was heard. Closer it came. Shuffling feet dragged the rocky soil, and then... they saw him. Upon his chest, the Loustofian crest. Fern and Reagal held their heads down.

"That you, sir?" Garrick ran towards the man arms stretched forward.

"No! Garrick, stop!" shouted Fern.

Garrick skid to a halt, twisting his ankle in the process, biting his tongue to stop from wailing in pain.

"But sir, it Phillip," replied Garrick, eyes and face scrunched in agony.

The empty shell that was once Phillip of Loustof gargled as saliva dripped from his mouth and down to his chin. He shuffled aimlessly through the Land of the Stone Trolls, his eyes, fixed and glazed, free from emotion. Garrick stood, his doleful face told his two companions that he finally understood. Phillip had been infected by the turgoyle resin. There was nothing they could do for their lost companion, nothing...except—

Fern pulled his sword from its scabbard and slowly walked past Garrick. Garrick, with eyes filled to the brink, watched as Phillip was taken from his misery. Reagal trotted gently to Garrick and patted his back softly. Fern slumped towards them, head dropped, wiping his sword with downward swipes on his trousers, streaks of Phillip's blood striping his pants.

"Can you—" Fern paused, swallowing the lump in his throat. "We need to bury the body."

"Do not worry, my young Majesteek, I will retrieve poor Philleep from dee ground."

"No, sir!" exclaimed Garrick, tears trickling down his cheek. "He my brother Loustofian, I get him."

Reagal nodded his head, grinning in respect. Garrick's chest tensed as he lifted Phillip's unusually cold, limp body from the ground. Although, Phillip was light, Garrick's breath labored. The three companions searched the area, Garrick still holding the body in his arms, until they found it...the boulder that held Randal's body, crushed against the rock. Sufficing as his final resting place, and using their swords, Fern and Reagal dug a shallow grave next to where Randal had perished. Garrick gently lay Phillip inside the rocky hole, and with his giant hands, swept the dirt and stone over his corpse, patting it softly.

Garrick stood, surprisingly stoic, and spoke.

"They good men, loyal men. Phillip and Randal, good soldiers, good brothers. They be missed."

Fern and Reagal both gave their respects and laid their hands upon the graves looking back at Garrick with sympathetic smiles.

The company gathered themselves quickly, not lingering long, before setting off through the treacherous land once more. Taking no chances, they moved through the rock at a crouch, keeping out of sight. Suddenly, out of the corner of Fern's eye, he saw something move past a rock high on one of the cliffs a distance away.

"Reagal, it seems we're going to have a busy day," said Fern in a whisper as he pointed towards the boulder. "Did you see it?"

"No, but I am sure I just eard someding. It sounded like a soft clicking coming from dat direction." Reagal pointed towards the cliff.

The band halted and found cover behind a large outcropping of rock that gave them a good vantage point of the cliff.

"Garrick, can you see anything," asked Fern.

"Yes, sir, something move up there, but I not know what it is."

"What do you dink?" asked Reagal.

"I figure if it was a troll, we would be able to see it from this position, and if it saw us we would've been attacked by now," replied Fern. "It must be some other creature."

"But what kind of being would be foolish enough to travel in dis part of dee world?"

"Besides us?" Fern asked, almost laughing.

Garrick's eyes suddenly burst open wide.

"I see it!" he whispered. "It a horse...no, wait." Garrick's head bobbed up and down like a duck in a pond, trying to get a better look. "It like...like...you, master Reagal."

Fern stood and leapt onto Garrick's shoulder to see for himself, making sure not to be spotted. He quickly jumped back down.

"There's a centaur upon that cliff, no doubt. It doesn't look like he's seen us yet. Do you think it could be Galeon?"

"Our doughts are dee same, but der is only one way to find out. I will go to greet my kin. You and Garrick must remain out of sight, for it might be a trap," answered Reagal.

"Reagal, you should know me better by now," replied Fern. "I'll not let you face any peril without me."

He turned to Garrick and the giant nodded his head in agreement. Reagal looked at them both as he shook his head, knowing all too well there would be no use in arguing.

"Very well, my stubborn friends, but stay a distance behind, in case it is an ambush. Der is no need for all of us to be captured." replied Reagal.

Reagal lead them, dashing behind rock and boulder as quietly as possible. Garrick was at a crawl, making sure he was completely hidden, until they were directly beneath the cliff. Hooves could be heard clacking on the rock above. Reagal, nearly dragging himself against the stone, inched his way around the face of the cliff towards a narrow incline. It circled around until he came to a level area at the top. Just beyond sat several boulders. The sound of the hooves started to fade as he made his way towards them. Fern and Garrick stood a few yards back keeping their eyes peeled for anything suspicious. Reagal quickened the pace. He moved swiftly, taking cover behind one of the boulders. Turning to Fern, Reagal motioned him to stay hidden. He then stepped out from around the boulder into the open. Having an unimpeded view, Reagal could see the centaur peering over the cliff surveying the surrounding land. To his elation, he immediately recognized the centaur.

"Aadoo!" shouted Reagal.

The centaur spun around, startled by the unexpected voice.

"Capteen Reagal! By Valom's Star, you are alive!"

The centaur came galloping towards Reagal with amazing speed.

"I av been searching for you and dee Majesteek for days! I ad all but given up ope!"

Aadoo suddenly looked around, noticing Fern was nowhere to be seen.

"Capteen, where is ee?"

Just then Fern and Garrick stepped out from behind the rock. Aadoo nearly jumped back off the cliff at the sight of Garrick.

"My young Majesteek, Garrick, come meet one of my fader's most valiant guards," said Reagal as Fern and Garrick quickly made their way up to the cliff.

Aadoo bowed quickly at the introduction. Fern was astonished at how much larger he was compared to Reagal. He stood just slightly taller, but his broadness was immense. His coat was jet black from head to hoof, making the whites of his eyes piercing. His face was like Reagal's, only wider, and he was fully armored carrying a spiked flail.

"Please, Capteen Reagal, I do not mean to be disrespectful, but we av no time. I must get you to your fader as quickly as possible." Aadoo spoke in a deep foreboding voice with great urgency.

"Then you know where they are hiding?" interrupted Fern.

"Yes, of course, and we must not dawdle. Dee Stone Trolls are out in numbers and would kill us wid pleasure if dae find us out ere unprotected," replied Aadoo. "Follow me, I will explain everyding on dee way."

He turned and quickly led them off the cliff. As they made their way down through the jagged rock, Aadoo revealed that the three armies had all met in Dundire as planned and were preparing to invade Loustof. But an army of dragons attacked them before they could make it out the gates, forcing them to retreat into the mountain. Reagal quickly interrupted Aadoo, informing him that Timal was the evil behind the plot for world domination, and that Edinword was nothing but a scapegoat.

"Den where is Edinword?" asked Aadoo.

"Dee young Majesteek as released im. We do not know what as become of im," replied Reagal. "Tell me, Aadoo, where as my fader retreated to, and are dee oders wid im?"

"Yes, dae are all united, dae av taken refuge benead dee ground. We are actually very close to dee entrance."

Reagal looked quite shocked.

"Are you telling me dae are in dee lairs of dee Stone Trolls?"

"Yes, Capteen, we av pushed dee beasts out of der omes into dee wild and av taken control of every underground lair in dese lands. King Soleece as been meaning to rid our kingdom of does orrid creatures for some time. Ee figured, what time would be better den now, especially wid dee elves and dwarves helping us. It was quite easy, actually. Our casualties were few, and now we av a iding place dat no one would suspect."

"But how did you get here without Timal's army of dragons spotting you?" asked Fern.

"Anoder easy task. Dee dwarves av secret tunnels dat form a complicated system of roads idden undernead der mountain, which connects to all our lands. Dae had no choice but to reveal dim to us, given dee circumstances. Dae are so well idden dat not even dee keen eyes of dee elves could spot dim. Timal will av no chance at finding us."

"Amazing!" Reagal and Fern said in unison.

"But where Soma?" asked Garrick suddenly.

"And Galeon, did ee make it to my fader," asked Reagal, not giving Aadoo a chance to answer Garrick's question.

"I am afraid dat Galeon as not been eard of since ee was taken by dee soldiers of Loustof, and to be honest, Capteen Reagal, I am not sure your fader would welcome im. Der as been no sight of Soma as well," answered Aadoo with a puzzled look upon his face.

Reagal took a heavy breath and shook his head, hoping that his brother was still alive.

"Please tell me Capteen, as Prince Galeon escaped dee dungeons of Loustof?"

"Yes Aadoo, dee young Majesteek as freed im."

Aadoo immediately turned to Fern with his fist to his chest and bowed in great appreciation.

"Den it is as your fader ad foreseen," exclaimed Aadoo.

"Foreseen? What has he foreseen?" asked Fern.

Reagal looked to Aadoo with a stern expression upon his face.

"I am sorry, I should not av let my tongue loose. We are forbidden to reveal our king's readings before dae fully come to be. Please forgive me."

Great, thought Fern, *another question that will go unanswered.* Suddenly, he drew his sword.

"Trolls!" he whispered.

In front of them sat two Stone Trolls with their heads hanging down on their chests. In between them was an opening, barely noticeable, naturally concealed by overhanging stones. The stones cast shadows over the ground in front of the opening, making it invisible from above.

"Please, put your sword away. Dae are noding more den decoys. Dese are two slaughtered trolls from our earlier battle. We are using der bodies to deter anyone from coming close to dee entrance. And as you can smell, dese disgusting bodies won't last much longer."

Fern sheathed his sword, and they all followed Aadoo into the lair of the trolls. As they walked through the entrance, Fern could feel the temperature drop rapidly. The cool air was welcoming to all. The only light present was from the opening, which quickly dissipated as they walked further underground.

"Aadoo, I can't see in front of me," said Fern.

"Old on to my tail. We are nearly der," replied Aadoo.

The troll's lair was nothing like the tunnels of the quaggoths. The ground was unleveled, and the walls were jagged with dull protruding rocks, which Fern and Garrick discovered with their heads every few steps.

"How much further, Aadoo, I don't think my head can take much more of this constant pounding," said Fern.

"I am sorry, I did not realize yours and dee giant's eyesight was so poor. Do not worry, we will be der soon."

I did not realize the centaurs could see so well in such darkness. Fern thought it funny how little he knew about his friends, but enjoyed learning everything he could.

Aadoo and Reagal came to a halt, causing Fern and Garrick to bump into them.

"We are ere," announced Aadoo. "It might take me a few moments to remember dee combination to dis door. Dee dwarves are clever beings who seem to delight in confusing less ingenuitive creatures like myself."

Fern could not see what invention the dwarves had created, but was later informed by Reagal it was a set of stones that had to be inserted into numerous openings in the lair wall. Each stone was placed at a certain angle and pushed in, releasing internal levers that opened a hidden door.

Aadoo finally managed to remember the combination, and several loud clicks later, a large door slowly slid open, sending a flood of light towards Fern's face. The four companions walked through the doorway into an enormous underground base. Dwarves, centaurs, and elves crowded the cavernous area, all clad in armor and bearing weapons. The clanks of metal and sounds of voices made it difficult to hear one's thoughts. Aadoo shouted as he pushed his way in like a plow, leading the group through.

"Please make room! Prince Reagal, son of Soleece has arrived!"

The centaurs, those who could hear through the noise, pushed their way forward and bowed to Reagal.

Forcing their large frames in front of Aadoo, they parted a path through the crowd. Reagal was closely behind them, followed by Fern and Garrick. Thousands of warriors gathered throughout numerous underground lairs. Fern could barely believe the sight of the massive armies all congregating together peacefully beneath the earth. Astonishment was an understatement, as they made their way deeper underground as the sights became even more impressive. Dwarves could be seen hammering on red molten steel, fashioning new weapons for their armory. Makeshift stables of wood and stone housed unicorns and horses in shimmering armor. The beautiful beasts calmly awaited their dwarven and elven riders. Fern quickly noticed the spiral horns of the unicorns clad in a sheath of silver armor. Stone tables, once used by the trolls, now seated elves and dwarves as centaurs stood around them conversing about strategies of war.

Fern smiled watching Garrick as they continued to make their way deeper underground. The giant's mouth stretched open as he walked at a slight crouch trying to clear the ceiling. Reading his lips, Fern watched as he mouthed, in silence, *wows* and *amazings*.

Through their numerous conversations, Fern learned that Garrick had always wanted to become a knight. He also knew he was never allowed to become a warrior when he was in Loustof, and that King Edinword personally told him that becoming a gate keeper would be his only accomplishment in life. It was easy to imagine his emotions as he passed through the ranks of soldiers standing before him, knowing this might be his chance to live out his dreams. Reagal, on the other hand, seemed quite nervous. He continued to look around as if he was searching for someone or something. Suddenly, Fern noticed his eyes as he found what he was looking for.

"VILORIA!" shouted Reagal.

Fern was amazed at the strength of his voice as it rose above the crowds and made its way to the ear of its target. A centaur came hurtling through the multitude of warriors straight to Reagal. Fern discerned no difference in this centaur from the rest until it removed its helmet and long dark hair flowed down to its back. She stood stern, with high cheekbones and a thin face. She had light brown eyes that tilted slightly inward toward a small nose that fit perfectly above her full-lipped mouth.

Pulling Viloria to his chest, they embraced. Fern could barely hear them as they spoke in their language, and could not understand what was told, but understood the emotion. Reagal suddenly stopped and turned to Fern and Garrick as Aadoo continued walking, not realizing that they had stopped.

"May I introduce you to my life mate, Viloria."

Fern and Garrick both bowed. Fern could not believe Reagal had never mentioned he had a wife.

"I see she's a warrior," said Fern.

"Of course," whinnied Reagal. "I would not give my art to any lesser."

"I'm sorry my friend, I didn't mean to offend," replied Fern quickly. "I've never met a female warrior before; we don't have them where I come from."

"Well den, my young Majesteek, now you av met dee best."

Viloria blushed slightly.

"I am only as good as my training allows, my love," replied Viloria with confident pride.

Aadoo interrupted, yelling as he came galloping back to the company.

"Please, Capteen, you must not linger, we need to get you to your fader wid aste!"

"Of course, of course," replied Reagal as he turned to Viloria. "Viloria, my love, I will see you after I meet wid my fader."

She bowed to them without argument and retreated into the crowd as the company followed Aadoo once again.

Aadoo approached a large blank stone wall at the back of the lair and grabbed a torch that hung to his right. In front of him was another set of stones, but instead of inserting them into the wall, Aadoo began setting them into openings carved out of the ground. Each opening had a symbol engraved in the center of it. Aadoo picked up the first stone and placed it above the torch. When the stone encountered the flame, a symbol matching one on the ground was revealed. Aadoo proceeded to lay the corresponding stones in each opening until all were in place. Fern could hear slight clicking noises as the last stone was laid into the ground. A hidden door appeared in the center of the wall and slid open. Fern could not believe the engineering of the dwarves. Ever since Dundire, his admiration for them was great, and after seeing the ingenious design of the secret doors, his admiration only grew.

Aadoo led them through the doorway and into a large circular room. Fern immediately noticed numerous tunnels leading out. In the center of the room was a circular stone table, around which stood the three kings.

"Ah hah, son, dank Valom you are still alive!" said Solace as he came galloping towards Reagal. "And young Majesteek, I am pleased to see you are still wid us." Solace gave Fern a strange look after saying it, confusing him greatly, before turning to Garrick. "And who might dis large fellow be?" he asked, looking up at the giant.

"Dis is Garrick. Ee is a great warrior, and I would not be standing ere if not for im," exclaimed Reagal.

Garrick immediately blushed and bowed to Solace.

"It is I who should be bowing to you, my mighty friend."

Solace bowed to Garrick, making his face turn a darker shade of pink than even Fern had witnessed. By this time, King Ardin of the dwarves and King Dandowin of the elves were standing amongst them.

"Oi, me boy, it does us good to see both of you alive and well," bellowed King Ardin. "And it is even better to see we have a giant joining our ranks."

"Yes, it is a welcoming sight, considering their dwindling population," said King Dandowin as he bowed to all. "But we must commend Aadoo for finding them."

"I dank you for dat, King Dandowin, but in all honesty, dae found me," replied Aadoo, bowing to the elven king.

"Oi, very well, very well, now that we have done away with the silly pleasantries, we must find out what life-saving news our three companions have brought for us," interrupted King Ardin.

Both Reagal and Garrick turned to Fern. He began explaining everything for what felt like the hundredth time.

"I'm sorry, my kings; I've failed you. Without the Ulmeck Rock, I can't see a way to defeat Timal's army," said Fern after his long recap.

King Ardin stepped forward and placed his hand on Fern's shoulder.

"Me boy, you must not think yourself a failure. After all, without you we would have never figured out that blasted Timal was leading the turgoyles. Not only that, but we might have a dragon of our own on our side."

"I'm not sure about Paliden," replied Fern. "He was supposed to contact me when I left the marshes, but I haven't heard a word from him since we parted nearly two days ago."

King Dandowin stood directly in front of Fern.

"Ardin, you might as well confess to the young Majestic."

"Confess! What on harth are you talking about, silly fellow?" bellowed King Ardin, shaking his head as he walked away.

"Very well, if you will not tell him, then I will," replied King Dandowin, slightly annoyed.

"Tell me what?" questioned Fern.

"I am sorry to say that your quest to retrieve the Ulmeck Rock was unnecessary."

"Unnecessary? What are you talking about?"

"Do you see these tunnels leading in all directions?" asked Dandowin.

"Yes, of course," replied Fern.

"Well, our stocky friend over there, and his ingenious band of dwarven engineers, have constructed a secret system of tunnels throughout our lands, one of which leads straight to the base of the Ulmeck Mountains. If he would have divulged this earlier, it could have saved you and your companions a great deal of trouble."

King Ardin came scurrying over to interrupt.

"Yes, yes, this might be true, but you must look at it in a different light. If I had revealed the tunnels to them, they would never have known of Timal's ambition, or found their giant friend, or saved the centaur, or met the dragon! So, you see, I have done them a great service!"

King Ardin pushed his chest out in pride.

"My dear dwarven king, your head is about as hard as the Ulmeck Rock we seek," replied King Dandowin, shaking his head in disbelief.

"But that means there is still a chance of making the arrows!" shouted Fern with growing hope.

King Dandowin looked over to King Ardin, whose chest had deflated, as King Solace entered the conversation.

"It as already begun" said the king of the centaurs as he trotted over to King

Ardin and patted him on the back. "Once Ardin eard of your misfortunes, ee sent is dwarves to collect dee Ulmeck Rock and bring it back to dese caves. Is dwarven smids av been forging dee arrows for days now."

"But ow did ee know of our misfortunes?" asked Reagal, astounded by everything that was just revealed.

"Soma," answered King Solace.

"Den she is ere?" shouted Reagal.

"No, I am afraid not, my son. I av sent er out again, looking for your broder, but she as not returned as of yet."

Reagal turned to Fern only to see him pacing the room lost in thought.

"My young Majesteek, please share your ponderings."

Fern stopped immediately and abruptly turned to everyone.

"We can win this war. Now that we have the Ulmeck Rock arrows. We can win!"

"Not so fast, me boy," King Ardin said with concern. "We haven't told you of the dragons we retreated from back at my kingdom."

"What about them?" said Fern, trying to think what else could possibly hinder their victory.

"The dragons that attacked us at Dundire wore armor made from the very same stone we are forging our arrows from."

The hope that came so quickly to Fern diminished. He knelt, realizing this entire time Timal had known about the Ulmeck Rock. Fern could not believe he was so naïve as to think he was the only one to have discovered it, and he suddenly realized that Paliden's chains, and the battle axe used to free him, were made from the rock. *How could I have been so blind*, he thought. Fern sat reliving every moment since the day he met King Edinword, not believing his missteps and wasted time. Lost in his own self-pity, he suddenly felt a hand on his shoulder. Fern looked up to see Reagal and Garrick both wearing wide smiles.

"You must not lose faid. We cannot change dee past, and dwelling on it will only lead to despair. Rise, my young Majesteek. We av dee advantage. Danks to King Ardin's tunnel system, and your knowledge of Timal's whereabouts, we can take our enemy by surprise." Reagal's reassuring voice was calming, and Fern rose to his feet.

"I'm sorry. You are right my friend, now is not the time to lose hope." Fern paused and looked directly into the eyes of his friends. "I've lived all my life without the companionship of friends, and now that I have you, I don't want to lose you. You have both saved my life numerous times. I promise you I'll repay that debt, and I'll do whatever it takes to help stop Timal from destroying your lands."

"Good, good, me boy, that is what I like to hear!" bellowed King Ardin. "Now, enough with the emotions, let's get down to my plan of attack."

"*Our* plan of attack, my modest friend," said King Dandowin as he pointed to the round table in the middle of the room. "Please gather 'round."

Reagal and Fern made their way to the edge of the stone table. Garrick stood back, trying to stay out of the way. Laying on top of the table were two rolled up maps secured with strands of unicorn hair.

"Garrick, this involves you as well. Come join us," said Fern when he realized Garrick was missing from the company.

Garrick could not believe he was being asked to participate in something so important. He hesitantly made his way over to Fern moving with shuffling feet, almost expecting to hear the kings order him back, but no one did. Instead, the kings of the world parted and gladly let Garrick stand amongst them. Fern stood by his side with his hand placed firmly on the giant's lower back, which still caused him to stretch his arm to its limit. Garrick gazed at his company grinning from ear to ear.

King Ardin reached for one of the maps and unrolled it, laying it flat on the stone table to reveal the entire dwarven tunnel system. King Dandowin held its corners as King Ardin unrolled the second map, laying it directly over the first. This map was a thin layer of Glass Spider hide, a transparent depiction of every kingdom, and when placed directly over the first, showed the exact route each tunnel traveled. Fern spotted their current position almost the exact moment King Ardin placed the second map on the first. King Dandowin placed a stone on each corner of the maps to hold them down.

"As you can all see, this map lays out the exact route of every tunnel and its exit into each land."

King Ardin suddenly interrupted. "All but the Fairy kingdom. Those blasted sprites have a powerful spell barring anything from entering without their say."

"Furthermore," continued Dandowin, slightly annoyed by the interruption. "You will notice there are three separate tunnels leading north to the Land of the Drakes. One to the southern part, another in the east, and finally one entering its western border. If what the young Majestic has told is true, and Timal's army is still within this land, then we will be able to attack him on three fronts. We have decided we shall lead our armies in these separate directions. I will go to the southern exit, King Ardin to the western border, and King Solace to the east."

"But where are we in all of this?" asked Fern.

"I have been contemplating that question ever since you arrived, and I have come to an answer. Your mention of the Dragon has intrigued me. If you could find him and persuade him to join us, we would be that much closer to victory. I suggest you take Garrick and scour these lands. Find Paliden, fly to the closest tunnel exit, and wait for our army."

"But what if we can't find him, or better yet, convince him to join us?" asked Fern.

King Dandowin looked at Fern and Garrick with a stern face.

"You must figure that out for yourselves."

"But what bout Reagal?" piped Garrick.

King Solace stood next to his son and placed an arm around him.

"Reagal will be coming wid me, ee as an army to lead."

Reagal stepped back from King Solace.

"I am sorry, fader, but I will not forsake my friends, I wish to join dim on der search."

"No, my son, you cannot!" shouted King Solace to the astonishment of all. "I am sorry for my outburst, but I cannot grant your request. You must command your soldiers; dae will expect it!"

"I can leave dat audority to Aadoo. Ee is well respected amongst my soldiers. I will announce it to dim myself and dae will serve im in my stead," argued Reagal.

Aadoo stepped forward and bowed to Reagal.

"It would be an honor, my Capteen."

"No! You will lead your army yourself!"

Everyone stood perplexed, knowing King Solace was normally in control of his emotions. First the strange look, now this. *What does he know? What has he seen in the stars?* Fern stood, wondering what could be causing the king of centaurs' sudden waywardness. And what's more, Fern could not believe Reagal's defiance. He knew his friend's unbounding loyalty to his king. *He can't truly be doing this for Garrick and myself.* Fern could not imagine that another soul would risk so much for the likes of him.

"Reagal, my son, please, you must do as I command. I am your king."

Reagal stepped closer to his father and stood tall.

"I am well aware of dat, and never av I gone against your word, but I av gone too far wid my friends to abandon dim now, and I owe boad of dim my life. My elp will be ders, and I *will* be accompanying dim. Dat is my final word."

King Solace stood with his head hanging as he paced the floor.

"You will do dis to me? Av you already forgotten your broder? NO! I cannot grant you dis! If you go, know dat you go against dee commands of your king."

King Solace marched from the room, hands clasped behind his back and head slumped.

"Huh, strange!" bellowed King Ardin. "I have never seen him so unhinged before. He must know something we do not. I suggest you be on your guard, my four-legged friend."

Reagal nodded to Ardin and turned facing Dandowin.

"Excuse me, King Dandowin, but when do you plan on setting out?"

"We will leave in the morning. Our armory is fully stocked, and our warriors fully equipped. There is no reason to linger any longer."

"Good, then we shall leave in the morning as well," replied Fern, looking to his two companions. "With any luck, we'll be waiting for you with a dragon on our side. As for now, I suggest we all get some rest, it's going to be a long day tomorrow."

With everyone in agreement, the two kings left the room to prepare their armies, leaving Fern, Reagal, Garrick, and Aadoo standing around the stone table.

"Well, sirs, I not sure 'bout you, but I could eat mountain troll right now," said Garrick as his belly rumbled with hunger.

"Yes, we should all get some food. We'll need as much energy as possible. There's no telling how long it'll take to find Paliden," answered Fern.

Aadoo stepped forward.

"Follow me, I will show you where to find someding to eat. Dee elves av brought more food den can be consumed by all. Aldough, now osting a giant, our supplies might run short," laughed Aadoo.

Fern stared at Reagal as Aadoo led the group out of the circular room and back through the crowded lairs to another tunnel. Reagal's solemn face quieted the group, and his slumped posture ached Fern's heart. *My friend could use a stiff drink*, thought Fern.

They reached a large open cavern where soldiers stood feasting on elven breads and drinking a sweet elven brewed beer called Atroot Ale, made from the At trees found in the forest of Alkyle. Garrick's mouth started to water as he came into the room and saw piles and piles of food and neatly stacked kegs of beer against a stone wall.

"Please, my friends, elp yourselves," said Aadoo.

Garrick and Fern both made their way through the masses. Loud, boisterous, speech filled the caverns, and chuckles, and downright gut-busting laughter, rang in the stale air. *Not sure if this is the proper activity that should be happening on the eve of battle*, thought Fern. Meanwhile, Aadoo held Reagal's arm, leading him back into the tunnel.

"Please Capteen, forgive my audacity, but I must explain your fader's actions. King Solace as confided in me is foresight. Ee knew Galeon was released from dee dungeons of Loustof by dee young Majesteek, and ee as seen a most tragic end to is son's life in is star readings…ee as seen your dead. It involves dee young Majesteek. Dee king does not know ow it will appen, or when, but ee is convinced what ee as seen will come to pass."

"Aadoo, you should not av told me dis, it goes against everyding we av ever been taught. If it is my fate to die fighting next to my friends, den die I will. I am not going to abandon dim."

Reagal marched back into the room, his mind cramped with worry. His saddened eyes lifted as he saw Fern and Garrick eating a large loaf of bread, each holding a mug of beer.

"Ah, Reagal, where did you go off to?" asked Fern.

"Oh, I was just giving Aadoo instructions on leading my men into battle."

Garrick reached back, grabbing another loaf of bread from the top of the pile and handed it to Reagal while Fern passed him a mug of the elven brew.

"I suggest we be light on the drink. I would like it if I had my head tomorrow." Fern gave a grin as he gulped a swallow of the brew. "And I know you are a stout man, my friend, but I'm afraid ale is all we've got." Fern smiled as Reagal took a swig from his mug.

"Yes…yes, ale will av to suffice," replied Reagal with downturned eyes and a solemn grin. The pain of defying his father, and the added weight of Aadoo's reveal, left Reagal pondering much.

Fern could feel his sorrow from a mile away. It was time to cheer up his good friend.

So, for the next few hours, the three friends sat talking about the joys in their lives, and what they would do after the war was over.

Hoping that his skills in battle would impress, Garrick spoke his dreams out in words."

"King Ardin maybe make me commander of dwarf army, that be fun…or…or, King Dandowin maybe let me join elves as knight! I always want be knight." Garrick's dreams continued to grow the more beer he consumed.

Fern never stopped his consumption of ale, and listened to Garrick as the giant continued to talk. *I wonder if any amount of drink can submit such a man*, thought Fern with a smile. But at that moment, Garrick began speaking about becoming the new king of Loustof, and Fern realized his question had its answer.

"I be gooooood king, and, and, and, nice kingy-wingy. Lah, lah-lah-lah-lah-lah. Kingy-wingy!"

Reagal smiled crookedly and slapped Garrick upon his knee as he swallowed a large chunk of bread, nearly choking on it as Fern dropped to the floor in laughter.

Reagal lifted Fern from his hysteria and took a gulp of brew as he began to reveal his own aspirations. "I want noding more dan to raise a family wid my life mate Viloria," he said. "My only ambition is to av a son, whom I can teach and raise in dee ways of my forefaders." Fern was not laughing any longer, even though Garrick continued to sing 'Kingy-wingy' in the background.

Furthermore, Reagal admitted, once he drank enough that is, that a daughter might be nice as well, one that looked like Viloria.

Strange, not once has he mentioned becoming king, thought Fern.

By the end of the night, Reagal had plans for at least twelve children, eight boys and four girls, and all with names already decided. Of course, a list of names is available, if one is interested in such things.

Fern belly laughed, with Garrick barely able to keep his eyes open, (still singing 'Kingy-wingy,' of course), and advised Reagal that he might want to discuss his thoughts with Viloria first.

"Ah, my young Majesteeeeek, If-if leefft t-to Vilooorriia, weee avvv twenty ch-ch-childreen."

Fern nearly choked on his bread as he rolled to the floor again, laughing like a crazed lunatic.

Suffice it to say, no one listened to Fern's suggestion about drinking in moderation. They were all too far gone, and Fern crawled from the ground pulling himself to his seat, and sat, balancing like the top potato on a steep pile; the slightest touch wound send him tumbling to the ground.

Realizing how intoxicated they all were, Fern began telling his friends how grateful he was, and how honored he felt that they would be fighting side by side. He confessed that his longing desire was to know someone that he would be willing to die for.

"I-I-I l-l-ove yoooouu booth, you are good f-friends!" Fern smiled like a village idiot as he gave Garrick a large kiss on his forehead.

Suddenly, Garrick slumped forward and hit the top of a keg that they were using as a table. Fern and Reagal laughed hysterically, propped their giant friend up against a stack of kegs and grabbed another beer. Within seconds, Garrick was fast asleep, snoring like a buzz saw, and drool slipped from his lower lip as his mouth hung open. Reagal smiled and stood, wobbly as a newborn baby horse.

"M-m-y young Ma-j-jesteek, ahh will paaart your cooompany for dee remaindeeer of dee night, for I-I av a beautiful waaarrior waiting for me dat I av not seeeen in sometime. I will see yoouu in dee morning."

Reagal bowed, nearly falling on his face, and left Fern sitting next to a snoring Garrick. Fern could only think of Lillia as he swayed like a reed. The kindness she showed him at the fairy palace, her soft caress and gentle manner, soothed his mind. His heart begged for her presence as he eventually rested his head on Garrick's knee and fell asleep.

12

AN UNEXPECTED ALLY

Fern awoke in an empty cavern, alone on the floor. The solitude that had accompanied him his entire life was now frightening. Memories of his loneliness as a child gripped his mind as his blurred eyes searched the room for Garrick and Reagal. He felt like a complete fool seeing only empty chairs and vacant tables. *How could you let yourself do this? If you can't even control your actions in moments like these, how do expect to help your friends when the time comes. You're a fool, Fern Majestic! Pull yourself together!* He grabbed a fallen stool and hoisted himself to his feet just in time to see Reagal and Garrick enter the room. A sigh of relief burst from Fern's chest.

"Good morning!" chuckled Reagal. "I see dee elven brew as rested you doroughly, but do not worry, it as no ill side effects." Reagal laughed loudly as he and a grinning Garrick approached.

Fern brushed dust from his shirt and ran his fingers through his matted hair, realizing that he felt amazing. *I drank like a drowning rat...the elves are extraordinary*, he thought as he pulled bits of bread from his disheveled clothing.

"As you can see, our armies av packed all der provisions and set out," Reagal said as he handed Fern a new set of clothes. "Take dese, and change quickly, for we must also be off if we expect to find your dragon friend in appropriate time."

"Then you really are joining us?" asked Fern, slightly surprised as he stepped behind some wooden barrels to change.

"Yes, of course. I av spoken wid my fader earlier dis morning and ee as agreed

215

wid my decision to accompany you and Garrick."

Reagal's eyes shifted back and forth as he spoke, and he stood like a pane of glass; Fern could see straight through his friend's words, and the look on Reagal's face made it clear that King Solace never conceded to his will. Fern accepted his explanation nonetheless, and even admired him for his selflessness. He couldn't help but think how excruciating it must have been for Reagal to defy his father, but Fern said nothing more on the matter.

The three companions gathered what provisions they had and headed toward the entrance. As they approached the opening, they were surprised to see Kings Dandowin and Ardin standing outside talking to one another.

"Your Majesties, I thought you were leading your armies to the north?" questioned Fern. He noticed a magnificent unicorn standing next to King Ardin.

"Oi, good morning to you all," bellowed King Ardin turning to Fern. "It is only Solace who has departed, for his way is longest. We shall be leaving soon, but we wanted to see you off first."

"Your unicorn is an amazing creature," exclaimed Fern, staring in awe.

"Yes, she is quite splendid," answered King Ardin. "Her name is Celestial, but I call her Celest for short. She is the fastest of my mares."

Celest stood tall staring at Fern, almost as if she knew him. Her coat was pure white, but her mane was light blonde, as was her tail. Her eyes were dark as the midnight sky, giving meaning to her name, and she wore no armor, only a finely-crafted brown leather saddle sat on her back. Fern continued to stare as he unwillingly spoke.

"What I wouldn't give to ride a unicorn!"

"Funny you should say that, me boy," said King Ardin as his mustache rose to his cheeks with a smile. "For she is yours."

Fern nearly fell back in shock.

"I don't know what to say," replied Fern.

"No need to say anything, me boy, let's just say it's my way of rectifying things."

King Ardin handed Fern the reins and gave him a quick wink and slap on the back. King Dandowin huffed and rolled his eyes at the dwarf's gesture and handed Fern a quiver of arrows, an elven bow, and a sword.

"These are Ulmeck Rock arrows forged by the dwarves, and a bow crafted by my finest bowyer made from the silver leaf wood found only within my kingdom." King Dandowin placed the bow upon Fern's back, pride beaming from his face. "Here also is a sword, made from the same rock, and crafted by the dwarven smiths."

He turned to Reagal, handing him a scimitar.

"A perfect weapon for a centaur, made from Ulmeck rock, with a curved blade designed for slicing enemies from horseback."

To Garrick was given a massive Ulmeck rock warhammer, crafted tirelessly throughout the night to fit in his giant hands. It took both Dandowin and Ardin to lift the weapon. Garrick's eyes grew enormous as he grasped the hammer's leather wrapped grip and easily lifted it above his head.

"Thank you so much, sire! I cherish it!" Garrick was in a world of his own, fighting as the hero, crushing the enemy singlehandedly and winning the day. Fern watched as his giant friend's eyes peered into dreams, and he smiled.

"I have news for you," said King Dandowin, turning back to Fern. "My elven scouts have spotted your dragon just this morning. He has been circling the skies to the east, above the land of Valom. He must be in search of you. Go now and do your best to recruit him. We wish you luck, and haste."

"Yes, haste," bellowed King Ardin. "We must be going now as well. I hope the next time we meet, victory will be close at hand. Until then, farewell."

Fern, Reagal, and Garrick watched the two kings disappear back into the lair. Mounting Celest, Fern looked his companions in the eyes, nodded, and headed east.

Fern sat astride his newly acquired unicorn searching the skies and wondering why Paliden had not tried to contact him. After all, the land of the Stone Trolls is part of Valom, and he was spotted just east of their position. Reagal suddenly interrupted Fern's thoughts.

"I was dinking about your encounter wid dee Elders at dee fairy kingdom. I believe dae av bestowed you dee power of transformation."

Surprised by Reagal's sudden thoughts, Fern responded with a slight squint of his eyes and tilt of his head.

"Yes, Reagal, I thought that as well, but I feel no difference, and they gave me no explanation or instruction as how to use this power, if, in fact, it was given," replied Fern in a frustrated tone.

"Yes, it is very curious," said Reagal. "But I remember you telling me dat Lillia spoke of fairies who had dis ability and could transform only when dae fear der lives are in danger. Maybe it is dat you av not yet been in dee right circumstance."

217

"I don't know...maybe, but I'd hate to be in such a circumstance to find out," replied Fern with a slight grin.

Fern could not help but think that even if this gift was bestowed upon him, how he could bring it forth? He has never feared death, and has even welcomed it at times, considering the abuse he had taken his entire life. If the power only happened when one feared his or her life was in danger, would he be able to transform when the time comes?

His thoughts were suddenly trapped by a large shadow passing over them. The three companions' heads snapped skyward just in time to see the tail of a dragon disappearing behind the clouds.

"Was dat im, was dat Paliden?" asked Reagal.

"Not sure, he hasn't tried to contact me, and I couldn't catch the color of its tail. It was moving too quickly," replied Fern.

"Can you not try to speak wid im?"

"I've been trying ever since we left the Marshes, but it seems I need more practice." Fern continued staring into the sky with concentrated squints.

"What if not Paliden?" said Garrick suddenly. "We should not be in open."

"You're right," replied Fern. "Reagal, you know these fields and lands better than anyone. Is there anywhere to travel that's not so obvious?"

"I am afraid not. Fields of grass as far as dee eye can see are my ome," replied Reagal. "We centaurs need no structure to shield us from dee elements, and prefer dee open land. You will find no cover ere."

"I'm convinced that that dragon has spotted us," said Fern. "We've been in the open since leaving the land of the Stone Trolls, and if it was Paliden, he would've contacted me by now. I suggest we draw our weapons. The clouds are heavy this morning and will give this dragon every opportunity to catch us by surprise."

The company traveled further east, keeping a watchful eye on the sky. The clouds became dark, and a heavy rain began to fall as no sign of the dragon was seen. For hours, the three traveled, walking through mud and puddles as wind began to blow, causing the downpour to fall like needles.

"I'm beginning to think this plan is as good as all the others I've been a part of!" shouted Fern, trying to make his voice heard over the pounding rain. "I've not sensed Paliden nor heard any word from him all day. I'm at a loss, and I'm drenched from this damned rain."

"I am starting to feel dee same, but if dat dragon was foe, we surely would av been attacked by now." shouted Reagal as he watched the clouds darken and the rain swirl.

The storm raged, and the group traveled close together, barely able to see through the thick blanket of water. Fern and Garrick were soaked to the bone and shivering. Reagal trotted through the storm not missing a beat. Fern wrapped his arms around himself, his drenched clothes sticking to him as if they had been glued to his skin. Garrick grumbled, and the hair on the top of his barrel head looked like a shiny bowl as the rain dripped into his squinted eyes. His heavy feet sank into the earth crushing the grasses, embedding the green blades deep within the mud.

"My friends, I miserable!" complained Garrick. "This rain pounding my eyes like hammer, and my clothes heavy like stone!"

As Garrick wiped his eyes with his vibrating hand, a powerful wind began to blow. Within an hour, the rain passed, and the sun began to shine down, drying the huddled, teeth-chattering, men's clothes.

"Well, I guess when giants complain, even Mother Nature listens," said Fern, smiling up at Garrick.

The sky was now clear of clouds, which gave Fern hope of finally spotting Paliden. As they traveled further into Valom, he noticed Celest's body begin to shudder. Fern stroked her neck to calm her, but the vibrations of her body became more severe. Fern immediately drew his sword.

"Reagal, Garrick, draw your weapons. There is something wrong with Celest, she seems nervous."

Celest suddenly reared up kicking her hooves. Mud and water flung in the air as a large green dragon swooped down from the sky. Lifting Fern off his leather saddle, the dragon carried him away. Fern's legs dangled free, as claws grasped tightly around his shoulders. Reagal and Garrick stood in shock as they watched their friend disappear into the distance.

"Paliden!" shouted Fern. But there was no response. Fern could sense nothing, and nothing was said between the two as Paliden carried Fern through the air for nearly an hour. Fern's shoulders ached, and his legs were numb. Confused and frustrated, Fern finally felt Paliden begin to descend. He could view the clearing in the Feral Forest, and the quaggoth holes, as Paliden landed. He released Fern to his feet and an uneasy feeling gripped Fern's mind. Paliden turned to face him. The green dragon sat tall on his hind quarters with a strained look on his face. He stared into Fern's eyes and breathed heavily, his large chest heaving, his nostrils flared. Fern finally understood. Paliden was trying to communicate with him, but could not.

"My friend, I can't hear your thoughts," spoke Fern aloud. "Are you able to hear mine?"

Paliden shook his head no.

"Then listen to me," requested Fern. "Our allies are marching to the north as we speak. King Ardin and his dwarves have an underground tunnel system, which should give us the element of surprise, but we still need your help. Will you join us?"

Paliden began to etch something into the dirt with his talon: *What happened to you after our departure? Why can you not speak with me?*

Suddenly it dawned on Fern.

"The Elders!" he shouted aloud.

Paliden's eyes grew large and without warning he swung his massive claw, striking Fern on his left arm. The pain was excruciating. What felt like lightning, shot through his body as he dropped to his knees. He glanced down to his arm, eyes trembling, and saw a long gaping gash from his elbow to his wrist. Blood began to flow from the wound, but to Fern's astonishment, it was not red, it was a pale blue. Not only this, but he watched as the wound closed like a trap. Fern looked to Paliden; he could see anger building in the green dragon's face. Paliden rose, standing, hind legs flexed, poised for liftoff. His chest filled with air as he sprung from the ground. His mighty wings flapped, sending the dirt from the forest floor whirling into a dust storm, blinding Fern. A tremendous roar that shook the trees like a hurricane came from the dragon as the dirt settled back to the ground. Fern watched as Paliden shot into the air.

"PALIDEN, NO...WAIT!"

Fern stood, confused and alone, staring into the sky. Suddenly, the ground beneath him began to shake. He braced himself and drew his sword. Dozens of turgoyles exploded from the quaggoth tunnels screaming and swinging clubs above their slimy heads. They quickly surrounded Fern. He grasped the hilt of his sword tightly. He was not about to let the turgoyles capture him again. He gave them no warning, rushing into the horde, his sword cutting and slashing the turgoyles down one by one. He felt power he had never felt before. The turgoyles could not defeat him. An unexpected voice came reverberating from the center of the battle.

"I HAVE YOUR CENTAUR AND GIANT!"

The turgoyles stood still and backed away from Fern. He studied the crowd as it parted, noticing Timal walking towards him, smile on his face and blond hair blowing in the breeze. Five red dragons clad in black armor descended from the sky. They landed, surrounding Timal, crushing the turgoyles that stood in their way.

"Surrender your weapon or your friends die!" shouted Timal.

Fern cocked his head as his eyes focused on Timal's.

"I have them, the giant and donkey. I have them both."

"How?" questioned Fern, suspicion heavy.

"Don't be a fool, silly boy! I have been tracking you ever since you departed the land of the Stone Trolls. I took them the moment you left," shouted Timal as he stood grinning like a mad man. His cape dragged the ground as he strutted closer to Fern. "I know about your newfound power, and I know your allies are marching in the wrong direction."

Fern grasped his sword firmly, his eyes popping and mouth slack-jawed. *How could he know so much?* Timal immediately saw Fern's confusion.

"You are quite naïve," he said, now laughing. "I have been ten steps in front of you this entire time. I have lead you by a leash, controlling your movements the moment you entered Loustof. I told you, Majestic, I have more power than you can imagine. Now relinquish your weapons and surrender to me, or I will slice their limbs from their feeble bodies as you watch."

"Where are they!" shouted Fern.

"They are where you left them, child." Timal now stood face-to-face with Fern. "You are trying my patience. Now lay down your blade."

Fern's grasp loosened around his sword. He shook his head in a daze, hair dancing around his sweat-drenched shoulders. *How can I let my friends suffer?* His brows furled deep, and his breathing intensified. Fern studied Timal's eyes. *He's lying, he'll kill them regardless!* Fern felt he had only one choice. His grip tightened around the hilt once more and he raised his sword, plunging it into Timal's chest.

The turgoyles charged, snarling and cursing Fern.

"Stay your weapons, ignorant rabble!" shouted Timal.

The turgoyles halted as Timal stepped back, Fern's sword sliding from his chest. He showed no pain, shaking his head and peering at Fern.

Timal leapt onto one of the red dragons, and without a word, lifted from the ground and ascended into the sky as the hordes of turgoyles rushed forward. The remaining dragons followed their master. Fern swung his sword, slashing into the crazed creatures, shouting to Timal as he flew away.

"Coward! You coward! Stay and fight!"

But it was no use, Timal disappeared within moments.

Fern's strength was wearing as he continued to strike down the army of turgoyles. Dozens more poured out of the tunnels. Fern's chance of victory was slim, even with his newfound power, but as luck would have it, unlikely help would soon arrive.

An ear-piercing noise suddenly sounded from deep within the Feral Forest. Drums started to pound, and the earth began to tremble. Within moments, minotaur's rushed from the trees into the battle. Dozens of them surrounded Fern, carrying large flails and maces, swinging them with unbounded accuracy. The turgoyles screeched in pain as they flew into the air. Fern's strength returned, and new confidence surged through his body. He fought with every ounce of stamina left in his being. The minotaurs began pushing the turgoyles back, sending them retreating into the tunnels. The battle was over quickly.

When the last turgoyles scurried out of sight, Fern dropped his sword and fell to the ground, exhausted. His chest heaved and sweat washed his face, dripping down upon his legs. A minotaur stood above him and grabbed him by the arm, pulling Fern to a standing position as the other minotaurs returned to the woods without a word.

"Hello, Fern Majestic."

Fern instantly recognized the voice to be Dominance.

"It's good to see you," replied Fern, nearly out of breath. "How...how did you know I...I was here?"

"I did not," replied Dom. "We minotaurs can smell those filthy turgoyles from miles away, and we do not tolerate them in our land, and it was a good thing we came when we did. You did not look like you could hold out much longer."

Fern nodded, but did not waste time with conversation as his thoughts were of haste.

"I greatly appreciate your help, but I need to get back to the land of Valom as quickly as I can. My friends are in danger and will die if I don't reach them. I must leave."

"Yes, of course. Follow me, I will show you the way."

Dominance dashed into the woods as Fern tried to follow him. Thoughts of deception were clearly in Fern's mind. *Is this such a clever idea? Why should I trust him now? He could be leading me to further danger. No...no, he is no ally of Timal, he just saved my life. Follow him.*

The dense woods seemed thicker than Fern remembered as he tried his best to keep pace with the mighty minotaur. Tree branches sliced Fern's face, and the thorns that were all too vivid in his memory jabbed his skin, the wounds healing instantly as he started to fall behind. He could not help but wonder what other unknown powers the elders bestowed upon him and hoped he would be able to discover his full abilities before it was too late. Fern's strength waned, and the distance between himself and Dominance started to lengthen.

"Dom, please slow down, I can't keep up," shouted Fern.

His exhaustion from the recent battle made it impossible to run faster. Dominance abruptly halted and drew his flail. Fern, unblinking, stared into the forest, but could see nothing. A flash of brilliant white suddenly appeared in front of them. Dominance raised his flail.

"Stop! That's my unicorn!"

Fern stood, eyes wide and bewildered. *How could she know I was here?* Celest reared up neighing to Fern and jerking her neck from side to side. Her shimmering yellow mane caught the only light in the dense forest. Dominance lowered his weapon as Fern mounted her back. Celest wasted no time, pivoting on her hind legs and galloping through the forest. Fern trusted her; she was taking him where he needed to go. He looked back at Dom as he rode away.

"Thank you again, my friend, but I think she knows where she is going!" Dominance started to fade in the distance. "I will repay you for your help someday!" yelled Fern.

Fern could barely see Dom raise his hand as he darted out of sight.

Celest raced through the Feral Forest with ease, dodging trees as if she knew the land better than the minotaurs. Her speed was incomparable and seemed to quicken with every stride. Fern noticed sunlight beaming in the distance through the trees.

"We're nearly there, girl!" Fern grasped the unicorn's mane.

Within moments, Celest burst into the fields of Valom. Faster she galloped. Fern could see dragons flying in the distant sky; fire spewed from their mouths down upon the ground. The sounds of war became deafening as Fern and Celest flew through the grasses. They were almost upon the battlefield. Dwarves on unicorn-back battled turgoyles and trocks, while centaurs launched arrows into the sky at the fire-breathing dragons. Elves on magnificent steeds skillfully cut down the onslaught of green. Fern could not understand how his allies were there, and had no time to question it.

Celest leapt into the fray with Fern upon her back. To Fern's everlasting joy, he spotted Garrick, bulldozing his way through the battle, crushing everything in his path. Without warning, an army of turgoyles on hogback, led by Lord Orgle, came charging into sight. Fern directed Celest, plowing down the wall of enemies and straight for the turgoyle lord. From behind, minotaurs came swooping in, flanking the turgoyles on hogback. Dom led the ambush swinging his flail, crashing it down on the turgoyles skulls cracking them open like egg shells. Dragons started to fall from the sky, thundering down like flaming meteors as the centaurs found the imperfections in their armor; Celest dodged the dead beasts with ease.

Fern watched with utter amazement, and inspiration, as he witnessed Garrick leap into the air as a dragon passed low in the sky. The giant grabbed the beast by the tail yanking it to the ground before jumping to its shoulders. Garrick's large powerful hands grasped the dragon tightly around its throat. The dragon fought hysterically, its arms scraping the giant's sides and its legs kicking violently in the air. Garrick's vice-like grip tightened, and with a quick wrench of his wrists, he snapped the dragon's neck. Fern stood frozen by his friend's abilities. Garrick tossed the red corpse into the horde of turgoyles, crushing their bodies with its massive weight. Appearing around the fallen dragon was Lord Orgle, carrying a massive halberd. He spotted Fern and raised his weapon as he kicked his heels into the warthog's ribs. Charging towards Fern, the turgoyle lord's jaw dropped open as he roared. His yellow teeth, crooked and sharp, stuck out like swords. He swung the large axe, grazing Fern's shirt. Fern leapt from Celest's back onto the giant warthog.

"Take a good look, lord. Mine will be the last face you'll ever see!" With a clenched fist, Fern jabbed the turgoyle across his jaw. Lord Orgle lost his balance and tumbled from his ride, bouncing into the grass. Fern squeezed the warthog's snout and yanked its head towards him as he slit its throat with his sword. He leapt from the stumbling beast as it crashed to the ground, landing on his feet in front of lord Orgle. The large turgoyle stood quickly grabbing his halberd.

"No stinking Majestic will defeat me!" Lord Orgle yelled, raising his axe with his puny wings spread open.

Fern wasted little time, swinging his sword with lightning speed and slicing

Orgle in the gut. The turgoyle lord jumped back and hovered in the air, wings sputtering frantically as blood spilled from his belly.

"You'll have to do better than that, Majestic scum!"

Orgle flew wildly, zigzagging movements hard to follow as the blade of his halberd found Fern's left arm. Orgle grinned, yellow teeth clamping shut as saliva splashed the air. The blade sunk deep into bone. Fern roared as the ax imbedded in his forearm. The pain grew like a torrid thought in his mind. Blue blood spilled out as Fern jerked the weapon from Orgle's hand, still deep in his bone. Fern clinched the handle of the halberd; his jaw muscles flexed as he gritted his teeth and ripped it from muscle and tissue. Searing pain burned through him like fire. He staggered backwards as the agony finally diminished. Fern looked down at his arm as the wound closed. Orgle's mouth dropped. Unarmed, he watched his opponent's injury vanish. Fern, with sword in one hand and halberd in the other, leapt high in the air. Lord Orgle turned, retreating like a scolded dog. The turgoyle lord stumbled and his tired little wings could not lift him as he dropped to his knees. Fern's mercy was swift. He scissored the two weapons together, stealing the turgoyle leader's head from his neck. Orgle's body fell to the ground, his severed head tumbling like a jagged rock from a cliff. Orgle's tongue drooped from his mouth, licking the blood-soaked ground, his eyes rolled back in his skull. The turgoyle army screeched in anger at seeing their lord's head come to a halt. Their rage made them stronger as the battle continued into midday.

Without a second thought, Fern leapt onto Celest and rode back into the battle. The last Majestic slaughtered the turgoyles effortlessly, regardless of their newfound rage.

More dragons flew in from the north, replacing the fallen. Their breath lit the sky with clouds of fire. Reinforcements of Stone Trolls, bounding from the west, poured onto the battlefield like a giant stampede. The centaurs were unprepared as the trolls attacked from behind. Fern dove from Celest's back into the sea of his enemy. The flanking trolls' attention turned away from King Solace and his army of archers. Fern finally had his chance to exact revenge on Phillip's and Randal's murders. It was swift. Still holding Lord Orgle's halberd, Fern quickly planted it in a troll's forehead. The creature fell dead with a thud, tripping multiple trolls with its large corpse. Fern stabbed, hacked, sliced, and plunged his sword. Body parts flung like loose blades of grass in a storm as he mowed through his enemies.

The centaurs, rarely missing, found the dragon's hide with their Ulmeck Rock arrows, scattering the flying serpents to the ground. Ardin and Dandowin could be seen pursuing the turgoyles, forcing them into the horde of anxious minotaurs.

Meanwhile, Fern was back astride Celest scouring the battlefield for Reagal, but there was no sign of the centaurian prince. The worry for his friend built as the war raged on. *Does Timal truly have him? But...I saw Garrick...he wouldn't have let him take Reagal.*

Suddenly, from deep within the fury of battling warriors, came a cry. Fern turned toward the sound. Soma burst towards the sky, swirling like an aerial dancer, wings closed, with a turgoyle in her grasp. Quickly she soared until she was amongst the dragons, clutching the turgoyle between her powerful paws. With a swift downward movement, she plummeted towards the ground, releasing the turgoyle.

Dragons circled the fields high above the battle out of the range of firing arrows. To everyone's amazement, and Fern's utter bewilderment, the dragons were not engaged in the fight any longer. They simply watched.

Darkness started taking over the sky, and stars sparkled like diamonds, but no pause in the fight was granted. The moon was full as it shone yellow light on the countless numbers of turgoyles continuing to pour onto the fields of Valom. The once-green waves of tall grass were now matted clumps of bloody earth.

The battle began to shift, and Fern could see his allies dwindling. They were desperately outnumbered, and the outcome of the war was becoming all too obvious; hope was sparse.

They fought like heroes, how could it end like this? The sparks from metal against metal forced Fern to blink his eyes. *Was it all in vain?* Thoughts of Lillia flashed in his mind, and...Reagal. *Where is he?*

"Arrrg!" he shouted as a massive force plowed into his back, flinging him across the battlefield like an unwanted piece of scrap.

A Stone Troll came into view as Fern lay flat on his back, sword ten feet away. Rolling on the ground, Fern dodged the grey, clammy feet of the troll as it tried to stomp the life from him. The troll's head suddenly exploded into brains and blood as a war hammer cracked across its skull, squashing it like a grape. Hovering over Fern was Garrick. The giant grabbed Fern by his arm, hoisting him to his feet.

"Thank you, my friend," shouted Fern through the screams and yells.

"No problem, sir," replied Garrick, smiling and handing Fern his sword. The giant stood by his friend's side, clothes shredded and dirty, face splattered in their enemy's blood.

Fern could hear the horn of the dwarven king sounding from behind.

"Let's go!" he shouted to Garrick.

His allies started to gather together for one last push. King Dandowin rallied his elven troops while King Solace and his army of centaurs lined behind their ranks ready to cast their last arrows into the charging turgoyle horde. Celest, finding her owner, galloped to the dwarven king, Garrick close behind. King Ardin looked at Fern and nodded in respect. The dwarven army, astride their unicorns, reared up for the final charge. The horn sounded, and the last hope for victory rushed forward. Fern raised his sword.

Valiantly they fought. The clash of steel and the roars and screams of the stricken echoed. They were hopelessly outnumbered, and their forces were nearly depleted. Fern could still see Garrick towering above the battlefield, fighting with all his might, but to no avail. Soma flew, showing her acrobatic skills as she dived down striking the enemy with deadly force. Her talons pierced their skin like butter as the chamrosh crushed their bones in her grasp. But with every downed enemy came multitudes of others. Fern and his allies showed no sign of retreat; they were going to fight until the end.

Loud drums began to beat, and battle cries drowned out the noises of war. The turgoyles suddenly drew back from Fern and his allies, forming into ranks. Without warning, armored men on horseback flew past Fern, crashing into the sea of turgoyles. A flag bearing the Loustofian crest could be seen as a soldier rode into the moonlight. The soldiers of Loustof fighting against Timal's army! *How can this be*, Fern thought. Then the unimaginable happened. Through the smoke and raging war Fern saw him: Edinword in full armor astride a shimmering black horse clad in brilliant steel. The Loustofian king, wielding a gleaming sword and shield, sliced down the turgoyles with amazing skill. He did not miss his targets. Each swing of his blade spilled blood, parting the horde as he shouted for Timal.

"Where are you, false king? Where are you?"

Thousands of men joined the battle, and hope was rekindled. Gallantly they fought. Fern had not witnessed such ferocity in men; this was the miracle they needed. Loustofian soldiers upon armored steeds plowed through the turgoyle army like farmers through fields. The turgoyles dropped like flies, crushed underneath heavy hooves.

Fern, though glad of the turn of events, was skeptical of the Loustofian heroes. *How did Edinword reclaim his army? Are his intentions true?*

As the enemy dissipated, Fern dropped his weary arms, the tip of his sword resting on the bloodied ground. Lord Orgle's halberd slipped from his grip and dropped flat by his feet. Fern stood gazing at the stars, blood-soaked clothes dripping in a cool breeze, heaving chest slowing like the wind from a passing storm.

13

TAKEN

Dawn approached, and the turgoyle army, depleted and scattered, fled into the shadows. The dragons, who never resumed the fight, could be seen retreating to the north as the sun started to rise in the east. Stone Trolls and trocks lay dead on the battlefield, changing the once-beautiful fields into a boulder-ridden landscape. Massacred bodies and the charred remains of turgoyles, dwarves, centaurs, elves, and men decorated the blood-soaked ground. The injured cried for help in agonizing screams as their comrades rushed to their sides amidst the dwindling fires and rising smoke.

The mood lay heavy, and the battle was finally over. Victory was had, and Fern stood surveying the aftermath. He spotted Garrick sitting atop a dead troll and galloped toward him. Amazed to find him unharmed, he slid down from Celest with open arms to greet the giant.

"Garrick!"

But Fern was abruptly interrupted by King Solace shouting as he leapt over the bodies of the dead.

"Majesteek! Majesteek! Ee as my son! Timal as Reagal!"

Fern turned to Solace. His arms dropped along with his heart. Garrick's head slumped to his chest in anguish as Fern turned to the king of the centaurs.

"Please, lead me to Timal, lead me to my son before it is too late."

Just then, Kings Ardin and Dandowin arrived from the battlefield.

"Halt, Solace," commanded King Dandowin. "You cannot race towards such danger; it will be your death. Please, my friend, think logically."

Fern remounted Celest and guided her to King Solace's side, placing his hand on the centaur's shoulder.

"I'll give my life for his, if need be."

"Preposterous!" shouted King Ardin. "You are the last of your kind. There will be no lives given freely on my watch, that I can assure you."

"Yes, we cannot allow you to sacrifice yourself and give in to this evil," replied King Dandowin. "We must face Timal together. Only with our combined strength do we stand a chance of defeating him."

King Solace looked at each of his friends and breathed a deep sigh as he slowly sat to the ground. His aged face grimaced in self-pity as he grasped his dark hair in his hands.

"I suppose you are right," replied King Solace. "Never av I made a rash decision out of emotion."

Garrick bounded into the conversation. "Yes, now we stand chance for victory. Specially since have King Edinword and army on our side."

"Ah, yes, Edinword, dank goodness for im. Ee will make a good ally."

Fern had nearly forgotten the reason for their recent victory, but his hate for Edinword lingered.

"We can't trust him. Don't you remember what he's done? For goodness sake, he stole your son right from under your nose," said Fern at almost a yell as he turned to King Solace. "Not only this, he made him fight for his life in a dungeon as a slave. No...we can't trust him."

King Solace stood, understanding in his eyes. "My dear Majesteek, if it were not for Edinword, no one ere would be drawing bread. Ee was dee one to tell us of dee turgoyle army's whereabouts, and ee was dee one who won back dee control of is men. At is own personal risk, I might add."

"But how?" asked Fern. "How could he do all this?"

"Does are questions dat need to be asked of *im*," replied King Solace.

"But how can you forgive the man who took your son?" Fern's understanding was vacant as Solace stood and flapped his tail to shoo the buzzing flies from his backside.

"Ee as begged for my forgiveness, and I av seen dee remorse and sincerity in is eyes." He looked directly into Fern's eyes with unwavering poise. "I cannot, and will not, deny anyone forgiveness when repentance is honest and artfelt. I suggest you do dee same. It will do your soul good."

Fern shook his head, still unable to see past his emotions. He was steaming as he turned to Garrick.

"Tell me what happened to Reagal! How did Timal capture him?"

Garrick's back arched, his head slumping down, chin resting on his chest, and his eyes filled with water.

"It after you taken away from us by dragon," he said with a sniffle. "We start run in direction you fly when sudden from behind, two more dragons attack us. First pick master Reagal up and flew away. I try grab him, but dragon very fast and I too slow. Second try to do same with me, but I much too heavy and it unable to lift me from ground. I grab it and break its back. I so sorry. I couldn't save master Reagal. I just so sorry!"

Fern, cooled by Garrick's sorrow, nodded his head with a sigh. "You fought bravely, and I'm very proud of you, Garrick."

Fern released another breath, turning, and looked compassionately at King Solace. His brows slanted outward, with his blue eyes large and sympathetic.

"Don't worry, your son's still alive," he said, placing his hand on Solace's shoulder to give comfort. "Timal won't kill him, not yet, at least. He wants me and needs me alive for some reason. He'll use Reagal to get to me, I'm almost sure of it. I must face him before all is over."

Soma flew down amongst the company, landing next to King Solace, and Fern remembered Galeon. "What of your son, Galeon? Did Soma find him?"

King Solace merely shook his head. Soma nuzzled her master, squawking softly as if giving consolation.

"I'm truly sorry," replied Fern.

Everyone stood quietly with heads lowered. King Ardin cleared his throat to break the silence. "So, me boy, do we have a dragon on our side yet?" he asked, looking hopeful.

"I'm afraid not, sire, and I don't believe we will. My meeting with Paliden went nothing like I'd planned. I could no longer communicate with him, and he became angry with me and flew off. I'm not sure what to make of it, to be honest with you."

"Oi, pity. It would've been a pleasant change to have a dragon breathing fire on our enemy for once instead of on us," chuckled King Ardin.

"Well, there is no reason to dwell on things we cannot control," said King Dandowin. "It is time we plan our next step. Solace, can you command Soma to fetch King Edinword? We will need his insight."

Fern interceded, yanking Celest's reins. "What?! Why do we need *him* in our council? He's too close to the enemy, and certainly can't be trusted."

"Regardless of your personal feelings, King Edinword is now our ally. We will need his help if we stand any chance of defeating Timal," replied King Dandowin. "And do not worry, we will be cautious."

"And the victory we experienced was only a small one," added King Ardin. "Our forces have been severely weakened, and Timal still has Ratlarp's army and whatever other rabble he might have recruited in his ranks, not to mention the dragons."

Fern huffed and shook his head as he watched Soma lift from the ground and part company.

A few moments later, the chamrosh returned, closely followed by Edinword. The Loustofian king sat astride his beautiful black steed, but his stature had faded. The once-proud man of Loustof sat slumped on his saddle with hands fidgeting the reins. His age seemed to leap from his face, tired and wrinkled. Fern noticed it as he glared at Edinword.

Edinword glanced at Fern standing amongst the kings. His head immediately dropped to avoid the young Majestic's piercing gaze. Fern gritted his teeth, his jaw muscles tensed.

"There you are Edinword," exclaimed King Dandowin. "Come and join our council. We need your wisdom in our decision making."

Wisdom?! How could the king of the elves, a being of such grace and intelligence, be so quick to accept an obvious deceiver into their council, even with caution, thought Fern. *He can't be serious? Edinword wise? How could they forgive and forget so easily?*

Fern shuffled on his saddle, huffing and puffing, as the Loustofian king greeted everyone. Edinword cautiously approached Fern. The anger in the Majestic's eyes was plain.

"I am truly sorry for all I have done." Edinword bowed slightly as he spoke, his shoulder-length white hair slipping over his ears. "I know I have a lifetime of sins to make up for, but please, let me try," he pleaded, fighting to keep the tears from breaking free.

Fern said nothing. Edinword shook his head, breathed a heavy sigh, and turned to the others.

"My kings, let me know what it is that you need of me, for I shall grant it without hesitation."

"Good!" interrupted Fern as he jerked on Celest's reins again. The Unicorn neighed, irritated at Fern's sudden lack of respect. "Tell us, how'd you know that Timal's army was going to be here, and how can we trust anything you say?"

"There is none I can think to make you believe my word. I can only tell you my story and let you decide whether it is so."

"Very well, tell us your story," sneered Fern in a sarcastic tone.

Edinword breathed another sigh and began to speak.

"I will start by saying thank you to the young Majestic. He has spared my life and given me the chance for a new one."

"I don't need your thanks, nor do I want it! Just go on with your tale," commanded Fern.

King Edinword continued with a heavy heart, deep in thought as he spoke, reliving every moment: *He pulled himself up from the ground on that fateful day when Fern Majestic saved him from the ogre.*

Edinword watched as Fern disappeared into the woods. Wallowing in self-pity and anguish over the loss of Mallock and his abundance of sins, he had given up the will to live. "Please, just let some foul creature appear from the darkness and take me from this world," he cried. He had no strength to take his life himself. Edinword dropped to his knees, crying into his hands, the tears pooling the soil with sadness. He crawled like a wounded rat, gripping the ground through the rock and dirt until he made his way to the cave entrance. The morning sun was rising, and the light graced his face. Edinword suddenly remembered the words Fern spoke to him before he broke the chains binding him to the cavern wall: My pity for you is slight. The word pity *echoed in his mind. After everything Edinword had done, Fern still showed him pity... compassion. Edinword pondered that thought, face planted on the dirt, blowing dust into the air with every labored breath. His eyes slowly opened wide,* I will not waste this gift that was given! *Hope was rekindled, and Edinword rose to his feet. The sins that he carried dangled from him like the bloodied shreds of his shirt. Shaking free from his sorrow, he stared through the trees towards his kingdom. Edinword wanted absolution, but what he wanted most...was Timal.*

His immediate instinct was to return to Loustof and reclaim his army. If only he could. His adrenaline flowed like a raging river as he started to sprint through the forest.

Through the town of Burdensville he raced, slipping past homes and townsfolk. Only a few recognized the king dressed in tattered clothing and missing crown as he dashed past residences and businesses. Their eyes popped from their sockets, their mouths hung open as they pointed and whispered, not sure of what they were witnessing.

Edinword, letting nothing distract him, tore through the streets with inhuman stamina along the long and winding road. Flocks of crows burst from trees with warning calls as the king kicked loose stones from under his feet. The sun was setting, and finally he saw it dazzling in the distance: the kingdom of Loustof. His kingdom.

Edinword crept through the streets like a thief in the night, only to find his kingdom completely void of inhabitants. Up the stairs and into his palace he went, frantically searching every room, corner, and tower until he came to the double doors to the courtyard. There he saw him: Fern, standing frozen and staring at a green dragon chained to the ground. He kept out of sight, peering through the doorway but never hearing a word, when suddenly, Fern turned from the dragon and darted toward the doors. Edinword leapt into the darkness, holding his breath as Fern burst through the entrance and sped down a hallway. Edinword kept in the shadows, following Fern through the corridor. "Clank!" Knocking into a decorative urn, Edinword quickly grabbed it, spinning from a side table to his right. Cursing inside his mind, Edinword flattened himself on the ground in the dark hallway. That was close, he thought as he slowly placed his hands on the plush carpet and pushed himself to his knees.

Edinword soon found himself standing three cells down from where Galeon was imprisoned. He listened as the centaur rejected Fern's request. A pause...the conversation was over. Galeon came bursting into the hallway. Edinword darted into an empty cell, nearly trampled by the stampeding centaur. Tattered and torn, Galeon glanced at the trembling king, paying him no attention. He didn't recognize me, thought Edinword as his wide eyes strained. A sudden epiphany struck the king like a lightning bolt as he looked down at his disheveled clothing and dirt-encrusted skin. His stealthiness was not as skill-driven as he initially thought, the prisoners of his dungeon did not give him away, because they did not know who was running through their halls. To them, he was just an escaped captive trying to find a way out.

Edinword wiped sweat from his brow as he lay huddled in the corner of his cell waiting for Fern to pass. He laughed quietly to himself, realizing his surroundings. An understanding of what life was like for the pathetic dungeon inhabitants flooded his heart as a rat scurried passed his dusty boots. A resolution to release each one developed in Edinword's thoughts, and he vowed to himself to implement his plan the moment he returned.

It wasn't long before Fern, running and screaming for the return of Galeon, came bolting down the narrow corridor. Edinword, keeping his distance, followed as Fern abandoned his chase and quickly changed course. Going room to room, he watched as Fern searched for something. Back down the spiral staircase he followed, tiptoeing like a child in the dark. Edinword crept to the arena doors. His eyes went wide as Fern quickly ran towards him with a battle-ax in his hands. Edinword's heart leapt to his throat. "I have been spotted, he is coming for me." Edinword hid in a dark corner, back against the wall with eyes clamped shut as he prayed. Fern dashed past, mind fixated on his goal, oblivious to the cringing body in the darkness.

As soon as he was away, Edinword slumped down to his backside breathing heavily. His heart pounded inside his chest, thundering like bass drums in his ears. He pushed his back against the wall and shimmied to his feet. Up the spiral staircase he raced and out to the courtyard, just in time to see Fern on the back of the green dragon ascending into the sky.

Edinword, dismayed, shook himself free of any discouragement and quickly averted his attention to Galeon. Backtracking, he swiftly found the centaur's dusty tracks. The hoofprints trailed west towards the Blue Marshes.

It had been two days of pursuit when Edinword found himself lost on the outskirts of the Blue Marshes. The centaur's tracks vanished in the mucky ground, and Edinword wandered aimlessly along the border searching for any sign of his lost champion. He came upon a large weeping willow, its swaying branches revealing two silhouettes, one small and the other massive, standing ten yards away. Edinword made his way to the trunk of the tree, grabbing its dangling branches and moving them aside to get a better look. To his absolute astonishment, he saw them: Fern and the green dragon, staring at each other without a word spoken. Confusion mounted as Edinword waited. He marveled at Fern; any other man would have retreated in terror being so close to such a dangerous creature. Of course, he also wondered why the dragon had not eaten Fern.

Moments went by, and Edinword had yet to hear a sound coming from the two unsuspecting souls. He watched as the dragon finally rose from the ground. The power from its flapping wings sent gusts of wind barreling through the willow. Edinword could see Fern as he entered the marshes. He followed. Darkness came. The powerful magic that was overwhelming Fern had no effect on Edinword. Why? One might never know. But some say Agers have abilities far greater than mortal men. Good thing too, for Edinword would need every advantage he could muster.

The Loustofian king, wet and weary, watched as Fern began slamming himself *against the willow trees. "What on harth is he doing?" Before he could devise an answer, Garrick came bounding through the mist. Edinword dropped to his belly, submerging himself in the water. Swimming like a snake, he slithered his way through the marshes as he followed Fern and Garrick to an expansive curtain of willow branches. As they vanished behind the curtain, Edinword jumped from the water like a fish. He parted the branches only to find more trees, marsh, and no sign of Fern or the giant. Edinword would change his course once more. Timal became his only objective.*

Within hours, dawn came. Keeping the sun to his back, Edinword found his way out, and by midday, he was into the Ruins of Liffland. This is where he would rest. Laying his head down on the ground, Edinword fell into a dream-world of sleep. Flashes of his son Mallock appeared in his mind, begging him for acknowledgement. Timal, behind him, whispered evil in his ear. Queen Amber on her knees pleaded for his protection, pleaded to live.

Edinword jerked up in the night, sweating profusely, heart pounding in his chest. In the pitch black he could see the light from the moon reflecting from hundreds of beady eyes. They were leading away. A turgoyle war party, marching rapidly towards the Land of the Stone Trolls, gave Edinword sudden hope. He sprang to his feet. This was his key to Timal's whereabouts. Quickly he gathered himself and followed. For hours they marched, keeping on the border of the troll's land. Lack of rest and food began to gnaw at Edinword's stamina, and he was lagging far behind. He had lost them.

Edinword plopped down on a boulder, parched, hungry, and disheartened. Twisting his neck and swiping the hair from his face, he stared to the passing clouds. Out of the corner of his eye, high on a cliff, stood a centaur. Galeon, he wondered? "No, it can't be. This one is much larger; I know my Galeon. What! How?" Edinword began to tremble, his heart rate soared, his mouth slack-jawed. Fern and Garrick, hiding behind a pair of boulders! How could this be? How could he have found them again? He wanted to run to them, announce his presence, but they would think him mad. He remained quiet behind cover and watched. "Another centaur!" It was Reagal, slowly making his way up an incline, to meet the other centaur. Edinword's mind was all a flutter. He crept behind them, yards apart, never taking his eyes away. "Be careful!" he whispered, though wanting to shout. "Stone Trolls!" But no, only decoys. The four companions disappeared into the caves.

"So, you see, my young Majesteek, is story olds true," spoke Solace as Edinword held his head down.

"Yes, but what did he do and where did he go after seeing my companions and I enter the caves?" asked Fern.

Edinword took another heavy breath, exhaling through his nose.

"I saw you enter the troll's lair," he said, "and again, I waited. Morning came, and Dandowin and Ardin exited the cave. Shortly after, I saw you conversing with the two kings before departing with your companions. I waited for nearly an hour before working up the courage to enter. I finally decided to reveal myself and found Dandowin readying his forces near the opening. I divulged everything I had witnessed to him, and Dandowin sent his swiftest elves to retrieve Solace and Ardin. That is when I departed. I was still determined to find Timal and my men. Dandowin was kind enough to lend me a horse, and off I went. Taking the elven king's suggestion, I traveled north towards the Land of the Drakes. I was no more than half a day into my journey when I came upon them. An army of men. My men! I was as shocked to see them as they were to see me. They admitted that they were sent by Timal and ordered to join the turgoyles in Valom. They were told to leave no one alive. To my everlasting joy, they had already decided to defy Timal, so no convincing was necessary. The captain of my army was already leading them away. They were on a course back to Loustof. I was overjoyed and told my men everything that had happened. Everything." Edinword paused as he looked at Fern. "They forgave me my weaknesses and followed me back to Valom to aid you and your allies. I am only sorry that we did not come sooner."

Fern studied Edinword's eyes suspiciously.

"It's a very convenient story, but I'm not sure of its validity," said Fern. "I, for one, haven't been met with so many fortunate events as you, and find it hard to believe you were unaided in your ventures. How do we know it wasn't Timal who sent you here to infiltrate our ranks and learn of our plans?"

"I can only give you my word," replied Edinword.

"Heh, your word," laughed Fern. "What is that worth?"

"Please, speak with the captain of my army, Grail. He is an honorable man. He will convince you of all I have told."

"I have already done so," interceded Ardin. "And I find him as you say."

King Ardin turned to Fern, his eyes peering and genuine. "He speaks the truth, me boy."

"Don't you understand what this man has done?" replied Fern in frustration. "It's because of him that Timal was allowed to gain strength. His thirst for power

237

and greed for wealth has led to all this. He allowed his own son and wife to be murdered by that evil bastard, not to mention the countless creatures murdered in his dungeon arenas. What's more, you will welcome him in our company without reservation? I don't understand."

"Oi, it is time to leave the past in the past, me boy," replied King Ardin. "Edinword has proven himself to all but you. Look beyond your hate, lad, and show the compassion you once gave him in the Ulmeck Mountains. We cannot afford conflict amongst ourselves. We have far too much else to worry about. Now, let's embrace forgiveness and do what needs to be done."

All looked toward Fern and nodded. Fern shook his head in disbelief.

"Very well," he said. "But don't let your guard down!"

Fern dughis heels into Celest, turning from Edinword. The Loustofian king veered in front of them.

"I will prove myself to you before all is over," he exclaimed.

"Very doubtful," replied Fern, rolling his eyes as he pulled Celest's reins and forced himself around the king.

"Wait!" shouted King Solace. "Where are you off to? We av yet to plot our new course. What about my son? Surely you will not abandon your friend?"

Fern quickly turned. "No, I will not. I will go to face Timal. He's retreated to the north, I'm almost sure of it. I promise you that I'll do whatever it takes to free your son, and I trust you will decide the correct plan of attack without my help. I've learned the way to the north and the Land of the Drakes courtesy of King Ardin, and I've made my decision to leave. I fear while you gather your remaining forces, Reagal will be enduring pain of torture in the hands of Timal and the turgoyles. I must do my best to find him as quickly as possible. Garrick has volunteered his services and will accompany me. We'll await your arrival in the Land of the Drakes."

The kings shook their heads in unison as Fern galloped away, Garrick bounding close behind.

King Solace motioned to the others to follow Fern.

"My friend, let him be," said King Ardin as he held Solace's arm to halt his pursuit. "He must go his own way. He will learn to relinquish his hate someday, but we have more important things to deal with."

King Solace dipped his head as Ardin released the grip on his arm.

"It is not is ate I worry about. I av foreseen dee dead of my son, and it involves the Majesteek. I fear der is noding I can do to stop it."

The kings looked at each other, masked in confusion.

"You are breaking your own law by telling us this," exclaimed Dandowin.

"Yes, I am quite aware of my infraction, but my ed as not been level since I witnessed dis vision."

King Dandowin's face remained stoic, and no sympathy accompanied his response. "You know as well as I that the future cannot be altered by any means that we possess. Your son's destiny is cast in stone, as was mine. I speak *your* words, my friend. You must come to this realization, or you will drive yourself mad."

"Good grief, Dandowin, show a little compassion!" exclaimed king Ardin. "The man's son is in danger!"

"Yes, as was mine those many years ago when he told those very same words to me. Or do you not remember his fate in Liffland when Lord Orgle took his life from me?"

"Yes, yes, I do not forget such dings," replied Solace with tears in his eyes.

"Oi, your son. I nearly forgot myself, very tragic." King Ardin said, looking away.

King Edinword stepped forward, raising his shield.

"I have felt the pain of losing a son. I know that I did nothing to alter his course, but I do not believe Mallock's destiny was set in stone. If I could have had warning of his demise, I am sure I could have changed his future." King Edinword bowed to King Solace. "I have stolen your eldest son for my amusement, and have done little to gain your trust, but I vow to you that I will give my life for Reagal's. I will join the Majestic, whether he agrees or not, and return your son...or die trying."

Without another word, King Edinword pulled the reins of his horse and galloped in the direction of Fern and Garrick.

King Ardin shook his head, huffing erratically, and began to shout.

"BUT WHAT ABOUT YOUR ARMY?"

Edinword was already out of sight.

"This is becoming ridiculous!" shouted King Ardin. "What does he expect us to do? We have very few supplies, and even fewer warriors. How are we supposed to march upon Timal with such a meager army?"

"Pardon me, my lords."

A soldier astride a blond horse galloped from the battlefield, halted in a cloud of dust, and bowed. "I am Captain Grail, I have been ordered by my king to lead our men in his stead."

"Ah, thank goodness!" exclaimed Ardin. "Now this makes sense!

14

THE FIRST STEP

Edinword raced across the fields of Valom, determined to catch Fern and Garrick. The glistening hair of his black steed shimmered in the light as it cut through the morning mist. Edinword pushed the horse to its limits, but Garrick, with his large strides, and Celest, who was known to be the fastest creature on land, would be nearly impossible to catch. Edinword knew he would not be able to stop, even for a moment, if he stood any chance of reaching them.

By midday, the Loustofian king, weary and hungry, could not get his mark in sight. Determination was his driving force, and it had never been stronger. *I will catch them if they stop for the night. I will...I must!* The sun was at its highest point in the sky, and Edinword began to sweat. His armor became an oven. Peeling himself from the cumbersome weight, Edinword let his beautifully crafted armor fall to the ground. The day waned as he continued his journey to the north. The sun began to set in the west, and his determination remained steady. The pounding of his horse's hooves echoed in his ears, and the thundering of his own heart sent rippling waves through his chest. Thoughts of his son's final moments haunted him. Mallock's face, bodiless, pale, and cold, spoke words of disappointment, taunting the Loustofian king. *Why father, why*, it said. Edinword closed his eyes and clenched his jaw. Tears welled beneath his lids, puffing his eyes red. Mallock's voice rose to an unbearable tremor. He shouted.

"I will not fail again!!"

Meanwhile, Fern and Garrick, making it through the fields of Valom, stood at the edge of the Land of the Stone Trolls. The "T" path was before them.

"Garrick, we must not stop for night," said Fern. "We'll veer north towards Dundire and continue on until we reach the Land of the Drakes. With any luck, we'll reach Timal and his army by tomorrow evening."

"But what our plan when we get there?" questioned Garrick. "We only two."

Fern laughed. "I'm afraid I haven't a clue...I...I suppose I'll know once we arrive."

"I agree we not stop for night, but if you want me keep pace, I need eat."

Fern could hear Garrick's stomach grumble as the giant smacked his belly with an opened hand.

"I suppose you're right, my friend. We must be quick, though. I don't want to linger too long. Even the land of Valom is no longer safe from foul creatures, and we're far too close to wandering trolls for my comfort."

Garrick gave a quick nod of agreement, and the two companions sat side by side and pulled some elven bread from pouches secured to Celest's saddle. The unicorn lipped up the fallen crumbs, strolled to the only patch of brown grass and grazed.

With night fully upon them, Fern became guarded knowing their vulnerability as they sat in the open. Celest's head suddenly jerked up from the grass as she let out a low snort. Fern immediately stood to his feet and drew his sword.

"Garrick, arm yourself, we have company approaching."

Fern could hear the hooves of a galloping horse closing in. Within seconds, he could see the silhouette of the steed carrying its rider.

Edinword slowed his pace as he came closer.

"Majestic, please lower your weapon. I am only here to aid you in your quest," shouted the king.

Fern, arm held ridged, sword raised high, stood resolute as Edinword trotted forward into the moonlight.

"Go back!" commanded Fern. "I don't want your help, nor does Reagal. Besides, you'll only slow my efforts."

Garrick stood by Fern, lowering his own sword.

"I am sorry, Fern, but your giant is not as fast as you might have thought, or I would not have been able to catch you."

Garrick's head dropped in shame, heaving a sigh of embarrassment. His look of humiliation angered Fern, and he kept his sword poised and lunged forward at Edinword.

"I will not tell you again!" commanded Fern as he raised his sword higher.

"Then you must kill me." Edinword maneuvered his horse closer to Fern. "I will not retreat."

The two men stood staring at one another, deadlocked, waiting for the other to recoil. Neither moved.

"Sirs, please, I know I not smart giant, but I know we wasting time." Garrick eased his way in between Edinword and Fern like a massive wall. His sheepish look calmed each man, and his sincere speech sliced through the tension like a knife. "Can both bear each other company for master Reagal sake?"

Fern lowered his sword and placed it back in its scabbard.

"You're right, Garrick," answered Fern. "This so-called king isn't worth my time."

Fern mounted Celest and motioned Garrick to follow.

"We won't wait for you if you fall back," yelled Fern as he rode into the blackness of night.

King Edinword grinned triumphantly and kicked his horse.

The night seemed short, and morning crept up like a sword in the back. The stabbing pain of what was about to be seen was sharp and terrible.

Fern and company reached the kingdom of Dundire. The base of the dwarven stronghold came into view and Fern's heart plummeted. Garrick, with his small, glimmering eyes, held back the moisture that begged to be released. Edinword trailed behind, his head held low.

The sight of the once-quaint village lay in ruins. The handsome little homes stood burnt to a crisp with charred heirlooms and belongings strewn amongst the skeletal remains of lumber and stone. The massive walls of Dundire still stood intact, but the gates of the mighty fortress lay unhinged, broken into scrap metal and scattered. The remnants of a great battle were present in every direction. Bodies of dwarves, trocks, and turgoyles littered the streets. Spears implanted in the ground pointed towards the sky, bloodied. Pools of red dotted the earth, and the clean water of the river was now pink as blood soaked-corpses floated downstream, bobbing and weaving around stones. Fern noticed Garrick, pale and sluggish, as he tried to keep his eyes off the tormented souls of Dundire. They had not slept in days, and Garrick was becoming weary and began to slow to a stagger.

"Majestic!" shouted Edinword. "We should rest, or we will fall before we reach Reagal. Besides, no one can keep up with a unicorn's pace."

Fern spurred Celest on, ignoring Edinword.

"You must listen to me!" shouted Edinword. "If not for my sake, for the giant's."

Fern turned his head, seeing Garrick, sweat pouring down his face. He pulled up on the unicorn's reins and came to a halt.

Garrick shuffled his large feet as quickly as possible, stumbling to Fern, wheezing and out of breath.

"I...sorry...sir...I...not...keep...up."

Garrick dropped to one knee and held his head down trying to catch his breath. Edinword sat quietly astride his horse waiting for Fern to speak.

Fern watched as Garrick gasped for air and wondered why the giant was so exhausted. After all, it was Garrick who carried Reagal across his shoulder back in Burdensville, and he never showed any sign of exhaustion; he even took him as far as the Blue Marshes. What was causing this?

"I'm sorry, my friend, I didn't mean to run you ragged," said Fern with concern. "Please, rest."

Garrick smiled and collapsed where he knelt. His large, lumpy frame slammed the ground like a block of stone, sending veins of cracks throughout the path. Within seconds, the giant was asleep snoring so strongly it made the leaves of the surrounding trees rustle as if there was a storm approaching. Fern dismounted Celest and sat next to Garrick. He felt no exhaustion and quickly found himself lost in thought. Fern did not notice Edinword take a seat next to him. It was only when the king offered him a piece of elven bread that he finally realized his presence.

"Why are you here?" questioned Fern suddenly, squinting his eyes as he peered at Edinword.

"To aid you and the giant."

"Yes, yes, this you've told me, but what are your true intentions?"

Fern stood after speaking and began to circle the king with swift strides. Edinword leapt to his feet and stood in front of Fern, forcing him to stop.

"I know, and understand your feelings towards me, Fern Majestic. Justified you are, but please, I beg of you...let me redeem myself."

"I don't believe you understand," answered Fern. "It's because of you that my family was murdered. It's because of you that my life was ruined, void of friends and looked down upon by all."

Slightly confused, Edinword furled his brows as he swallowed a lump the size of his fist.

"I told you, it was Timal who..."

Fern erupted as anger took over his body.

"YOU WERE THE ONE WHO ALLOWED HIM TO MAKE THE DECLARATION ABOUT MY PEOPLE WITHOUT QUESTION! YOU WERE THE ONE WHO ALLOWED MY PARENTS TO BE SLAUGHTERED BY THOSE DAMNED TURGOYLES! IT WAS YOU WHO STOOD IDLY BY AND LET THAT EVIL RISE TO POWER! YOU ARE THE ONE I BLAME FOR EVERYTHING! AND IF MY FRIEND DIES, I WILL TAKE YOUR LIFE!! NOW YOU UNDERSTAND!!"

Edinword stood silently, eyes wide and still. He slowly collapsed next to his horse with his head slumping down and chin on his chest.

Fern lay next to Garrick, his eyes wide open. His trust for Edinword still eluding him, he was taking no more chances. Edinword remained awake, sitting with his face down on crossed arms.

Fern propped his head against his giant friend's torso and drifted off into a dreamlike state. His eyes suddenly began to flutter. He could neither see nor speak. The Elders appeared in his mind. They spoke to him in a language he had never heard before, but understood nonetheless. Through the clouds he soared, watching the world from a separate set of eyes. He knew not where he was, but it was breathtaking.

It was midday when Fern finally stood up. His mind seemed as if it was functioning for the first time in his life.

Refreshed, he shook Garrick's shoulder with his foot. "Come on buddy, wake up." Garrick opened his eyes slowly and grunted, stretching his massive arms in the air.

"Where king?" asked Garrick, looking around.

To Fern's absolute shock, Edinword and his horse were nowhere in sight.

"How's it possible?!" questioned Fern aloud. "I didn't close my eyes for a second!"

"And I not open mine," said Garrick with a smile.

The companions walked around for a moment searching for Edinword, but the only signs found were horse tracks leading north.

"So, I was right after all," said Fern under his breath. "Garrick, your king has deserted us. He's gone to warn his master of our arrival."

Garrick nodded, disappointment in his eyes as he dropped his head.

"You think we catch him?"

"No, *we* can't. I'm afraid he has too much of a head start on us. The only chance of catching Edinword is if I leave you here and pursue him myself."

Garrick's eyes clamped closed as a heavy sigh escaped through his nostrils.

"I understand...you leave me behind."

Fern smiled. "Garrick, my good friend, I'll never abandon you. You must know this by now."

"But if king get to Timal before we do, they know we coming."

"Don't worry, Timal expects my presence regardless. Edinword's betrayal has no significance; it was also expected. Now get up, my friend, we've already wasted enough time."

Garrick smiled in gratitude, and Fern mounted Celest. Both traveled quietly, and before long, Fern began to hear Garrick wheezing. The sound reverberating from the giant's chest sounded like a reed in the wind.

It was not long before Fern noticed Garrick lagging a distance behind. He slowed Celest to a trot to let the giant catch up. Garrick staggered, and his boot toes dragged the ground with each step before he collapsed like a house of cards. Garrick sprawled across the path, his long, bulky arms stretched over his head, and Fern finally noticed the reason for his friend's lack of stamina. On Garrick's right side, just beneath his armpit, was a growing bloodstain.

"Garrick!" shouted Fern. "You're wounded!" He leapt from Celest and hurried to his friend's side.

"Oh...yes, but...not w—worry, it only...sm—small wound," replied Garrick, barely conscious, his face white as a ghost. The giant's head lay to his side, and his breathing was shallow.

"Do you have any of the healing potion?" asked Fern frantically.

"No, I-I use...I use on...on hurt w—warriors in Valom."

"I did the same," replied Fern. "But why would you keep this hidden from me?"

Garrick opened his eyes and looked into the distance shaking his head as the dust from the path settled in his hair.

"I n—not want be l—left be—hind."

Garrick slowly rolled to his back and placed his hands over his dirty face.

"Let me see your wound," asked Fern.

"No, it—it only s—slow you m—more. You n—need save master R—Reagal."

"*We* will save him, but first, I need to treat that wound."

Garrick gave a crooked smile and raised his arm to reveal a tear in his armor nearly two feet long. Fern opened the dangling chainmail to discover a gash the size of Garrick's own hand, which was considerable.

"No wonder you were slowing down," said Fern. "I can't believe you could even stand after an injury like this." Fern studied the wound for a moment and stood back. "It'll take some time, but I think I'll be able to close it."

Fern hustled over to Celest and plucked a single strand of hair from her mane. Using his Ulmeck Rock sword, he cut a link from Garrick's chainmail, attached the unicorn hair to it, and began to stitch his friend's side.

Garrick's eyes slammed shut as he bit his lip whimpering in pain, but remained strong with each puncture of his skin.

"Talk to me, it'll keep your mind off the pain.

"W—What you l—like t—talk about?" Garrick looked up at Fern and gave another crooked smile as he winced once more.

"I'll let you choose the topic."

Garrick's eyes rolled to the sky in thought.

"I—I wonder about t—time in fairy k—kingdom. I r—rem—member Reagal speak a—about Elder Fairies bestow p—power on you. You tell m—me bout that?"

Fern shook his head and smiled before replying. "Garrick, the whole point was for *you* to talk...not me."

"B—But I listen b—better than talk," replied Garrick.

"Very well," said Fern as he looped the link through a dangling piece of bloodied flesh. "I *do* believe the Elders bestowed their power onto me."

"That m—mean you can t—turn into dr—dragon?" Garrick's eyes lit up.

"I'm not quite sure, but I've started to feel power I've never felt before. For example, when we were in the battle in Valom, I felt as if my strength would never end; the wounds I received healed as quickly as they were dealt. It was amazing!" Fern stopped stitching for a moment and stared into the distance lost in thought. "However, I still do not understand how the Elders expect me to comprehend something that was unexplained. And if I can transform into a dragon only when I fear for my life...I'm still not sure I'll be able to do it."

Garrick looked up at Fern with a puzzled expression.

"Why you n—not fear d—death?"

"Because...I've never had a reason to live," answered Fern, eyes barely open as he looked to the ground crestfallen, memories of his broken childhood swirling in his mind.

"Until n—now," said Garrick.

Fern set the last stitch, covered the wound with leather bindings, and looked up at Garrick, scrunching his face.

"What do you speak of?"

"You n—not see? You has friends t—to live for. Friends who d—die for you. You are great m—man, I give l—life to save yours." Garrick paused for a moment and grasped his wounded side. "I fear d-d—death."

"But why?" asked Fern, disconcerted.

Garrick looked up and stared at Fern, misty eyed.

"Because your friendship."

"*My* friendship?" said Fern, not seeming to understand.

"Yes, you my f—friend, and I not have one b—before you. Now, I have m—many friends. I would give l—life to protect. It reason I go w—with you; I want h—help my friends."

Fern stood quietly and stared down at Garrick, handing him a pouch of water. His respect for the giant had grown beyond reckoning. He could not believe the wisdom his friend had gained, but, on the other hand, he could not quite understand it. Fern had lived for so long with just Edgar Jacobs, the old blacksmith, who cared for him, only to lose him to death a few years later. It never entered Fern's mind that someone could care for him the way Garrick had just described.

The giant gulped a large swig of water, emptying the pouch, and wiped his mouth.

"Garrick, I'm not quite sure what to make of you," said Fern glancing to the giant with a gleam in his eye. "Your wisdom baffles me."

"I no have w—wisdom, sir. I only say what I—I f—feel."

Garrick, color returning to his face, rose to a seated position. Fern slowly strolled over and mounted Celest, his head bobbing. *He never ceases to amaze me*, thought Fern starring with admiration. *He is a devoted friend.*

Garrick made it to his feet and shuffled over to Fern's side. Fern handed him a second pouch, this one containing some of the elven brew, and told him to drink. The two friends walked slowly, talking and eating elven bread. Fern had not forgotten Reagal but needed to allow Garrick some time to recover before they set off at a faster pace.

During their conversation, Fern's eyes stretched open as he learned how Garrick obtained his injury. In the battle at Valom, when Garrick struggled with the dragon, a talon pierced his side.

"I not feel it," said Garrick as he poked his bandage. "Only after battle I see blood. I think it enemy blood til I feel pain."

Even with his injury, Garrick fought until battle's end, thought Fern, *his valor's greater than twenty men*.

"My friend, you astonish me each day I know you."

Of course, and for the thousandth time, Garrick's cheeks gave off a pinkish hue.

Their conversation lingered as evening approached. They were not much further to the Land of the Drakes as they had been in the morning, and Fern's concern for Reagal was growing.

"Garrick, ready or not, we must quicken our pace. I fear Reagal doesn't have much time remaining."

Garrick nodded. "Not worry bout me, I able to keep up."

Garrick was true to his word and stayed close to Fern and Celest as they raced through Dundire. With his wheezing and shortness of breath behind him, Garrick's stamina had returned.

Their time in the dwarven kingdom was nearing an end; the Land of the Drakes was beyond the horizon.

King Ardin informed Fern of his path, but Fern had no idea when he would be crossing into the land of his forefathers, or when he would come face to face with Timal again.

The sunlight was dissipating quickly, and the stars started to appear in the night sky. As concerned and worried as Fern was for Reagal, his anticipation of finally stepping into his ancestral land for the first time was at its height. He wondered if he would see a sign or warning marking the border between Dundire and the Land of the Drakes. As they crossed into the north, the landscape became desolate and barren. So dry was the ground that it opened like a parched mouth begging for water, cracks and crevices everywhere. Even with Fern atop Celest, and Garrick with his large strides, leaping over the massive openings was precarious at best.

In the starlight, Fern and Garrick could see dry heat rising from the cracks. They could feel it like summer sun as they traversed carefully through the unforgiving kingdom.

The sight of his motherland saddened Fern. It was far from what he had imagined. *So...this is where my people come from. Huh, figures.* Suddenly, Fern began to wince in pain. The inscription on his arm burned deep into his bones, throbbing. Fern lifted his sleeve to see the writing glowing like a candle in the dead of night.

The pain abruptly vanished.

"You ok, sir?" questioned Garrick as he noticed his friend's pained expression.

"Yes, yes, no worries Garrick, just an old bother that shows itself from time to time."

"You know, sir, I have big wart on foot. It hurt me sometimes. I put Sunfire dung on it to stop pain. You should try."

"Sunfire dung?"

"Oh, I sorry. Sunfire is big red bird that live in kingdom. Its poop good for healing."

Fern giggled in response.

"I appreciate the advice, Garrick, but I think I'd prefer the pain."

Having lost the path after entering the Land of the Drakes, Fern and Garrick continued to travel north. No sign of the turgoyle army was seen, nor any dragon in the sky. Their pace was slowed due to their treacherous surroundings, and Fern began to realize Reagal's rescue would not be soon enough.

The land was vast and flat, but in the far distance, Fern could see the silhouette of a mountain range. The mountains were their destination.

The moon was behind them, and the stars shone bright, making the Land of the Drakes visible to all. Dry rotted trunks of fallen trees that Fern imagined flourishing once upon a time lay scattered in every direction. A dry river bed, riddled with large skeletons of fish, curved through the crusty ground leading to the mountains. Scaly reptiles, similar to snakes, with dark boney spikes lining their sides blended in with the dirt. Large beetles and centipedes by the dozens crawled in and out of the cracked earth. The only signs of plant life were small tumbleweeds blowing past them, occasionally catching a strong gust of wind and lifting high above their heads. *Well, I should've known this is what I'd get for a homeland,* thought Fern as the dead ball of branches flew by his face. *Why would it be any better than my life's been so far? I guess I should stop expecting—*

"Garrick, draw your weapons, and keep them drawn," whispered Fern. "I see turgoyles in the distance."

Garrick nodded as Fern pointed to the left of their path. A few hundred yards ahead sat a platoon of turgoyles camped around a fire. A putrid-smelling slop that caught Fern's and Garrick's noses dripped down the chins of the resin-covered creatures as they raspily spoke in their language. Their eyes, glowing in the moonlight like radiant beams, glanced at Fern and Garrick.

"They're looking right at us."

But no advancement came. Fern and Garrick inched away quietly in the night until the turgoyles could no longer be seen.

Creeping around the broken earth, they moved slowly towards the mountains. Steam, unexpectedly, would shoot up from the cracked ground, singeing the hairs from their arms. *Damn this land! By the time we make it to the mountain, we'll be as bald as a trock!*

"Look!" Garrick said in a whisper. "Trolls!"

Fern saw them. Stone Trolls shuffling their large, grey feet along the ground, grumbling to themselves as they carried massive spiked clubs. They stood only a few yards in front of Fern and Garrick.

"We attack?" asked Garrick.

"No," replied Fern as he studied the beasts' movement. "They're watching us, but they don't seem to be bothered by our presence."

"But why?"

"I believe they were ordered to give us safe passage."

"I no understand."

"I think I might," said Fern, looking unruffled. "Timal wants me alive and unharmed. That explains why he did not attack me in Earthingland, and why he allowed me to live when I fell from Paliden amongst the turgoyle army. It's also why his dragons pulled back, just when his army was about to overtake us back in Valom. He's been gathering information about me. I can't be sure, but I think he was testing my abilities."

"But why?"

"Timal told me he knew of my newfound power. I think he was trying to find out if I can transform into a dragon, and I think he's worried."

Garrick looked down at Fern and shook his head. He scrunched his brow as if confused. Fern caught his baffled expression.

"What is it?"

"Well, you talk bout Paliden. I wondering where he be, and why he leave you," replied Garrick.

"I wish I knew. It's something I've been pondering since it happened," answered Fern. "I just hope he remains on our side, if ever we meet again."

The mountains were growing larger, and Fern noticed the number of their enemy begin to grow, but still there was no advancement or show of aggression.

Swarms of turgoyles, some dragging large bear-skin bags full of makeshift weapons, marched by grumbling and cursing. The trocks and trolls congregated amongst themselves in small groups of three or four. They stared at Fern and Garrick, drool trickling from their open mouths, eyes fixated. More and more enemies surrounded them as they kept their distance. Timal's army was growing.

Staying guarded with weapons drawn, they finally made it to the base of the mountains. Clouds moved in from the west, blanketing the sky. Dust from the ground began to lift with the wind as the two companions tried to locate a feasible path up the mountains. Fern stopped abruptly.

"What wrong?" asked Garrick.

"Nothing, just a thought," said Fern, scratching his head. "When we finally come face to face with Timal, I'm afraid you will be targeted first. Remember that I'm the one who must deal with him, he doesn't need you alive."

Garrick's eyes widened.

"I need you to locate Reagal and retreat from this place," continued Fern. "You must promise me you'll flee if things become more than you can handle. Our allies should be close behind. When you leave, find them."

"But...I not abandon you."

"You must! I'm the only one who can possibly defeat him."

"But Timal can no be killed. He has ruby on neck."

"I'm aware of this, Garrick, but I must find a way to destroy it." Fern suddenly turned to his right, startled by a large figure approaching.

"Hello, Majestic." A deep raspy voice echoed in Fern's ear.

In front of them stood a large turgoyle as tall as Fern. His head was large with no appearance of a neck, and his nose was crooked and turned up (rather than curved downward like the typical turgoyle), revealing protruding hair coated in dripping snot that ran down to his lips. His yellowing teeth were visible, even with his mouth closed, and were as jagged as the Crags of Malice. His breath was powerful with a stench of decay. He was clothed in royal fabrics of green and brown, and he held a sword identical to Lord Orgle's. Upon his head sat a crown immediately recognized by Fern. It was the crown of Loustof...Edinword's crown. The turgoyle smiled as he noticed Fern staring at it.

"Yes, Majestic, it is a rancid piece. Isn't it?" The turgoyle presented Fern with an evil grin as a beetle crawled in the creature's right nostril and exited its left.

"Who are you, and what do you want?" commanded Fern in an irritated tone, brows furled tightly.

"I'm Lord Ratlarp, of the Ulmeck Mountains, and I've come to escort you to the ruler of this world." The turgoyle's slimy tongue crept from its mouth. The beetle scurried to Ratlarp's chin to avoid the gooey appendage.

"He might rule these lands, but he's not the power to rule the world!" replied Fern as Ratlarp caught the beetle with his tongue, chomping it down with a crunch. Green beetle guts oozed from between the turgoyle's teeth as saliva squirted upward and out.

"Hahaha, you speak in the present, Majestic, but you will soon discover my master's true strength." Ratlarp swallowed with a gurgling gulp. "Now, follow me," he said.

Fern dismounted Celest, speaking quietly to the unicorn.

"Thank you, my magnificent guide, for your service. You must leave me now. Go to the west of these lands and find King Ardin."

Fern patted Celest's neck and signaled her to retreat with a quick smack to her hind quarters. She followed his command and sped away. Fern watched as turgoyles appeared from the darkness chasing after the unicorn with raised weapons. *Hah, good luck trying to catch her, you grotesque turkeys.* Celest kicked the dirt from the broken ground, leaving her pursuers in a cloud of dust. Fern smiled.

Lord Ratlarp spun around.

"Follow me," he said with a motion of his hand.

The turgoyle waddled like a pudgy short legged bird, and its puny wings looked shriveled like deformed prunes. Fern remembered the Crags of Malice and Lord Orgle's comments about his "flightless cousin." *He's kind of pathetic, isn't he*, thought Fern. *I wonder how he demands respect from his army?* Ratlarp halted. He swiveled his head, looking at Fern, and gave a quick jerk to the left.

A hidden passage up the mountainside appeared in front of them. Steep, jagged steps twisted and turned, fading high up the rocky earth. Ratlarp, taking short calculated steps, began to climb. Fern looked back at Garrick, giving him a piercing look of warning. He turned, peering at the summit of the mountain. *Impressive*, thought Fern. *Must be twice as high as the Ulmecks.* Fern's eyes drifted down until they caught sight of Ratlarp's wings again. *I should stab this wretched creature in his back and be done with it. He's probably leading us on a wild goose chase anyway.* Fern glanced back at Garrick, who looked oddly confident. *I wonder what he thinks about all this?* The steps continued to curve around the face of the mountain as the two companions glanced at each other from time to time wondering if they were being led into a trap.

Lord Ratlarp stopped.

A distress call, resonating from below, sounded like a screaming siren and shook rock from the mountain as it echoed across the land. The ear-ringing noise carried and faded as the turgoyle lord creaked his head around.

"Ah, your soon-to-be-dead friends must be arriving. I must leave you now. Follow the stairs. My master is anticipating your arrival."

Lord Ratlarp waddled his heavy torso around and scurried down the mountain, disappearing into an opening in the rocks.

"Did you hear that, Garrick? Our allies have come." A sense of comfort overwhelmed Fern, knowing his friends were close. "Listen to me, once we find Reagal, you must take him to his father; don't hesitate to leave me. I'll face Timal alone. You must promise me this."

"But—"

"NO! You must give me your word," commanded Fern, more adamant than ever before.

Garrick's head fell to his chest as he answered.

"I promise, sir, but that not what I want talk bout. I wonder how turgoyle lord knew bout our friends."

"Edinword," whispered Fern aloud. *How could I not have realized? Edinword has been following me since Loustof and knows everything. He informed Timal of the tunnels. My allies are walking into a trap!*

Horns began to sound within the mountain and the ground began to shake. Fern and Garrick watched as hidden passages opened all around them and hordes of turgoyles poured out like an avalanche down the mountainside. Fern raised his sword, but the turgoyles ignored the two companions as some opened their wings and glided down to the ground. Formations gathered quickly, and the largest turgoyle of each group acted as platoon leader. Lord Ratlarp atop an armored warthog rallied his troops. Thousands more poured from the mountain, joining what was now a massive army. Ogres and trolls appeared from the shadows to join the ranks. Trocks accompanied them, pushing large wheeled catapults. The ground near the army of turgoyles began to crumble and collapse into large holes as hundreds of quaggoths emerged from under the earth. Fern and Garrick glanced at one another, each with their own look of worry, knowing their allies were marching into a desperate situation.

Cut the head from the snake, thought Fern. *I need to kill Timal. Maybe...just maybe his hold on the dragons will be released, and Paliden can reclaim control of his kin.* Fern's gaze turned outward, peering over the vast waste land of the north. *But where is he? Why did he leave so angry?* Fern's luck would have to change dramatically for any of his hopes to come to fruition.

Fern motioned to Garrick and the two continued their climb up the jagged stairs. They both felt helpless as the number of enemies continued to grow. It seemed a near endless supply; Fern could not believe how it was possible. *Timal must have been gathering, and possibly breeding, his armies for centuries!* "Hurry, our time is running short!" Fern bounded up the winding stairs, gaining speed with each leap.

Garrick kept Fern's pace easily, but their ascent up the mountainside was taking longer than either was hoping for. Further and further they climbed for hours without a hint of an opening or entrance into the mountain. Their breathing became shallow as the air became thin. The ground below was now far beneath them, and Timal's army looked no more threatening than gathering ants. Fern's eyes surveyed the ground, searching for his allies and their armies; only the desolate land of his ancestors stared back.

"Garrick, I've a feeling we've been sent on a wild goose chase. I see no sign of an entrance, and we're just getting further away from our friends. I fear Timal's deceived us once again."

Fern had barely finished those words when the face of the mountain began to shake. Two enormous slabs of rock slowly spread apart, sounding as if the entire mountain was going to collapse. The ground beneath Fern's and Garrick's feet vibrated like an earthquake, and the two companions lifted their arms and bent their knees trying to balance themselves. Intense heat rushed out from the opening, causing Fern and Garrick to cover their faces. A glow of deep crimson emanated from cracks in the mountain walls. Fern looked at Garrick broodingly, and they both stepped inside a tunnel large enough to fit a fully-grown dragon.

The scent of death was immediately caught by both, and a feeling of dread hung heavy as stone as they traveled deeper. Turgoyles could be seen scurrying out of sight through spiral tunnels bored into the mountain. Strange violet winged creatures that resembled small sharp-toothed fish with legs, known as Chitlings, flew from the ceiling, missing the two companion's heads by mere inches. Torches inserted into swirling metallic dragons hung on the wall every few yards. Steam coming from cracks blew out like geysers. The bursts of moist heat shot in every direction, making it difficult to breathe.

Fern and Garrick had their weapons drawn and held their cloth undershirts over their noses as they crept slowly through the tunnel. No sign of Timal or the dragons were sensed. The floor beneath their feet slanted slightly, sloping into the belly of the mountain. Solid black granite, surprisingly clean of debris, and smooth, gripped their footsteps well. The cracked jagged curved walls rose to a rounded ceiling decorated with small pointed diamonds. *Even here beauty can be found. Maybe there is hope for my land...if I can rid it of this intruder.*

The tunnel began curving to the left, spiraling down, but never branching off. No more turgoyles or chitlings were seen, and dead silence gripped the innards of the mountain. Time stretched like a bowstring. *Will this blasted tunnel ever end,* thought Fern? He was beginning to wonder if they were ever going to find Timal.

Time was difficult to keep inside the tunnel, and it was not long before both Fern and Garrick lost track of it. Hours continued to pass, and Fern wondered if his allies were fighting for their lives as he and Garrick wandered aimlessly into the mountain. He abruptly turned to Garrick as a low grumbling noise echoed a short distance in front of them.

"Garrick, that was either your stomach or a dragon is nearby."

"It not me," whispered Garrick.

"Aw, Majestic, come forth into my view!" came a voice in the same direction of the grumble.

Fern and Garrick gave each other a quick nod and walked around one last curve and into the belly of the mountain. It was massive in scale, a world of its own. Giant crystal-clear stalagmites and stalactites jetted from the floor and ceiling. Beautiful white flowstone decorated the vast floor of the dragon kingdom. There were cave formations of every size and shape as far as the eye could see. Small streams of clear water flowed along the cavernous floor. Large cave columns shot to the ceiling, giving the dragon kingdom a royal ambiance.

Fern walked slowly in complete wonderment as he took in his surroundings, his eyes glared and his mouth agape. Garrick, on the other hand, noticed more than just the cave formations. High above them, near the ceiling of the mountain, were numerous pairs of large glowing yellow eyes staring at the two companions as they made their way around the large structures.

"We being watched," whispered Garrick as he pointed to the ceiling.

Fern's eyes slowly turned up.

"Yes, my friend, those are dragons," he replied as he took out his bow.

"No need for that...come, come," said the voice, now sounding from around some low hanging cave drapery just a few feet ahead.

Fern and Garrick made their way around the drapery and into a large open cavern. In the middle lay a black granite platform raised ten feet from the floor with steps cut out in the center. On the top of the platform, carved from one of the crystal stalagmites, was a throne, and on it, sat Timal. The lord of the north was dressed from head to toe in chainmail armor with a black cape draping from his back. On either side of him sat a red dragon the size of Paliden. They were marvelous creatures that shimmered in the glow of the mountain. Their scales rattled at their slightest movement and their breathing echoed, bouncing off the cavern walls. Their long tails twitched with anxiety as Fern watched their eyes follow his every step. Their massive black talons gripped the ground, cracking dirt and rock between their fingers. And their teeth shone, bright white, as they snarled, smoke rising from their nostrils. Horns from their armored heads sprung erect as Fern came closer. The dragons wanted nothing more than to devour him.

"Ah hah, you have finally arrived, and you have brought the giant. How convenient," exclaimed Timal.

"Where is Reagal?" shouted Fern.

"Patience, young Majestic, patience. I will bring him forth soon enough. Now, let us all sit and speak of your surrender. That is, after all, why you came."

Fern chomped down his teeth, lips curling and nose crinkling as he tried containing the fire inflating his chest. His eyes veered from side to side searching for the Prince of Centaurs. Nothing.

"You will not find him here, silly fool. Only I know his whereabouts, and I will not share those with you until an agreement can be made."

Timal spun on his heels childishly with a click, turning to Garrick, his eyes weighty. "Garrick, my old friend, have you come to join me in my plight? I have just the right place for you in my ranks."

Fern interceded before Garrick could give any response.

"Leave him alone, Timal! You can't control him any longer. Stop the mind games... tell me what agreement you speak of!"

"The terms for your surrender. Do you not pay attention, goofy boy?" Timal spoke softly. "And let the giant speak for himself. If I recall, he has always wanted to become a knight. His big opportunity has arrived!"

Garrick stepped forward, Fern grabbed onto his arm, shaking his head.

"You not my prince, you evil man, I never serve you."

Fern immediately stepped in front of Garrick as he caught the sly grin on Timal's face.

"And there will be no surrender! NOW RETURN MY FRIEND!"

Fern's powerful voice echoed through the cavern, shaking the stalactites that jetted from above. The dragons rumbled with growls and shifted their large bodies. The rattling of their scales sounded as if a thousand rattlesnakes hung from the ceiling ready to strike. The noise sent chills down Fern's and Garrick's spine.

"Now, now, Fern Majestic, I am surprised you are not the least bit curious about what I have to offer. A naïve child such as yourself must be slightly intrigued. For what I have to give...is much!"

"I could accept nothing from you. You are deceptive and evil, and if you do not release my friend now, I will kill you and every last dragon of this world!"

"Doubtful, but what optimism!" replied Timal with a growing smile, still as calm as ever. "You will, however, surrender to me, ooorrr, watch your friends suffer. It is *your* choice. Now, come, sit with me. We have much to discuss."

Timal motioned to the dragon on his right with a quick flutter of his thin fingers. The dragon threw its head back and release an incredible roar that shook the very floor of the mountain. It took all Fern and Garrick had to stay on their feet.

Shortly after, two skinny green goblins scurried out from the darkness carrying a round table and two chairs. Long strands of black hair sprouting from their bodies flopped about as they ran. They quickly placed the furniture in front of Fern and scampered away.

"Come, child, use your head. Place your emotions aside and be rational. Take a seat and you might save your friends' lives tonight." Timal stood from his throne and marched down the stairs towards Fern.

"Garrick, you must retreat now, I don't believe Reagal is alive, and Timal will kill you if you don't go," said Fern in a low whisper, keeping his eyes fixated on Timal.

"He will go nowhere without my leave, and your precious Reagal is alive as we speak, that I assure you."

Fern and Garrick stood shocked and wide-eyed as Timal came closer.

"I want to see for myself that he is alive," commanded Fern.

"Oh my goodness..." Timal cocked his head for a moment and rolled his eyes. "So be it, impatient boy! But if I grant you your request, you must grant me mine," replied Timal.

Fern stood stiff, locking eyes with Timal.

"Fine!" he exclaimed.

"Your word," said Timal his smile everlasting.

"My word! Now, where is he?"

"Excellent! Bring forth the prisoner!" shouted Timal.

15

The Battle of the North

Soma flew high in the sky, clouds streaming by, the sun warming her feathered wings as she surveyed the land of the north. The command of King Solace echoed in her ears, pushing her into the barren landscape. Loyalty to her master masked the chamrosh's fear as she soared deeper into dragon territory. Turgoyles, trocks, trolls, ogres, and quaggoths could be seen gathering below into a massive army. Soma watched as her enemy broke off into separate legions, each one larger than her allies combined forces. She hovered in the air as they separated and headed in different directions. The trap was set, and Soma knew she had to reach her master with this news before her allies arrived in the Land of the Drakes.

She pulled her wings in close to her body and dove towards the ground like a shooting star. Her speed was unmatched as she aimed towards an outcrop of rock. Her wings opened like gliders as she landed on the perimeter of a stone formation just inside the borders of Dundire. She quickly ran over to a large boulder and sniffed its surface. Her large, curved beaked scraped the face of the stone. She paused, nearly dead center, and lifted her paw, pressing into an indentation in the stone. The section sunk inside the boulder and a secret door in the ground slid open. Soma swiftly entered the tunnel, and within seconds the door slid shut behind her. Her padded paws hit the cold, dusty tunnel floor as she ran, head tilted up, nostrils sucking stale air. The scent of her master was faint. She halted, standing where the tunnel branched off in three different directions. Lifting her head, she opened her mouth slightly and inhaled. She immediately recognized

259

her master's spoor. She turned right, heading northeast.

Her pace was hurried, yet she seemed to enjoy the chase as she bounded off the tunnel walls, leaping forward trying to gain momentum. It wasn't long before Soma could see a dim light appear in front of her. Shadows in the distance marched quickly and sounds of clinking metal echoed. The hindquarters of centaurs, tails swiping the still air, came into view. Soma squawked. The loud reverberating noise traveled quickly, and the centaurian soldiers twisted their necks in shock, their hooves coming off the tunnel floor.

"SOMA!" they yelled. "MY KING, MY KING! SOMA HAS RETURNED!"

The centaurs parted, making a direct path to King Solace. Soma jetted to his side.

"Ah, my loyal friend, do you bring news?" asked Solace.

They spoke in whispers, just long enough for Soma to reveal all she had seen. King Solace jerked up, calling Aadoo forward. The acting captain galloped through the ranks of warriors.

"Aadoo, we are walking into a trap, Timal knows where we and our allies will be arriving, and ee as us outnumbered by many. You must not exit to dee nord. Take dee border exit into Dundire and try flanking our enemy, catch dim by surprise. I must leave you now. I place my army, and my faid, in your capable ands. I will be back as swiftly as I can. You must old out until den."

Aadoo, frozen in dismay, slowly thawed and bowed to his king. Solace, with a stern face, gave him a confident nod and galloped through his army of stunned soldiers. The sight of their retreating king left them whispering words of despair. Aadoo turned, determined in his orders, and commanded his army to push forward towards the Land of the Drakes.

Soma dashed to her master's side and back towards where the tunnel branched off. The urgency to reach King Dandowin and King Ardin before they stepped onto the battlefield was known to both.

The dust storm they left in their tracks engulfed the entirety of the tunnel, and they only stopped when they arrived at the divergent paths.

"My feadered friend, you must go and warn Ardin before it is too late. I will go to Dandowin. Be safe." The look on Solace's face spoke a thousand words.

Soma obeyed and quickly headed west towards the dwarven king. Solace watched as his friend sped from his sight, but he did not immediately leave. Something suddenly dawned on the centaurian king, and he turned to the southern exit and galloped faster than he had ever galloped before; Dandowin would not be warned.

Soma never looked back; she swiftly ran, leaping every few yards, gliding through the tunnel. Ardin was further away than Solace had been, and Soma knew it would take some time before she would reach him. The chamrosh's determination was stout, and there was nothing that was going to come between her and her pursuit.

Leaving the centaurian army behind, the winding tunnel was dark and lonesome, and the smells, numerous and faint, were distinguished one by one in Soma's mind. Her eyesight excelled in the dark, and she could see the smallest insects as they scurried down the tunnel walls. Tiny black rodents the size of one's thumb, scampered about, trying to escape Soma's watchful eyes. Normally sweet morsels of meat, she ignored the mouse-like creatures as she inhaled their aroma. The tunnel stretched for miles, and any sign of Ardin had yet to be detected. Soma's worries of failure urged her on.

Hours passed like leaves in the wind, and Soma's strength, although substantial, was beginning to dissipate. Soma surveyed the tunnel floor as she flew, her speed lessening, studying the indentations in the soil. Footsteps! To Soma's elation, she began to pick up the dwarves' tracks. She leapt in the air, pouncing with new hope as she stretched her wings and dashed through the tunnel.

The tracks became fresh and her speed replenished when she was abruptly halted by a fork in the tunnel. To Soma's astonishment, the tracks vanished. She stood, confused, cocking her head left than right, the feathers on her head ruffling. Studying the ground for quite some time, she sniffed the air; she had lost the dwarves' scent and could not understand in what direction they could have traveled. Soma became anxious as she paced in a circle; her hope was beginning to dwindle. She decided to sniff the air one last time before guessing on a direction. As she lifted her head, she suddenly noticed three circular stones in the ceiling of the tunnel. The stones were larger than her paws and placed in a triangular pattern.

Being an inquisitive creature, she flew up and hovered for a moment analyzing the stones. Inserted into the ceiling, they were each adorned with a cross carved in the center. Three symbols spread out in equal distances were positioned around their perimeters. Soma noticed each stone had the same three symbols: the first, an eagle, the second an arrow pointing right, and the third was a drawing of an earthworm. The chamrosh studied the stones for a moment. She then placed her claw into the cross and began to turn each individual stone until the arrow symbols met in the middle. A sudden clicking sounded from within the wall and an opening in the tunnel appeared. A large round stone rolled from its mouth, closing the path to the left. Soma studied the passage leading right, but still could not pick up the dwarves' scent. Once again, she began to turn the stones until the eagle symbol met in the middle. Clicking noises were heard, and the stone rolled back into the wall, reopening the second path, and a hidden door in the ceiling slid open. Morning sunlight poured down, causing Soma to squint. She cautiously poked her feathered head through the opening, twisting and turning, as she peered outside. To her surprise, she was staring into the Land of the Drakes. A large army of turgoyles stood twenty yards away, and Soma slowly ducked her head into the opening with just her eyes and the crown of her head visible. No sign of the dwarves appeared as she surveyed her surroundings. The sun vanished. A massive Stone Troll suddenly startled Soma as it bounded over her head towards the turgoyle army. She immediately ducked back down into the tunnel without being noticed and quickly turned the stones. When all three earthworm symbols met in the center, the ceiling door slid shut and a path quickly appeared in the floor.

To Soma's relief, the scent of the dwarves wafted from the entrance, and to her surprise, an unexpected spore accompanied it.

Hope rekindled, Soma hurried. The tunnel dove down, then rapidly veered north at a slight incline until the ground became level again. Soma ran swiftly, hoping she would catch her allies in time. The dwarves' scent became stronger with each step and the second became undeniable as she continued to gain ground. A junction appeared in the distance. When she arrived at the intersection, she let her nose lead the way. Soma veered right and was overjoyed when her keen ears began to hear the sounds of both the dwarves and...the elves. The unexpected scent she had been detecting was none other than Dandowin and his army.

Within moments, she saw them, marching in tight formation, both kings leading the way. She quickly flew above the dwarves, bouncing from helmet to helmet, until she saw King Ardin. She squawked loudly, getting the dwarven king's attention. Soma noticed King Dandowin coming into view marching just a few feet in front of Ardin. Astonished to see the chamrosh, Ardin shouted.

"Blast it! How did that goofy bird find us?"

Soma flew directly to king Dandowin, knowing he would understand her best.

"Soma! This is fantastic news," exclaimed Dandowin. "Solace must know of our situation. Please, my friend, tell me all that you know."

Soma and Dandowin marched side by side as they spoke to one another. Information was quickly shared. Soma urged a change of course; the centaurs were going to need their help.

"Blast it, man! Speak so we can all understand!" bellowed Ardin as he puffed out his chest in frustration.

"Yes, yes, patience, my friend. I was just about to tell Soma that we are already on our way to meet the centaurs."

Now speaking in common tongue, Dandowin explained that King Ardin had seen the same turgoyle army outside the tunnel exit as Soma. Realizing Timal knew their plans, the dwarven king used a secret tunnel within his secret tunnels to find king Dandowin.

"Oi, Timal has more wits than even I anticipated," bellowed King Ardin. "The filthy buzzard knew we were coming, and furthermore, he has us hopelessly outnumbered."

"The only consolation," added King Dandowin. "Timal does not know where the doors leading out are located, even if he does know which direction we are coming from."

"I just hope old Solace can hold them off until we get there," huffed King Ardin.

"Let us hope, my friend," replied Dandowin, eyes cloaked with worry.

Soma nudged the elven king in his thigh and asked a question.

"Ah yes, Captain Grail of the Loustofian army," replied Dandowin as he looked down upon the chamrosh. "No, he has not been told. His path was not through the tunnels, and with good luck, Timal does not yet know of their betrayal. They are traveling above ground and should be heading in a northeasterly direction. Hopefully they will arrive to aid your master before we do."

Soma, with her beak opened and ready to ask further questions, was suddenly interrupted by the dwarven king.

Ardin, frustrated he couldn't understand a word the chamrosh was squawking, furled his brow. His bushy mustache twitched as he pursed his chapped lips, and he began to point his plump finger at Soma.

"Can you ask that bloody peacock what plan those damned centaurs might have? They'll be facing our enemies alone!"

Soma might not have been able to speak common tongue, but she could quite understand it. Her large curved beak snapped shut as she stared menacingly at Ardin, and a low growl shook her chest.

"My dear dwarf," began Dandowin. "You should respect our friend, she has been known to bite the appendages off creatures she dislikes, and if I might be so bold...the finger you are currently pointing at her would make a tasty treat."

King Ardin jerked his hand away, placing it in his pocket as his eyes shifted to Dandowin's.

"Be that as it may, ask the question!" he huffed as he took a step back.

Dandowin gave a sly grin and began to speak with Soma.

Meanwhile, far from his allies, Aadoo cautiously led his army of centaurs to the tunnel's exit. As they approached their destination, his anxiety grew into a monstrous pain, pounding in his chest. Loud voices of turgoyles and clanks of metal sounded like taunts as they came closer. Aadoo had done as his king commanded; beyond the tunnel was the Land of the Drakes, and their enemy. The Centaurian leader realized there would be no turning back; they had to face whatever evil appeared outside the exit. He suddenly halted his army and turned to face them.

"My brave warriors, listen to me now! We av been commanded by our king to face an enemy dat as arisen in our world! One dat must be stopped at all costs! We must not give in to dis evil, we will burst drough dis doorway into an unforgiving land, into steel and shield! We will destroy dis foe or die wid honor! By Valom's Star! By Valom's Star! By Valom's Star!"

The centaurs chanted, slamming their swords against their shields until the sound became deafening. The ground above shook as dust and dirt rained from the tunnel ceiling. Aadoo quickly inserted a set of stones into slots in the wall. Two large slabs of rock parted. Beams of daylight burst through the opening as Aadoo galloped into the barren wasteland without hesitation. The pounding of his powerful hooves cracked the dry ground. His scimitar glistened in the light as it slashed the awaiting turgoyle army. He was followed by a stampede of centaurian soldiers still chanting the words of their captain: *By Valom's Star, by Valom's Star, by Valom's Star!*

The small band of turgoyles sent to guard the border were taken by surprise as Aadoo rushed out into the sunlight. A large stone troll standing in the center swiftly sounded an ivory horn. The alert soared throughout the land, quickly being received by the turgoyles to the east. It would only be a matter of time before more forces joined the battle. Aadoo fought as if it was the most important moment in the war, his army following suit.

The Centaurian leader was magnificent, wielding his sword like a master painter wields a brush, every stroke precise. The troll holding the ivory horn spun his head. Aadoo had been spotted. The dull-witted creature broke through the ranks, flinging turgoyles to the ground as he lifted a large wooden club above his bald head. Three long, sharp spikes, already tainted with blood, projected from the end. The troll swung the weapon as Aadoo charged forward. The wind whipped through Aadoo's long black hair, and the club missed its target. The centaur was far too quick and agile for the bumbling troll, sweeping to the side to easily dodge the strike. Aadoo spun his body in a semi-circle, his arm outstretched, his sword slashing the air. The troll roared in agony as its legs buckled from cut tendons.

"Take dat, you foul beast!" he yelled as he leapt above its hurling club.

The troll ground its teeth as blood poured from its legs, a pool of bright crimson fed the parched earth. It tried once again to strike Aadoo with the spiked end of its club, missing wildly. Aadoo reared up as the troll stumbled trying to get to its feet. Lunging forward, he plunged his sword deep into the troll's chest. He watched as the collapsing beast crushed the bodies of turgoyles standing too close.

Aadoo's army, nearly as skilled as he, made short order of the turgoyles.

A low drumming sounded from the east. Aadoo's face tensed, his eyes squinted, and he could see how desperate their situation was becoming.

Long spears jetted from the hands of armor-clad enemies, marching towards Aadoo in the distance. Not only turgoyles occupied the swiftly approaching hordes, but stone trolls as well as giant cave ogres from the nether regions of Earthingland, slamming mystic cowhide drums. The beats sounded with Aadoo's pounding heart. In the center, he saw a legion of quaggoths, blinded by the sun and driven from underneath the earth by threat of torture, stumbling as they followed the sound of the drums. Aadoo rallied his men around him.

"My soldiers, you av fought valiantly, but dee battle is far from over! We av much more to show dis evil, and show dim we will! Our true capteen is not wid us dis day to lead, but you will fight as if ee were beside each of you! Show Capteen Reagal what you are made of! Fight for im! Die for im!" Aadoo turned and charged the turgoyle masses.

Back in the dwarven tunnels, Kings Ardin and Dandowin hurriedly led their armies to the eastern exit. The hope now was that the centaurs had made it to the border and had drawn the turgoyles towards them. Little did they know that their hopes had been met, but the acting captain of Solace's army needed dire help. Aadoo's forces were being pummeled by the sheer number of their enemies.

They needed reinforcements, and they needed them now. Thankfully, the exit was before them. Within moments, Ardin had the hidden door open, and their forces began filing out into the sunlight.

King Dandowin immediately noticed tracks from the turgoyle army.

"Soma, you must fly to your master and inform him of our arrival. He will need the reassurance. Now, fly swiftly."

Soma leapt into the air without a moment's hesitation. The warm breeze ran through her feathered head, and she flew through wispy clouds until she could see them. The battle was in full swing, and closer than she expected. Diving towards the mayhem, she tried to locate King Solace. With no idea that he had taken an unknown route out of the tunnels, and had yet to return, the chamrosh zigged left and right, up and down, searching. She suddenly spotted Aadoo charging a cave ogre. She veered down towards the beast as Aadoo engaged. The chamrosh swooped in front of the ogre, sinking her talons into its face and tearing eyes from their sockets as Aadoo thrust his sword through its belly, the ogre's intestines spilling like cooked noodles from a pot.

"Soma, tell me you av brought us good news!" shouted Aadoo. The centaur's powerful voice easily reached Soma's ears. "Tell me my king is on is way wid reinforcements!"

Soma was shocked to hear King Solace had not returned. Knowing there was no time, she quickly disregarded the news and revealed to Aadoo of his allies' approach.

"Not a moment too soon, my loyal friend! Dank you!"

A language as old as Harth, but younger than the stars, echoed throughout the battlefield as Aadoo shouted of their allies' approach.

His men fought until their arms were wrought with fatigue and could hold their swords no longer. Their strength was all but gone when they heard King Ardin's horn sounding in the distance. Before long, dwarves and elves could be seen swiftly approaching. Two kings led their soldiers into the fray, slashing turgoyle flesh like knives through jelly.

King Ardin, astride a beautiful armored unicorn, waylaid the turgoyles with controlled fury. He was flawless in technique and as accurate with his sword as any warrior in the land. King Dandowin fought by his side riding his swiftest mare. She was a blonde beauty with a tanned, flowing mane that danced with her graceful movements. She carried Dandowin as he slaughtered the turgoyles with little effort.

Aadoo burst through the onslaught of turgoyles.

"My friends, it is nice to see you av joined dee party!" shouted Aadoo with a slight smile as he sliced a turgoyle's head off. "Av you seen my king? Ee left us to find you some time ago, and as yet to return!"

King Dandowin looked to King Ardin. The burly dwarf shrugged his broad shoulders, nearly losing his head to an ogre as he temporarily lost concentration. Quickly regaining his form, he sliced the ogre's belly open, spilling its innards to the ground.

"Oi, me boy, I am sorry, we have not seen nor heard from him since our departure, but have faith in your king. He will not forsake his people!"

Aadoo nodded his head turning his full attention to the fight. The battle was quickly shifting in their favor. The turgoyles were being pushed back towards the mountains, and the trolls and ogres were now only few. The quaggoths retreated into the earth.

Sadly, the shift was short lived, as two more armies suddenly appeared in the distance; one coming from the south, the other from the west, both as large as the first.

King Ardin sounded his horn, rallying his men together. Aadoo and King Dandowin quickly followed suit as the remaining turgoyles retreated to their approaching kin.

The three commanders ordered their men to fall back. They met in the center of their armies, Soma as well.

"Sires, what is our plan of attack?" asked Aadoo.

"Oi, not sure we have one," replied King Ardin with a grimace, looking to Dandowin. "Where are our blasted Loustofians? They should have been here by now! Our numbers were small enough *with* their help!"

"Have faith, my dwarven king, they will arrive soon. In the meantime, we need to do what's necessary to survive," replied Dandowin.

"Oi, like leave this place!" bellowed Ardin.

"Retreat is not an option, you know this. Timal will not stop until each of us is dead. Our only choice is to fight. So please, catch your breath, our enemy has just grown threefold."

Dandowin pointed towards the west. Two large armies could be seen merging as they marched towards the already massive army in front of them.

"MY KINGS!" came a voice from just beyond their sight.

Suddenly Captain Grail of Loustof galloped forward on an armored horse followed by the Loustofian army.

"About damn time!" shouted Ardin.

"I apologize, my lords, but I have been delayed. I bring news from King Solace," replied Captain Grail as he removed his helmet from his head, disheveled brown hair falling to his shoulders.

Soma leapt into the air in joy knowing her master was still alive.

"Well then...tell us this news, boy!" bellowed Ardin.

"He has gone to get reinforcements," exclaimed Captain Grail.

"What reinforcements?" asked Dandowin, extremely confused.

"He did not divulge the identity of our new allies, but he reassured me he would return as soon as he can, with or without them," replied Grail.

"Wonderful!" exclaimed Ardin sarcastically. "It sounds to me that he is not even sure of these reinforcements. So, we are short a skilled sword...and unsure of any help."

Aadoo stepped in front of King Ardin and looked down with a stone face and stern eyes. He was still quite a bit taller than the dwarf, even with Ardin being on the back of a unicorn, and looked very intimidating.

"No disrespect to you, sire, but av faid in my king. Ee as never failed my people, and ee will not fail yours!"

"This might be so, me boy," replied Ardin as he tried sitting up on his unicorn to gain height. "But if he does not hurry, we will not be around to see his triumph."

Aadoo smiled at the dwarven king. "Sire...dat would define failure. Ee will be ere."

Aadoo's confidence gave little hope to King Ardin as the dwarf looked out at the barren land and saw the approaching army.

"We will need more than reinforcements if we stand a chance at defeating that," replied King Ardin. "The dragons have yet to show their foul faces."

16

ENOUGH IS ENOUGH

Bloodied wrists wrapped in rusted shackles hung from chains. A large wooden cross secured to a wooden base slowly rolled out, two large ogres pushing from behind. Reagal's lower body, twisted and slumped, lay sideways on the splintered device. His head was limp against his chest, and his breathing was low and shallow. There was no movement. Fern and Garrick gasped as the ogres came to a halt. Gaping slashes glared from Reagal's sides with streams of blood flowing to the ground. Around each of his ankles were spiked shackles that bore into his flesh. Blood dripped down onto the wooden platform reminiscent of raindrops splashing into a puddle. Fern immediately turned to Timal, placing his sword to the other man's throat.

"RELEASE HIM, NOW!" shouted Fern as he choked back tears.

"My young naïve Majestic, I am afraid we have been through this already. Your sword will have no effect on me, and I am not about to let the donkey free without your surrender. Now please, silly boy, sit, and we will negotiate his release. Oh yes... do not forget, you have given me your word."

"And you said he was unharmed!"

"No, no, I said he was alive," replied Timal. "Now, if you would like, I can change that, but if you want your beloved friend to still draw breath, then you must sit and speak with me, as you have promised."

Look what he did to him! This bastard, thought Fern. A feeling of being trapped grabbed his chest. Fern stood speechless, still holding his sword to Timal's throat.

269

"Very well, my spunky child," spoke Timal. "If I must show you my resolve to convince you to speak with me, then so be it. Bring forth Edinword!"

Forgetting that Edinword could possibly be there, Fern's arm dropped, the tip of his sword striking the ground with a clank as his mouth went agape. Two more ogres wheeled Edinword out on an identical torture device as Reagal's. The Loustofian King hung from chains, body riddled with blood and clothing shredded. Edinword held his head up to Fern, commiseration plastered on his face.

"Can you believe this fool!" exclaimed Timal smiling as he spoke. "He dared to come into my kingdom to try to save your precious centaur, single handedly. What's more, he tried to steal my property."

Shaking his head with a boyish grin on his face, Timal strolled over to Edinword, and with a playful hop, stepped onto the wooden platform. Edinword ignored him and spoke directly to Fern.

"I am truly sorry for everything that has happened to you, Fern Majestic. I know now that I am the one who has brought forth all this evil. I have tried my best to atone for my sins, but I am afraid I have fallen short."

Fern could finally see the Loustofian king for who he was. Misjudged and broken, Edinword pleaded with his eyes for Fern's forgiveness, and Fern ultimately realized he had been wrong. He looked Edinword in his misty eyes, studying the king's aged face, but did not speak. Fern nodded, giving him a compassionate smile. Edinword returned the gesture, understanding Fern's silent exoneration.

Timal crept around to Edinword's back like a predator circling its prey.

"Ah, forgiveness, it is something that should be given freely. Do you not think?" Timal said looking to Fern. "It was something I granted this king a long time ago, and he thanked me for absolution by trying to have me killed."

Without warning, Timal drew his sword and plunged it into Edinword's back, out through his chest. Edinword screamed in agonizing pain as he arched his body. Blood spurted from his mouth as he contorted in torment, eventually going limp. Fern dashed towards Edinword, his sword aimed towards Timal, screaming in anger.

"You bastard!"

Garrick, already amongst them, yanked the two ogres guarding Edinword into the air and smashed them into the stone floor with twin thuds. Timal leapt like a frightened jack rabbit, landing behind the platform as dragons started to descend from the ceiling. The two by Timal's throne surrounded their master, shielding him from harm. Timal clapped his hands in the air, and the ogres guarding Reagal snapped their whips, striking the centaur on his blood-soaked sides. Reagal wailed in pain, the excruciating sound reverberated throughout the cavern. Fern's and Garrick's ears burned, and they immediately ceased their attacks.

"My patience is growing thin," said Timal. "Now sit, or would you like to hear the donkey scream once more?" He lifted his hands again as if to clap.

Still speaking with relative calm, Timal's body language told a different story. His muscles tensed as he cracked his neck, and his easygoing stride became stiffer as he dropped his arms and began to pace the floor.

Fern ignored him regardless and leapt onto Edinword's platform, striking the chains that bound the king's arms. Edinword collapsed to the ground, flopping with a thud. Fern bent down, grabbing the king around his arms to lift him. Edinword's eyes surprisingly showed life as they met Fern's.

"Leave...me," he said through labored breath.

"Not here," replied Fern.

"Listen...to me. You...must realize...that your life is...is worth more...more than you know."

Blood started to fill Edinword's mouth, causing him to choke. A spritz of the red liquid dotted Fern's face, slowly dripping to his jaw. Fern lifted Edinword to a seated position, propping his head against the wooden platform as Garrick stepped forward. The two remaining ogres began to approach.

"Leave them be!" commanded Timal, watching Fern curiously.

The ogres shuffled back to their positions, scratching their heads in confusion.

"Garrick, my loyal guardsman...please come closer," said Edinword as he choked and sputtered, heaving his chest to catch air and wiping his mouth on his forearm. The giant knelt in front of his king, eyes misty and snot dripping from his crooked nose.

"I have never treated you with any kindness...and for that...I am sorry. I allowed your family...to die in my arenas...and I am now paying the debt...that I owe to all. Please forgive me...my faithful giant."

"I forgive, sire," replied Garrick as tears poured from his eyes.

Edinword strained his neck, letting his head fall to the side.

"Majestic...if you die...your friends will lose...a piece of their souls." Edinword stared, thoughts of Mallock crowding his mind. "I will never...they...they will never be whole again. You must not let...you must not let this happen...Majestic, Majestic?"

"I'm here, Edinword," answered Fern.

The Loustofian king looked towards the ceiling, eyes glazed.

"I...I am truly...I...I am sorry."

Edinword's eyes began to close, his body limp. Fern gently placed him down on his back and slowly stood up.

Fern turned to see Timal sitting at the round table, his legs crossed and a devilish grin decorating his face.

"Garrick, stay here."

Fern marched to the table and sat down, eyes burning holes into Timal's.

"Now that you have seen my resolve, we can talk," said Timal as his smile widened.

"The only thing you've shown is your lack of a soul. You're the pure essence of evil, and I promise you that before the night is through, I'll have your life." Fern surprisingly spoke as calm and collective as his adversary.

The smile on Timal's face faded as he disregarded Fern's threat. He jerked up, popping from his chair like a spring. Walking around the table, he threw his hands in the air.

"Fern Majestic, the last of his kind! Valiant and brave! A devoted friend of friends! Now he sits in my presence, not knowing who he is or where he came from. All he knows is what he has read from the inscription upon his arm."

Fern jumped from his chair, knocking it to the floor.

"What could *you* know of the writing on my arm?" he shouted.

"Everything," answered Timal. "I...know...everything!"

"Tell me then!"

"Sit, silly boy, and I shall reveal all."

Fern lifted the chair from the ground and lowered himself back down as curiosity took him over. *Be careful Fern.* He was taking Timal's words with a grain of salt.

"Tell me, Majestic, do you remember how you came to be in the town of Burdensville?" Timal clicked his heels together, stopping in front of Fern and looking down as if he were the teacher and Fern his student.

"No, I don't."

"Of course you do not!" replied Timal as he started to walk around the table once more. "You do not remember because you were lying dormant under the harth before the town of Burdensville even existed."

Fern followed Timal with his eyes. *What's this mad man talking about,* he thought. *Buried in the ground?* Timal glanced at Fern and saw the perplexed look on his face.

"You are the son of Fernand Majestic, the first king who ever ruled these lands. The very same man I gave my blood to over two-thousand years ago."

"You're crazy!" exclaimed Fern, shaking his head in disbelief.

"Yes, that I am," replied Timal. "You can thank your father for that, but what I say is true. The magic of dragons goes far beyond just strength and healing abilities. My kind has the power to lay dormant for thousands of years before hatching into life. Your father knew this. He also knew that he too had the ability to harness this power. Once he had my blood running through his veins, any child of his line would have this ability. He hid you from me, burying you in the ground where you lay in a deep slumber for two-thousand years, ensuring his bloodline's survival. Little did he know that I would devote my life to the demise of every last Majestic."

A small armored goblin came scurrying from around a cave column panting and out of breath.

"Master...master?"

"Ah, Frag, what news do you bring?"

"Beg your pardon, master, but we have pushed the enemy's forces back into Dundire."

"Good, good, but remember, I want no survivors. Kill every one of them!"

"Of course, master."

Frag turned and dashed out of sight as Timal turned back to Fern.

"You see, child, there is nothing left for you to do. Your only option now is to surrender to me."

Fern stood dumbfounded, not able to hear a word. His mind pounded from the barrage of latest information, and he could not determine whether it was fact or fiction.

"Why...what does all of this have to do with the present," questioned Fern, finally able to come back from the trance he was under.

"Do you not think it is important?" replied Timal. "Besides, it is only fair you understand everything before your surrender."

"Why do you need my surrender? Why not kill me and be done with it?"

"You are not very quick, are you? Have you not figured it out yet?"

"Figured out what?"

"I NEED MY BLOOD BACK!" shouted Timal.

Fern stood from his chair, drawing his sword, and for the first time, he saw his enemy lose control. Timal quickly calmed himself, and Fern caught a glimpse of fear in Timal's eyes as he backed away.

"I am sorry, please sit down," said Timal, speaking in a soft tone once again. "I know what power the Elders have bestowed upon you, but I also know you do not yet understand how to harness this power. Please, do not think you can defeat me, now sit down."

Fern placed his sword on the table with a clank and sat back in his seat. He now realized Timal did not want to threaten his life; Timal's fear of the Elders' gift worried him greatly. *But how could he possibly know of this*, he thought.

Timal began to pace, trying to fully regain his composure, shaking his limbs and relaxing his breathing as he took short gulps of air.

"I need you to grant your blood to me willingly. If you do not, then I cannot return to my permanent form."

"Very well, take my blood," said Fern sarcastically, "and I'll kill you in your dragon form."

Timal laughed and tilted his head down, shaking it slightly.

"I cannot obtain your blood as I have the others. I must tear the heart from your chest and consume it. Only then will I be free."

"Why, why am I different from the rest?"

Your blood is now infused with the Elder's blood. It will not bind with any others, but my pure blood still flows deep within your heart. The only way I can obtain this is to consume it. Now, I have said enough. You need to come to a decision, or see your friends suffer before their death."

Fern paid little attention, still wanting clarification.

"And you expect me to let you tear the heart from my chest willingly?"

"If you desire to see your friends and allies live, then yes. You must realize you are hopelessly outnumbered. Your friends are being slaughtered as we speak. The donkey is on death's door, and the only reason the giant is still standing is because I have allowed it. Give me what I desire, and I will call off my forces, your friends will be allowed to walk free, and this whole ordeal will be over. It is all in your hands...or, rather, it is all in your heart."

Fern stood from his seat and paced the floor contemplating his options. He skidded to a halt, spinning to Timal with a sly grin.

"Give me the red ruby that hangs around your neck and I will surrender myself," Fern's tone was rather arrogant as he slid his sword back into its scabbard.

"The ruby? What could you possibly want with this, foolish child?" Timal pulled the chain out from under his shirt to reveal the glowing stone. "You do not even know what it is."

"Perhaps you tell me then."

"With pleasure," replied Timal. "This is the blood essence of every Majestic that ever was. I have personally extracted it from their beating hearts. It was an arduous task, learning their weaknesses and exploiting them, but I have found one way that never failed." Timal smiled as he peered at Reagal hanging from the torture device.

Fern stepped back staring at his friends as he had a sudden epiphany.

"I understand!" said Fern looking at Timal and nodding his head slowly. "You threatened the lives of their loved ones to get their compliance. You had to take blood from them willingly, the same way my father took it from you...and I'm the last piece to your puzzle."

Timal said nothing; he merely stood and smiled. Fern took a deep breath and exhaled. He looked towards Garrick and Reagal, and realized his situation. *What must I do? I can't watch them die, it will be the end of me, but how can I let Timal live?* As hopeless as it seemed, Fern refused to give in. His mind cramped as he desperately searched his thoughts for some way out.

Timal paced the floor, anxious for Fern's response.

"Your decision?"

Fern could not answer.

"Very well," said Timal. "The lengths I must go to."

He spun on the heels of his boots, his cape swiping the air, pushing a gust of wind towards Fern, and walked away. Vanishing behind some cave formations, Fern could hear Timal's muffled voice speaking with someone. Confused, Fern turned to Garrick, but before he could speak, Timal reappeared, walking with a fully-armored centaur, his hand upon his shoulder. The centaur carried a long spear and came into the light.

"Galeon?" questioned Fern, squinting his eyes. "What are you doing here?"

Galeon said nothing and galloped towards Reagal with his spear pointed towards his brother's chest. Fern was amazed to see Reagal raise his head to look at Galeon. His tortured eyes released a pair of tears that fell to the ground, splashing into his blood.

"Maybe this will make your decision easier," spoke Timal. "If you do not agree to my terms, I will have the donkey murdered by his own brother."

Fern watched in terror as Galeon pressed the spear to Reagal's chest. Garrick's pleading eyes looked to Fern, stunned, waiting for a wink, a nod, a slight motion of his hand, something to let him know what to do.

Suddenly, Frag, the messenger goblin, came running up to Timal, barely able to breathe.

"Master! Master! We need reinforcements! Our forces are being defeated!"

"What?" shouted Timal in disbelief. "How?" The charming aura that surrounded Timal vanished, and his body language became agitated. He stomped towards his gangling messenger like a charging bull and halted.

"Tell me everything, maggot!" he shouted.

"The fairies have arrived riding on top of giant bears! They are slaughtering us!"

Timal's chest filled like an overinflated balloon ready to burst. His head tilted back, and his mouth stretched open far beyond mortal capability. A roar that could only be described as terrible burst from deep within Timal's chest. His dragon legion sprung from their perches to join the battle. Stalactites rained like missiles, crashing to the ground. Fern and Garrick dodged the shattered fragments and watched as dozens of crimson dragons swooped from the cavern ceiling, twisting and spinning through the air. Fern's eyes bounced back and forth as the last of Timal's guard disappeared through the exit. *Now, now is the time!*

"GARRICK!" shouted Fern.

Without hesitation, Garrick leapt onto the platform, flying headfirst into Galeon like a battering ram. Reagal's brother shot through the air as if he had been hit by a ton of bricks. His body slammed into a cave column, crashing to the ground. Galeon lay unconscious, spear still grasped in his hand.

Gripping Reagal's chains in his giant hands, Garrick pulled. His muscles pulsed on his forearms, and his wrists twisted. The giant grunted as sweat began to drip from his brow. The chains binding Reagal's hands sprang free, and the centaur collapsed to the wooden platform, splashing into a pool of blood. Garrick scooped his arms under his friend's body and gently lifted him over his shoulder. Blood drenched Garrick's back.

Turning towards the tunnel, Garrick was immediately met by the two guarding ogres. The beasts raised their whips, striking simultaneously. Garrick spun to his side, protecting Reagal, and accepted the searing pain. Fern drew his sword and tore across the cavern to help his friend. Timal stood back, hands clasped behind his back as he playfully balanced on his heels, calmly watching everything unfold.

The ogres, blindsided by Garrick's massive frame, did not see Fern until it was too late. He quickly buried his sword through one of the beast's back. The instant kill gave the ogre no chance to scream and it collapsed to the ground.

"Go! Garrick...GO!" shouted Fern as the second ogre spun around and charged Fern, its whip snapping the air. Garrick, eyes strained, shook as he laid Reagal gently on the ground. The giant bounded towards the battle, his thoughts now on helping Fern.

"No, Garrick! Leave now!" shouted Fern.

It was too late. Timal stood where Reagal lay. His menacing shadow blanketed the wounded centaur, and his eyes were wild as his devilish smile grew into a maddening chuckle. His sword dug into the wounded centaur's throat, and a trickle of blood began to find its way to the ground. Fern quickly finished off the remaining ogre with one fatal swing of his blade, slicing its neck open like a split melon, its blood pouring to the cavern floor. The thick red liquid splashed upon the ground as the ogre slumped to its knees before flopping onto its face. Blood flowed towards Fern, reaching the tips of his boots. Garrick stood frozen as Timal raised his sword and looked towards them, laughing hysterically.

"NO, PLEASE...WAIT!" shouted Fern, dropping his sword and holding his hands in the air. Timal's smile changed into a sneer as he swung the sword. His cape blew like a flag in the wind and his blond hair rose from his shoulders. Fern could only watch as the blade came down. Slow motion took over reality as he dashed towards Reagal, trying to come between Timal's blade and the centaur's neck. The air from his lungs suddenly left him as he was flung backwards. His attempt to save Reagal was thwarted by the giant, and Fern watched helplessly as Garrick threw himself over Reagal's body. Timal's sword sliced deep. Garrick rolled to his side, lying on the ground next to his friend, clinching his chest. The giant squirmed in pain, his large legs kicking the dust from the ground. Blood squirted between Garrick's fingers as he grasped his wound. The giant choked as his eyes widened and filled with tears. Timal stepped back in pure glee as he cackled like an old hag. Paying little attention to anything else, Fern ran to the fallen giant's side.

He knelt, crashing into Garrick, anguish gushing from his eyes. The giant looked up at his friend with tears streaming down his face. Blood spurted Fern's cheeks like a canvas as he tried placing his hands to the gaping slash wound. There was no use, the damage ran deep to Garrick's heart. His life was fading quickly as he struggled to speak. Fern cradled his friend's massive head in his arms.

"Forgive me...my friend," spoke Garrick as his skin went pale. "I sh-should no... have...disobey y-you."

"Don't be silly, you owe me no apologies," replied Fern as he let the tears flow.

"T-T-Tell Master R-Reagal...that I-I sorry...I not s-save him...from d-d-dragon. I..." Garrick looked to the ceiling. "I...w-w-will miss...I will m-miss...my friends."

Garrick's eyes rolled back in his head and a final breath echoed through the cavernous innards of the mountain. Fern wept on his knees uncontrollably. *No, no, no, no, NO, NO! How could I have let this happen? Why Garrick? Why him?* As Fern sat in Garrick's blood, drenching the ground further with his tears, he remembered Edinword's final words. Fern could feel his heart tearing open like a thin piece of parchment; a part of himself was being ripped from his soul. As Fern held his friend in his arms, thoughts of losing another, Reagal, began to consume Fern. For the first time, he felt fear, but not of death...no, death would never threaten Fern...he feared for his friends. They had become everything, they had become his family, they had become his *life*.

Fern pulled Garrick's face to his until their foreheads met. *You are a true hero, Garrick of Loustof. I will not let you die in vain.* Fern gently rested Garrick's head upon the ground. He stood. Clinching his sword in his hand, knuckles white and teeth grinding, he began to walk towards Timal. His eyes burned with vengeance as he snarled. Timal remained standing over Reagal, his sword raised, smile never leaving his face.

"Predictable. Naïve and predictable," laughed Timal as he raised the sword high above his head. "Now stop! Surrender to me willingly, or I will finish him."

Enough is enough! The sword in Fern's hand slid free from his grasp, clanking to the floor as he froze in his tracks. Timal's eyes brightened with triumph and he lowered his sword to his side. Fern's body tensed and his chest pounded like the hooves of wild horses galloping. He could not breathe. Flames of brilliant blue illuminated his eyes. His bones creaked and cracked as his skin stretched like rubber. Memories of Garrick's joyous face, and thoughts of the giant's pure-hearted kindness spun in his head as power suppressed them deep inside his mind. His legs lifted from the ground as they pulsated and grew. His arms spread and widened, and his fingers elongated as claws protruded from their tips. Shining black horns burst from his back, ripping his skin like paper as they lined his spine. A massive tail sprung from the base of his back, whipping dust from the floor. His arms spread to wings and grasped the air around him. His eyes turned black as midnight and his skin...scales, painted blue and vibrating as he drew breath. His head broadened, and his face shot forward as large pointed teeth chomped down with powerful jaws. Monstrous he grew, larger than Paliden himself. He hovered in the air, staring at his enemy with glassy black eyes. Timal, unblinking and stunned, stood still as stone, holding his sword in the air.

Without warning, the blue dragon snapped its tail like a whip, flinging Timal across the cavern floor as if he were as light as a feather. The dragon circled Reagal, guarding him like treasure. Fern was not himself, the power that engulfed him controlled his mind.

Timal placed his hands upon the ground, pushing himself to his feet and brushed the dust from his chainmail.

"I was hoping we could avoid this, you silly, silly fool, but now I have no choice. I will kill you, and all you care for. GALEON!" shouted Timal.

Awake from his fall, the centaur charged from behind. The blue dragon grasped Reagal in his monstrous talons and shot to the ceiling. He placed Reagal on a ledge as gently as a dragon can and dove back towards the ground. Timal stood clear from danger as Galeon galloped towards the blue dragon.

17

THEY FINALLY CAME

Dark clouds rolled over the mountain range of the north, trailing Timal's army like an ominous shadow. King Ardin raised his sword above his armored head, each allied commander following suit. The charge was given, and the armies rushed forward towards the enemy. Thick clouds of dust rose behind them like tidal waves. Lightning crashed down, and heavy rain began to pour as the decisive battle began.

Roars of thunder drowned out the cries of war as centaurs trampled the turgoyles into the muddy ground. They fought for their world with unbound bravery. Dwarves astride unicorns skillfully battled their enemies while elves sent arrows soaring through the drenching rain, the sharpened heads finding their marks. Loustofian soldiers fought to prove themselves worthy of their great company, and Soma flew above, diving down on the enemy.

Trolls and trocks heaved and grunted as they grasped long wooden handles of catapults. Made of timber and steel, they cast fiery boulders through the air. The blazing rocks came crashing down to the sloppy ground like giant grenades, breaking into fragments as they shot through the battlefield. The shrapnel sliced into the allied warriors. Body parts scattered, bloody and torn. Aadoo reared, his front hooves kicking the raindrops just as a lightning bolt came shooting across the sky. He bounded through the hordes of enemies, followed by Reagal's life mate, Viloria. Both aimed for the trolls and trocks loading their catapults. Wielding a sword in both hands, Viloria severed a trock's head from its neck as she galloped past. Her long black hair, drenched and shimmering, slapped her back as the trock's headless corpse splashed into the muddy ground. Aadoo smiled at the sight of his fellow soldier's success and speared a troll through its chest.

"You take dee left, my friend, and I will take dee right," shouted Viloria as she leapt high in the air, bringing her swords down on the wooden neck of a catapult, cutting it from its base.

Aadoo nodded his head and swiftly galloped back around. Drawing his sword from its scabbard, he disabled another catapult with one mighty swing of his blade.

Their effort, sadly minute, was overshadowed as numerous trolls shot flaming boulders toward their allies. Quaggoths emerged from the broken ground, pulling horses and men down into their would-be graves. Dozens of turgoyles, flicking their puny wings and barely clearing the ground, replaced the fallen. The onslaught of enemies gave King Dandowin and his elves little time to reload their bows. Ogres swinging massive clubs flung men into the pounding rain as the pale beasts plowed their way towards the Loustofian cavalry.

Captain Grail of Loustof rode atop his armored steed, shearing the arms from ogres one by one. Flanking the allied armies from the west, turgoyles on hogback charged, catching the Loustofian captain by surprise.

Wielding a mighty two-handed sword forged by the Loustofian smiths, Captain Grail cut through the turgoyles like a hot knife through butter. The blade caught the light from the lightning crashing all around him. Its gleam lit like a torch and shined bright for only a moment.

Although his skills in battle were great, Captain Grail could not withstand the numbers that quickly engulfed him. He was struck from his horse by none other than King Ratlarp.

Captain Grail plunged into the mud, though quickly regained his feet as the rain tore further into the earth. The ground had consumed his sword. He frantically searched for it, dropping to his knees and combing the watery surface with bare hands. King Ratlarp snarled as he reeled around astride a massive warthog. His nasty molding teeth shone clear as he smiled; Edinword's crown still grasped firmly upon his head. Both rider and swine were armored from head to toe in rust-permeated chainmail that hung loosely on their bodies.

Ratlarp charged Captain Grail. With sword in hand, the turgoyle lord sunk his blade deep into the unarmed captain's body.

"How does it feel, worthless bag of vomit?" laughed Ratlarp as he twisted his blade and jerked it from the captain's chest. Blood flowed freely as Captain Grail fell to the ground, face frozen, and eyes lifeless. He was crushed into the mud by a passing troll, and the hilt of his sword tilted up from the mud, inches from his limp hand.

The war raged into the night, and the storm grew. There was no relent as Timal's army began to push the allied forces back towards the border of Dundire.

Meanwhile, King Solace galloped from his errand. As he approached the barren land of the north, he could hear the sounds of war. Swords waved like conductors' batons as screams of agony danced with roars of thunder. Crashing steel against steel played like a thousand cymbals, and the drumming of pounding hooves beat the ground like a marching band. The centaurian king swiftly arrived and leapt into the chaos without thought of life or limb. He arrived...alone.

King Dandowin quickly spotted his friend. His keen elven eyes watched the Centaurian king's rage as he trampled his enemy to their deaths, and the name "Solace" was suddenly unbefitting. Dandowin fought his way through the battle to greet him.

"Solace!" he shouted over the noise of battle and raging storm. "Please tell me you bring good news!"

The centaurian king spun as a turgoyle on hogback charged them both.

"I av none, I'm afraid!" replied Solace, quickly dispatching his enemy with a swift jab of his sword.

"None?"

"Not yet, but I am still olding out ope dat my plan will work!"

"What plan do you speak of?" asked king Dandowin as his great white steed danced around the slashing blades of numerous turgoyles.

"It is too much to tell on dee battlefield, but all will be revealed if we survive dis night!" shouted Solace.

The two kings fought side by side, carpeting the earth with corpses. The ground beneath them suddenly started to collapse. Quaggoths emerged from muddy openings, slashing with their claws, sending clumps of rock and dirt flinging in all directions.

"My fellow king, we need to make our way to the surface or we will be swallowed alive by the ground."

Dandowin's warning fell on deaf ears. The elven king, astride his horse, was alone. As he tried to navigate out of the massive hole, his ride lost its footing, tumbling amongst stone and mud. The earth continued to crumble beneath them. Dandowin slipped from his saddle, landing on his feet. Through the chaos, he watched as his horse was slaughtered by the underground beasts. Dandowin trudged through the mud, fighting heroically to reach his loyal steed, but the quaggoths were too many.

King Solace, separated by dozens of enemies, quickly bound up the side of the craterous hole, leaping with his powerful hooves. Clawing his way to the solid ground above, his final leap sent him to the surface. Jerking his torso around, he searched in vain for Dandowin; nothing could be seen through the strengthening storm and monstrous horde. *I ope ee as made it safely*, he thought as lightning flashed, revealing his furled brow and clenched teeth.

The night waned and the war intensified. The rain slowed and eventually stopped, but the storm was far from over. Timal's army seemed to grow as the allied forces dwindled. Further into Dundire they were pushed until the battle was solely on dwarven land. Lightning struck the forests, setting them ablaze, illuminating the battlefield as if the stars were as large as the sun. Ardin could be seen astride his unicorn gathering what dwarves remained and retreated deeper into the woods. Joining his dwarven ally and rallying his elven warriors, King Dandowin had made it out of the quaggoth hole, muddied and disheveled.

"OI! You've look better, my friend!" chuckled Ardin as Dandowin came hustling over.

"Haven't we all?" he answered straight faced.

"Where is Solace? Is that blasted centaur still out on the battlefield?" bellowed Ardin.

The centaurs continued to fight, not noticing the retreat of their allies. Soma, with a turgoyle grasped firmly in her paws, realized their position. Rapidly, she swooped down to her king.

With news of retreat, Solace quickly called to his men. Gathering in a row, they stampeded their way to King Ardin and King Dandowin. As the three commanders met, Timal's army was in hot pursuit; there was little time for conversation.

"Solace, where are our reinforcements?" asked King Ardin as he let out a deep sigh of relief seeing the centaurian king alive and unharmed.

King Solace lowered his head, shaking it.

"I am afraid my plan as failed. It looks as if we are on our own."

"Then we are doomed!" bellowed the dwarven king as burning trees began falling in front of them. "This is madness! Our numbers cannot withstand much more, and the enemy is at our heels! If we do not think of something fast, we will surely perish!"

King Dandowin suddenly pointed to the forest. The three kings observed the trees crashing down all around them, forming a burning barrier between them and Timal's army.

"Look, my friends, mother nature is on our side. The trees are giving us the necessary juncture. It will take some time for Timal's forces to make it through."

"MY KING! MY KING!" shouted voices from the distance.

Aadoo and Viloria came galloping up to them out of breath and drenched in the blood of their enemy.

"Ah, Viloria, Aadoo! It is nice to see you still alive!" shouted King Solace as they came to a halt and bowed.

"Sires, dee Loustofian Capteen is dead, but is men remain on dee battlefield. Dae are being slaughtered!" shouted Viloria.

"By Valom's Star!" replied king Solace. "Soma, go now! Warn dim of our retreat before it is too late!"

Without question or hesitation, Soma leapt into the air, soaring back into the battle.

King Ardin shook his head, looking down to the ground.

"Oi, how could we forget them!" bellowed the dwarf.

"It is war, my friend, and war is chaos," replied Dandowin. "We will make more mistakes before this night is over."

King Ardin puffed his chest out and looked to his friends.

"Well, be that as it may, I will not give in to this madness! We must find a way to defeat these bastards!"

King Dandowin looked up at the dwarven king, grinning from pointed ear to pointed ear.

"I thought we were doomed," he said as he let out a slight chuckle.

King Ardin grumbled something under his breath as King Solace began to speak.

"Our ope is in dee young Majesteek."

The centaurian king lifted his head towards the sky as a light rain began to fall. "I av come to terms dat I will lose my son tonight, but I old out ope dat Fern Majesteek will not let is dead be in vain."

King Dandowin placed his hand on Solace's shoulder with a firm grip.

"My dear friend, I am not sure what you saw in the stars, but I have come to believe, as King Edinword had suggested, that our lives may not be set in stone. If I had known all those years ago that my son would perish at the hands of Lord Orgle, I might have changed his course."

King Solace's eyes dropped to the ground as his chest caved with a heavy sigh.

"I am truly sorry for your loss. I av always regretted dee laws of my forefaders," replied Solace. "But even if what you say is true, we cannot elp my son now."

"Yes, that maybe be so, but your faithful guard Aadoo informed me that he has revealed your readings to Reagal himself."

"WHAT?" shouted Solace as he turned to Aadoo. "Is dis true?"

Aadoo stepped forward as a bolt of lightning flashed in the distance and a crack of thunder sounded.

"I beg your forgiveness, my king, but Dandowin speaks drue."

Lost in hopeful thought, King Solace simply nodded his head. Though, his ruminations were short-lived as Soma came flying in from the rain.

"Ah, dear Soma, are dee Loustofian soldiers retreating?" asked Solace.

Again, unable to understand a word spoken, king Ardin's face flushed red with frustration.

"Well?" bellowed the dwarven king as his patience grew thin.

"Dae av retreated but are being pursued by Timal's army. Dae av broken far away from our position and are being drawn into dee nord. We must go to der aid, or dae will be surrounded by dee enemy and stand little chance of survival," replied King Solace.

"The only problem," said King Dandowin, "is that our blockade of burning trees protecting us from our enemy now prevents us from aiding our allies."

King Ardin suddenly gave his friends a large smile.

"OI! Do you think that I would retreat into the middle of a forest fire without a means of escape?" he chuckled. "You forget, this is my home; I know every inch of it, and I have many secret places throughout."

King Ardin, sitting tall upon his unicorn, back arched and ridged, motioned the others to follow. His arrogant posture made Dandowin and Solace give each other a quick roll of the eyes. Ardin and his unicorn, prideful as he, pranced to a gathering of boulders. Within moments, they were filing down into another underground tunnel.

"This was not on your map," said King Dandowin, brows strained, looking at the dwarf with suspicion.

"Come now. Did you expect me to inform you of all my secrets?" he laughed.

"Well, can you at least tell us where it leads?"

"Of course!" bellowed King Ardin. "It leads to my mountain kingdom, but it has many exits. We can take any of them to escape this inferno."

"But won't it take us furder from dee battlefield, sire?" asked Aadoo.

"Unfortunately, yes, but it is better than walking to a fiery death," replied King Ardin. "Plus, we could use the rest from battle."

"I just ope dee Loustofian soldiers can old out until we arrive," said King Solace.

"They are mighty warriors. They will survive," added King Dandowin.

The dwindled armies, down to mere hundreds, marched through the underground tunnel. Silence gripped the soldiers, and thoughts of the injured and the lost grasped their heads. The smells of blood and flesh still sat fresh in their noses, and visions of death and destruction danced like specters in their minds.

Like dwarves always do, King Ardin finally broke the silence.

"Dandowin, I have been pondering something since entering the Land of the Drakes."

"Please share your thoughts, my friend."

"How has Timal been able to gather such a force, and why haven't we seen the dragons yet?"

"Have you not noticed? Timal does not need the dragons to win this war," replied Dandowin with a smirk. "But, I believe we have been fools for many years in allowing these turgoyles free rein of this world to come and go as they please, and to tolerate their plundering of other lands. They grew strong...stronger than any one of us could have ever imagined. We have been blind."

King Ardin stared into the tunnel, nodding his head and stroking his blood-stained beard.

"I suppose you are right," he finally responded. "And now, we are paying for our blindness."

"But our eyes av been opened!" added King Solace with optimism.

"Oi, my friend, I am afraid it might be too late to do anything about it," said Ardin. "But I will not go down without a fight."

The three kings nodded to each other as the silence took hold once more.

"AH HAH!" shouted King Ardin as a slight bend in the tunnel came into view. "This is it!"

He dismounted his unicorn, sliding down with a pounce, and shuffled to the wall of the tunnel. The hefty dwarven king bent over, belly to his knees, and picked up a long steel ladder from the ground, propping it against the wall. He carefully climbed to the very last rung of the ladder, balancing precariously, and felt the ceiling for something.

"Yes, yes, here it is," he said as he found what he was looking for.

Plunging his hand deep into his pocket, King Ardin pulled out a large golden ring filled to the brink with brass keys. It took nearly five minutes before he found the one he was looking for. Placing it into a keyhole, and with a snap of his wrist, a loud *click* was heard. A large slab of stone lowered down to the tunnel floor like a drawbridge, shaking the ground as it slammed with a *crack*. Light rain immediately started to fall through the opening, and thunder and lightning filled the sky. Night was still upon them as they filed out into Dundire. Trees, still blazing in the distance, though lessened by the drizzle, clouded the sky further with black smoke.

The allied forces quickened their pace, following King Ardin, back towards the battlefield. Rain pounded their armor like drops on a tin roof. As they came closer, all noticed a distinct smell.

"What is dat stench?" shouted King Solace.

"Oi! It smells like wet dog!" bellowed King Ardin.

King Dandowin nodded in agreement as they all observed the battlefield. What they witnessed would never be forgotten: thousands of giant Sun Bears with riders in shimmering blue armor carrying blue steel swords crushing their enemies.

Astride the powerful furred creatures, fairies soared above the turgoyles, crashing down upon their frail bodies. The muddy ground became a grave site as the fallen sunk into the earth.

The skill of the fairies was incomparable. In unison, they vaulted from the backs of the sun bears, swords twirling in their hands. The display of gymnastics was eye-popping as Ardin and his companions looked on, slack-jawed. Severed heads and limbs flung about like confetti, and bodies dropped like flies. Within moments of the onslaught, the fairies were back upon their bears, riding like cattle rustlers herding their enemy to their will.

"Ah, my plan as worked! Our reinforcements av arrived!" shouted King Solace.

"How?" questioned Dandowin, eyes still wide and mouth agape.

"Does it matter?" replied Solace.

"But who are they?" asked Ardin.

"Dae are dee fairies!" shouted Solace as he charged into the fray.

Dandowin and Ardin glanced at each other with a puzzled look on their faces and darted after their friend.

The Loustofian soldiers were still in the midst of war when the three kings and their forces came bulldozing into the enemy. The rain began to come down in sheets, but was barely noticed as they pummeled their adversaries.

With the help of the fairies, the tides quickly began to turn. The Sun bears were fierce as they ravaged the turgoyle army. Large, razor-sharp teeth clamped down, ripping the winged creatures' limbs from their bodies, as the fairies swung blue-steeled scimitars at the ogres and trocks unarmored necks. The enemy had been pushed back into the Land of the Drakes. Unfortunately, no celebration was had, for they all knew their most dangerous adversary had yet to appear.

All thoughts were on the dragons as Timal's army began retreating to the mountain. The allied forces withdrew, knowing at any moment the drakes from the north would be descending from their home.

The leaders met in the center of the battlefield with Soma staying by Solace's side. Rain danced and twirled off their armor like sprites at a spring party, and dangling hair, flying in the wind, whipped like sails.

"Oi, my fellow kings and warriors, we all know what to expect next from our enemy, but I fear that even with our new allies, we will still come short of victory," spoke the dwarf in his baritone voice.

Forona and Reannthane of the fairies were present at the meeting, taking command of their fairy army. Forona stepped forward as she removed her helmet. Her long, shimmering hair flowed through the wind, and to the shock of all, stayed dry as bone as the rain found no hold.

"My friends, it has come to our attention the young Majestic presently faces the lord of this land. It is in Fern that we must place our hopes. If he cannot defeat this enemy, our efforts on the battlefield will be all for naught. We must face whatever comes out of that mountain and contain it until the Majestic has accomplished his task."

King Ardin looked at the fairy commander and smirked.

"I will not leave my hopes to one man!" shouted the dwarven king. "It was not Fern Majestic who brought us this far; It was the blood of our men! And little thanks to you!"

King Dandowin quickly interceded.

"Now, now, my stout friend, let us not lose our heads. They are here at our request, and we are very grateful, but you are right. I, as well, will not leave my hope to just one man. We will defeat Timal with or without the success of the young Majestic."

"I respect your resolve," replied Reannthane, his eyes squinted above high cheekbones. "but I think all of you have underestimated your opponent."

"WHAT?" screamed Ardin as he steered his unicorn closer to Reannthane, who sat atop a giant Sun Bear. "You, who have not fought for our world in nearly two thousand years, are going to lecture us about what *we* have done wrong!"

King Solace quickly galloped between the two leaders.

"Please, Ardin, Reannthane, dis is not dee time for arguments! You boad know dee outcome if we cannot work togeder. Our entire world is at stake!" Solace quickly turned his attention solely to King Ardin. "My dear friend, you must control your feelings. We will stand no chance widout der elp. Trust me, I av ad a grim time convincing dim to come to our aid. We must do what we can to keep dee peace between us. After all, isn't dat what we are fighting for...peace?"

"Peace? I am not fighting for peace! I am fighting because an evil bastard has threatened my livelihood; that is what I fight for!"

King Ardin turned away, shaking his head and taking deep breaths. Forona and Reannthane placed their helmets back on their heads, looking at each other and laughed as they rode towards their army.

King Solace stepped back, looking towards the mountain. The storm had passed without any of the commanders' notice, and the stars began to shine bright in the night sky. The ground beneath their feet was no more than sludge, and large rain puddles dotted the barren land. Steam from the larges cracks in the ground rose and hung like a fog above the battlefield, concealing the carnage of the landscape.

King Dandowin turned to his friends with his eyes peering. "Who has taken command of the Loustofians?" he asked.

King Solace suddenly spun around.

"Ah, yes, I av taken it upon myself to appoint Aadoo as commander to dee Loustofian soldiers. I ope everyone ere is in agreement wid my decision. After all, I dink it only fair, considering what dae did to my son. I dink it will be a good lesson for dim," replied Solace. "And I will lead my army from ere on out," he added.

They all nodded their heads and looked to the mountain as an ear-piercing roar shook the earth. Timal's army stood forming into ranks at its base. A rumble deep within its belly sent shockwaves through the ground, and a sudden wind blew in from the north. Timal's army charged without warning.

Ardin galloped to his dwarven warriors, kicking up the muddy ground as Dandowin ran towards his ranks of elves. Solace signaled his centaurs to charge. Soma flew into the sky high above her master to get a better vantage point. The Sun Bears and their riders were the first to meet Timal's army, crashing into them like boulders.

Dozens of red dragons suddenly burst into the sky, breathing fire down on their enemy. The scene resembled grand fireworks, exploding in a dazzling finale. No glee our celebration could follow such a display. Fairies engulfed in flames, leaping from their giant bears, rolled frantically in the mud trying to extinguish their melting flesh. Screams of harrowing pain and slow agonizing deaths roared above the clash of steel and battle cries.

The elves swiftly released their Ulmeck Rock arrows into the sky, but the dragons had learned from the battle in Valom, avoiding the barrage of arrows. Their wrath was swift as they dove down, grabbing the elven archers in their massive talons. Upward they flew, twirling like aerial dancers high in the sky before releasing their enemies to their deaths. There would be no mercy from them this time.

18

THE DEATH OF A DRAGON

Garrick's enormous body, pale and cold, lay motionless on the blood-soaked surface of the floor as Reagal wavered in and out of consciousness. Fern, in his monstrous dragon form, lifted from the ground as Galeon charged. The last Majestic was still lost deep inside his newfound power and had no control over his actions.

Timal paced the floor behind them, watching as Galeon raised his spear. The dragon's belly filled with fumes that were ignited into flames as he released his breath towards the charging centaur.

Dodging the oncoming flames, Galeon quickly leapt behind the torture device that once held his brother. The wooden contraption was soon in ashes as the intense fire engulfed it. Galeon charged once again and released his spear. It pierced the air and found its mark. Timal crashed against the cavern wall, spear protruding from his chest.

Galeon spun around and stood in front of the blue dragon, hands in the air showing no weapons. Reagal's brother shivered. His heart pounded through his chest like a drum and sweat dripped from his brow like a faucet.

Staring at Galeon, the blue dragon looked him over. Its expression was blank as it cocked its head to the left and bared its teeth. Smoke exited its nostrils as a sizzling sound escaped its mouth. Galeon shuddered.

"Please, my friend, I am ere to save my broder, der is no oder reason!" he shouted as his legs began to quiver.

The dragon could not distinguish whether the centaur was friend or foe. It scraped the ground with its curved talons. The sound echoed inside the mountain like nails on a chalkboard. In an instant, the dragon swept its hand across the cavern floor, grasping the centaur in a vice-like grip. With a roar that shook the walls, it tossed Galeon across the cavern floor.

Timal had just made it to his feet when the centaur came hurling into him like a cannonball. Their bodies tumbled upon the ground, slamming into a cave column. Timal chuckled as he pushed the unconscious centaur's body to the side and stood. The blue dragon gave him no time, shooting across the floor in a puff of dust.

Grabbing Timal in its claws, it grasped him firmly. The dragon's belly inflated with fumes; its jaws unhinged, and its mouth stretched open. An orange-red ball as bright as the sun grew deep in its throat. Heat emanated from its mouth like a furnace, and the dragon's breath smoked. Grunting noises followed. An explosion of fire launched from its mouth like a boiling geyser. Timal blackened as his flesh was charred, and the spear projecting from his chest disintegrated into a burst of searing flame. The dragon flung Timal's blackened body against the wall like a rag doll and calmly walked away on all fours.

The blue dragon strolled casually towards Garrick's body, tail flickering upon the floor. Gently lifting the giant from the ground, the dragon spread its wings. Although massive, Garrick was surprisingly hoisted up with ease and placed on the ledge next to Reagal.

Timal stood, grunting like an elderly man, and shook his head as he brushed the soot from his body. His undergarments and cape had all been turned to ash, and he was left wearing nothing but his chainmail armor. He marched stiffly, cracking his neck, and looked up towards the dragon, shaking his fist.

"The power that has you will soon take control, silly fool! You will no longer know yourself, and the Majestics will be no more!"

Timal lowered his hand, smirking and wild-eyed. But it was not an expression of satisfaction. Timal had lost his calm demeanor.

Suddenly a weak voice came from the ledge.

"My...young...Majesteek..."

The dragon's head jerked down as Reagal lifted his. The centaur examined the black empty eyes. He searched for his friend...he searched for Fern...he could not find him.

"Please...my friend, Fern Majesteek, you...you must take back your...mind. You must take...control." Reagal spoke, his words broken as he lay barely conscious. "You must not let...dee power consume you. Remember what Lillia told you. Remember!"

Reagal dropped his head and his eyes closed as his strength slipped. His breathing was labored, and his eyes flickered open once again. Garrick's pale face met him. The giant's eyes, glassy and dead, stared at Reagal. A tear trickled down the cheek of the centaurian prince as he choked back the rage building in his chest. Garrick, stiff and lifeless, gave him no peace.

Fern remained lost deep inside the dragon as Timal circled the floor, stomping furiously and staring towards the ledge. The blue dragon seemed content staying guard while Timal's frustration grew.

Timal began to pace back and forth, mumbling. His demeanor was changing rapidly as he argued with himself. *This will not stop me! I will take back my blood! I will! His heart is MINE!*

His anger burned through his skin as if he were on fire. His teeth ground and eyes seethed with rage as the dragon remained on the ledge. Timal abruptly stopped and pointed his trembling finger toward the dragon. His face contorted, and his breathing intensified.

"Fern Majestic! Find yourself! Take control of this power! Or you will forever be lost!"

Timal's anger was at its peak. Reagal, now fully conscious, but still badly wounded, listened to everything. He could not understand why Timal wanted Fern to be in control of his power, but could not argue with him.

"Listen, come back to us!" pleaded Reagal. "Fight dis power dat as you! You are too strong to let dis defeat you!"

The dragon stared at Reagal's battered face, its head cocking like a confused dog. A glimmer of light flickered in the blackness of its eyes, and it was gone.

Timal's exasperation continued as he began to shout once more.

"Majestic! I will kill all you care for! Starting with the donkey! I know of your relationship with the kings of this world! They will suffer before they die by my hands! And I know of the fairy maiden you hold dear! Lillia will suffer most of all before I rip the heart from her chest!"

The light in the dragon's eyes reappeared with a vengeance, bursting into a blaze of blue. Fern exploded from the ledge. His wings spread like sails as he roared, shaking the entire mountain with his mighty voice. He spun in the air to face

Reagal. Fully conscious, Reagal nodded, a weak smile gracing his bruised face.

The last Majestic hovered in the air, trying to adjust to his new body. The immense power was now under his control. Though maintaining it would be a different matter entirely.

He flew down to the cavern floor where Timal once paced.

"Turn around, massive fool!"

Fern swirled his large body around, his tail nearly smacking his own face as it couldn't catch up with his backside. Timal stood over Galeon with his sword to the centaur's chest. The point of the blade pierced the skin as blood began to flow from the wound, slowly dripping into a crimson pool on the floor.

"This is your last chance, silly boy! You will surrender your heart to me!" shouted Timal.

Fern looked up towards Reagal as the centaurian prince hung his head over the ledge. Fern could not speak. *Tell me...tell me what to do, my friend.* Reagal could see the desperation in his eyes.

"My fader as seen dee stars, he knows one of is sons will die dis night! I trust your judgment. Do what is necessary, and I will old no blame to you!" shouted Reagal.

Movement from the corner of Fern's eye caught his attention. A blood-soaked arm wrapped itself around Timal's shoulder. King Edinword stood behind Timal and grabbed the ruby from around his neck, ripping it from its chain.

"You forget, my friend, I am an Ager, I do not die easily!"

The whisper tickled Timal's ear as Edinword shoved his sword through Timal's back. Launching the ruby towards Fern, Edinword immediately collapsed to the ground. Timal stumbled forward with the Loustofian king's sword protruding from his chest.

"You have no power now, you evil bastard!" shouted Edinword as he lay on the ground next to Galeon, a slight smile of victory plastered on his face.

Timal began to laugh like a man who had just lost his mind. His head shook wildly as he arched his back, the blade of Edinword's sword vibrating like a tuning fork.

"You idiot! All these years and you thought it was the ruby that gave me my powers?" Timal pulled the sword from his back and dropped it to the ground. "The ruby is nothing but a trophy. It represents all the Majestics who have given their lives to me! Nothing more!"

Timal hauled his leg back and snapped it forward, kicking Edinword's sword across the floor. It spun like a top until finally resting in front of Fern.

Fern opened his hand and stared at the ruby. He couldn't help but wonder why it had given him healing power back at the Crags of Malice, and if it was not the ruby that gave Timal his power, what did? As Fern let the ruby slip from his hand, Timal revealed the answer.

"I have already uncovered the reason for my eternal life. It is my curse! I must walk this world forever in this abominable human form, because of his kind's lack of purity." Timal pointed towards Fern. "YOU CANNOT KILL ME!"

Timal suddenly dashed towards Galeon and King Edinword, his sword raised. Fern was far faster. Scooping them up in his talons, he flew them to the ledge. With no bargaining chips remaining, Timal walked calmly and plucked the ruby from the ground. With a satisfied smirk, he looked up towards Fern.

"Ahh, thank you for returning my trophy. I hold it very close to my *heart!*"

A maddening laugh echoed as Timal raised the ruby high into the air. Ripping it from its chain, he quickly plunged it deep within his chest. The red gem entered Timal's throbbing heart as he dropped to the ground. His body began to convulse, and tremendous roars from within his chest burst free from their confinement. Ambivalent, Fern could only watch.

Wings ripped free from Timal's shoulders, jetting towards the ceiling. His legs pulsated and grew. His arms tore from their human flesh into massive scaled limbs, and a monstrous tail, lined with black fins, burst from his spine. Timal flopped upon the ground like a fish from water as he grew into an enormous dragon. He became still.

Rising from the ground, Timal arched his long neck and peered through piercing blue eyes. Fern descended. The last Majestic hovered in complete shock. In front of him was a monstrous green dragon.

"PALIDEN?!" screamed Fern, still coming to grips with reality. "HOW?!"

"Ah hah! Excellent! We can speak to one another again. I was hoping for this!" exclaimed Paliden. "The Elder's power had masked my blood running through your veins, causing us our lack of communication, but now that we are both dragons, we can hear each other's thoughts once more."

It suddenly hit Fern like a ton of Ulmeck Rock. *That's how he knew...that's how Timal knew so much! He's Paliden!* Fern dropped to the ground with a crash.

"I see you are speechless, silly fool, but do not worry, I have plenty to say for the both of us," Paliden's mouth curved into a gleeful smirk. "I will start by telling you that your moment of victory ends now. You will watch as I kill every last one of your allies, singlehandedly, before I rip the heart from your chest...with or without your compliance!"

Paliden suddenly dove down towards the exit tunnel, twisting and whirling through the air. His agility and aerial acrobatics were immediately recognized by Fern.

Fern glanced towards the ledge. Reagal peered over the edge, still helpless and unable to move.

"GO!" Reagal shouted with whatever remaining strength he had. "YOU MUST END DIS NOW!"

I can't leave you, my friend, I can't! The battle within Fern's mind was as fierce as the war taking place outside. On one hand, Fern had Reagal to protect, but on the other, he had his allies, oblivious to Paliden's wrath that would soon find them. *What should I do?* His head pounded as the conflict swelled. Reagal suddenly spoke as if he could read Fern's thoughts.

"Do not worry about me, young Majesteek! If you do not stop Timal, ee will destroy everyding we av fought and died for! Now...please...GO!"

Fern winced, and his heart sank like a rock. His saddened eyes teared as he came to his decision. *Yes...yes, my friend, you are right. You have always been right. I will listen this time, I will trust in you.*

Fern nodded his head and dashed through the exit tunnel. He flew, slamming into walls and bouncing from the floor as he acclimated to his new form.

The night sky dazzled with diamond stars, twinkling brilliantly as wisps of white clouds breezed by. Fern marveled at its beauty, seeing it for the first time through his new eyes. His ears rang, and the allure of nature became tainted with the sounds of war. Terrible screams of torment gripped Fern's heart as he spun in the air to view the carnage. Red dragons rained fire down on his allies. He watched helplessly as soldiers ran like living torches, trying to extinguish the flames. The fairies with large, gleaming blue shields repelled the blazes as the elves shot Ulmeck Rock arrows through rising smoke and scattering embers. Soma circled above, dive bombing the dragons with her outstretched talons and easily avoiding their counterattacks. Unfortunately, she was little more than a nuisance to them, doing little harm.

Fern searched the skies, unsteady. His wings, although powerful, were not yet obedient to his will. Fern felt like an infant learning how to walk. He was erratic to say the least, but his determination was stout as he scoured the land below. *Where has he gone? Why would he retreat?* Paliden was nowhere to be seen. *No... wait!* Fern bit down with his monstrous jaw as anger and worry boiled his mind. *He has returned to the mountain! Reagal!*

Fern spun in the air like a hurricane. Folding his wings to his side, he dove to the mountain entrance. His chest began to pound, and his heart raced. *He is playing me like a fool!* Fern suddenly halted in midair. Barricading the cavernous opening, Aadoo and Viloria stood with shields in hand and weapons raised, the Loustofian army behind them. Paliden hovered above. He turned to glance at Fern. With a sudden movement nearly too fast to follow, Paliden was amongst the warriors. The Loustofian soldiers charged. Fern flew as fast as his body could take him, all too aware that Reagal's loved ones were in dire danger.

Paliden snatched Aadoo and Viloria in his vice-like grip and exploded into the air, dodging swinging swords and flying arrows. Aadoo hacked the dragon's flesh like an ax to a tree. Paliden's skin sliced open, though healing immediately. Aadoo's jaw dropped with shock.

Viloria, arms pinned to her sides, wriggled like a worm for freedom. Paliden tightened his grip. She screamed soundlessly as the breath was squeezed from her chest. Aadoo plunged his sword deep into Paliden's arm. Cracks of splintering bone sounded like eggshells as the centaurian warrior's body shattered from the inside. Paliden grinned as his talons dug into Aadoo's ribs. Blood sprinkled from the sky like raindrops. Aadoo, stronger than most, endured the pain. He was not about to give Paliden the satisfaction of hearing him scream.

"Viloria, hold strong!" grunted Aadoo as he grimaced and contorted his face.

Paliden suddenly released Aadoo from his hand, tossing him towards the face of the mountain. Fern, now just yards behind, quickly changed direction, flying to intercept the injured centaur. Paliden's teeth clenched together, shining bright in the moonlight. With a roar of glee, he released Viloria in the opposite direction and dove toward the tunnel.

Fern caught Aadoo's feet before hitting the mountain and dashed towards Viloria as she plummeted to her death. Her screams echoed in his ears. *I'm not going to make it!* Flashes of Reagal's pained face spun in Fern's mind. *No, no, not this!*

Like a spirit from the heavens, a chamrosh swooped from nowhere, grabbing Viloria by the shoulders and bringing her to a soft landing. To Fern's amazement,

Soma was not Viloria's savior. His large dragon eyes sprung open wide as he looked up to the stars. Dozens of beautiful chamroshs, flying in from the south, crowded the sky. Fern wasted no time, quickly descending to where Viloria and the chamrosh stood. Laying Aadoo on the ground, he pivoted on his hind legs and darted toward the tunnel.

Fern barreled through the air, slamming into the side of the mountain. *Blast it, Fern, calm yourself and control your movements!* The Loustofian army scattered for cover as an avalanche of rock and stone tumbled from above.

Fern gathered himself and entered the cavern. The winding tunnel was void of light, but to Fern's astonishment, he could see perfectly. His eyes were like beams of lights, shooting streams of luminescence upon the ground. Fern opened his wings and thrust them to his sides. He steadied his body, gliding around the bends and curves of the tunnel. He was learning.

The path seemed short as Fern emerged from the darkness and found himself standing in the open cavern facing Timal's throne. He immediately snapped his head towards the ledge. They were gone. *I'm too late!* Fern's heart cramped, and his eyes went misty as thoughts of Garrick's death swirled in his mind. *Now Reagal... Edinword! He has no mercy!* Emotions formed into tears as he screamed the green dragon's name.

"PALIDEN! PLAIDEN! Show yourself you cowardly serpent! Sho—"

Paliden was a wrecking ball, slamming into Fern. The air from Fern's lungs ceased to flow, and his vision went dark as something clamped around his neck. Paliden grasped Fern's throat with his razor-sharp talons as the two dragons tumbled, wrestling into cave columns. Stalactites shot towards the ground like bombs, exploding into fragments, sliding in every direction. Fern grabbed Paliden's wrists, prying the talons from his throat, the fresh breath of life inflating his lungs once more. He filled his belly with fumes, igniting them into his enemy's face like a fire storm. Blinded by the flames, Paliden's only recourse was to push away. Fern's powerful chest acted like a springboard as Paliden kicked his hind legs forward. The green dragon shot towards the ceiling, swirling his body, wings guiding his movements. Fern regained his footing, but only for a moment. Paliden hit Fern like a battering ram. Fern's body cracked as it blasted through formation after formation. An avalanche of rock and stalactites buried him in a heap. Fern burst from the rubble with a mighty roar, his wings spread. Paliden stood in front of him. He plunged his claws into Fern's chest. Wrenching with pain with eyes clamped shut, Fern gave a tremendous roar as blue blood squirted into Paliden's face. The green dragon smiled.

Fern's eyes crept open. His crushing grip held Paliden's wrist. The two dragons stared at each other, snout to snout. Paliden struggled to push his hand deeper into Fern's chest as Fern tried to retract it.

"I will have your heart!" shouted Paliden as blood started to flow rapidly. "It is inevitable!"

"I'll never..."

Fern was weakening.

His strength is unbelievable...I can't give in, not now!

Fern's breath labored and sweat began to drip between his dragon eyes.

"Where...are...my...friends?" he said struggling to speak.

"You are about to die, and all you can think about are those insignificant beasts? They will be your DOWNFALL!"

"You're wrong!" shouted Fern. "They'll be my...*strength*!"

Fern's adrenaline exploded. His forearms pulsed as he slowly pulled Paliden's claws from his chest.

Grabbing the green dragon around the torso, Fern rose from the cavern floor. His momentum grew as he flew higher. Paliden struggled to free himself, jerking his long, scaled neck from side to side, but there was no escaping Fern's grip.

With Paliden's back facing the ceiling, they hit with devastating impact. The dragons blasted through the ceiling like an erupting volcano. Massive boulders hurtled into the air, landing on the outskirts of the battlefield. The armies paused and stared into the sky as the two aerial acrobats rolled and twisted in mid-air.

The red dragons fled to their master's aid, but were immediately intercepted by dozens of chamroshs swooping up from below. The battle that would become known as the War of Wings began.

Fern clamped tightly around Paliden's body. The air was thinning rapidly the higher he flew, and Fern began to feel light-headed. His eyes rolled back, and his grip loosened. Paliden broke free. Fern began to plummet towards the battlefield, his back downward and wings pushed up, fluttering like loose pieces of skin. He was losing consciousness. In seconds, Paliden's arms wrapped around Fern's body. The two dragons were a meteor about to crash. The squealing noise from the rapid fall pierced the ears of those both fair and foul. Paliden released Fern, spreading his wings, and ceasing his rapid descent. Fern plowed into the ground like a ball from a cannon. A gigantic crater sent a wave of dirt and debris pummeling everything in its path, blanketing the land.

"I have been a dragon for thousands of years and can withstand all the elements of nature!" shouted Paliden as he hovered over Fern. "You cannot begin to understand my abilities! Now, surrender and my offer will stand!"

"What did you do with my friends?" asked Fern again.

A voice so pleasant, and unexpected, replied.

"Have no fear, they are in good hands!"

Hanging over the edge of the crater was Lillia in full armor astride a giant Sun Bear. "You must destroy Paliden now!" she shouted "He will not be in his dragon form for much longer. He is vulnerable! Finish him!"

But how, thought Fern.

"You must attack his—"

Without warning, a fireball shot towards Lillia. The sphere of burning rage spun through the air, a tail of blazing orange behind it. The speed was instant. It struck. Lillia was a living projectile, ripped from her saddle and ricocheting across the ground. Her body was broken, eventually coming to a halt amongst shattered rock and bloodied corpses.

Fern roared. Quickly, he rose from his back, exploding from the crater. Lillia lay a few hundred meters away on her back. Next to her was her Sun Bear's dead body, burnt beyond recognition. The smell of singed hair and charred flesh wafted in the air as Fern slammed the ground next to Lillia. He searched for signs of life. Lillia's eyes slowly opened to a slit. Fern tried to smile, but a searing pain suddenly grabbed his shoulders. His body lifted from the ground, and Lillia became a tiny ant as the distance between them grew. Paliden's talons sunk deep, and Fern's anger burned through the pain.

The stars were growing large in the midnight blue as Fern whipped his tail back, slamming Paliden in his face. Paliden's grasp was powerful, and his concentration even more so. His eyes clamped shut as he cut through the thin frigid air. The ground beneath them was a globe as they hovered in the lower atmosphere of Harth.

Fern twisted and clawed. *I can't break free! There must be some way I can distract him. Think, Fern, think!* His face suddenly brightened. He smiled. Fern's eyes rolled upward.

"So, you can't keep your form for long?" he taunted.

"Your female sprite will pay for her loose tongue when I am finished with you!" shouted Paliden.

"Yes, yes, everyone will pay," chuckled Fern in a sarcastic tone. "Just like Reagal, who now is beyond your grasp, and Edinword, whom you failed to kill. Hah! Even the Majestics...you have yet to finish them off! Your diabolical scheme is not very sound. Wouldn't you say?"

Paliden's claws shifted and his breathing heaved.

"Do not think you can outwit me with mind games!"

"I won't need to outwit you, I'll only need to kill you!"

Fern spread his wings open, and with a sudden jerk, he ripped his shoulders free.

Fern hovered in front of Paliden, breathing the thin air as his new body acclimated to the extreme altitude.

"So, Majestic, I see you have adapted quickly. I must rethink my options," said Paliden, smiling.

"I won't give you the chance!" shouted Fern as he became a blue streak, shooting through the air.

Like a bolt of lightning, he struck. His jaws clamped around Paliden's throat. The green dragon roared. An echo bounced from the mountain side. Paliden clawed Fern's chest and belly, ripping scales free. They fell from the sky as shards of glass, light from the stars and moon reflecting on them like diamond shields.

The dragons plummeted, locked in a death roll like two giant crocodiles. The earth shook and broke as they crashed into the battlefield. Fern lost his advantage as Paliden's throat dislodged from his mouth. The dragons battled ferociously, neither gaining the upper hand. Fern was the stronger of the two, but he lacked coordination and experience.

The War of Wings intensified as Fern and Paliden fought for domination. The battle surrounding them still raged, and its outcome was uncertain.

Breaking free, Fern rose from the ground to face Paliden. His wings flapped as his chest expanded and collapsed. Their fight came to a standstill, and both dragons contemplated their next moves.

"Majestic, why continue a battle that you cannot win?" said Paliden as he rose to meet Fern. "You cannot kill me, and as you try, your friends are being massacred. Take my offer, sacrifice your heart to me...end this conflict!"

Fern grinned as he slowly landed on the ground and caught his breath. "I'm finished listening to your deceptive words," he replied. "I see the reality of things.

Your confidence isn't what it was." Fern spun around with his arm stretched and his hand open like he was presenting a gift. "My allies are equal to yours, they'll not give in to your armies so easily, and I've dismissed your offer long before now!"

"You are sadly mistaken, Majestic," replied Paliden as he observed the battlefield.

"No," answered Fern in a calm tone. "You're the one who has made mistakes. The first was taking Garrick's life, and I swear to you, I'll be there when you make your last. That is when I'll kill you."

Anger began to radiate from Paliden's body like heat from the summer sun. The green dragon's head tilted down as the muscles in his hind legs tensed. His bright white teeth scissored together as steam rose from his nostrils, and his talons grasped the air.

"If I cannot have the heart from your chest, then I will take the heart from your life!" shouted Paliden.

I've gotten to him, thought Fern as he braced himself.

Tremors invaded the earth as Paliden released an ear-piercing shriek. He charged. Fern followed suit. The two titans barreled towards one another, their determination unmatched. Swerving at the last possible moment, Paliden veered right.

Fern spun around to see his rival flying at near impossible speeds directly towards Lillia. Fern's roar broke in distress as he dashed to catch his enemy. *He's dead! I'll kill him!*

Fern roared in agony as he witnessed Lillia being roasted alive. But as the fire from Paliden's throat diminished...*I don't believe it! Reagal?!* The Centaurian prince, holding a blue shield high above his head, stood over Lillia's body.

Fern tore into Paliden like a savage demon. Turgoyles and quaggoths scattered trying to avoid the wrestling dragons as they tumbled to the ground. Their massive bodies rocked the north. The fight was masked by steam bursting into the sky. It danced like ghoulish devils, egging the two dragons on. Fern suddenly heard a soft voice echo in his mind. *Lillia!*

"*My Fern, you must take his heart from his chest while the gem remains inside. It is the only way to end this.*"

"You fool!" shouted Paliden. "Does the ignorant sprite think I cannot hear her thoughts?! I will not allow you to kill me! I will be the only one taking a heart tonight!"

There was worry in Paliden's trembling voice, and Fern's hope grew into a bright light.

Breaking free once again, Paliden ascended into the night sky. Fern was on his tail, but the speed of the green dragon was far greater. Paliden increased his distance. With a sudden turn, he dove towards Fern with his arm outstretched. Fern reached into the air as if grasping for something. He pushed his ability to its limits. The two dragons clashed, plunging their claws deep into each other's chests. Blood burst from their bodies like water from a geyser. A shockwave swept the battlefield as they roared simultaneously. The armies froze to watch the sky. Fern could feel Paliden's claw grip his heart. He held Paliden's arm tightly around the wrist. No worry was in Fern's mind.

Paliden's eyes widened with fear as his face scrunched, and he pleaded to Fern. "NO! MAJESTIC!" he shouted as he felt Fern's hand tighten around his own heart. "Please! Do not do this! I have yet to reveal som—"

"It's OVER!" shouted Fern. "No more lies!"

"PLEASE! You do not understand! There is a threat you need to know about. Larger than any this world has ever known. We can defeat this evil, *together!* PLEASE, do not end my life! You must listen to me! This comes from your father's own words. Do what he could not...join me."

Fern, calm and heartbeat steady, stared into Paliden's eyes. "Don't worry, I'll do what my father could not."

The last Majestic slowly extracted the beating heart from Paliden's chest, but trying for one last ditch effort at victory, Paliden tightened his grip.

"I WILL HAVE YOUR HEART!" he shouted.

"You already ripped the heart from my chest when you took Garrick from me," said Fern, eyes piercing, brows furled deep as he held Paliden's throbbing heart in his claw. The green dragon's life was fading.

Paliden's wrist was glass, shattering in Fern's tightening grip.

Pulling the limp claw from his chest, Fern watched as the piercing blue color from Paliden's eyes faded to black. His lifeless body plummeted to the earth, landing amongst his army with a thunderous boom.

No wound, not even a scar, tarnished Fern's chest. He held Paliden's still-heart in his hand. His grip tightened. A burst of blood exploded through his fingers like jelly until nothing remained but the red ruby. He looked down to see the remains of Paliden's army retreating into the distance. The dragons had vanished from the sky, and Fern's allies were cheering as the morning sun rose in the east.

19

THE KING OF THE NORTH

"LILLIA!"

Fern's eyes burst open as sunlight beamed through a window to his right. He sat up, a plush down blanket slid down to his lap. He scanned his surroundings finding himself in a small room on a soft bed dressed in a light blue silken robe. Around his neck was a golden chain, and hanging from its middle was the red ruby.

The window was open as a cool morning breeze rushed in. Birds sang sweetly, and the sound of running water could be heard in the distance. The sun was shining brightly, warming Fern's face. *This is odd*, he thought as he suddenly realized he was back in his human form. Fern sat for a while looking around the room. *Was it all a crazy dream?* He smiled as he took a second glance. *No, this is definitely NOT my workshop.*

He dressed in the simple clothes draped over the bedside table and made his way to a silver wooden door. His hand had just grazed the handle when a knock was heard on the other side. Fern opened the door. Standing before him was Lillia and King Solace. Fern's heart burst with joy as a gigantic toothy smile covered his face. He embraced them.

"Glad to see you're alive," said Fern as he released his hold.

"Dee feeling is mutual," replied Solace with a wide grin.

"Where am I?"

"You are in the fairy kingdom, of course," answered Lillia with a pleasant smile.

"Once you vanquished Paliden, you changed back into your human form in mid-air and plummeted to the ground. Solace carried you to our kingdom. You were grasping the ruby firmly in your hand when we found you."

Fern stared into Lillia's eyes for a moment, lost in thought, reliving every harrowing moment from the night before.

"How did you know of Paliden's weakness?" he finally asked.

Lillia smiled, her soft lips catching the light with a glisten.

"He was cursed for eternity to walk in the form of the creature he bestowed his power to; he was invincible in his human form...but not as a dragon."

"But how did you know of the ruby...wait, how did you even know of Paliden?" Fern's eyes widened.

"Soma relayed the information to me about the ruby, the second question *I* will not answer," replied Lillia. "And to be honest, my Fern, what I told you on the battlefield was only a guess; I was not entirely sure it would *kill* Paliden."

Fern shook his head. *What crazy luck!*

"But how did Soma know the ruby was in Paliden's heart?" he asked, still bobbling his head in disbelief.

"Reagal told him."

Fern looked down the hallway, his heart pounding in his chest like a hammer. "Where is he?"

Fern's eyes filled with worry. King Solace smiled.

"Ee will live, danks to you. And danks to King Edinword, I am pleased to say, boad of my sons av returned to me alive."

A tear of joy rolled down King Solace's raised cheeks as he grinned from ear to ear.

"So...Edinword is alive as well?"

"Yes, ee is ealing next to my sons as we speak. We av come to escort you to dim."

Fern did not move. He was frozen as he gazed out the window in his room, his eyes swelling with tears.

"What is wrong, my Fern?" asked Lillia.

"Where is Garrick?" he whispered, choking on a lump in his throat.

Fern slowly shuffled around, his head hanging like the mournful mood at a burial. Tears streamed down his face as the overwhelming pain clinched his constricted heart.

Lillia sighed as she wrapped her arms around him in a loving embrace.

"He is here, laying peacefully in a casket of glass, but you will be the one to determine his final resting place."

She wiped the tears from his eyes and brushed his auburn hair from his face. The feel of her soft, supple lips kissing his forehead made Fern smile, but only for a moment.

"What about Viloria...and Aadoo?"

Solace dropped his head in anguish, a heavy sigh escaping his chest.

"It is sad news, my young Majesteek. Aadoo perished on dee battlefield. Is bones ad been crushed by dee green dragon's grip, yet ee was able to save my son's life-mate wid one last eroic action. Using is body as a shield, he took a blast of dragon fire. Ee now lays benead dee ard in dee burial grounds of our most revered warriors of dee past."

A tear for Aadoo trickled down Fern's face. *I won't forget him.*

"But der is much to rejoice, my young Majesteek. Many survived, and Aadoo will be remembered as a ero."

A slight grin developed on Fern's face as he raised his head.

"And you'll be appy to ear dat King Dandowin is alive and well and in Alkyle at dee present. Dough, ee will be arriving soon. And I must say, noding can kill dat stubborn dwarf. Ardin is downstairs. Now, follow me, dae are all anxious to see you."

Lillia slid her hand across Fern's palm, gently grasping it.

Escorting him down a staircase through a well-lit hallway, they made their way to the main chamber of the fairy kingdom.

Fern stared at Lillia as they strolled leisurely, captured by her beauty.

"I've been wondering...how did you speak with me on the battlefield?" he asked.

"I told you, my Fern, I have felt a connection to you the moment we met," replied Lillia.

"So, you've used the method of transference before?"

"Not exactly," laughed Lillia. "It is an ability all fairies have, of course, but I have never had a need to use it, and it is much different than dream sharing. I was not even sure you would hear me."

Fern smiled, his head a constant shake as they came to the bottom of the stairs. He abruptly stopped. His eyes concentrated as his ears brimmed. The name *Majestic* could be heard chanting from every mouth inside the expansive room.

The kingdom was bursting with fairies, centaurs, dwarfs, men, and elves, and all began to applaud and bow as Fern walked behind Solace. Above them hovered dozens of chamroshs. One, in particular, could be seen flying in circles ecstatically before landing next to Fern. Fern patted Soma on her head as the chamrosh emphatically rubbed against his leg. Her feathers ruffled with excitement, and her tail wagged like a ribbon in the wind.

Praising him for his heroism, Loustofian soldiers slapped the last Majestic on his back as he walked passed. *Maybe I am dreaming.* Fern wore an awkward smile and thanked everyone he could. Lillia was still holding his hand, squeezing it tenderly. She could sense Fern's discomfort and laid her head upon his shoulder as Solace took the lead.

Parting the crowd, Solace trotted briskly. Fern was relieved when he stopped in front of two silver doors. Solace knocked gently. A nurse slowly opened the doors, and they entered.

Solace escorted them into medical chambers, much like the one Fern had stayed in when he was recovering in Dundire. Overflowing with the wounded, the room was lined with beds. Nurses carrying bloodied bandages scurried about, family and loved ones sat on small stools comforting the injured. Fern's heart was ravaged with pain by the sight of it all. His head hung like dead weight and his eyes welled with tears. *Oh, my dear friends, may you heal quickly*, he thought.

Noticing his anguish, Lillia gently placed her hand on his back.

"Do not feel sorrow, my Fern, they will all recover completely. It is, after all, what we fairies do best," she said, smiling.

Against the back wall of the medical chamber, and separate from the rest, stood three beds. In the middle, snoring soundly and nicely tucked beneath the blanket, was Edinword. On either side of him lay the sons of Solace. On the right, supported by a massive Iron pine bed, was Reagal. Viloria stood watching over him, gently combing her fingers through his long, dark hair. On the left of Edinword, and wide awake, was Galeon. The centaur sat high in his bed, staring at Fern.

"Good morning," he said. "I see you are well. Dough, I am afraid I cannot say dee same for myself. Of course, you should know my injuries better den I. After all, you gave dim to me."

Galeon smiled like an eager child, waiting anxiously for a response. Fern's eyes squinted, and his head tilted. He remembered nothing before he took control of his power and had no idea what Galeon was talking about.

"Do not mind my son, ee is lucky you did not kill im," replied Solace.

"Did I not tell you, my young Majesteek? My broder is part bull!"

The voice of Reagal danced around in Fern's ears like beams of morning light upon the ocean waves. Fern was a top, spinning on his heels to greet his friend. A tear rolled down Fern's face, and a mile-wide smile stretched across it as he tackled the centaur.

"Reagal! I can't tell you how happy I am to see you!"

Tears flowed steadily as the two companions embraced.

"How did you make it out alive?" questioned Fern as he released Reagal from his bear-like hug.

Reagal smiled, wincing, as he looked at Soma, who had snuck in behind Fern.

"I ad a little elp from my friend," replied Reagal as Soma strolled to his bedside. He scratched the underside of her neck as she nuzzled his arm. "Soma and er kin came to our aid dee moment you and Paliden flew from dee mountain. Dae carried all of us to safety, including...Garrick."

The sadness in Reagal's eyes as he said the giant's name glared.

"OI, OI! Look what the dragon dragged in!" shouted a bellowing voice from behind.

"Ah, King Ardin, I was wondering where you ad gone off to," replied Solace.

Ardin pounced over to Fern and smacked his back with a clap.

"It does me good to see you, me boy. Though I must say, you are much better looking as a dragon!" Ardin's belly was a large ball, bouncing as he laughed.

"You do realize people are trying to get some rest?" asked a familiar voice.

Fern turned and saw King Edinword sitting up in his bed with a blood-stained bandage wrapped around his chest. No words were exchanged between the two men, they merely looked at each other with a smile and a nod.

"I am sorry to break up this wonderful reunion," bellowed Ardin. "But we have one last counsel to hold before we all make our departures. King Dandowin will be here shortly and—"

"I am here now!"

The king of the elves, followed by Forona, Reannthane, and Gathriel, marched adamantly towards them.

"We have prepared a table for everyone. Please follow us," said Forona as she bowed to Fern.

Fern looked on with shock as Reagal began to rise from his bed.

"Reagal, NO, you must rest!" ordered Fern.

"Do not worry, I av enough strengd for all," replied Reagal with a wink and a smile.

Reagal wrapped his right arm around Viloria and gave Fern a gentle pat upon his back.

Edinword, grunting like a bull, stood from his bed and cloaked himself in a blue robe. He grabbed a small wooden chest from a bedside table and shuffled in the rear of the company. Fern noticed his crouched posture. *Huh, I see it now... Mallock.* He sighed as the memories flooded his mind. Galeon remained behind and watched as they left the room.

The cheers and bows were still abundant as they re-entered the main chamber. The crowd quickly parted as the company made their way to a large Silverwood oval table in the center of the room. They all took their seats. Forona glanced around the table.

"My friends, we are here today because of our unrelenting spirit. The evil that has infected our world has been vanquished, and we owe much of that victory to Fernand Majestic."

Everyone stood from the table and began to bow to Fern as the chamber room exploded in applause. The sudden visions of townsfolk screaming appeared around Fern like spirits in the night. He tried to shake free. The noise became muffled, and Fern stood from his seat waving his hands in the air.

"PLEASE, PLEASE! DO NOT CHEER FOR ME!" shouted Fern.

The crowd grew silent.

"If it wasn't for my friends, and everyone here, this day wouldn't be possible. You're the ones who should be receiving the applause, not I."

Fern slowly slid down in his chair, brows furled and eyes perplexed.

"Oi, you are a modest fellow!" bellowed King Ardin. "But even I have come to agree that without the loyalty you have shown your friends, we would have never been able to defeat our enemy. Learn to be humble enough to accept credit when credit is due. Now, stand and receive the applause that is rightfully yours."

Fern was a lost puppy as he glanced at Reagal. The centaurian prince grinned, pushing Fern to his feet.

"Get used to it, my friend," he said with a chuckle.

The crowd began to cheer at once. Their chanting nearly blew through the ceiling as it shook the walls.

"Please, please!" Forona shouted unavailingly.

"QUIET!" bellowed Ardin as he stood on his seat, his hands raised in the air.

Forona, taking her hands from her ears, yanked King Ardin back to his seat. The room was as quiet as a tomb.

"Thank you King Ardin," said Forona as the dwarven king cursed under his breath. "But we have not joined together to hear only applause, we have also congregated for a needed explanation."

"Explanation?" puffed King Ardin. "From whom?"

"Be patient my dwarven king, we fairies will be giving the explanation," exclaimed Forona.

Fern quickly turned to Lillia, puzzlement spreading over his face. A reassuring look was her reply as she smiled with a gentle nod.

"We believe the time has come to free our people of the shame that has haunted us for thousands of years," explained Forona. "And we believe everyone has the right to know the truth. I am here today to tell you who our enemy truly was. Some here might know that all dragons, save one, were once fairies of this world." Forona paused, glancing at Fern. "Our power to transform was created for protection... and never meant to be used as a weapon."

A deep breath entered Forona's lungs, and the full attention of everyone present held the kingdom captive.

"The human we all know to be Timal was once Paliden, the supreme ruler of all fairies. For a thousand years, he ruled our kingdom in peace. But he became ambitious. He said fairies, whom he believed were the purest and most worthy, should rule the world. Deity, the oldest and wisest of our kind, and the creator of transformation, led a secret order of fairies known to us as the Elders, to overthrow Paliden."

Fern sat frozen in his chair. *Finally, an explanation to all this madness.*

"The plan was a success, and Paliden was cast from the fairy kingdom along with any like-minded fairies. He was ordered never to return. Unfortunately, his ambition did not cease with his defeat. Paliden and his followers became angry and discontented. All but Paliden lost control of their power, permanently transforming into dragons. Paliden searched the world trying to build an army; he found the Majestics. He promised them great wealth and power if they helped him destroy our world, but little did he know how far our relations had stretched across the lands. The King of the Majestics had a great friendship with our savior Deity. Fernand Majestic, the first king of the north, came to him prior to Paliden's banishment and asked to be granted the power of transformation. He desired the great power that was envied by so many. Deity revealed the effects that would be bestowed upon any fairy who gave power to another being, something that only Deity knew, and the king of the Majestics was denied his request."

So, I'm truly the son of the last Majestic king. Paliden was telling the truth. But what do I do with such a title? Fern shook his head as he continued to soak in the information that his heart desired his entire life.

"When Paliden came to Fernand with his ploy, and his gift of dragon blood, the Majestic king willingly accepted. Paliden paid for his ambition as the effects took over his body, changing him into his human form and causing him to walk this world for eternity. To add additional turmoil to an already cursed soul, the Majestics betrayed Paliden and drove him from their land. Paliden disappeared, and was nearly forgotten."

Huh, so Timal betrayed the Majestic king hundreds of years later for their treachery. If only he could have shown forgiveness. Fern laughed at himself for his hypocrisy as he remembered Edinword.

"We fairies vowed never to appoint a supreme ruler again," continued Forona, "and Deity placed a powerful barrier around our world, permitting any dragon from entering. To our everlasting shame, Paliden resurfaced to the land of the north hundreds of years later calling himself Crull of the Crag Mountains and deceived the new Majestic king. He murdered him and took over his people with the assistance of a massive turgoyle army. He declared war on our world and we were forced to take up arms. Our kind was nearly destroyed until the Majestics broke free from Paliden's rule and helped the fair folk of this world defeat Paliden and his army. He retreated and again was not heard from for hundreds of years. After the war, we fairies made another vow. We locked our arms beneath our kingdom and swore never to lay hand to sword or shield again. It was only recently we learned that it was Timal who declared death to the Majestic race and devoted his eternal life to their demise."

Forona turned to Fern as Reannthane and Gathriel stood from their seats.

"On behalf of all fairies, we give our sincerest apologies to you, Fernand Majestic, and to your entire race. We thank you for all you have sacrificed, extend our friendship to you, and promise to aid you in time of need. We hope you will accept this new vow."

Fern could only nod in response as he once again became lost in thought.

Questions began to accumulate in his head.

The three fairies sat back down in their seats as silence took over the room. Fern quickly interrupted the quiet.

"If you knew of Paliden, why did you let me continue to associate with him? You saw us together at the border of your kingdom."

"You misunderstand. We warned you about the deception of dragons. Furthermore, a dragon is all our eyes could see, something we did not know Paliden was still capable of. Not even Deity knew it was possible to regain the power of transformation once it was taken away. If you recall, you did not reveal Timal to us. We believed Edinword was behind the war. We had no idea Paliden had returned, and you never revealed the dragon's name. It was only when King Solace divulged this information to us that we decided it was our obligation to fight."

"But the Elders knew of Timal, and of Paliden. How is it that you could not have known?"

"The Elders had many abilities that were lost to the rest of us. One ability was transference. We can only assume they could read your thoughts."

"But why did they not share such vital information with their own people?" argued Fern.

"Fern Majestic, you must realize that fairies do not live and die like the rest of the inhabitants of this world. We decide when we leave this realm. When a fairy comes to the end of his or her time, that fairy chooses one soul to bestow their wisdom and life force to. Once given, they vanish from this world to begin an eternal life in Ethrealm, a dimension far beyond our own. In the Elder's case, they chose you to be granted this gift. You now carry the life force of all the Elders of our kingdom. So, you see, they were no longer here to inform us of Paliden's return. But they must have held unbound trust that you were the one to finally end his reign of evil."

Fern sat, face of stone and eyes fixated, staring into space. His mouth was clamped shut and he could not move, thinking about what the Elders had done for him, and what faith they must have had to trust him with such a great gift.

King Ardin suddenly jumped from his seat.

"Oi, are we finished here?" he bellowed. "I am overjoyed the fairies have decided to clean their collective conscious, but I have injured dwarves to attend to, and a kingdom to rebuild. I really must be off!"

"Yes, yes, my impatient friend," replied King Dandowin as he stood from his seat. "We all have important business to attend to, but we also have important business to discuss...now."

"What business?" bellowed Ardin.

Dandowin raised his hand to halt Ardin, and the dwarven king rolled his eyes and sat back down.

"Fernand Majestic, please rise and come forth," exclaimed Dandowin as he moved from the oval table and parted the crowd.

Fern slowly stood and hesitantly walked toward Dandowin.

"Take a knee," commanded the elven king.

Fern peered around the room, in obvious confusion. *What's going on? Didn't they just...am I being executed?* Fern laughed in his mind trying to make light of the situation.

"Please, my young Majestic, do as I ask," spoke Dandowin softly.

Fern reluctantly obeyed and knelt to one knee.

"King Edinword, come forth!" commanded Dandowin.

Edinword stood from his chair and limped slowly towards Fern. In his hands was a small ornate wooden chest.

"King Ardin! King Solace! Come forth!"

Solace trotted over quickly. Ardin, taking his time, scooting his seat under the oval table and stroking his aged beard, finally made his way to the kings' side.

Dandowin stepped behind Fern and placed his hands upon Fern's shoulders. Edinword lifted the lid of the wooden chest, slowly raising an ancient crown into the air. With a loud commanding voice King Edinword spoke:

"Let it be known to all that Fernand Majestic, the rightful king of the north, reclaims his throne upon this day! All will bear witness to this momentous declaration, that his people will rise once again in his light and prosper once more! Stand, King Majestic, and turn to face your audience!"

Fern stood and slowly turned to the awaiting crowd. Edinword placed the crown upon Fern's head, and roars and chants of his name were deafening as his eyes became the size of the sun. Without warning, the inscription upon his arm suddenly began to burn.

Fern pulled the sleeve of his shirt up to his shoulder and looked down to see the ink slowly vanish from his skin. The ruby began to glow with great brilliance and a soothing warmth engulfed his body. He immediately knew his journey was not over as a pressing need to gain back his land suddenly gripped him. *Maybe a holiday first*, he chuckled under his breath.

Whimsical music began to play, and the crowds began to rejoice. Food and wine carried on the backs of chamroshs filled the room, as dancing and laughter erupted.

Edinword appeared in front of Fern, capturing his eyes with deep emotion. Taking him by the hand he knelt.

"My dear Majestic, I vow to you that my sword and my swords to come are yours. If ever you need my allegiance, I will grant it without hesitation. You have taught me more in our short acquaintance than I have learned in my entire life. My gratitude will be forever lasting. Until we meet again."

Edinword stood, and the two men shared a moment of understanding as they searched each other's eyes. As Edinword departed the fairy kingdom, King Ardin stepped forth.

"Oi! What can be said that has not already been said, me boy? You have proven your name worthy of your ancestors. Let your land bloom with life, and may your kingdom prosper as mine has. Though, I must say, after seeing the north…not sure if that's possible."

Ardin smacked Fern on his shoulders with both hands bellowing in laughter as he departed.

Dandowin came forward and bowed quickly.

"*King Majestic*. I am proud to be part of this historical moment. I could never have imagined when we first met in the forests of my land that you would come to this, but you have earned the right to call yourself king. Never forget that!"

Dandowin bowed again and departed.

Solace was last and bowed the deepest before speaking.

"I cannot dank you enough for all you av done. My sons' lives are owed to you. It is a debt I can never repay. If ever you need anyding from me, it will be yours. Please call on me from time to time. You will always be welcome in dee land of my faders. Take care, young Majesteek, and peace be wid you and your kingdom."

Solace parted company and vanished into the crowd. When all had said their praises and blessings, Fern sat back in his seat next to Lillia. He remained with the fairies, staying close to his friends as the party stretched into the night.

Hours had passed, and the merriment of celebration had all but died. The main chamber was clear of spectators, and Fern, Lillia, Reagal, and Viloria were all who remained.

Still sitting around the oval table, Fern held his crown to his eyes. Quite plain, he thought as he studied it. As Fern spun the crown in his hand, he suddenly noticed words inscribed on the inside. His eyes sprang wide as he jumped from his seat like a startled cat. *I don't believe it!*

The inscription read: *You are Fernand Majestic, the son of a great people. May they rise again through your life, and may you lead them to prosperity once more.*

Fern dropped the crown to the floor. *How's this possible? I need answers.*

Lillia, Reagal, and Viloria stared at Fern, shock plastered on their faces.

"Is all well, my Fern?" asked Lillia as she bent down to retrieve Fern's crown.

"Yes...yes, of course." Fern paused, his eyes circling as he contemplated his future. His head snapped still, and he looked to Lillia. "It's time. Please take me to Garrick."

Lillia nodded, and without question took Fern by his hand. Reagal and Viloria followed closely behind.

Lillia led them through the chamber room and out the main doors. The sun was shining brightly as the group stepped onto the lush green grass. A beautiful variety of four winged blue birds fluttered in the air, hovering like halos around the company's heads. Their musical chirps played like hymns.

Their walk through the fairy kingdom was brief, and they soon found themselves standing outside a clearing surrounded by giant birch trees.

Releasing Fern's hand, Lillia pointed forward. Fern strolled into the clearing, enjoying a warm breeze as it touched his face. He suddenly halted; he was a block of ice. A glass casket upon a large blue marble stone slab in the center of a beautiful meadow stood before him. Only a few trots behind, Reagal proceeded forward. He placed his hand on Fern's shoulder and gripped. Fern awoke from his daze. They made their way through a thick fescue lawn until they arrived at a set of steps.

Garrick's body had been laid inside the glass housing on several white pillows. He was clothed in beautiful silver silken garments, and his hands were folded together on his heart. Upon the giant's body, beams of morning sunshine shone down between low, puffy clouds. A smile graced Garrick's face; he was at peace. Fern felt Reagal's palm leave his shoulder, and a tear dripped down his cheek. A sense of comfort engulfed Fern as he turned to Reagal.

"My friend, I'm thankful you're still with me," said Fern with a smile as he spun back to Garrick. "He gave his life for us both, and I'd like to do one last thing for him before he's placed in the ground."

Fern stared into Garrick's face and smiled.

"He told me once that he'd always wanted to fly on a dragon. I'll grant him that wish and fly him back to the only home he's ever known. He'd be proud of his king who now dwells there, and would be honored to have Loustof as his final resting place."

Fern looked to Reagal, tears flowing steadily down both cheeks.

"Will you meet us there?" he asked.

"Of course," replied Reagal with slight confusion. "I am sorry to ask dis, and I mean no disrespect, but ow can you change into your dragon form? I dought it was only on dred of one's life?"

Fern smiled.

"The Elders didn't bestow power of transformation on me. They bestowed the wisdom and life force each held in their soul. The power was great, giving me the ability of rapid healing and unbelievable stamina. It also made me see things clearly, and cloaked the blood running through my veins, which, in turn, cast a barrier over my thoughts from intruding minds."

"But ow did you figure all of dis out?" questioned Reagal, taken aback by Fern's abundance of knowledge.

"As I was sleeping one night, I dreamt that I was flying amongst the clouds with the Elders in their dragon forms. They spoke to me about my power and cleared my mind further. I don't believe it was merely a dream, though; I believe the Elders knew the true secret of unlocking this magic, and they were finally sharing it with me. I began to better understand this as I was faced with losing what I hold most dear; it's in those moments when one truly knows who they are. Of course, I didn't entirely realize the secret to this magic until Garrick lay dying in my arms. It was he who taught me the value one person holds in this life. The moment he died, I knew what I had to do, and I believed I could do it." A solitary tear slowly formed. Fern blinked his eyes sending the drop of emotion down his cheek as he continued to speak. "I realize now I had the power of transformation all along, and it was not the threat of losing my life that made me transform, it was the belief in myself and the belief that people held in me that gave me the power. I must admit, it was still a challenge to control, once I gained this knowledge. The power is strong and continually tries to test me, but I could hear your voice, telling me to fight. Your belief in me helped tremendously in gaining the upper hand, and I will be forever grateful."

"But Timal ad control of is power as well, did ee not?" asked Reagal.

"Yes, he did. His belief in himself was indeed great, but it was powered by arrogance, and because of this, his power was inferior to mine."

"But ow did Paliden regain is ability of transformation?" asked Reagal.

"The ruby holds the answer. When placed in his heart, it temporarily transformed him into his dragon form. It is his blood, and the blood essence of every Majestic that has ever lived, bar one."

The two friends smiled at each other as Fern backed away from Garrick's casket. Fern peered to the edge of the clearing where Lillia and Viloria stood patiently.

"Meet me in Loustof, ask Lillia to accompany you there, I have much to discuss with you both."

Reagal nodded, lifting the glass lid from Garrick's casket, and retreated to Viloria and Lillia.

By the time he had made it to the edge of the clearing and turned around, Fern was in his dragon form with Garrick on his back. The blue dragon lifted into the air, and as the two friends faded into the distance, Reagal began to sing:

Lay my son of Loustof
Down upon your head
Lay my son of Loustof
Nothing you shall dread

Dream the dream of heroes
Dream the dream of men
Dream the dream of soldiers
For soon your wounds will mend

Battles we have faced
Times of war we've seen
Many men have died
On battlefields of green

Soaked in blood the victory
Peaceful times are near
Celebrate the Kingdom
With women, wine and cheer

James Stevens

Lay my son of Loustof
Down upon your head
Lay my son of Loustof
Nothing you shall dread

Dream the dream of heroes
Dream the dream of men
Dream the dream of soldiers
For soon your soul ascends

THE END